THE LOST HOURS

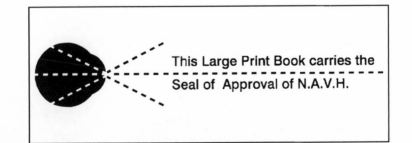

This Large Print Book carries the
Seal of Approval of N.A.V.H.

THE LOST HOURS

KAREN WHITE

THORNDIKE PRESS

A part of Gale, Cengage Learning

GALE
CENGAGE Learning·

Detroit • New York • San Francisco • New Haven, Conn • Waterville, Maine • London

GALE
CENGAGE Learning

Copyright © Harley House Books, LLC 2009.
Conversation Guide copyright © Penguin Group (USA) Inc., 2009.
Thorndike Press, a part of Gale, Cengage Learning.

Thorndike Press® Large Print Core.
The text of this Large Print edition is unabridged.
Other aspects of the book may vary from the original edition.
Set in 16 pt. Plantin.
Printed on permanent paper.

LIBRARY OF CONGRESS CATALOGING-IN-PUBLICATION DATA

White, Karen (Karen S.)
   The lost hours / by Karen White.
     p. cm. — (Thorndike Press large print core)
   ISBN-13: 978-1-4104-1960-6 (alk. paper)
   ISBN-10: 1-4104-1960-6 (alk. paper)
   1. Women in horse sports—Fiction. 2. Accident victims—Fiction. 3. Equestrian accidents—Fiction. 4. Grandparent and child—Fiction. 5. Grandmothers—Fiction. 6. Family secrets—Fiction. 7. Friendship in children—Fiction. 8. Self-actualization (Psychology)—Fiction. 9. Large type books. I. Title.
PS3623.H5776L67 2009b
813'.6—dc22   2009022896

Published in 2009 by arrangement with NAL Signet, a member of Penguin Group (USA) Inc.

Printed in the United States of America
1 2 3 4 5 6 7 13 12 11 10 09

To my beautiful grandmother,
Grace Bianca.
Thank you for sharing your stories.

ACKNOWLEDGMENTS

Thank you to my daughter, Meghan, and her trainer, Jen Bishop, for reminding me what it's like to love horses again. And yes, Meghan, I do watch.

A huge thanks to Andi Winkle for your generosity in sharing your time and knowledge about horses with me. I hope you don't mind being the stable manager at Asphodel Meadows or that I wrote in your broken nose but made it more glamorous than walking into a glass wall. Any mistakes about horses and equestrian events are completely mine.

And thanks to talented authors Wendy Wax and Susan Crandall, whose support and willingness to bump ideas with me is priceless. Thank you for always being honest, and for being my two-person pep squad when I need it.

As always, thank you to Tim, Meghan, and

Connor for allowing me to follow my dreams.

The golden moments in the stream of life
    rush past us and we see nothing but
    sand;
The angels come to visit us, and we only
    know them when they are gone.

                 — George Eliot

CHAPTER 1

When I was twelve years old, I helped my granddaddy bury a box in the back garden of our Savannah house. I didn't ask him what was in it. The box belonged to my grandmother, so I didn't care. Long before the Alzheimer's got her mind, a fear of living had taken hold of her spirit, convincing me that my grandmother had no stories worth listening to.

I squatted by the edge of the shallow hole in the middle of my grandmother's peonies, smelling sweat and summer grass as I dug my fingers into the dark earth and held up my handfuls of dirt briefly before opening my clenched hands, the clods raining shadows onto the box below. The dirt struck the tin with soft patters like little fists against the sealed box, demanding the release of its secrets. I yawned and turned away, the box and whatever it might contain forgotten by the time the screen door of the back porch slammed shut behind me.

I hadn't thought about that hot afternoon for over a decade: a non-event in a busy life filled with friends, parties and my never-ending quest for accolades and excitement in the saddle on the back of a high-jumping horse. I had thought myself indestructible, immune to the fears and disappointments that had stolen the color from my grand-mother's face the same way the setting sun creates a world of shadows.

My delusion was understandable to my grandfather, who knew the source of it. After all, he was the one who'd told me that being the sole survivor of an accident that took the lives of both my parents meant that God was saving me for something impor-tant. I took this to mean that I had already experienced the greatest tragedy of my life and nothing bad would ever happen to me again. My grandmother claimed I was merely tempting the devil. But I was content to exist in my make-believe world, where I was infallible until the day came when I was forced to realize how very wrong I'd been. Life is like that, I suppose: always slapping you in the face when you least expect it.

The doorbell rang, erasing the smells of summer grass and damp earth. I rose slowly from my chair in the front parlor, scanning my eyes over the worn furniture with the eyes of a person who hadn't become accustomed to its growing shabbiness for over twenty years. The house still smelled of flowers although the last of the wilted funeral arrangements had been put out at the curb the previous evening with the rest of the garbage. I had hoped that keeping the flowers in the house would help me feel the grief I knew was living somewhere under my skin. I had done enough grieving in my life by the age of six that I guess my body figured I just couldn't do it anymore.

The doorbell rang again and I walked stiffly to the door, my back and right knee protesting every step. Humidity hung over Savannah in the summer like a veil, antagonizing my injuries as much as any cold weather would. I'd long since reached the conclusion that there was no climate that would coddle my bruised bones, so I might as well stay in this ancient city and old house that had been in my mother's family for four generations.

I swallowed back my disappointment as I pulled open the door and revealed my granddaddy's lawyer, a man about ten years younger than the grandfather I had just buried. His skin was tinged gray like the color of dried marsh mud and he had down-turned eyes that always seemed to look anxious.

"Mr. Morton," I said, stepping aside to allow him through the doorway. "This is a nice surprise." I had hoped it would be one of my old friends from my equestrian days, the friends whose visits had trickled down to a slow drip in the last years. They'd gotten tired of asking me when I was going to ride again, and stopped visiting, as if whatever I'd contracted that kept me on the ground might be contagious. I had no classmates, having been homeschooled for most of my life, and my friendships had centered around the show circuit. A few had made an appearance at the wake, but that was all. Even Jen Bishop, my oldest friend and closest rival, had merely sent a flower arrangement and a note.

Mr. Morton grunted and led the way to the parlor. I indicated for him to sit only a moment after he'd taken his place in my favorite chair, the same chair my grandmother had sat in each evening with her endless knitting.

"Can I get you something to drink?"

"Why don't you get me something to drink, dear?"

I paused, wondering if it would be polite to suggest he put in his hearing aid.

14

"What would you like, Mr. Morton? Tea or lemonade?" I watched as he ran his finger across the dust on the side table, etching out a single line of accusation about my lack of housekeeping skills. "Or maybe arsenic?" I added softly.

He blinked slowly up at me, and for a horrible second I wondered if he'd actually heard me. "A Co-Cola would be nice. It's a hot day."

I left the room and returned with two glasses of Coke filled two-thirds with ice. I'd only had a partial can and rather than try to go through the motions of explaining this to Mr. Morton, I figured it would be easier to just go with what I had.

"Thank you, Piper," he said as he took a long sip, then wrinkled his nose before setting it on a coaster.

"What can I do for you, Mr. Morton?" I asked loudly, sitting on the worn sofa next to his chair.

He placed his briefcase on the coffee table in front of him and made a big show of opening it and taking out a large manila folder. "I've got some papers for you to sign concerning your grandfather's estate." He slid the stack in front of me and handed me a thick black pen. "There're also papers regarding the continuation of your grandmother's care that you'll need to look at and sign."

I looked up at him, realizing for the first time what my grandfather's death would really mean for me. Along with the deed to the house, all its furnishings and his 1988 Buick LeSabre, I had apparently also inherited the care of the grandmother who no longer recognized my face.

I signed the papers where he indicated and slid them back to him. With meticulous precision, he stacked the papers and placed them in his briefcase. But instead of standing up and taking his leave, he sat back in his chair and took another sip of his watery drink and blinked at me through thick glasses.

"Is there anything else, Mr. Morton?" I asked.

He looked at me, not comprehending. Placing his bony hands on his black-clad knees, he said, "There's one more thing, Piper."

I didn't bother to reply.

"As you know, I've been acquainted with your grandparents since I was an errand boy in my father's law practice. They were good people." He looked down for a moment as if to compose himself and I wished that I could borrow some of his grief.

16

He continued. "Annabelle — your grand-mother — was a beautiful young woman. Her father was a doctor of some reputation. He treated patients regardless of their social class or the color of their skin — a rarity in those days." He lowered his head, his bushy eyebrows like avenging hawks in a down-ward spiral. "And Annabelle was no differ-ent. Always putting others first and taking care of people." His voice softened when he said her name and I glanced up at him, but his eyes didn't give anything away.

I looked down again, impatient, and curled my toes inside my shoes to keep my feet from tapping as Mr. Morton took his unwanted stroll down memory lane in my parlor. My gaze strayed through the window to East Taylor Street out front and to Monterey Square beyond it with its statue of Revolutionary War hero Casimir Pulaski. This view had been my world since the time I was six years old and moved in with my grandparents. The sound of the bells at St. John's in nearby Lafayette Square mixed with the gentle conversation of my grand-parents on the balcony below my bedroom had been my nighttime lullaby. For a brief while my talent for jumping higher and faster on the back of a horse had taken me around the world. But my horse was long since gone, and I was back where I started from, staring at the statue in Monterey Square and the implacable face of General Pulaski.

"When you first came to live with them, your grandmother planned to give you something that had meant a lot to her when she was a young woman." He paused briefly, his brows furrowed with seeming incomprehension. "I guess she never found the right time to give it to you because your grandfather gave it to me for safekeeping when he put Annabelle in the home. I thought that you should have it now."

I dragged my attention away from the window, aware that he was awaiting a response from me. I struggled for a moment to capture his last words. "Something from my grandmother?"

Mr. Morton took a sealed envelope from the inside of his jacket and handed it to me. There was a small lump inside and my name had been written with my grandmother's meticulous cursive. I glanced at Mr. Morton and he nodded his head in encouragement before I dug my nail under the flap of the envelope and ripped it open.

I peered inside, looking for a letter or a note. I cupped my hand and tipped the envelope over, shaking it until whatever had been stuck at the bottom came tumbling out into my palm.

Mr. Morton leaned toward me and we both stared at my prize, a gold charm of an angel holding an opened book. I shook the envelope again, waiting for the chain to fall out, but the envelope was empty.

"There's not even a note," I said, turning the charm over in my hand, wondering why she had held on to it for so long without giving it to me and feeling an odd disappointment.

Mr. Morton took my hand, squeezing it hard enough to almost be painful. "No, there wouldn't be. Annabelle had always planned to give it to you in person. It's a part of your grandmother's history — part of her life she would want you to know."

I stood, uneasy with his intensity. "I'll take good care of it. And I'll look for the chain, too. Maybe it's somewhere in her old room."

He stared at me for a long moment and I thought he hadn't understood what I said. While I prepared to paraphrase slowly and clearly, Mr. Morton said, "You do that, young lady." He stood and faced me, a concentrated look on his withered face. "You never know what you'll find."

Uncomfortable, I waited for him to gather his things, then quickly led the way back to the foyer.

"You're a pretty young lady, Piper. I'm sure your grandfather would want you to move on. To find a young man and get married. Start a family of your own."

"You mean sell the house?"

Mr. Morton shrugged. "That's certainly a possibility. Even after making allowances for your grandmother's care, with the remainder of your parents' and grandparents' estates, you'll have a nice little nest egg. Maybe you'll want to travel for a bit."

I opened the front door, hearing the distant sound of the church bells. "There's no place I want to go. Besides, with my back and knee, I don't think long-distance travel would be a good idea."

He regarded me quietly. "It's not always the distance of a trip that determines its value. Sometimes the best trips are only as far as the circumference of your heart."

Before I could ask him what he meant, he said, "Speaking of trips, Matilda and I are going on a four-month excursion around the coast of South America. It's been a dream of hers for a long time and I finally figured that now's as good a time as ever. You might be able to reach me by e-mail, but that would be sporadic at best. If you need something immediately, you can call my office and George will be happy to take care of you."

"Thank you," I said, trying not to flinch at the mention of George's name and impatient now for Mr. Morton to leave. His words had unsettled me and all I wanted was to go back to my darkening parlor and think about all I had lost.

He stepped outside onto the brick steps and pulled an old-fashioned gold watch out of his pocket. A gold key fob dangled from the chain as he studied the clock face and frowned before shoving it back in his pocket. "One more thing. Matilda asked me to find out if her family tree is ready yet."

Dabbling in genealogy and delving into other people's family secrets had been the riskiest behavior I'd allowed myself to be involved in since my riding accident six years earlier. I frowned, knowing that my answer would not be something Mrs. Morton would want to hear. "Tell her almost. But I haven't been able to find any connection between her family and the British royal family as she thought there might have been. Although I have found a family connection to sheep farmers in Yorkshire."

He stared at me blankly for a long moment. Finally, he said, "I'll let you tell her that yourself."

"Just feed me to the alligators instead," I muttered to myself as he turned away. I imagined his imperious wife, whose aspiration to grandiosity was equal only to her disdain for me for having had the bad taste to have been born north of the Mason-Dixon Line, regardless of the fact that both my parents had been born and raised in Savannah.

Mr. Morton faced me again abruptly, almost making me startle. "I heard that, you know."

I smiled, my face feeling stretched and unused to the movement of turning up my lips. "Good-bye, Mr. Morton," I said as I closed the heavy door with the black wreath hanging from it.

I watched him through the leaded glass of the door, trying again to find the tears for the grandfather who had raised me since I was six. I absently fingered the small charm in my hand and blinked hard, willing the grief to find me. But I could only stand there, dry-eyed, as I watched Mr. Morton slowly make his way down the walk toward the square with the statue honoring a fallen war hero. And I wondered, not for the first time, if dying in the quest for glory wasn't far better than surviving with the livid scars of failure for all to see.

CHAPTER 2

I woke up with a stiff neck and something small and hard pressed into the side of my hip. I'd fallen asleep on the sofa again in the absence of a grandfather to tell me to go upstairs to bed. I sat up, rotating my neck while digging under my hip for the protruding object. It was the small gold charm and I picked it up, a misplaced sense of excitement filling me for a moment. I wasn't sure why. Maybe because a quest for the missing chain might distract me long enough that I might forget about the rest of my life.

I shuffled to the kitchen, my knee and back joining in protest with my neck. I opened the refrigerator for my morning Coke, belatedly remembering the sad display of hospitality I'd shown to Mr. Morton with the remnants of my last can of Coke rescued from the back shelf. Covered casseroles, assorted salads, and a large ham, courtesy of a misplaced sense of duty on behalf of neighbors, my grandfather's former business associates, and church members, crammed the small space. It was the Savannah way of feeding bereavement, as if all that grieving required extra caloric input. I hadn't so much as lifted a corner of foil wrap, feeling guilty for not having earned any of it. I had yet to shed a single tear.

"Dang it," I said to the empty kitchen as I slammed the refrigerator door. Something clattered on the wood floor and I belatedly realized that I'd been holding the charm in my hand and had dropped it when I'd slammed the door. With unaccustomed alarm, I got down on all fours, forgetting to favor my right knee, and began to search for the charm.

I found it resting on the floor, propped next to the overflowing plastic garbage bin, as if a reminder that it needed to be emptied. I picked up the charm, then held it in the light from the kitchen window. Squinting, I studied the back of the opened book, my attention caught by thin black lines etched across the covers. Moving my head closer, I realized that the lines were actually writing but the words were too small for me to read. With as much enthusiasm as I could muster, I walked across the foyer to my grandfather's study, pausing only a moment as the smell of pipe smoke made me think that I should have knocked on the door first.

I rifled through the desk drawers until I found the magnifying glass still resting on the top of the desk, where my grandfather had read the Sunday paper. A shadow of sadness drifted over me, stilling me for a moment as I willed the grief to come. But I remained as numb and helpless as I had been for the last six years and even that thought couldn't bring the tears I needed to shed. I held the metal handle in my hand, imagining it still warm from my grandfather's touch. Instead it felt cold and impersonal as I brought it over to the window to see better.

I held up the charm and the magnifying glass and brought them closer to my eye. Turning the charm around to see the inscription on the book's covers, I read it out loud. *Perfer et obdura; dolor hic tibi proderit olim.* I looked up, hearing the words as I'd read them. Wasn't that Latin? I read the inscription again, racking my brain for the high school Latin that I'd done my best to forget in the intervening years.

Putting the magnifying glass back on my grandfather's desk, I turned to the shelves of books in the off chance that any of my old Latin textbooks might have been saved over the years. Granddaddy never wanted to have anything to do with computers and I didn't feel up to climbing two flights of stairs to get to my own. And by looking through the library, I was guaranteed that my search would eat up most of the empty morning.

With breakfast forgotten, I spent an hour going through my grandfather's books and finding nothing remotely resembling anything that would help me translate the Latin phrase. I was about to leave the room when I spied the antique sea captain's trunk under one of the windows.

My grandmother had used it to keep her knitting projects, including the sweaters and scarves she'd made for me that never quite fit or suited me and which I'd never worn. I had never been curious about the trunk's contents before, but something made me pause before it, a fleeting memory of my grandmother kneeling before it with creaking knees to place something inside.

Slipping the charm into my pocket, I knelt on the floor and lifted the lid. The overpowering stench of mothballs made my eyes sting as I averted my face for a moment to allow the contents to air out. I began rummaging through the trunk quickly, pushing aside old knitting projects and half-used balls of brightly colored yarn that even at the time when my grandmother was knitting, had seemed so out-of-character for her. She always wore drab browns and grays yet all of her projects for me were created out of bright pinks and yellows, pale blues and the amber hues of the marsh at sunset.

My fingers sifted through the soft wool until they scraped the bottom of the trunk and my fingernail flicked something small and hard. I tugged on it and found myself lifting out a very small pale blue sweater. My finger had found one of the mother-of-pearl buttons that closed the sweater in front in a tiny, neat row. I looked at the sweater for a long time, wondering who it could have belonged to.

My reverie was broken by the sound of the phone ringing. I picked up the old black princess model on the desk. "Hello?"

"Hello, Piper. It's Mr. Morton. Matilda and I are heading for the airport shortly but I wanted to give you a call before we left just to make sure you're all right."

"That's very kind of you, Mr. Morton. Thank you," I said, meaning it, my annoyance at the phone's intrusion into my solitude forgotten.

"I know you haven't had a lot of time to think about our conversation yesterday, so I won't ask about your plans just yet. Just wanted to know if you had any last-minute questions before I leave the country."

I was about to say no when I had a sudden thought. I dug the small charm out of my pocket. "Actually, I do. Being a lawyer, you probably know a bit of Latin, right?"

There was a long pause, and then Mr. Morton said, "I don't really follow baseball, Piper, so I don't know how the Marlins are doing."

I bit my lip, but before I could repeat my question, Mr. Morton let out a low chuckle.

"I'm pulling your leg, Piper. I heard you the first time. Matilda makes me wear my hearing aid while I'm traveling with her because otherwise I drive her crazy. What she doesn't know is that I can turn the thing off and leave it in my ear and she won't have any idea."

I smiled into the phone. "I promise it'll be our secret, Mr. Morton."

"So, what did you want translated?"

I brought the charm up to my eye, squinting as I read out loud, *"Perfer et obdura; dolor hic tibi proderit olim."*

He cleared his throat. "That's Ovid. It means 'Be patient and strong; someday this pain will be useful to you.' " He paused for a moment. "Where did you hear that?"

"It was on the charm from my grandmother that you gave me."

I heard him take a deep breath. "It sounds like something she'd say."

"Funny," I said, leaning back against the desk, "I was thinking just the opposite. I mean, Grandmother wasn't really the type to be profound or even sentimental enough to have a favorite verse put on a charm."

He was silent for a moment. "And that's where you would be wrong, Piper. Very wrong."

"Pardon me for disagreeing with you, Mr. Morton, but I just don't see it that way."

"No, I guess you wouldn't. You never really knew your grandmother."

I swallowed my irritation. "Mr. Morton, I lived with her for six years and have been visiting her almost daily since I was twelve. I think that qualifies me as knowing her."

"Studying the cover of a book doesn't qualify you to discuss its contents, you know."

I felt my anger rise as my stomach grumbled, reminding me that I hadn't eaten. I didn't reply.

"Is there anything else, Piper? Matilda has grabbed her umbrella, which means she's ready to go."

I wanted to tell him where he could stick that umbrella but I held back. I remembered the sweater and reluctantly spoke again. "I found something else in my grandmother's trunk. A small knitted blue sweater. As far as I know, both my mother and I were only children with no brothers. I was just wondering if you had any idea who it might have belonged to."

There was a long pause but this time I knew that it wasn't because he couldn't hear me and I felt a tingle of anticipation dance down my spine, raising the hair on the back of my neck.

"Mr. Morton?"

"Our taxi is here and I really have to go now, Piper."

"Mr. Morton, do you know something about this sweater?"

I heard the sound of a honking horn and then Mr. Morton spoke again. "Your grandmother was a lot stronger than you think, Piper. Maybe you should go visit her."

The sound of a car honking sounded again through the receiver.

"I really must go now, Piper. Don't hesitate to call George if you should need anything. Good-bye, dear."

I kept the receiver pressed against my ear,

30

listening to the dial tone for a long time, trying to figure out what in the hell Mr. Morton had been trying to tell me and why I should even care.

I made myself go to the grocery to buy more Coke and frozen dinners, the thought of heating up a casserole just for me completely unappealing. My conversations with Mr. Morton and my discovery of the blue sweater had made me think of my grandmother and I found myself purchasing cornmeal, okra, and green tomatoes — the old comfort foods that she had made for me as a child.

I knew that I should visit her, but her presence at my grandfather's funeral had been exhausting as I fielded her repetitive questions and reintroduced her to relatives and friends she'd known for fifty years. She'd been utterly lost, and after a while I stopped reminding her whose funeral we were attending. To her, Granddaddy would always be alive, and it gave me some comfort to know that she would never be truly alone.

But I needed to go visit her. I would do it soon, if only to ask her why she would have thought to caution me about patience, strength, and pain.

I placed my grocery bags in the backseat

of the old Buick, trying not to see my grandfather in his worn straw hat at the wheel, signaling his turns with his left hand because the fuse for his blinkers had blown out and he hadn't wanted to part with the cash to replace it.

As I drove around our square toward East Taylor, the moss-draped oaks teased me with intermittent sun and shadow, the old houses staring stoically at the square and at me as I passed, defying time and climate simply by remaining. In front of my house I paused, the antique beauty of the Savannah gray brick town house and delicate wrought-iron railings never lost on me. I think it was because the first time I'd seen it, it had been a place a refuge following the death of my parents. Even afterward, when I'd begun to think of my grandmother's house as a place of sadness and shadows, it was still the place I called home. If it held any secrets, I was kept blissfully unaware of them.

I pulled into a spot on the curb, belatedly remembering that I had given my front-door key to the funeral director so he could unload the funeral flowers and place them inside for the wake while I wasn't home. I sighed heavily, eyeing the three bags in the backseat and deciding whether I could balance all three while I cut through the side garden and made my way to the backyard.

I had set down one of the bags in an empty flower bed in the backyard to readjust the load when I heard the front doorbell ring. Leaving the bag on the ground, I unlocked the back door and ran inside, dropping the two bags on the kitchen counter before rushing through the house to the front door.

George Baker, an associate in Mr. Morton's law firm in addition to being Mr. Morton's grandson, stood on the front steps with an appropriate look of condolence on his face and a blue-and-white seer-sucker suit on his thin-framed body. He wasn't a bad-looking man, but his relentless pursuit of me since I had returned to Savannah six years before had made me wary and I avoided any contact with him with the same amount of effort I applied to avoiding any reminders of my past. He was also the only person of my acquaintance who insisted on calling me by my given name instead of the nickname my grandfather had given me the first time I'd sat on a horse.

"Hello, Earlene. I'm glad I found you at home." He held up a foil-wrapped casserole dish. "Mama thought you might get hungry, so she sent her tomato-okra casserole for you. There's a lot of food there, so if you don't think you can eat it all, I'd be happy to stay for dinner and help you out."

I took the casserole and forced a smile on my face. "Thanks, George. That was real sweet of your mother to think of me."

He stood facing me, obviously waiting for an invitation to come inside.

I indicated the space behind me. "I left a bag of groceries in the back garden and two more in the kitchen and I need to go put them away before they spoil."

"You know you're not supposed to be carrying anything too heavy. Let me help you."

Resigned to submitting myself to his company, I moved back to allow him in. "Let me put this casserole in the fridge if you wouldn't mind getting the bag I left outside."

He followed at my heels like a lost puppy as I made my way to the kitchen and he went out the back door. I added the casserole to the collection in the refrigerator and started unloading the bags. When George returned he began organizing the groceries on the counter by the section of the kitchen where they would be stored. It annoyed me and I pretended not to notice his system when I put the can of peeled tomatoes in the pile with frozen peas and ice cream.

"You gave a beautiful eulogy at the funeral, Earlene. You're a very strong woman, saying those words and not crying at all. I said that to my grandpa Paul and he said that you would have made your grandfather proud."

"Thank you," I said stiffly as I stuffed a plastic bag inside another. How could I explain to him that it wasn't at all because I was strong? To be strong I'd have to feel something.

He stacked the two boxes of Froot Loops on the counter. "Do you really eat this for breakfast?"

A sarcastic comment came to my lips but I bit it back. I simply didn't have the energy to apologize later. "Yes, as a matter of fact, I do."

He pursed his lips. "I think your doctor would agree that a diet filled with fresh fruits and vegetables as well as whole grains would contribute to your healing process a lot quicker than all these processed foods."

I gritted my teeth and began folding the plastic bags, knowing what was coming next.

"You know, your accident was close to six years ago. You should be walking with a lot less pain by now. Maybe you need to go back to your physical therapist to go over some exercises. . . ."

"Thanks for your concern, George. I appreciate it. Really. But I can take care of myself."

His perusal of the kitchen countertops with crumpled fast-food bags made me a liar but I chose to ignore him as I bent under the kitchen sink to throw in the pile of plastic bags.

"Have you thought much about what you're going to do now?"

I rose slowly, looking out the window over the sink into the bare garden, its beds as abandoned and neglected as a childhood dream. His grandfather had asked the same thing and I think I hated them both a little bit for it. For so long I'd existed with a wall between my present and my future and I had neither the will nor the strength to tear it down. It was so much easier to simply be.

I turned to face him. "It's really none of your concern, George."

"You know that I'd like it to be."

I closed my eyes for a long moment and took a deep breath.

"There's another reason I stopped by today."

My eyes fluttered open with dread, half expecting a small ring box.

He reached inside his jacket pocket and pulled out a small manila envelope. "My grandfather meant to bring these to you when he stopped by yesterday. For some reason they were kept separately from the envelope he already gave you. I think it's because these were given to my grandfather for safekeeping last year, when your grandfather first knew he was ill." He shoved the envelope at me and distracted himself with storing the frozen food in the freezer, stacking the peas and broccoli with military precision. "I don't think he meant for you to find them before he died. Which is why he instructed us to give them to you after his death."

I stared down at the envelope with the law firm's preprinted return address in the upper-left corner. Only my last name, Mills, was written in an unfamiliar handwriting on the front. I flipped it over and pulled out two letter-sized envelopes followed by a heavy silver key that slipped out of the envelope and clattered to the floor. I stared at it for a moment before picking it up. It was an old-fashioned key, like all the other keys that protruded from locks throughout the old house. None of the doors were missing keys, and as I turned it over in my hand, I wondered what it could go to.

I then turned my attention to the two envelopes, both of them sealed and both of them addressed to a Miss Lillian Harrington at Asphodel Meadows Plantation, Savannah. I recognized my grandmother's handwriting, but not that of the person who had scratched through Lillian's name and address and written, "return to sender." I didn't know who Lillian was, but I knew of Asphodel Meadows. A former rice plantation built in the early eighteen hundreds on the Savannah River about thirty miles south of the city, it was now, and had been since around nineteen twenty, a horse farm. I'd never been there, although it hadn't been for lack of interest on my part. Considering my past history with horses, I thought it odd now that my grandfather had never taken me there, or that our paths hadn't crossed in the nearly incestuous equestrian community of Savannah.

I glanced up at George, who looked back at me with undisguised curiosity. I shoved the key in my jeans pocket and put the letters back inside the larger envelope before tucking it under my arm. Smiling brightly at George, I began to lead him back to the front door. "Thanks so much for the casserole and for helping me with my groceries. I really do appreciate it." I yanked open the door. "I'll be sure to call you if I need anything. I promise."

His mouth jerked open and closed like a goldfish who'd sought sanctuary outside of his bowl as he tried to come up with something that would get me to invite him back inside. I put my hand on his arm and gently guided him through the doorway.

He put a hand on the doorframe, overly confident that I wouldn't shut the door with his hand in the way. "You have my cell number, right? Call me anytime. Day or night. You hear? If you need anything, please call me first."

I nodded. "I will, George. Promise." I began to close the door and was grateful when I saw him yank his hand away.

I carried the envelope into the study and emptied the contents onto the mahogany desk and sat down. With my grandfather's ivory-handled letter opener, I sliced open the smaller envelope. Carefully unfolding the heavy stationery, I read:

September 30, 1939

My Dearest Lillian,

My words are so inadequate, but I have no other means to reach you. I know that circumstances dictate that we not have any contact with each other, but my conscience dictates that I at least attempt to reach you using whatever means I have to ask your forgiveness. I don't know if I can live the rest of my life without it, so I must at least try.

What happened was an accident. You were there and you know the desperate situation we were in, but the end result was the same. And for that, I cannot forgive myself but must rely on your clemency to release me from this guilt that claws at me every day without mercy.

Forgive me, Lillian. Forgive me for loving too much and for trusting too much. With God's mercy and your forgiveness I might have hope again. *Dum vita est, spes est,* remember?

Please let me know that you have received this. You can send a message through Paul at the law offices. I see him often and I know that he can be trusted.

Remember how happy we once were? How much is changed, Lillian. I don't know if I can ever feel happy again after all that has happened. But with your forgiveness I know that I can try. Josie always told us that the more we loved, the more we lost of ourselves. I think she's right. I've lost so much that I don't think I can ever find myself again.

Your friend forever,
Annabelle

I read the letter three times, trying to hear my grandmother's voice, the one I remembered from my childhood, but couldn't. Who was this Lillian? And Josie? And what had my grandmother done that was so horrible that she was begging for forgiveness? If I hadn't recognized her handwriting, I would have denied it was written by her. This young woman in the letter was passionate and forceful. The grandmother I knew was neither.

Slowly, I slid the opener into the second envelope and pulled out the letter and began to read.

December 15, 1939

My dearest friend,

My first three letters to you have been returned to me unopened. I don't blame you, for I deserve no better.

But I have loved you like a sister, as I loved Freddie and Josie, and my loss of all of you has killed something inside of me. I only hope that one day you will find it in your heart to forgive me and we can be as sisters again. Until then, I will not rest, nor weep, nor smile, nor love; I cannot, for a heart is required to do all those things.

Do you remember when we were not much younger and we talked about the men we would marry and the daughters we would have, and the stories we would tell them when they were old enough to hear? I pray that you will have a daughter one day, and that I shall, too. Then we can share our stories with them so that what has happened will never be forgotten and we aren't so all alone in our sorrow. That is my wish for both of us.

Good-bye, sweet friend,
Annabelle

My eyes stung with tears I couldn't shed for a woman I thought I had known. I caught sight of the little blue sweater I had left folded on top of the desk. I lifted it up to my face, smelling nothing but dust and old secrets, and for the first time in my life I realized that my sad, quiet grandmother might have a story to tell me after all.

CHAPTER 3

I hated the smell of nursing homes: the mixture of antiseptic cleaners, stale cooking odors, and old dreams. I hadn't learned to hate it until my long stay in the hospital six years before when I'd begun to associate those same smells of the hospital with all of my own lost dreams.

The nurse on duty greeted me as I signed in and escorted me to the Alzheimer's wing, where she had to use a code to open the door. My grandmother had a private room, as private as living in a nursing home could be, and it was at the end of the corridor at the back of the building, giving her two large windows to look out and see the gardens. This was what my grandfather told me when we had moved her in, and I never thought to mention to him that every time we visited she sat facing the wall.

She was asleep when I entered, so I sat in a chair near her bed and watched her sleep.

She slept on her side with one hand tucked under her cheek like a child, and her long white hair tied back in a braid that lay on the pillow beside her like a remnant from her past life. My grandmother had always been old to me. I'd seen pictures of her when she was younger, of course, but I could never quite reconcile those pictures of the beautiful bride or young mother with the sad old woman of my childhood.

She stirred, a word lost on her lips as she struggled between sleep and wakefulness, awaking from dreams she couldn't remember or share. I often wondered what she dreamed of — if she were reliving happier times before the smiling woman in the photos became the old woman, or if her dreams were as blank and empty as her mind had become.

I waited as she opened her eyes and gradually came awake. Her gaze settled on me and I held my breath wondering if she would recognize me today. But her eyes continued on to the window behind me as if I had been nothing more than a piece of furniture.

"Grandmother?" I said quietly, not wanting to startle her.

Her brown eyes shot back to me and widened, but I knew that she still did not know who I was.

"Grandmother," I said again. "It's me. Piper. I've come for a visit." I stood and helped her sit up, then fluffed her pillows.

"Yes, Piper," she said, repeating my words without comprehension. "Where's Jackson? He said he would come." She looked at me suspiciously. "Have you seen him?"

"No, Grandmother. Granddaddy is dead, remember? We buried him on Saturday, at Bonaventure Cemetery, where Mama and Daddy are. You wore your black dress with your mama's cameo at the neck."

Her eyes blinked slowly as she continued to stare at me silently. Eventually her gaze traveled back to the window behind me. "Jackson brings me flowers. He knows that moonflowers are my favorite." She suddenly turned her head to face me. "Have you seen Jackson? He always brings me flowers."

I stood, trying to see the grandmother who'd taught me to garden inside this woman who didn't know who I was. I felt sorry for this old woman, yet I didn't know her. Her presence in my life had become like a soft wind that moves your hair and then is forgotten by your next breath. I walked to the window to stare down at the pretty garden somebody had hoped would resemble an English one with geometrical patterns and precisely pruned hedges. Pink roses dotted large green bushes bordering the small square space, highlighting the trellises with climbing wisteria and white wooden benches for weary spectators. I felt sad, recalling the beautiful garden my grandmother had tended in our backyard that now lay sleeping under tired dirt.

I remembered the small blue sweater and the manila envelope in my shoulder bag. Turning back toward the bed, I pulled out the sweater. I would wait to ask her about the key and the letters until later as I had learned that she could only absorb one thing at a time. I wasn't really expecting her to recognize the sweater or even to reveal anything to me. But when I had been standing in my grandfather's study the previous day, it had finally come to me how very alone in the world I was — how many years had passed since my grandmother had written that last letter. And I had to at least try.

"Grandmother? I found something yesterday in the house, in your trunk in Granddaddy's study, and it looks like something you might have knitted. Do you recognize it?"

Her brown eyes blinked slowly as if trying to focus on my face and then I watched as her gaze slowly traveled to the bundle in my

46

hands and stopped, her eyes sad and unblinking. I came closer and sat at the edge
of her bed, her gaze never leaving the blue-
yarn sweater. Her hand, as delicate as a
fallen leaf, reached out and grabbed a fistful of the soft fabric, the blue veins in her
hands like roadmaps of her life. Slowly, she
pulled it toward her and buried her face in
the sweater as I had done, and I wondered
what memory she was smelling.

"Do you know whose this was?"

She didn't respond, but kept her face
buried in the sweater. After a moment her
shoulders began to shake and a keening I
had never heard before erupted from her,
the sound bringing back to me all of my
own lost hopes and dreams.

With a hesitant hand, I touched her
shoulder, appalled yet compelled to reach
her as I witnessed a depth of emotion I
never thought her capable of.

"It's okay, Grandmother. It's going to be
okay." The words were as empty of meaning
as my incessant patting on the sharp bone
of her shoulder that protruded from her cotton nightgown. It wasn't okay. And for a
brief moment I wished that I had never
found that sweater in the trunk or read the
letters, that I had been allowed to continue
in my numb existence in the quiet house on

47

Monterey Square. But I had found the sweater and brought it here to show her. And I had remembered the words that haunted my dreams the night before, words my grandmother had told me long ago that I thought I'd forgotten. *Every woman should have a daughter to tell her stories to. Otherwise, the lessons learned are as useless as spare buttons from a discarded shirt. And all that is left is a fading name and the shape of a nose or the color of hair. The men who write the history books will tell you the stories of battles and conquests. But the women will tell you the stories of people's hearts.*

I thought back to my own mother, dead now for more than twenty years and how she'd left home at eighteen and never gone back. I remembered her only from an old Polaroid of her standing in front of the Golden Gate Bridge with my father — a picture I always thought was to show the world how very far from home she wanted to get.

My grandmother's sobbing stopped as abruptly as it had begun and I thought for a moment that she'd forgotten what she was crying for. But when she turned her reddened eyes up to me, I saw within them a clarity that I had not seen for years.

"He's gone," she whispered, her fingers

like claws as she hooked them into the sweater. Tears fell down withered cheeks but she didn't blink or take her gaze away from me. She let go of the sweater and grabbed my hands, her fingers cold and brittle. She leaned toward me and very quietly whispered so close to my face that I could feel her puffs of breath. "Every woman should have a daughter to tell her stories to."

My grandmother looked away and let go of my hands, distracted now. She leaned back against her pillows and closed her eyes. "I'm sleepy," she said, keeping her eyes closed.

I wasn't ready for her to go to sleep yet. I leaned forward and spoke quietly. "Who's Lillian, Grandmother? Who're Lillian and Josie and Freddie?"

Her eyes rolled violently under her lids but she didn't open them. Instead she turned her face away from me, but I saw her hand tighten into a fist before tucking it under her chin.

"Grandmother?" I whispered.

She didn't move. I stayed on the edge of her bed for a long time, watching the shallow rise and fall of her chest with a growing sense of unease — the same feeling one gets upon leaving home for a long trip and knowing something has been forgotten.

Finally, I stood and leaned over to kiss her cheek. I startled when her hand closed around my wrist and her eyes opened. "My box," she said. "I put it in my box but now I can't find it."

"What box?" I asked, remembering the smell of summer grass and the feel of dark earth in my hands and knowing the answer already.

But she had closed her eyes again, her breathing settling into the reassuring rhythm of a peaceful sleep. I touched her cheek, vainly seeking a connection with this woman who had raised me, and wishing again that I had never read her letters or discovered the light blue baby's sweater in the trunk.

I didn't even pause to change my clothes or shoes when I returned home. I did stop in the kitchen to gulp down two pain pills, not really bothering to wonder if I was doing so from habit or just from the need to soften the edges of reality for a while. Then I went directly to the gardening shed and pulled out my grandfather's shovel, then made my way through to the back garden to the spot where I remembered burying my grand-mother's box.

I considered for a moment calling George, but the thought of his overeager smile and his insistence that I think about my life made me hesitate. If I found that my back and knee wouldn't allow me to use a shovel, then I'd take another pain pill before calling George for help.

After swatting at the sand flies that had begun to swarm around my neck and ankles, I lifted the shovel high, stabbing the earth with the tip as I'd seen my grandfather do, and gritting at the wave of pain that grabbed my spine. I wasn't used to doing more than walking around in my house and leaning over a computer desk at various libraries as I researched, despite the insistence of George, my grandfather, and my physical therapist that I be more active. Using my good leg, I pressed down with the heel of my foot and embedded the entire head of the shovel in the dusty ground of my back garden.

Starting to feel the light-headedness I associated with my medication, the pain seemed to ebb, its edges soft and bubbly like that of an oncoming wave sliding onto shore. I wiped a bead of sweat that had begun to drip down my forehead, then lifted the shovel with a full load of dirt and dumped it behind me.

It didn't take long; the hole had only been as deep as the shallow box required. But by the time the shovel finally hit metal my blouse and pants clung to my skin with sweat and I had begun to see spots before my eyes.

I knelt in the sparse weeds beside the gaping wound in the earth and reached inside for the tin box, my fingernails scraping red clay as my fingers found their way around it. Impatiently I lifted it out of the hole, eager to have it over with, and relieved that it wasn't too heavy to lift by myself. I brushed off the top, then lifted it open, the old hinges hardly protesting.

I sat back with the box on my lap, the unearthed dirt and small rocks clinging to my pants, and I looked inside. A bundle of raw-edged scrapbook pages, stacked beneath a worn and cracked front cover and wrapped in a frayed black grosgrain ribbon, lay nestled inside. On top of the pile, as if placed as an afterthought, was a framed sepia-colored photo of three young girls, two unrecognizable but the blond one uncannily familiar. I wasn't sure at first. In the photo, the girl had a sparkle in her eye as if she knew a secret and her smile was full of mischief. But the wide eyes and slightly snubbed nose were definitely my grandmother's; I recognized them mostly because I saw the same eyes and nose every time I looked in a mirror.

I pried off the stiff cardboard backing, not feeling the pain when my nail tore back. Pulling the frame in closer to block the sun with my shadow, I peered down at the back of the photograph where someone had scrawled in amateur calligraphy three names: Lillian Harrington, Josephine Montet, and Annabelle O'Hare. I startled, recognizing the first name as the name on the letters my grandmother had written. My eyes flickered down to the words written beneath the names: *Dum vita est, spes est —Cicero.* I frowned, recalling the quote written on the wall of my high school Latin teacher's classroom and often repeated by her. I stared at the words for a long moment, remembering that my grandmother had written the same ones in her letter to Lillian. *Where there is life, there is hope.* I had never understood its relevance and still didn't.

I lifted out the pages and gave them a cursory flip, my perusal slowing as I noticed the brutally torn edges of each page, as if they'd been ripped from the spine with force.

Sweat dripped onto a page and I stood to bring the bundle in the house for closer inspection. I must have stood too suddenly;

my head swam and my vision blurred as I lost my grip on the pages and fell to my knees. I put my head down to my chest and waited for my head to clear before opening my eyes again.

The scrapbook pages lay scattered on the bare earth and encroaching weeds, the pages fluttering like moths. Crawling on my hands and knees I began gathering them up, shaking off the dirt before stacking them. As I lifted a page that had been nearly torn in half, I spotted a small newspaper clipping that was stuck facedown to the back of it. Yellowed glue with paper remnants coating its top clung to the side facing out as if the clipping had once been glued between two scrapbook pages.

Carefully, I pulled it off and read it, feeling my skin growing colder and colder despite the pressing heat of the summer sun.

The article was from the *Savannah Morning News* and dated September 8, 1939. It read:

The body of an unidentified Negro male infant was pulled from the Savannah River this morning around eight o'clock a.m. by postman Lester Agnew on his morning rounds. The body was found naked with no identifying marks and has been turned over to the medical examiner to determine the cause of death.

I felt ill, either from the pain pills or the heat. Or maybe it was from facing a past that perhaps would have been better remaining hidden. I lay down, pressing my face against the cool earth. I tasted dirt and weeds and stubborn grass but I didn't have the energy to turn my head. I stayed that way for a long time until my stomach settled and my head stopped spinning. I opened my eyes and pulled myself up on my elbow, catching sight of the upturned tin box, where something glinted from an inside corner. Slowly, I reached out my hand and pulled it toward me, unsure of what I was looking at.

It was a necklace of sorts, with a thick filigree chain halfway filled with a mismatched assortment of charms that bore little resemblance to one another. They reminded me of the angel charm Mr. Morton had given me and I sat up to examine the necklace more closely, clenching my eyes shut for a moment to stop the spinning. I dangled the charms in my hand, studying them and wondering why most of the chain had been left empty. I fingered the figures like a blind woman uncoding

Braille, trying to read the stories behind them until I reached the last one.

I looked down into my palm and saw a tiny gold baby carriage, its spokes delicately molded, and wondered what all of these charms meant. The sand flies continued their invisible attack as I stared down at this buried treasure, biting me without mercy and as persistent as old grief.

The necklace slipped through my fingers and into my lap and I inexplicably began to cry. I wasn't sure if my tears were for the old woman whose stories remained untold, or for the girl I had once been who had believed herself invincible but who had grown into a woman who no longer believed in anything at all.

CHAPTER 4

Lillian Harrington-Ross sat at the window in her sitting room and stared at the letter in her age-spotted hands, deliberately overlooking the fingers that resembled more the knotted trunks of live oaks than the graceful fingers of a woman who'd once taken so much pride in her hands.

The sound of hooves beating on dried, packed earth drew her attention out the window to the lunge ring, where her grandson, Tucker, had brought the recently rescued cherry bay gelding, the vivid scar bisecting the horse's flank appearing like a caution sign. Tucker held the lunge whip out, expertly guiding the reluctant gelding around the ring, coaxing secrets from the animal's unknown past.

Lillian rarely opened her blinds, preferring the darkness, but she'd wanted to watch her grandson and the new horse to surreptitiously study them both to see if either one of them showed any sign of healing. She sat back in her chair and looked out at her grandson through half-closed eyes, seeing another man in the shimmering heat, another man who'd known how to speak to horses and who'd had no tolerance for broken things. She let her eyelids shut completely, feeling the tremor in her old hands, imagining that it had been the power of a horse felt through the pull of the reins. But that had all been so very long ago. And she wondered again how she had let something so precious exit her life so easily. Like the moment a parent realizes their child is too big to be carried yet not remembering how long it had been since the last time.

Dum vita est, spes est. The letter shook in her hands as the words danced in front of her eyes. *Where there is life, there is hope.* Was it really possible to have once been so young as to believe in hope? And in friendships that were meant to last a lifetime? But it was more than the passage of years that had made her a cynical old woman; grief and loss could poison more than just time.

Peering again through her bifocals at the letter, Lillian read it for the third time.

Dear Mrs. Harrington-Ross,
　　I'm not sure if you received my previ-

ous three letters. In case you haven't, I'm Piper Mills, the granddaughter of Annabelle O'Hare Mercer. I have recently discovered pages from a scrapbook that belonged to her along with a photo of my grandmother, you and a girl named Josephine among other things.

You may or may not be aware that my grandmother passed away last month after having battled with Alzheimer's for many years. Her scrapbook has left me with many questions and I'm eager to speak with you to help me answer as many as I can.

I can be reached at the number below and would be happy to either speak with you over the phone or set up an appointment to meet with you at Asphodel Meadows.

I've never met you although I lived with my grandparents for many years. I'm left to assume that any friendship you had with Annabelle must have ended some time ago. Please know that the reason or fault is of no interest to me. I'm simply trying to get to know the person my grandmother was before I was born, and perhaps to find some meaning to the death of a woman who I feel I never really knew at all.

I look forward to hearing from you.

Sincerely,
Piper Mills

Lillian sighed, her chest tightening. *So Annabelle is gone.* The years seemed to rush at her like an incoming tide, the memories like a picture show in vivid color, each one moving forward like a sewn hem, and each stitch a mouthful of grief. But never regret. The one thing she attributed her longevity to was her stubborn ability to never confuse grief with regret.

There was a soft rap on the door behind her before it was opened. Lillian smelled the dust and the sweat and horse before Tucker spoke. Her bones and her eyesight might not be as strong as they had once been, but her sense of smell had not yet deserted her. She closed her eyes again, remembering the man who'd once carried the same scent and found herself smiling softly.

Tucker kissed her on the cheek and she looked up at him, seeing more of her son-in-law than her daughter in his olive skin and nearly black hair. He had her late husband's height and broad shoulders and her own dark green eyes. But his aura of regret was his own, and settled on his

60

shoulders like an ill-fitting coat.

He moved to the sideboard and poured himself a tall glass of iced tea. "Can I get anything for you, Malily?" His childhood name for her had stuck, and had suited Lillian at the time as she'd once considered herself too young to be called "Grandmother."

"Sherry," she said, watching his eyes.

He didn't even pause as he unstopped the decanter and filled a small sherry glass to the top. "I'm sure it's five o'clock somewhere," he said softly.

Tucker crossed the room and handed her the glass, then remained standing. Although long since grown, he knew better than to sit on Lillian's furniture when he was dirty from working outside.

After taking a long drink of his iced tea, he said, "That new horse is a tough one. He's got a big personality and the strength to match it. Who knows what kind of abuse he's gone through, though."

Lillian took a sip of the sherry, already thinking about how soon she could have another, and turned to the window seeing past the rings and stables, beyond the green pastures, and saw through years to three little girls sitting atop a pasture gate. She turned back to Tucker, noticing his fingers

61

wrapped around his iced-tea glass and how they were no longer the hands of a doctor. She thought of the horse with his scars and wondered if having them so visible wasn't preferable to the hidden kind where nobody knew how to avoid the parts that still hurt.

"I need you to do me a favor." Lillian avoided Tucker's eyes by taking another sip from her sherry, welcoming the numbness that seeped into her fingertips.

He sounded wary. "What is it?"

She paused for a moment, weighing her words. "I need you to write a letter for me. The granddaughter of an old friend of mine, a Piper Mills, wants to meet with me to discuss aspects of her grandmother's past." Lillian regarded Tucker before continuing. "As you know, I gave all of my papers to Susan for her research, and I don't have the heart to go search for them now nor do I expect you to do it. It's too soon. . . ." She looked away, unable to watch the color drain from his face. "And I'm afraid my memory isn't as good as it once was, and without the papers I doubt I can recall anything with any accuracy. I'd rather just tell this Piper that I'm not available. I was thinking that if you wrote the letter, she would assume I was too ill to speak with her and leave it at that."

Tucker returned to the sideboard and poured himself another glass from the frosted pitcher of iced tea. A drop of condensation dripped on the mahogany surface and he quickly wiped up the spot with a napkin before his grandmother had a chance to say anything. "Piper Mills. The name rings a bell."

Lillian took a deep breath, wrinkling the letter in her hands as she balled them into fists in her lap. "About six years ago she was regarded as one of eventing's sporting elite and an Olympic hopeful. The rumor was her grandfather had already bought plane tickets to Athens." She smiled ruefully. "Then at Kentucky she fell from her horse and he landed on her. Nobody knows for sure, but they say it was her fault, that she knew something was wrong when there was still time to pull back but she continued into the jump. She broke her back, shattered her leg and a few ribs, and punctured her lung. They had to euthanize her horse. She hasn't ridden since."

Tucker eyed his grandmother. "I remember now. I thought she died."

Lillian looked down at her glass. "She probably wished that she had."

Tucker turned away and Lillian regretted her words. But it was so hard to avoid pressing on his bruises. Since Susan's death, talking to him was like walking with two broken legs; anywhere you stepped it was going to hurt.

Tucker stared outside at the empty lunge ring. "If you were friends with her grandmother, why haven't our paths ever crossed?"

Lillian lifted her empty glass for Tucker to refill. "Because her grandmother and I ceased being friends a long, long time ago."

He took her glass but set it on the sideboard and she knew better than to argue with him about it.

"So why now? Why does she want to talk to you now?"

Lillian closed her eyes and leaned her head back, the warmth of the sun from the windows feeling like poison ivy pricking at her skin. "Because Annabelle — her grandmother — has recently died. I suppose it's not unusual for those left behind to want answers to questions they never thought to ask when they had the time."

Avoiding Tucker's troubled eyes, Lillian pressed on. "Those papers — the ones I gave Susan — they've caused us so much grief. I don't think I could stand to have someone else go through them."

Tucker returned his glass to the sideboard,

the crystal clunking hard against the wood. "I'll take care of it today." He crossed the room to kiss her on her cheek again. "I've got to go. We've got a truckload of hay and shavings coming in this morning and I want to make sure it's all good before they unload it."

When he straightened, she reached for his hand and squeezed it, hoping he would accept this mute apology for saying Susan's name aloud. He squeezed back, then left. As Lillian watched him go she thought again of the damaged horse and its unwillingness to trust and realized how very much alike the wounded animal and her grandson really were. She fingered the gold charm around her neck, the one she'd worn since she was ten years old, and as she listened to Tucker's footsteps fading down the hall, Lillian wondered if she was the only one who could still see his scars because she knew exactly where to look.

The bells of St. John's were ringing the hour as I tried to bury my face deeper and deeper into the cool cotton of my pillowcase. I lost track of the number of times they rang, but thought it was more than ten. Alarmed, I kicked off the covers, remembering that the Goodwill truck was scheduled to stop by before noon to collect the bags of my grandfather's clothing, which I hadn't yet collected or sorted. I'd donated all of my grandmother's clothing to the home where she'd lived the last years of her life, not being able to bring myself to go through it all and sort it. Anything of value had been left behind when she'd moved sixteen years ago, and anything she'd obtained since was nothing I wanted to hold on to.

My feet landed on paper as I slid them over the side of the bed. With a groan, I reached down and picked up the letter that I'd read at least a dozen times, my disappointment having now morphed into full-out anger. I relished the emotion; it was the only emotion I'd felt in a very long time.

Holding the crumpled paper in front of me, I read it again, curious to see if maybe reading it in the light of day after a night's sleep might change the way I felt.

Dear Ms. Mills,

It has come to my attention that you have been trying to contact my grandmother, Mrs. Lillian Harrington-Ross, in the hopes of talking with her about your late grandmother, Annabelle O'Hare Mercer.

Unfortunately, my grandmother is now

very frail and bedridden, and she is not receiving visitors. On your behalf I did ask her about your grandmother and it took several moments for her to even recollect that she had once known her.

I'm afraid that even if my grandmother were healthy enough to meet with you, she wouldn't be able to answer any of your questions at all.

My deepest condolences on your loss.

Regards,
William T. Gibbons

My gaze traveled from the letter to the newspaper on the bedstand. I hadn't yet canceled my grandfather's subscription and I found myself reading it from cover to cover as if to make up for my own lack of involvement. It was folded open to the front page of the people section — written the same day as William Gibbons' letter — where a large photograph taken at a charity horse event was the main feature. The photograph focused on an older woman, looking neither frail or bedridden — her only seeming nod to her age being a beautiful ebony cane — and a younger man flanking a young girl tricked out in equestrian garb and holding aloft a gold trophy.

The caption read:

Mrs. Lillian Harrington-Ross of Asphodel Meadows Plantation and her grandson, Dr. Tucker Gibbons, award the winner's cup to Katharine Kobylt of Milledgeville at the Twin Oaks Charity event.

I slapped the letter on top of the newspaper, welcoming the new wave of anger. I'd still only skimmed through the scrapbook pages, not completely understanding why I hesitated to read them thoroughly. But I'd seen the name Lillian Harrington on practically every page and from what I could tell, the pages spanned nearly a decade of my grandmother's life, beginning around the age of thirteen.

And then there was the picture of the three girls sitting atop a pasture gate, grazing horses visible in the background. Their arms were thrown around one another's shoulders, their identical expressions of joy, mirth, and friendship plastered on eager faces. I shut my eyes, having finally accepted that my anger was aimed at myself. I shifted uncomfortably on the perch of my bed, realizing that all the answers to my unasked questions were now buried along with my grandmother under the alluvial soil in Bonaventure Cemetery.

I felt something else, too — an undercurrent that wasn't anger or disappointment. It was what I imagined I'd feel if I looked up into the sun to find all the answers and found instead only blindness. I wasn't naive enough to assume that any answers I'd discovered would be what I wanted to hear.

Stumbling to the bathroom, my back and right knee aching with the sudden movement, I hurriedly showered and dressed, pulling my jeans out of the bottom of a pile of laundry I hadn't yet found the energy to wash. The burst of energy I'd discovered with my newfound purpose of contacting Lillian Harrington had fizzled, then gone flat like a bottle of Coke left open too long. William T. Gibbons' terse letter had taken care of that. My eyes stung as I pulled my hair back into an unforgiving ponytail and tried to think of anything else to get excited about beyond the arrival and departure of the Goodwill truck.

After limping down to the kitchen and rummaging through the cabinets to find large plastic garbage bags, I returned to my grandfather's room and opened his closet. Not allowing sentiment to cloud my progress, I dumped suits, ties, slacks, and belts indiscriminately into the bags. I paused only when I came to his straw hat. I didn't touch it, but left it on the shelf where my grandfather had last placed it, then watched as it quickly became the last item remaining, a lone survivor of a long life, my part in it no longer clear. I considered it for a moment, seeing the hat and myself as the last testaments to my grandfather's years on this earth and couldn't really decide which one he'd put more faith in. At least the hat had shielded his eyes from the sun. I'd only succeeded in letting him down.

Almost as an afterthought, I grabbed the hat, then closed the closet door, feeling only regret in the brittle straw in my hands as I firmly tucked the hat into the open plastic bag.

Glancing at my watch, I limped back down to the kitchen with the bags, quickly scrawling out tags for each bag and taping them to the outside. Then one by one, I dragged them to the back garden, settling them into what had once been my grandmother's herb garden, the rocks delineating the edges now mostly gone, the remaining ones bleached by the sun and placed as sporadically as tombs in a graveyard.

Sweating and out of breath, I leaned forward with my hands on my knees and felt something digging into my thigh. I reached into my pocket and found the old-fashioned key George had given me in the envelope with the letters to Lillian. I'd forgotten about it until now, and made a mental note as I returned it to my pocket to test all the doors in the house with it.

After returning the key to my pocket, I headed toward the kitchen door, glancing up at the back of the house as I made my way down the weed-covered flagstone walk. I reached the back porch and stopped, the view of the rear of the old house suddenly flashing through my head. Retracing my steps, I stood again in the deserted garden and looked up at the back of the brick house.

The row of windows on the upper story that marked my bedroom and the bedroom shared by my grandparents appeared as they always had: neat tidy rectangles of six-on-six panes with ripples visible in the old glass.

My eyes traveled to the attic level, where three shorter windows were centered over the upper story, the two brick chimneys on either side of the roof framing the windows like parentheses. I stared at them for a long time, fighting against the encroachment of my inertia as the excitement of my new discovery pressed me forward and into the house.

I took the stairs slowly, my knee aching

and urging me to sit down. But I pressed forward, feeling the key in my pants pocket and trying to imagine why my grandmother would think that pain could ever be useful.

At the far end of the upstairs hallway stood the door that led to the attic stairs. As I'd thought, the key protruded from the lock and the door was unlocked. I pulled it open, sneezing as the dust motes, disturbed from their resting place for the first time in years, drifted up to tickle my nose. I sneezed, then pulled the door open farther and made my way up the stairs.

I stood amid the old trunks and broken furniture, antique appliances and the Victorian doll house that my father had made but that my grandfather had relegated to the attic because it distracted me from focusing on horseback riding. On the opposite side of the room from the single brick chimney sat a large mahogany open armoire filled with my horse show ribbons and trophies. These had once been kept in the front parlor until my accident, after which I'd begged my grandfather to get rid of them. I hadn't known what he'd done with them and I was still too numb to care that they hadn't been thrown away. All I'd cared about at the time was getting them out of my sight, an unwanted reminder of the girl who had cheated death once and had been stupid enough to believe that there would never be anything else to lose.

This attic was the old stomping ground of my imagination back in the days of my childhood when I still had one and before life taught me that dreaming was only for those young enough to have not experienced too much of real life. But in all of those years of playing up here and digging in the trunks for old-fashioned dresses made of soft clingy fabrics and high-heeled shoes that were three sizes too big for me, I had never noticed that the two windows visible from the inside of the attic didn't correspond to the three windows seen from the back garden.

I walked to the wall where the third window should have been. The walls in the attic were plastered and painted a stark white and there was nothing remarkable about this wall except for the large armoire in the middle of it. Pressing my forehead against the plaster, I peered into the small crack behind the armoire and saw the door exactly as I'd imagined it.

My first thought was to call Mr. Morton and have him save me the trouble of moving the armoire by asking him to tell me what was behind the door. But he was on his trip and he'd already made it clear that he'd told me all that he was going to. Whether his choice had been to protect me or my grandparents, I wasn't sure.

After removing most of the larger trophies from the shelves of the armoire and stacking them on the floor, I leaned my back against the armoire and dug my heels into the old wood floors to give it a good shove, succeeding in doing nothing more than making the piece of furniture groan and my back and knee ache.

With a heavy sigh of resignation, I went downstairs to my bedroom and made a quick phone call to George from Mr. Morton's office, telling him only that I needed his help to move a heavy piece of furniture. Then I went down to the foyer and waited on the bottom step for the doorbell to ring before slowly answering the door.

Without preamble, I led George up to the attic and walked straight to the armoire. "Here's that piece of furniture I told you about. There's nothing in it but I still can't get it to budge. I was thinking that maybe with the two of us pushing on one side, we could slide it."

George eyed the massive piece of furniture speculatively before taking off his seersucker jacket and hanging it on an old hat rack that jutted out of a pile of packing boxes. "I think I can do this by myself, Earlene. I wouldn't want you to strain your back."

I bit the inside of my lip to keep from saying something I shouldn't. "Humor me, okay? I'm pretty sure it's going to take both of us."

With a furrowed brow he placed his shoulders next to mine so that we were standing next to each other with our backs against the armoire, George's frown changing to a smile as soon as he realized that he was standing closer to me than I'd ever allowed him.

Digging in our heels, I counted to three and then we both pushed as hard as we could and succeeded in budging the armoire about an inch. My back and knee protested but I felt encouraged by our progress. Turning to George I said, "Let's try it again. It shouldn't take too long."

With renewed energy, we continued to push an inch at a time until we'd completely uncovered a door that matched the rest of the doors in the house.

George raised his eyebrows. "Did you know this was here?"

"Not until about four hours ago," I said as I dug the key out of my pocket and fit it into the lock. It was old and unused and I had to use my whole hand to turn the key but finally I heard the click of the locking mechanism. I paused and put my hand flat against the door, then faced George. "Whatever we find in this room stays between you and me — do you understand?"

He pretended to zip his lips and throw away a key. I turned back to the door and pulled it open, the unused hinges complaining loudly.

The room was cramped, with a sloped ceiling and only enough space for a single bed, washstand and a small chest of drawers. I moved to the center of the room, slowly turning around and taking it all in, trying to get the four walls to give up their secrets. A basket by the lone window held faded and rumpled magazines. I peered at the one on top, a *Good Housekeeping* magazine dated June 1939.

George moved to close the door to make more room for both of us to stand inside. "There's no knob on the inside of the door."

I looked at him, feeling sick. "Don't shut it all the . . ." My voice trailed away as I spotted the small bassinet that had been behind the door. I approached in small steps, holding my breath.

"It's empty, Earlene."

I let my breath go as I stood looking down

at the white wicker of the bassinet, tiny dots swimming in front of my eyes. Inside the baby's bed, folded neatly and with care at the bottom, lay a small knitted blanket made of pale blue yarn.

CHAPTER 5

That night, I dreamed of the accident again for the first time in months. I was transported back as Fitz and I tackled the cross-country course and approached fence five, the flower basket. Officially, they said it was a misjudgment in striding that didn't allow Fitz to get his legs out of the way. To me, though, the reason why didn't matter. Because in the end, I had still lost everything.

In reality, my accident had been over in a matter of seconds, but my dream always progressed in slow and hellish detail, and I saw things I couldn't have. In the dream we're heading toward the obstacle, a jump through the basket handle, not considered one of the more challenging jumps on the course, and I sense something's not right. But Fitz is heading forward and I still think we can do it, that we'll catch up and everything will work out. When it's too late I realize Fitz is going too fast, his body is not up as high as it should be, he can't clear the jump. His body starts to rotate and I'm flying off in front of him. For a brief second I see he is now perfectly vertical in the air and when he falls it's clear that he's going to fall on me. But I can't move; I'm broken into a million little pieces and I wait there for what seems forever with my beautiful horse poised above me in a grotesque dance. I'm consumed with the absolute astonishment and disbelief that the worst thing that could happen to me could happen twice.

But this time in the dream I feel the sweat under my helmet, hear the sweet creak of the leather as I lean forward in the saddle, smell the reassuring scents of horse and grass and anticipation as I move toward the jump. And when Fitz clips the top of the obstacle I'm seeing everything from an impossibly high vantage point, not recognizing the doll lying in the grass is me. He lands on the doll, then rolls off and hits the ground, then bounces up three feet, coming back down. He struggles to stand and takes a few steps before staggering to the right and collapsing. Both horse and rider are eerily still but I feel nothing.

I float over the spectators behind the ropes

and see my grandfather. He's not screaming or rushing toward me. Instead, he's frowning with disappointment and saying something to the woman beside him. When I fly closer, I see that the woman is my grandmother and that next to her are my mother and father. Their faces are blurry but I still recognize them. They're wearing the same Christmas sweatshirts that they'd been wearing the last time I'd seen them alive. I continue to fly over the course, staring at the rag doll and motionless horse on the ground, so calm it appears both are sleeping. The noise of an approaching helicopter blocks out all sound, pulsing in my ears.

Then I look down and see my grandmother is alone, and that strikes me as odd because my grandmother hadn't been there in real life, hadn't even been to an event for a long time before it. But she's there now and she's moving her lips but no words are coming out. I float down slowly to get closer, and just as I'm near enough to hear what she's saying, I spot the blue baby blanket clutched in her hands. Her lips are still moving, and when I finally hear the words, they sound like gibberish or another language and I'm overcome with frustration that I can't understand anything my grandmother is trying to tell me. And then I'm back in my body on the ground, feeling again the agony, and I'm screaming, screaming, screaming.

My throat felt raw as my eyes opened in the bedroom of my grandparents' house, the sound of my screams still settling into the four walls like ghosts. I sat up in bed, shivering despite the warmth of the summer night. I stayed like that in the dark room for a long time, listening to the occasional car and tracing the headlights against the far wall. It was only as I was drifting off to sleep again that I realized what my grandmother had been saying to me in the dream. *Dum vita est, spes est.* And by the time the sun began to poke holes in the morning, I had almost come to believe that maybe my life wasn't over yet and that it might be time to finally listen to what my grandmother had to tell me.

By mid-June, the asphodels in Lillian's garden had shot through the earth and were pointing at the sky like bright yellow spears. They'd never been her favorite flower but she'd felt obliged to cultivate them in a nod to her ancestors, who'd named their plantation for the flower and for the Greek mythological meadow where indifferent and ordinary souls were sent to live out eternity after death.

The heat of the day simmered up from the soil in waves as she squinted under the large straw brim of her hat at the sound of tires on gravel. She watched as Tucker's Jeep approached through the alley of two-hundred-year-old oaks, and straightened as he pulled up into the circular drive, stopping in front of the large Roman sundial that had marked the time at Asphodel Meadows since 1817. Lucy and Sara, in identical eyelet sundresses, scrambled out of the backseat. The older of the two, Lucy, wore her somber expression like an accessory and held tightly to her little sister's hand.

Sara jumped up and down, creating a cloud of dust around her anklet socks and white patent leather Mary Jane's. "Malily! Daddy said we could have supper with you and Aunt Helen tonight."

Lillian smiled at the girls, then rubbed her lower back as Tucker approached. It was getting harder and harder to move anymore and she'd known since the beginning of that spring that these would be her last gardens. Even with Helen's help, it was beyond her physical limitations now. Her twisted and curled fingers couldn't hold a clipper any better than she could kneel or squat for any length of time and she grieved for her garden like the moon mourned the night sky at sunrise. But grief, she'd learned in her ninety years, was as much a part of life as breathing, and disappointment and regret its eager companions. So was guilt, which she tried not to think about anymore. Especially now, after receiving Piper Mills' letter. If only she'd been able to throw away the guilt with the letter. But guilt, she'd also learned, was a lot like tree sap: it stuck to everything and after a long time it hardened to stone, trapping unsuspecting creatures inside of it.

Tucker stopped in front of her, looking at her solicitously. "You shouldn't be out in this heat. Women half your age would have had heat stroke by now."

She smiled up at him, seeing the dark smudges under his eyes and noticing that his hair needed cutting. "We're from hardy stock. It would take a lot more than heat to knock me over." She ran a curled knuckle over his cheek, trying to erase the lines that had no business being on the face of a man just past his thirty-second year. Quietly, she said, "You know I love having the girls, Tuck. It would just be nice to have a little advance warning, that's all."

He glanced away. "Yeah, sorry. I just . . . Well, the new nanny — Emily — takes classes at night and couldn't stay. I figured you and Helen could keep them entertained."

Lillian looked toward the row of sweet-smelling English lavender she'd coaxed into growing along the short fence lining the drive. "What the girls need is more time with their father." She sensed his shoulders tightening. "You're welcome to join us, you know."

He reached out a hand toward Lucy and tucked her pale blond hair behind her ear. She responded by leaning into him like a daisy toward the sun, pulling her little sister with her. "I've got plans."

Lillian tilted her head back to stare into his face. "Plans?"

His lips tightened. "Yes, plans. That don't involve children. And if you can't watch the girls, I'll find other arrangements."

She watched as Sara squatted to smell the lavender, the bow on her dress untied and dragging in the dirt. Lucy simply stood next to her father wearing the same unreadable expression, the color blanched from her cheeks like sun-bleached shells on the beach.

Lillian kept her voice light, knowing Lucy

was listening to every word. "That's not necessary, Tuck. We'll be happy to watch the girls." She put her hand on Lucy's head, feeling the warmth through the fine strands of hair. "Just . . . try not to be too late. Maybe you can join us for coffee when you return."

"Maybe," he said, his eyes averted as he gave her a quick peck on the cheek before gathering both girls in a stiff hug.

Only Sara seemed oblivious to the awkwardness. She held out a sprig of lavender to her father. "For you, Daddy," she said, shoving it under his nose before kissing him heartily on the cheek.

"Thanks, sweet pea," he said softly as he straightened, tucking the sprig into the pocket of his starched buttoned-down shirt. His eyes met Lillian's for a moment, and they recalled that he hadn't called Sara by her nickname since Susan's death more than a year before. It was as if that one event had renamed them all and taught them to speak in separate languages.

"Good night, Lucy," he said.

Lucy kept her head down, her gaze firmly planted on the row of lavender.

Tucker turned and began walking toward his Jeep, then stopped. "Oh, before I forget — Helen and I rented out the caretaker's cottage. To a genealogist. She's doing research on families in the area."

Lillian struggled to keep her composure. "But I thought . . ." She swallowed back the wave of anger. "I assumed that with Susan no longer here to handle the rental property that we could just close it up. . . ." Her voice trailed away, and she was aware that she'd said those very same words more than once.

His hands fisted in his pockets. "I know," he said, his words clipped. "But then this woman called, and when Helen told me she was a genealogist, I felt obligated to Susan to say yes."

Despair settled on Lillian like dusk in the marsh; suddenly and completely she found herself in darkness. "Tucker — what about your practice? And your girls? Wouldn't they benefit from your time more?"

He studied her for a moment before dipping his gaze to his daughters, who stood mutely together, their hands held between them.

"I don't think I'm a good influence on anybody right now."

Despite the pain in her back and the need to sit down, she raised her chin. "Perhaps you're right. But don't wait too long. You don't want to give yourself something else to regret."

He glanced at her with what looked a lot like dislike in his eyes but she didn't shrink back. "Good night, Malily."

The three of them turned to watch Tucker climb back into his Jeep and peel out of the gravel drive, throwing up dirt and rocks behind him.

Lillian crooked each arm out, knowing the girls wouldn't want to touch her ruined hands, and waited for each to take an elbow before leading them to the door tucked under the front porch between the twin curving sets of stairs that led upward. She'd had the elevator installed nearly five years earlier when she'd found herself unable to tackle the steps. As the door closed on the sunlight behind them, she missed being able to enter her own home from the front doors, and the old familiarity of the four Doric columns that had always seemed to embrace her and welcome her home.

The sound of the television set blaring from the back parlor welcomed them as soon as they stepped out of the elevator. Sara skipped ahead, unable to curb her energy but Lucy held fast to Lillian's arm, making Lillian feel much older and frailer than she actually was. It seemed to her that the end of her life had come much too quickly, that there was still so much to be done. And now Annabelle was dead. For the first time in many years, Lillian wished she were young again. She wanted to scream and shout and throw things, and curse at the vagaries and unfairness of life. But even when she had been young and had the body and the energy, she would never have outwardly shown any of those emotions. Despite dreams to the contrary, Lillian Harrington-Ross had never done anything that was not expected of a gently bred Southern woman. Except once, and seventy years later she was still living with its ghosts.

Helen sat in the back parlor on the old settee with Susan's yellow Lab, Mardi, at her feet. The old dog had mourned for his mistress for a couple of weeks, refusing to eat and wandering aimlessly around the stables and house looking for her. And then in resignation he had attached himself to Helen. Maybe he'd viewed Helen's disability the way most people did, assuming that without her sight she was the most vulnerable of those Susan had left behind.

Helen patted the cushion on either side of her to let the girls know she wanted them to sit. Sara raced over and bounced into her seat while Lucy took the more leisurely approach by sitting gingerly on the edge. With the remote control, Helen flicked off what appeared to be the *Jerry Springer Show* and patted each girl on the head. "I guess Malily and I have company tonight. It's a good thing I put on my new dress."

Lillian eyed Helen's red silk cocktail dress, overdone, as usual, for another evening at home. Although five years older than Tucker, Helen was still long, lean, and stunning, her hair as dark as it had been when she was a girl and without benefit of Clairol. Being blind since the age of fourteen had neither blunted her beauty or her wild streak. And Helen would have liked to make everyone believe that she'd inherited both from her grandmother. Only Lillian knew how much of that was true.

Lillian sat carefully in her favorite stuffed armchair. "Your dress is lovely, Helen. Where did you find it?"

Helen smiled as she reached for her cigarette case on the table in front of her. "Thank you. I do like it. The new nanny, Emily, took me into town this morning and helped me pick this one out. I wanted red, and she promised me this was the reddest red dress she'd ever seen."

"It's definitely red," Lillian said, trying hard to keep the disapproval out of her voice. But it was a lovely dress, and the silk was finely woven. It had taken Lillian a while to understand Helen's reasons for the way she dressed but she'd eventually learned that it had everything to do with Helen's sense of touch. It was as if instead of her hearing or taste becoming stronger when she lost her sight, everything had become focused on what she could feel at the end of her fingertips.

"You shouldn't smoke, Aunt Helen," Lucy said somberly. "Daddy said it would make your lungs turn black and kill you. And he's a doctor, so he knows these things."

Lucy looked alarmed as Helen reached toward the coffee table for her lighter. Still smiling, she flicked the lighter and moved it to the end of her cigarette. "Sweetheart, that could be true for most people. But not for me because lightning never strikes twice. I figure being blind would be enough to make the hand of fate pass right over me when handing out bad news."

Lucy looked up at her aunt with eyes dark enough to be called black, and always appearing darker still when contrasted against her pale hair. "That's not what Mama said. She said bad things happened to good people all the time."

Helen blew out a puff of smoke and put her arm around Sara. "Well, then. We'll just have to try very hard not to be too good, then."

"Helen," Lillian said sharply. "Please."

Helen's smile faded, but not the light in her sightless eyes. "Sara, hand me the ashtray, would you please?"

Sara did as she'd been asked and placed it in her aunt's left hand while Helen stubbed out her cigarette with her right before sitting back against the couch with a heavy sigh. "I overheard your conversation with Tucker," she said to Lillian.

Helen recrossed her legs and settled her skirt. "I took the phone call from that woman who's renting the caretaker's cottage. Her name's Earlene Smith. Which I think is very odd."

"How so?" Lillian shifted in her chair, trying to find a comfortable position where all of her bones wouldn't ache. She could hear Odella in the kitchen preparing their supper but she couldn't muster any appetite. She hadn't had an appetite for a very long time.

"Earlene is an old lady's name. And the woman on the phone sounded very young."

"It must be a family name. That's not so out of the ordinary around here, Helen."

"Obviously. But most younger people come up with a nickname so they fit in better. Like Tucker, for example. So for this woman to be using that name, well, it struck me as odd, is all."

Lillian fingered the charm around her neck. "You're always seeing zebras when all we have is horses, Helen. Did the woman sound local?"

Helen leaned back in the couch, a long, slender arm around each of her nieces. Her red fingernails matched her lips and her dress and her high-heeled snakeskin pumps that were made for a night of dancing instead of one playing Chutes and Ladders. "Now, Malily, that's another thing that struck me as odd. Her accent was Savannah, born and bred, but she said she's from Atlanta. She did say that her mother was from Savannah, which could explain it. But still . . ." Her voice trailed away, her forehead creased with speculation.

Lillian shifted her position again. "Did you ask her what her mother's name was?"

"It didn't occur to me. My generation's not as obsessed with bloodlines as yours was, Malily." She smiled in her grandmother's direction. "Besides I was too busy answering all of her questions about the horses here and their proximity to the cottage. Apparently, she's deathly afraid of them and doesn't want to have anything to do with them while she's here. I explained that she'd be able to see them in the pastures from time to time, but that all of the stables and riding rings are behind the house. She seemed okay with that."

Lillian absently rubbed the charm hanging from her neck and realized how much her hands were hurting. She glanced out through the narrow slats of the shuttered windows toward the pregnant gray clouds that were moving in from the low lands. Lord knew the pastures and her gardens desperately needed the rain but how she hated summer storms. Maybe, if she were lucky, it would simply be a cleansing rain, nourishing the earth without punishing her with memories she could easily push away except when lightning flitted across the sky.

"How odd," said Lillian, "that she would choose our caretaker's cottage — in the middle of a horse farm — to come do her research if she's so afraid of horses."

Helen nodded. "I said the same thing. So Earlene explained that the Rosses were the core branch of the family she's researching, so it made sense to her to be here to have access to the family cemetery and any papers we were willing to share with her."

Lillian jerked her attention to Helen. "What did you tell her about the family papers?"

"I explained that some were private — meaning your scrapbook — but that she would be welcome to most of the rest. And don't worry, Malily. I wouldn't ask you or Tuck to get involved. I'll handle everything." Helen rotated her ankle, the snakeskin of her shoe glowing softly in the gray light from the almost-shuttered windows. "Besides, I could use a diversion. It's very hard for a woman my age to consistently lose at Chutes and Ladders. I need something else to focus on to lift my spirits." She squeezed the girls on either side of her as they giggled.

Odella walked briskly into the room, her soft-soled nurse's shoes squeaking on the heart pine floor. She was about fifteen years older than Helen and just as thin, but her parchmentlike skin and graying hair made her appear years older. She'd been married and widowed three times and raised eight children, which probably accounted for the weary expression she normally wore. But there was no finer cook in the entire Lowcountry than Odella Pruitt and no softer heart, although she did her best to hide it behind a tart tongue and salty attitude, neither of which Lillian minded. It was a small price to pay for excellent food and a firm hand to help Lillian's increasingly feeble body.

"Food's ready and it's not going to eat itself," announced Odella as she gently grasped Lillian's elbow and helped her out of her chair. "Girls, grab hold of your aunt Helen and take her to the dining room, would you please? Don't want her knocking anything over. Got enough to do as it is without having to clean up extra messes."

"Yes, ma'am," the girls said in unison, their eyes wide. They hadn't yet discovered the secret that was Odella Pruitt, and that was fine with Odella. Because once they realized what a pushover she really was, they'd have her wrapped around their small fingers.

"I'll be careful, Odella," said Helen with a deceptively meek voice. "You know how clumsy I can be." This made Lillian grin since Helen moved with the grace of a ballet dancer, and except for that first desperate year of Helen's blindness, she'd never knocked over a single thing.

But Lillian's smile quickly faded as she heard the first rumble of thunder. She grasped at the gold charm dangling from her neck and allowed herself to be led into the dining room. She kept her eyes focused in front of her and tried not to shudder with each flash of lightning that seemed to throw light into the forgotten corners of her memory, illuminating things she didn't want to see.

CHAPTER 6

The handheld GPS that I'd stuck to the inside of the windshield in my grandfather's Buick had long since announced that I was "off-road," apparently in a place where even satellites couldn't find me, my destination unknown.

I paused on the old gravel road, knowing from the blank map on the GPS screen that the Savannah River was somewhere to my right and a large golf course was on my left. But somewhere, in the vast dark space on the screen, lay Asphodel Meadows, once the queen of the Savannah River rice planta-tions, but now operating solely as a horse farm and private residence, its land de-voured by development and the encroach-ing river, its rice beds now a golf course.

Just when I thought I should turn around, I spotted the small marker tucked into the brush on the side of the road announcing my arrival at Asphodel Meadows. It was a brown National Trust sign, but it was hidden so well that I was left to believe that someone had done it intentionally.

As soon as I turned onto the road, I smelled the horses. Not the horses exactly, but their associated smells of cut grass, hay, and leather. Despite the heat, I turned off the air conditioner, trying to block the scent that never failed to rip through me with equal parts exhilaration and terror. I began to sweat in the stifling interior as the gravel crunched under the slowly rotating tires as I followed the drive to where it seemed to stop abruptly, disappearing into a steep green embankment. Finding it hard to breathe, I lowered the windows, hoping to find sight of the road.

To the right of the Buick, at a sharp angle, I spotted the continuation of the road as well as the turnoff I must have missed while staring straight ahead in the hopes of avoiding any sight of pastures. Gripping the wheel tightly, I angled the car and turned, finding myself suddenly enveloped in the canopy of an ancient live oak alley. I stopped the car, looking at the old trees that barely resembled the live oaks of Savannah's squares despite the generous shawls of Spanish moss. These trees were darkened and withered, despite enough leaves to show that they were alive. But the limbs were bent and gnarled, the knobs at the forks like the bent shoulders of mourners at a funeral.

Gulping the stagnant, humid air, I caught the scent of the river, too, and continued to drive forward through the short line of hulking oak trees toward the cream-colored columned house beckoning me at the end.

When I reached the circular drive in front of the house, I released my hands on the wheel and wiped my sweaty palms on my white linen pants, then dug into the side pocket of the door for a fast-food napkin to wipe my face. I sat there for a long time, pressing the napkin to my face and listening to my heart pound while I stared at the house in front of me.

The house wasn't the typical antebellum Greek Revival architecture found in my history books of the Savannah River plantations. Instead, it had been built in the English Regency style, with a raised first floor, flat roof, and twin sandstone staircases flanking the lower entrance. The steps rose to the front porch with its four Doric columns standing sentry to the double front doors. It would have been beautiful if not for the odd alley of grieving oaks that led to the house.

There was something else, too, that shimmered in the air here along with the humidity and the foreboding trees at my back. It wasn't neglect, exactly, or even the darkness that seemed to emanate from the oak alley despite the bright summer sun. It had more to do with the absence of light. I didn't believe in ghosts, but I did believe that this house could be haunted by its own past, its sorrows weeping shadows down the sandstone bricks and columns.

The saving grace was the front garden. I recognized the smilax and the lantana, and the fragrant tea olives that had once, long ago, decorated my grandmother's Savannah house. But whereas this garden oasis was neatly laid out with pristine edges and formed shapes, I recalled how the lantana in my grandmother's back garden had been allowed to grow unchecked until it started poking through the window screens. I couldn't imagine anything in this garden being allowed to grow beyond its boundaries. I pressed my hand to my face, the sweet, verdant smell now seeming more cloying than fragrant in the heat of the still summer afternoon.

"Hello, there."

The voice came from the top of the steps and I had to exit the car to be able to get a better view. I shielded my eyes from the sun with my hand and looked up. A beautiful woman with long, wavy dark hair who appeared to be in her midthirties stood with graceful hands folded on the sandstone balustrade. She was looking over my head toward the oaks as she spoke, and for a moment I thought the woman was addressing another visitor.

"Hello. I'm . . . Earlene Smith. I'm renting the caretaker's cottage for a few months. I was told to come to the main house to get the key from Helen Gibbons."

The woman smiled, illuminating her face. "I'm Helen — I spoke with you on the phone. Did you find us all right? Why don't you come on up for some sweet tea and we can sit for a while and get acquainted before I get the key for you?"

Feeling as if the oaks were watching me from behind, I began to climb the steps toward Helen, trying not to wince at the stiffness in my knee and back, and noticing the yellow silk chiffon dress Helen wore that seemed more appropriate at a morning wedding than spending an afternoon at home.

When I reached the top, I extended my hand. "It's a pleasure to meet you, Helen. And thank you for being able to accommodate me on such short notice."

Helen's hand remained at her side, but

she continued smiling, her eyes focused on my forehead. "Did you notice our trees? They spook people the first time they see them. I suppose that's one of the reasons Malily hasn't opened Asphodel Meadows to the public."

I let my hand drop, scrutinizing the other woman closely, wondering what it was that seemed to be missing. Reluctantly, I followed Helen's gaze toward the trees. "I've never seen live oaks like that."

"They are unique, aren't they?" she said, not quite smiling. "There used to be forty-eight of them. My great-great-grandfather and his generation called them the 'old gentlemen.' They had quite the reputation as being the longest and most beautiful oak alley in the South."

I tried to imagine it, but couldn't. "What happened?"

Her eyes reflected the sky and the trees as she spoke. "When they dammed the river a few decades back they changed its course and Asphodel lost quite a bit of property — and thirty-two trees. Men came and chopped those old trees down, then hauled them down the river on barges. My mama has a desk that was made from the wood from one of those trees, but it gives her bad dreams after she's spent any time working on it. We were compensated for it, of course, but the remaining oaks didn't take too kindly to the assault. Overnight they changed to how you see them now — like old men."

I shuddered and faced Helen again. "Do they know what caused it?"

Helen shrugged, her gaze focused again on my forehead. "They said the trauma of the earth-moving equipment and superficial damage to the roots caused by the removal of the other trees somehow disturbed the roots of the remaining ones." She crossed her arms and tilted her chin up. "Of course, there are those who don't believe that version of the story at all."

I was about to ask her what she meant when Helen extended her hand in the direction of the open front door. "You're limping, so you must be wanting to sit down. Why don't we go on inside?"

I had a sharp retort on my tongue when I noticed the long, slim metal cane Helen held in her left hand. My gaze jerked quickly up to Helen's eyes and I saw then what I'd been looking for earlier. Eyes the color of the marsh stared out at the world without focus or light, as if a curtain had been drawn across them. But there was something in the way Helen's gaze flitted about her surroundings, as if she saw something entirely different from everyone else and that what she saw might even be better.

I cleared my throat and nodded, then added hastily, "Sure. Thank you," and followed Helen into the house.

The foyer soared over two stories, with a curving staircase climbing along the outer wall, decorated by the frowning stares of painted ancestors. I wondered if they'd all been smiling at one time until the oaks had been removed and like the remaining "old gentlemen" had turned to grieving for eternity.

As I followed Helen toward the back of the house, I was vaguely aware of marble floors and dark paneling, crystal chandeliers and oil paintings of horses and jockeys. Tall windows marched across the top and bottom floors of the house, yet heavy shadows sat like furniture against the walls as we passed darkened rooms, heavy draperies covering up all light.

Helen led me into a formal parlor of high ceilings and intricate moldings with an antique piano in one corner and an ornate armoire in the other. Two sofas faced each other, flanking an empty fireplace, a mottled antique mirror hanging above the mantle. Dark wood plantation shutters were closed, allowing little sunlight to creep around the edges to chase away the shadows. Despite the elegance of the room and its furnishings, I felt the same uneasiness I'd felt outside, like a strong wind would bring with it the scent of rain.

After leaning her cane against the armoire, Helen asked, "What can I get you? We have sweet tea and homemade lemonade. Or I can fix you something stronger, if you prefer. As my brother, Tucker, is fond of saying, it's always five o'clock somewhere."

"Sweet tea would be fine. Thank you."

I watched as Helen deftly handled the decanters and glasses, neatly replacing the lid on the ice bucket after dropping several cubes into two tall crystal goblets. Then she unstoppered a ship's decanter filled with red liquid and poured it into a small glass until it was almost up to the top. She picked up my glass and held it up for me to take before picking up her own.

"Why don't you have a seat and rest a bit? My grandmother — I call her Malily but her real name is Lillian — will probably join us in a moment. She can smell her sherry like a shark can scent blood in the water."

I accepted the glass with a murmur of thanks, trying to disguise the sudden rush of adrenaline I'd felt with the mention of

Lillian's name. I sat down in an overstuffed wing chair by the piano and immediately felt something soft bump my hand. Startled, I looked down at the large yellow Lab, whose nap I had apparently disturbed. He bumped my hand again and I obliged by scratching him behind his ear.

"That's Mardi," said Helen, elegantly folding herself into an identical chair opposite. "He likes to think he's my Seeing Eye dog, so we just humor him. He's a real marshmallow. He's also, as you can see, a real watchdog, always alerting us to the presence of strangers." She took a sip of her tea, then raised her brows. "And you both have something in common — he's afraid of horses, too."

I stared hard at her, but Helen's face was open and her expression without malice. "Well, then," I said carefully, "we should get along just fine."

"Full use of the stables is included in your rental agreement, you know. That's why most people who rent it choose to come here in the summer instead of the beach. I don't suppose you'll be utilizing the stables, though."

"No," I said, feeling the mix of exhilaration and terror push through me again, "I won't be."

My attention was drawn to a movement in the doorway and I realized that Helen had already turned her head. The older woman whose picture I'd seen in the newspaper stood with her hand gripping the doorframe, the fingers bending in the wrong directions. She wore a striped silk blouse and matching skirt, her blond hair and makeup elegant yet understated. I knew Lillian Harrington-Ross was ninety years old but she looked at least twenty years younger. A fleeting memory of my own grandmother with her weary face and long, uncut hair made me wince.

"Are you pouring drinks, Helen?"

"Yes, Malily. Yours is waiting on the shelf." Helen gave me a wink and for a moment I forgot that Helen was blind.

I stood to greet the newcomer and realized my hand was shaking. Lillian approached with her glass, appraising me with eyes the color of emeralds.

"Malily, this is Earlene Smith. She's renting the caretaker's cottage for a few months while she does genealogy research. Earlene, this is my grandmother and owner of Asphodel Meadows, Lillian Harrington-Ross."

Lillian slowly took a sip of her sherry. "Yes," she said, pausing for a moment, "I remember you mentioning her." Her gaze took in my scuffed sandals, wrinkled linen pants, and pink button-down blouse with the coffee stain on the front courtesy of the idiot driver in front of me that morning on Abercorn Street. Lillian's eyes returned to my face and stopped for a moment while I held my breath. "Have we met before?"

I shook my head. "No. I don't think so."

The old woman stared at me for a moment longer. "You must remind me of someone else, then." She moved to the sofa and then added as an afterthought, "It's a pleasure to meet you, Miss Smith."

"Likewise," I said, my voice cracking as I resumed my seat. I glanced over at Helen and found the blind woman's empty gaze fixed on me. Mardi nuzzled my hand and I focused on scratching his large head. "And please call me Earlene."

Lillian sat up with a straight back and elegantly sipped her sherry. It was only one o'clock in the afternoon but I wished that I'd asked for something stronger than tea.

"Helen tells me your parents are from Savannah but that you were raised in Atlanta."

I bartered for time by taking a long drink of my iced tea, completely blindsided by my own shortsightedness. In all of my hasty preparations to come here, it had never once occurred to me that I would need an alternate background for Earlene Smith. There had once been a time in my life when acting before I could think of the consequences had served me well, but those days were long over and I needed to learn to stop thinking like the competitive jumper I no longer was.

I put my glass down on the table, missing the coaster and feeling Lillian's eyes staring at me coldly. I quickly stood, nearly tripping on the dog, and retrieved a cocktail napkin from the armoire to wipe up the drops of condensation.

"Yes," I said, trying to think calmly so I could remember whatever story was going to come out of my mouth. "I was raised in Atlanta. My father was a doctor there."

"In what hospital?" Lillian took another sip of her sherry but her eyes never left my face. "My grandson received his medical degree at Emory and was at Piedmont Hospital for his residency in general medicine."

I focused on the wadded cocktail napkin in my hands. "I . . . I don't really remember. He — well, both of my parents died when I was six. I moved to Savannah to live with relatives after that."

"I'm sorry," she said, her tone flat, as if at

her age the news of death was no longer news. "With whom did you live in Savannah?"

I looked over at Helen for some sort of reassurance but she seemed to be inwardly focusing on her iced tea. "My father's aunt and uncle. He worked for one of the banks on Bull Street and my aunt was a homemaker." I took another drink from my glass, trying to wash down the lump that had lodged itself in my throat. I'd never done this much lying in my entire life. "Harold and Betty Smith. They were originally from Augusta, I think."

An imperial brow lifted. "Augusta? I don't believe I know anybody in Augusta."

Nor ever saw any need to, I wanted to add. I'd taken an instant dislike to the old woman, my dislike having nothing to do with Lillian's aristocratic attitude. It had more to do with the words in the letter her grandson had sent. *On your behalf I did ask her about your grandmother and it took several moments for her to even recollect that she had once known her.*

"Yes, well, they're gone now, too." I lifted my glass to my dry lips only to realize that I'd already drained the last of the iced tea.

Helen stood. "Well, then, if you'll excuse me for a moment, I'm going to go rummage through my desk in the library and get the keys to the cottage for you."

"Yes, thank you," I said, trying to restrain myself from begging her to stay so I wouldn't be left alone in the same room with her grandmother. Even Mardi deserted me, moving as fast as the heat of the day would allow him.

"I understand you're one of those people who likes to dig into other people's business."

I stared at Lillian for a moment, not yet comprehending. "Oh, you mean a genealogist? Yes, I guess. In part you're right. But I really only dig as far as my clients want me to."

"And who are your clients now?"

I desperately wanted another glass of iced tea if only as a prop to give me time to formulate answers. I glanced over at the armoire and then over at Lillian and decided against it. "I'm afraid that my clients are confidential. It's part of my contract with them whether or not they want confidentiality."

"I see," said Lillian, although it was clear that she didn't. She considered me with steady, unblinking eyes and I was suddenly very aware that this woman missed very little. Despite being only three years younger than my grandmother, Lillian Harrington-Ross shared little else with Annabelle Mercer. A sharp stab of loss pricked at the place around my heart and I turned away from those eyes that seemed to see everything.

To change the subject, I blurted, "I was admiring your garden out front. What were those tall, yellow flowers?"

The old woman took a long sip of her sherry. "Those are asphodels — the flower this plantation was named for, which is why I cultivate them here."

"I don't think I've ever seen them before."

"It's doubtful that you would have. They're generally found in Greece, where they grow wild. They're mostly associated with the dead." She took another sip of her sherry, her eyes shifting from me to the shuttered window. "Do you know Greek mythology, Earlene?"

I swallowed, my throat tight and dry. "No. I'm afraid that I don't." I shifted uneasily in my seat, watching the shadows as they seemed to unfold and stretch themselves into the room. This old woman and her house made me feel as if I were pushing on the screen of a second-floor window, not sure when it would give way and send me tumbling to the ground below.

I shouldn't have come. I watched the dust

motes float across the window and thought of the scrapbook pages waiting in the car. On one of my brief perusals through the pages, I had paused long enough at yet another mention of the names Josie and Lily and a new one, Lola. And there, in my grandmother's girlhood writing, *Best friends forever.* But there was no connection now to the cold elderly woman sitting in front of me and the petite blond girl sitting next to my grandmother and another girl on a pasture fence in a faded picture with curling edges. *I shouldn't have come,* I thought again.

Lillian continued. "According to Greek mythology, Asphodel Meadows is where the souls of people who lived lives of near equal good and evil rest. It's a ghostly place and a less-perfect vision of life on earth." Her lips turned up with what resembled a smile. "Not quite hell, but not exactly heaven, either."

"The flowers are beautiful," I said, afraid I'd blurt out the truth if I didn't say something else. I glanced at the doorway, hoping Helen would return with the key so I could leave.

"My ancestors had a sense of humor," Lillian continued as if I hadn't spoken. Her words were slightly slurred and I wondered if the old woman was almost drunk. "Or maybe they thought that living in purgatory here on earth would shoot them directly to heaven when they died."

My knee hurt and my head was beginning to. *I shouldn't have come.* I wondered why I hadn't let George talk me out of it or why I'd felt the need to come in the first place. I'd told him everything, even showed him the scrapbook and newspaper clipping, but he'd still come up with a dozen reasons why my coming to Asphodel was a bad idea. Even I'd had my doubts. Knowing my grandmother's past wouldn't bring her back or give me another chance. And maybe the attic room with the empty bassinet and blue baby blanket had nothing to do with her. Or maybe they were never meant to be found.

I opened my mouth to excuse myself, to apologize for taking up their afternoon and to thank them for the tea before leaving as quickly as I could, when my gaze caught a flash of gold appearing in the neck fold of Lillian's silk blouse.

It was a small gold angel with outstretched wings and holding a book, pierced by two holes to allow a chain to pass through the charm. It was unremarkable, really, except that it was identical to the one I now wore around my own neck, safely tucked inside my shirt.

Helen finally appeared and I stood abruptly, finding it suddenly hard to breathe in the dark, stuffy room. "I'm sorry, but I really must leave now. If you'll just tell me where the cottage is, I'm sure I'll have no trouble finding it."

Without moving, Helen held out a key ring with a single key dangling from it. "That's fine. I'll call or have somebody stop by later on to see if you need anything."

I took the key, trying not to snatch it from Helen's grasp in my haste. After listening to Helen's directions, I said a quick word of thanks and my good-byes to both women, then left, ignoring the pain in my knee and quickly forgetting my doubts about why I was there. It wasn't the fact that Lillian Harrington-Ross had an angel charm identical to the one my grandmother had left for me; instead it had everything to do with the reason why an old woman who claimed not to even remember my grandmother would be wearing it around her neck.

Dum vita est, spes es. Where there is life, there is hope. With a grim determination I hadn't felt in years, I limped down the steps of the old house toward the garden with its uncanny familiarity. The scrapbook pages in the backseat fluttered as I pulled open the door, the sound like a whisper from the dead.

I put the car in gear and headed toward the front drive, my tires spinning on the gravel as I felt the cool gold of my angel charm pressing against my skin like an old memory, just as cold and twice as persistent.

Impatiently, I wiped my sleeves across my cheeks as I moved beneath the spiky shade of the old oaks, glancing at the GPS and seeing again that I was still out of satellite range, and that my grandfather's car and I were just a little blip on a huge screen of vast emptiness.

CHAPTER 7

The scratch of cricket wings chirped outside the casement window in the small living room of the caretaker's cottage. The setting of the sun had done little to ease the heat from the day and the only air conditioner was the window unit in the single bedroom. I pulled the damp pink knit camisole away from my skin one more time before focusing my attention on the marred surface of the coffee table and the scrapbook pages that lay on top of it.

My arm swept down the top page, a magic wand to peer into the past, my eyes moving over the handwriting of a young woman with precise A's and dotted I's. The letters were neat and tidy, just like the grandmother I'd known, yet I still couldn't quite picture the young girl bent over this scrapbook, her pen scratching against the thick paper.

I glanced up at the photo of the three girls I had perched against a table lamp I'd placed on the coffee table for better light. They seemed to be staring at me expectantly, waiting to begin their stories. With a deep breath, I turned back to the scrapbook pages, lifted the torn cover off of the first page, and began to read.

February 4, 1929

Today is the first day of the rest of my life. That's what Josie tells me anyway, and with her being more creative than I am, I'm going to borrow her words for this first page of our Lola album. The name and this scrapbook were all Josie's idea, but I get to go first because I'm the oldest.

We met Lola today in the window of a little shop on Broughton Street. It was supposed to be just Josie and me running an errand for Justine, Josie's mother, but little Lily Harrington tagged along, too, on account of my daddy needing to discuss some horse business with her daddy. I tried to pretend I wasn't listening, because I'm pretty sure I'm getting a new mare for my thirteenth birthday next month.

There were two mannequin busts in the window, right next to each other. I don't know what made the three of us stop at one time in front of the window. Maybe it was the way the sun hit the necklace on the first bust, making it sparkle like diamonds, or maybe it was the necklace on the other bust that was filled with gold charms. Josie was the first to notice that both necklaces were exactly the same except the second one was filled with charms. And that's why I think it caught our attention — the completely bare necklace made us all see the possibilities.

Josie had to wait outside while Lily and I went inside to ask about the price. I just about fainted when they told me. I knew it wasn't high-quality gold so I thought it would be cheap. We had all wanted it so badly that I guess it just didn't make sense that we didn't have the money to buy it.

It was Josie — of course! — who came up with the idea of naming the necklace Lola. And it was also her idea that we pool our money together to buy it, and then share it three ways, each of us having possession of it for four months out of the year. Lily tried to tell us that because she was an only child she'd never been expected to share anything and wasn't sure she could start now. Her father has the money to purchase it for her, so I got down on my knees like my mama always did when she had something important to say to me, and told her that this was about friendship and loyalty. And that this necklace would bind the three of us together forever, like the old-fashioned blood oath that warriors used to make with each other.

Being Lillian, she felt the need to argue. This habit of hers gets on other people's nerves, but I respect her for it. It's how she makes sense of a world I can tell she doesn't always agree with. She told me that we didn't need a blood oath or anything like that because we're only girls, and we're not expected to go out into any battles.

And that's when I shared with her the last thing Mama told me before she died: that our battles were the stories we kept inside the part of our hearts that men couldn't see, but that our loyal friends, sisters, and daughters would cherish forever.

Then Josie surprised us all by saying that to make our bond official, we needed to record in a scrapbook every moment of our lives while it was our turn to wear the necklace. We would be responsible for adding a charm to the necklace that would represent the four months it had been in our possession and that we should all start now by choosing one charm together that we would always wear except when we had Lola.

Josie picked the guardian angel because of the book in the angel's hands but I was the one who chose the inscription that would wrap around the angel's wings: *Perfer et obdura; dolor hic tibi proderit olim.* I'd learned it in Latin class and Mama had liked it enough to start a needlepoint sampler with it. She'd died before she finished it, so I thought it would be a sort of tribute to her, a way to finish her last story. The words are tiny, so they could all fit on the charm, but it doesn't matter if we can read it or not. We all know what they are and what they mean and that's the most important thing.

So Lola came home with me first and I slid my angel charm on the chain to wear for the next four months. Lily has a Brownie camera and said she'd take a picture of Lola when it's her turn. But I drew a picture on the next page to show everyone what Lola looked like at the beginning of our story.

I flipped the page and saw a pencil sketch of the necklace I'd found in the tin box my grandfather had buried in the backyard. Except this necklace only had the one, single charm of an angel holding a book and with pierced wings to allow a slender gold chain to slip through them. I tapped my fingers against the page, the sound echoing in the silent room, somehow knowing that to touch the necklace again would make this journey irreversible. But I thought of my dream, and the knitted blue sweater in my grandmother's trunk, and realized that this journey had never really had a return option.

Sliding the scrapbook aside, I stood and limped into the bedroom, where I dragged the box from under the bed, where I'd put it. I wasn't sure why I'd felt the need to hide it. The only person who would recognize any of the contents would be Lillian Harrington-Ross and I couldn't see the old woman coming inside the cottage to snoop. Maybe I'd only meant to hide it from myself.

I tossed the box on top of the quilted bedspread and slowly lifted the lid. I peered inside at the necklace, its once shining gold now burnished to a dull bronze. Picking it up, I let the odd shapes of the charms slip through my fingers like a rosary, the words forgotten. I spotted a bell, a musical note, a high-heeled shoe, a heart, a rearing horse, and a sailor's knot. My eyes blurred, obstructing my vision of the rest of the charms. "So you must be Lola," I said to the empty room, gingerly touching the forgotten memories and smiling at the innocence of young girls, wondering if I'd ever been so naive.

I put Lola back in the box, the tapping sound of metal against metal like impatient fingertips. My smile faded quickly as I spotted the yellowed news article. My hand hovered over it for a moment before delicately lifting it with two fingers, then held it as I read it again:

The body of an unidentified Negro male infant was pulled from the Savannah River this morning around eight o'clock by postman Lester Agnew on his morning rounds. The body was found naked with no identifying marks and has been turned over to the medical examiner to determine the cause of death.

I dropped the article back into the box

and lifted the lid to shut it, but my gaze caught on one of the charms on the necklace that I'd noticed once before. I studied the tiny needle-sized spokes of the wheels, the sunshade and handle of the baby carriage spun from gold and began to feel sick.

I slammed the lid shut and shoved the box back under the bed before flipping off the lights and closing the door. Fingering the gold angel around my neck, I returned to the scrapbook and closed the pages with a quiet thud. I stared at it for a long time, feeling as if Fitz and I had just taken that final jump again and were still falling in a timeless void, waiting to hit the ground.

Helen listened to the jangling of Mardi's collar tags to help guide her to the old tabby house, not that she really needed a guide. She'd lived at Asphodel Meadows her entire life and could easily have found her own way. But she pretended for Mardi's sake, because the Lab strongly believed that she needed his help.

Using her cane in front of her, she walked slowly but purposefully toward the Georgian four-over-four house that had been the principal residence of Harringtons while the main house was being built back in eighteen seventeen. It was where her parents had lived briefly during their endeavor at domesticity and the births of their two children and where they stayed on their infrequent trips home from whatever remote corner of the earth they were attempting to civilize. Even Malily's remodeling of the tabby structure and updating it with every modern convenience hadn't been enough to entice her only daughter to come home to stay.

It was where Tucker had moved two years ago with Susan and the girls after he'd given up his medical practice in Savannah in an effort to focus on Susan's needs. It really had never occurred to any of them how insurmountable her needs had been, or how the end of her life could offer no answers.

As Helen stood on the brick walk leading up to the house, she turned her face upward, picturing the double chimneys and graceful portico that had been added to the tabby facade in the last century. She remembered it as being a lovely house on the outside, but the interior during her childhood there with her parents had been decorated with loneliness and disappointment and even now she avoided it as much as she could.

She didn't bother to knock using the large lion's head knocker. She simply turned the handle and walked inside, then followed Mardi up the staircase to the upper level.

After pausing outside Tucker's door for a moment, she threw it open. One of the advantages of being blind, she always thought, was that people forgave a lot of bad behavior. It also allowed them privacy when they were lying in bed stark naked.

"Damn it, Helen. Why do you do that?" The words were accompanied by the rustling of bedsheets.

She smelled the alcohol in the room and it made her want to gag. As she made her way to the window to pull open the curtains and slide open the sash, she asked, "Are you alone?"

Her question was answered by a pillow being thrown at her back.

"You shouldn't throw things at blind people. It's mean."

Another pillow followed the first, hitting her on the side of the head as she turned to face the bed.

"Go to hell," Tucker mumbled, sounding as if he were burying his face back into the mattress.

She moved toward the bed and crossed her arms as Mardi leapt onto the mattress. "I could just follow you, couldn't I? You seem to be well on your way already."

When he didn't say anything, she turned away from the bed and felt her way to the bathroom to turn on the shower, then returned to the room to begin opening the rest of the windows. "It stinks like an ashtray that somebody poured bourbon on in here. At least you're alone."

The bed creaked as she pictured Tucker sitting up, listening to the bristling sound of his hands running over his face.

"I wouldn't do that. My girls live here."

"Yeah, well, not really. They spend more time at the big house than they do here and they weren't here last night. I thought you could at least show them the courtesy of having breakfast with them this morning. Malily and the girls just sat down, so if you hurry, you could make it."

With what sounded like a growl, Tucker stood and trudged to the bathroom. She followed him, pausing by the doorway. "Susan died, Tuck. Not you."

The steady beat of the water against slate tiles agitated the silence between them. "It's not that, Helen. It's never been that."

"Don't you think I know that? Regardless of what people might think, I see an awful lot. But guilt will only carry you so far. And your girls need you."

She heard him turn on the faucet and drop the cap to his toothpaste tube in the sink but he didn't say anything.

"I'll see you at breakfast, then."

He answered by shutting the door in her face.

"I love you, too," she shouted through the closed door before turning and leaving, allowing Mardi to lead the way.

As Helen made her way back down the brick walk, she heard footsteps crunching on gravel approaching her. She stopped and smiled. "Earlene?"

The footsteps stopped. "How did you know?"

"You're the only person I know of on the property right now who walks with a limp."

"Oh. Well. That makes sense, I guess." Earlene's voice was tight, like a dam had been built to prevent any words from tumbling out.

Helen smiled gently. Earlene Smith was a mystery to her. Helen usually prided herself on developing images in her head of the people she met just by listening to their voices and the way they moved. But when she tried to picture Earlene, a blank canvas flickered through her mind. "I'm sorry if I've made you uncomfortable. Being blind makes me notice things that seeing people deliberately overlook." She quickly changed the subject, sensing Earlene's discomfort. "You also sound out of breath. Did you walk all the way from the cottage?"

"Yeah, I did. Everything seems a lot closer on the map you gave me." She rattled the map in her hand. "I was looking for the old family cemetery. It's supposed to be near this house."

Helen nodded. "You're very close. This was the family home for a few years while the big house was being built. They needed a cemetery pretty soon after they moved in here, unfortunately. Smallpox epidemic. Took their two youngest children and a visiting cousin." She held out her arm. "If you'll give me your arm so that I don't trip on any roots or rocks, I'll take you to it."

Cool fingers touched her hand and guided it to Earlene's elbow. The skin was warm and smooth, and Helen's sensitive fingertips felt a long, raised scar on the inner side of the elbow. "Thank you. And I'm glad I ran into you. I forgot to ask you yesterday for your deposit check. Do you think I could have it today?"

Earlene was silent for a moment as Helen guided them both back toward the house. "Would it be all right if I gave it to you in cash?"

"Yes, of course. I normally don't even suggest it because I don't find many people carrying around so much cash."

"Yes, well, I'd rather just handle it that way."

Helen nodded, thinking it odd but somehow fitting in with the mystery of Earlene Smith. "We're going to cut to the right here and cross the lawn until we reach the live oak with the tire swing leaning on it. My brother made it for his girls last year although he hasn't hung it yet."

Helen heard Mardi dash past them, most likely in pursuit of a squirrel. She laughed. "I'm glad I don't depend on him as a guide dog. I might end up in a tree."

Earlene laughed, too. "I haven't had a dog in a long time." She paused for a moment and then added, "It's hard to remember what it's like."

Helen turned her head toward her companion, hearing the wistfulness in her voice, and something else, too. A forced aloofness, maybe, and a fragileness, too. Helen thought of the scar on Earlene's elbow and the limp and wondered if her internal scars were there, too, and if they were just as permanent.

Earlene brought them to a stop. "We're at the tree. Where next?"

"To the left. In about ten yards or so, you should see a small dirt path that will lead us into a wooded part. If you stay on the path there'll be a clearing with an iron fence around it. You should be able to see the tombstones from there."

Earlene pulled her arm in close. "Be very careful here. There're lots of rocks and debris in the grass."

"Thanks. And remember not to come out here at dusk. The no-see-ums are out then and those suckers can bite. Don't bother with repellent, either. That stuff is like vitamin water to them — makes them bigger and stronger, I think."

They continued walking, listening to Mardi's collar clink and his heavy panting as he bounded around them. The area around the cemetery was Helen's favorite part of the plantation. It was the place she remembered colors the most: the blue of the sky, the mossy greens and browns of the trunks of the sweet gum and hickory trees, the buttery yellows of the asphodels that sprouted untended inside the cemetery gates like flaming arrows thrown by the gods. The memory of faces had faded with time, but the colors remained, bright flashes of light against perpetual darkness.

Helen could tell by the way Earlene relaxed her hold on her arm that they had reached the clearing. Slowly, they progressed around the perimeter of the fence to the gate where Earlene paused. "It's beautiful here. The light here seems . . . I don't know. Softer."

"I know. When I was a little girl, I used to say that it seemed the sun was shining through angels' wings." Helen laughed. "I like to come here and paint sometimes when I can find somebody patient enough to bring my easel and paints and guide me in and out."

"You paint?" Helen could hear Earlene's struggle between politeness and curiosity.

"I haven't been blind my whole life — not until a high fever at the age of fourteen. I loved to paint before and found no reason to stop now." She could sense Earlene looking at her, hesitating. "What is it?"

Earlene took a deep breath. "I'm just . . . curious. Your grandmother's house — it's so dark. Being here, with this beautiful light, it just made me wonder . . ."

Helen reached out her hand and touched the cold metal of the wrought-iron fence, then slid her fingers up to the top of the arrows that pointed toward heaven and pressed her thumb down hard. "It's always been that way, even when Tuck and I were children. What makes you ask?"

She felt Earlene shrug next to her. "My . . . aunt. She was that way, too. After she went away to live in a nursing home, I ran around opening up all the blinds. I'm thinking that maybe as we get older, our eyes must get more sensitive to the light."

Helen pressed her thumb down harder, feeling a chip in the paint. "Or maybe our memories make us see things with such a bright clarity that we have to shield our eyes."

Earlene lifted the latch on the gate. "Maybe." The hinges squealed as she pushed open the gate, then led Helen inside.

There had been a fitful sprinkle of rain earlier that morning, just enough to torment the parched summer grass, and Helen could smell the moist earth and wet leaves that had piled up against the bottom of the fence. She'd have to remind Tucker that he needed to clean it out although she was pretty sure he'd have somebody else do it. Even as a child he hadn't liked to come here and had once told her that it reminded him of a monster's mouth, the white stones like sharp teeth waiting to catch him. She supposed that he had even more reason to believe it to be true now that he was grown.

Helen leaned against the closed gate. "So what exactly do you hope to find here?"

"I'm just . . . I was hoping . . ." Earlene fell silent.

Ah. "Maybe if you can tell me the last name your client is interested in researching, I might be able to help. My family has lived in the Savannah area since before the Revolution. It's in my blood to know every connection of every family going back at least two hundred years."

Again, Earlene paused.

"Or maybe you can tell me what you're really looking for."

Twigs and leaves crunched as Earlene shifted her feet. She sounded almost relieved when she finally spoke. "I'm actually doing this as a personal favor. For a friend." She paused again. "Her name's Lola. She's writing a history about Asphodel Meadows and the Harringtons. She tried to reach your grandmother but your grandmother made it very clear that she wasn't interested in talking to anyone."

"And since you're a genealogist who knows how to research, it made sense for you to come here and see what you could learn." Using the fence as her guide, Helen began walking around the periphery of the cemetery. "I'm not surprised that Malily wouldn't help your friend. She never talks about the past — even to us. She's not the cold woman she likes to portray to the world, you know. You'd never guess there's a lot more underneath that powdered veneer. Did you know that she used to be a well-known equestrian? Years ago, of course, but still. She told me once that she wanted to be a jockey when she was a little girl, and live in the stable with her horse." Helen paused to make sure that Earlene was following her. "Hard to believe, isn't it?"

"Yes," Earlene said slowly, "it is. I never would have guessed."

"I think it's a good example of how we're never really who we say we are." Helen turned her head to face the direction she knew Earlene was standing. "We're made of so many different layers, and each one tells a story." She stopped, remembering something her grandmother had said. "My mother hasn't been back to Asphodel for almost five years now. When she left that last time my grandmother said almost the exact same thing, something about how so many of our stories stay hidden under other layers. But how a daughter should know her mother's stories to pass on to her daughters."

"But she's been reluctant to share her story with you."

Helen shrugged. "I always thought that she was making me wait my turn, that my mother should go first. But I don't think

Mama's planning on coming home any day now and Malily isn't getting any younger."

Earlene's voice sounded small, the words barely having enough room to escape. "You should talk to your grandmother now, before it's too late. Ask her to tell you her stories."

Helen forced her voice to sound light. "Asking Malily to do anything is like moving a mountain. But maybe someday soon."

Earlene shifted, twigs and leaves crunching under her feet. "So what happened next?"

Helen shrugged. "My mother left. She told Malily that she already knew all she wanted to know."

"And she hasn't been back since?" Earlene's footsteps walked toward the center of the cemetery toward the large pyramid monument.

"No. But that's not unusual. Our parents are missionaries. We stayed here while they were out there, saving the world."

"I'm sorry." Earlene's footsteps returned. "That must have been hard for you." She took a deep breath. "My own parents died in a car accident when I was six. I don't remember them very well, but I still miss them. I was angry for a long time that they'd left me behind."

Helen touched Earlene's arm again, feeling the scar. "Is that where this came from?"

Earlene rapidly sucked in her breath. "No."

Helen dropped her hand, realizing she'd touched that fragileness, reminding her of a china plate wobbling on the edge of a table. She wanted to explain that in her world without light or colors, the boundaries between herself and others had become blurred. Tucker had once told her that instead of seeing people's faces, she could see directly inside their hearts.

Helen held out her hand again. "Well, if you want to learn about Lillian Harrington-Ross, this would be the right place to start. Her great-great-grandparents and everyone since are here, as is her husband, Charles Ross. The monument in the center is his."

Earlene's fingers were cool again as she took Helen's hand and placed it on her arm before leading her toward the tall, narrow pyramid. With her free hand Helen touched the marble monument, running her fingers over the engraved letters. "He designed the monument himself, but my grandmother added the words."

"But it's only his name, and his birth and death dates."

Helen brushed the letters again with her

fingers. "I know. My sister-in-law, Susan, pointed that out to me. We both thought it odd that there weren't any sentiments. My grandparents were married for over fifty-five years, after all, and had two children. You would think she had more to say other than he was born and died."

"Two children? So your mother wasn't an only child?"

"She had a brother, but he was killed in Vietnam. He's buried near his father."

Earlene pulled away and Helen felt her kneel. "It's the biggest monument, though. And somebody's brought flowers recently."

Helen let her hands trail down the monument until she was kneeling next to Earlene. "Yes, well, Malily comes here dutifully once a month and puts flowers on his grave. She's always been good with appearances."

"What do you mean?"

Helen stood and turned away, picturing the row of smaller headstones that rose from the earth like historical markers, indicating the periods of epidemics that took the lives of children and left the parents with cold marble in a cemetery. She faced Earlene again, not sure why she'd chosen this stranger to confide in. Maybe it was because they were both essentially orphans. Or maybe it was Earlene's admission that her parents' deaths had felt like a desertion worthy of her anger. And Helen knew all about that.

"The first time Malily brought me here, I was about seven or eight. She either thought I was too young to remember or to understand, but when she put down the flowers for Grandpa Charlie, she didn't say anything sentimental. Nothing like 'I love you' or 'We'll be together again.' "

"What did she say?"

Helen shook her head. "It sounded a lot like 'I'm sorry' and then 'Thank you.' Not that Malily is prone to sentimentality, but I've always remembered how strange it was to say that to a man you were married to for so long. Look, Earlene. . . ." She stopped, not really sure if she wanted to continue, recalling Earlene's words. *My own parents died in a car accident when I was six. I don't remember them very well, but I still miss them. I was angry for a long time that they'd left me behind.* She took a deep breath. "I'd like to help you with your research. If you'd like. I was helping Susan before . . . before she died. She'd found some old letters of my grandparents and other miscellaneous papers in the attic. I think that's what started her genealogy kick. Anyway, I don't think Malily would mind

139

you seeing them — at least after I speak with her. And if you think it would help, I could bring you over to the house for the two of you to get to know each other better. She might even offer information on her own once she gets to know you. At the very least, I could answer any of your questions that I can."

A rustle of wings disturbed the silence above them. "That's very generous of you, Helen, but I don't . . ."

"Please don't say no. It'll give me something to do besides helping Malily with the estate and painting. My brother's not much company these days and I'd welcome the distraction."

Earlene was silent for a long moment as if weighing her need to find information with her need to stay aloof. Finally, she said, "All right. Thank you. I promise not to take advantage of your generosity, though, and put you at odds with your grandmother."

"I'm glad to help. You're the most interesting thing that's happened here since . . . well, for a while."

"That makes two of us then. That's the first time I've been called interesting in probably as long."

They both shared a laugh until Helen heard Earlene's stop abruptly. Crunching leaves and sticks marked her passage to the far side of the cemetery. "Is this a moon-flower vine?"

"Yes, it is. But it refuses to bloom. I think Lillian's given up on it now, but she used to tell me that she'd come here at night to see if it would bloom, but it never did."

Earlene didn't say anything but Helen heard her take a few steps. "There's a grave here — but it's on the other side of the fence, outside of the cemetery, and it has fresh flowers on it. I can't read the inscription. Do you know whose it is and why it's there?"

Helen's lips began to tremble as they always did when she remembered. She could even still smell the scent of rain when they'd come to tell them that they'd found Susan in the river. Even now, she could hear Tucker calling Susan's name as he'd searched for her and taste her own tears on her lips. Odd, she thought, how something she hadn't seen could be so imprinted on all of her other senses.

"That's Susan's grave. My grandmother wouldn't allow her to be buried in sancti-fied ground."

Earlene didn't respond right away, but Helen could hear the rush of breath as she sifted through the possibilities.

"Why?"

Helen swallowed. "She killed herself."

Earlene's breath came heavier now. "Oh. I'm so sorry — I didn't mean to intrude. . . ."

"That's all right. You'd find out eventually anyway. It was very sad, especially for her children."

"She had children?"

"Two girls. Lucy and Sara. They're eight and five now. Young, but old enough to remember her." Helen paused, listening to the whir of cicadas hang in the summer air for a moment, suspended over them like anticipation, then evaporate into silence. "They actually seem to have come to terms with it. Susan wasn't . . . a happy person, I guess you would say. The girls probably see it as some sort of relief."

Helen heard Earlene approaching again. "Your poor brother." Earlene's footsteps stopped. "What about this one? It's a small stone angel stuck by itself in the corner." She paused and Helen pictured her leaning down to examine it more closely. "There's no inscription on it."

"It's a bit of a mystery, I'm afraid. Nobody seems to know what it is or how long it's been here. Susan was obsessed with it. I think that's why Tucker chose to bury her nearby."

She reached out for Earlene's arm and felt again the reassuring pressure of her hand as Earlene brought it to the crook in her elbow — the one without the scar this time.

"Did he love her very much, then?" Earlene began to lead her toward the gate.

Helen stumbled on something soft and small and stopped to pick it up. She held it out to Earlene. "It feels like a glove."

Earlene took it from her hand. "It is. It's a man's riding glove."

"It must be Tucker's. He comes here sometimes to clear the weeds and put flowers on Susan's grave. He's living at the tabby house, where you saw me coming down the path earlier. If you wouldn't mind, could you please stick it in the mailbox as we pass it?" Mardi began nudging her hand. "It must be eleven thirty — time for his treat. He doesn't like me to forget."

"Smart boy," Earlene said. "Can I take you back to the house?"

"No, just to the driveway if you wouldn't mind. Mardi and I can find our way back from there."

They walked back slowly in silence as Helen thought about Earlene's question and how she still wasn't sure how to answer it. When they reached the mailbox, Earlene stuck the glove inside and closed it.

Helen had her face turned toward the house, a small smile on her lips. "When Tucker and I lived here with our parents, we were pretty much allowed to run wild. Tucker was the most dedicated prankster I'd ever known, drove our parents crazy. He was always hiding things in the mailbox — like your toothbrush or left shoe. Once he put Mama's new kitten in there but the mewling gave it away. He got in a lot of trouble for that, I remember." Her smile faded a bit. "But he was so scared of thunderstorms. Whenever it rained, he'd crawl into my room and sleep by the side of my bed. Daddy found him there once and I told him that I'd been scared of the thunder and Tucker was there because I asked him to. I didn't want Daddy to be angry with him."

"And you're still close?"

Helen shrugged. "As close as he'll let me get, which isn't too close these days. It's like he thinks I couldn't see what was between them, that I didn't know. . . ." She stopped abruptly, remembering that she was speaking to a virtual stranger. She smiled brightly. "Well, never mind our family dramas. I'm sure you have your own to deal with and don't need to add ours."

Earlene was silent for a moment before

answering. "Yes, well, thanks again for your offer to help. I know my friend will appreciate any information I can find."

Helen tilted her head to the side. "You don't sound like an Earlene. Is that really your name?"

There was a brief pause before Earlene answered. "It is. But I've always gone by my nickname." She didn't elaborate.

Ah. "Then I'll call you Earlene until you tell me different."

"Thank you," the other woman said, gently releasing her arm from Helen's grasp. "I'll call you once I get my notes in order and maybe we can meet to discuss them."

"Sounds like a plan. Why don't you come by for supper tomorrow night at seven? I'm hoping my brother will join us and you can meet him."

"Thank you. I'll be there."

"Just wear a dress or a skirt and put some lipstick on. Malily cannot abide a woman in jeans."

"How did you know I was wearing jeans and no makeup?"

Helen smiled brightly. "I can hear the jeans rubbing as you walk, and as for the lipstick, well, that was just a guess."

"You're good," said Earlene, a smile in her voice. "Scary, but good."

"I'll take that as a compliment. See you at seven, then."

"Good-bye."

Helen waited with Mardi as she listened to Earlene head out in the opposite direction, her limp more pronounced than before. Using her cane, Helen began walking toward the house, knowing without a doubt now that whatever it was that had really brought Earlene to Asphodel Meadows hadn't been a friend's request and that the scars she bore were more than just the visible ones.

CHAPTER 8

Lillian woke with a start, the remnants of her dream still floating in the air around her like ghosts. She moaned, the pain in her hands and back throbbing through her body, her bones knocking against one another. But she wasn't completely sure if it was the pain or the dream that had brought her awake. More pain pills would bring relief, but they would also bring sleep. And sleep would bring back the dreams. She clung to the pain as it shot ripples through her skin, forcing her exhausted body into blessed alertness.

Stiffly, she pulled herself up in the large rice poster bed that she'd been conceived in and in which she would most likely die. It had been hers and Charles' through their fifty-five years of marriage — years in which he'd lain next to her in the large bed, years of dreamless sleep. It was as if he'd erased her past, a dam braced against the deluge, and once he was gone she'd drowned in the memories as easily as if she'd stepped off the banks of the Savannah River and slowly sank to the silt-covered bottom.

She moved to the large window that faced the front of the house, where in the daylight she had once enjoyed seeing her garden and the sundial that were as much a part of her now as her green eyes and the shape of her nose. Behind the half-closed blinds the summer moon hung full and sultry white, daring to illuminate the bitter oak trees in the alley. Tucker had tried to convince her that they needed to be replaced with younger saplings but Lillian wouldn't hear of it. She'd known them since her birth, had witnessed their transformation, and their humped shoulders and knotted limbs made her a kindred spirit. The years hadn't been kind to either them or her, although it had occurred to Lillian that in their case they hadn't done anything wrong to deserve their current state.

She braced her arms on the windowsill, the pain still intense but moving out now to other parts of her body, slowly dissipating. Her nightgown stuck to her skin despite the central air-conditioning she'd installed in the house when she'd redone the tabby house, but it was no match for the humid summer air and her dreams. Biting her lip, she pulled back the blinds, then slid open the window lock and raised the sash, letting the wet, sticky air hit her face. The smell of the boxwoods by the front door rose to greet her, reminding her as they always did of home, and a whippoorwill called out from the lane of oaks. Long ago, Josie had told her the legend of the whippoorwill, how they were lost souls come back to remind the living how tenuous was the line that separated them.

The whippoorwill called out again and Lillian shivered despite the heat. A horse whinnied from the direction of the stables, and she thought of the horse Tucker had been working in the lunge ring and wondered who was winning that battle. She hoped it was Tucker. He needed to win at least one.

Lillian sank down in the stuffed chaise lounge Odella had arranged for her in front of the window and felt her eyelids sag despite the pain. She was so very tired. She wondered why God kept her alive and she didn't like the answer when she thought about it. How did a person seek redemption for a sin committed long ago against people now dead? Lillian had always imagined that when Annabelle died her guilt would pack its bags and leave like an unwanted houseguest. But it remained, a suitcase of memories left behind.

She thought again of Annabelle's granddaughter and her letters and a thread of doubt began unraveling in her head. What if she'd done the wrong thing by turning her away? Shifting in the chair, her old bones rattled inside the loose flesh of an old lady. Funny, in her mind she was still the young Lillian Harrington, beautiful and lithe, the pride of her father. It was only when she saw herself in the mirror that the truth found her and she was confronted with the old woman she'd become, the lines on her face and crooked fingers the price she paid for keeping secrets.

Closing her eyes, she let her head sag against the back cushion of the chaise as sadness, like a moth, fluttered to her chest and settled there. Her useless fingers found the angel charm she still wore around her neck and she twisted the chain tightly until she could feel it pressing into the soft skin of her throat, a noose of lost chances and broken promises.

When Lillian woke again, the sun streamed through the open window and a dawn chorus from Carolina chickadees and song sparrows had replaced the nocturnal call of the whippoorwill. She kept her eyes closed, clinging to the respite of a dreamless sleep. For a moment she allowed herself to imagine that she was a girl again, to the time before knowing that growing older meant giving up things you loved, and that making choices could reach farther than into the next day. She teased herself with the thought that today was the day she would tell her secret, that she would at last be free from it. But she thought of Tucker and the shadow of grief that followed him, and of Helen who loved her and thought of her as the mother she never really had, and Lillian knew it was too late. Not now, when Tucker's grief was as raw as broken glass and Helen's love kept Lillian from dissolving her past in alcohol.

Her heavy lids drooped, and she allowed herself to drift off to sleep again, just for a few moments she promised herself. The music was already playing as her eyelids closed and she was dancing with Charlie and they were laughing because the first four names on her dance card were his. It wasn't until she opened her eyes and felt the wetness on her cheeks that she remembered where she was and that the worst thing that could happen to you could happen twice.

■ ■ ■ ■

I slid on a pair of cream-colored cotton walking shorts, checking the length to make sure they covered my scarred knee and then slid on my sandals. After gathering up my purse and notebook, I checked the hand-written map Helen had given me, looking for the best way out of the property. I studied the neatly drawn lines and lettering, precise enough that it almost didn't appear hand-drawn at all, and I wondered who'd made it.

I traced the line of the road I'd come in on, and it appeared that my GPS had taken me the long way. Glancing at my watch, I calculated how much time I had if I wanted to make it to the library in downtown Savannah before dinner at Asphodel Meadows at seven. The Bull Street branch of the Savannah library had a genealogy and local history room and I'd already figured that one morning and afternoon probably wouldn't be enough time to find all the information I needed, but it was a start.

I threw everything on the passenger seat of the Buick, then slid onto the hot vinyl seat, the backs of my legs through my shorts feeling scorched. After starting the car I blasted the air-conditioning and rolled the windows down all the way, sticking my face outside to suck fresh air into my lungs. The old familiar smells that always made me think of what could have been startled me at first, and made me remember where I was. I slumped in my seat, feeling my heart squeeze, remembering defeat like a phantom limb. It was like an old war wound that ached in cold weather, and being on a horse farm was like moving to a perpetually arctic climate. Quickly, I slid the windows up again and put the car into drive.

Slowly, I drove down the drive that I remembered from before, the golf course on one side and the oak alley of twisted trees on my right. Ignoring my GPS's commands to turn around, I followed Helen's map instead, and continued to drive down the red dirt road past the alley of trees. Shortly after that, the road became nothing more than two bald tire tracks on a pate of red clay, the grass on the sides tall and rising from marshy water. This made sense since Asphodel had once been a rice plantation with fertile bottomlands near the river. Although the old rice fields weren't marked on the map, I figured I'd found them, the first piece of history I'd actually discovered since coming here.

I'd driven less than a mile when the road abruptly ended in a stand of tall Georgia pines, the narrow road no longer visible. Throwing the car into park, I studied the map again, seeing no correlation to anything on it with this place I seemed to be. Annoyed now, I slid the gearshift into reverse and hit the gas. Mud splattered my rear window as the tires ground into the soft mud, leaving me in the same place I'd started.

Putting the car into drive again, I gently pressed on the gas. The car moved forward gently, than slid back down into the red mud, where it seemed to make itself comfortable. I tried reverse and then drive several times before finally admitting defeat.

"Damn," I said to the mud and the pines and my own stupidity, and banged my hands against the steering wheel. I climbed out of the driver's seat, my sandals sinking into the muck. "Damn," I said again and would have kicked the car if I didn't know from experience that doing so would mean only that I wouldn't be able to walk for a day or two.

I glanced inside the car to where my useless cell phone sat on the dash. I didn't know the number at the house or anybody who would be remotely nearby. I briefly considered calling George, but realized I would owe him more than I was prepared to give as a matter of thanks for making him drive from Savannah to save me.

With another *damn,* I left everything in the car, then tugged my sandals out of the sucking mud and walked about ten feet toward drier ground. My knee ached from the effort and I had to grit my teeth before continuing on.

Small insects darted around my head and ankles but none bothered to bite me. My grandfather used to joke that it was because I was too bitter. A fellow competitor once told me it was because I had steel running through my veins instead of blood like the rest of the mortals. And for a very long time, until that final jump, I had believed it to be true.

About ten yards from where I'd left the car, I came upon a railroad-tie fence. Tall weeds grew at the fence posts, confirming my opinion that it marked an empty horse paddock. And, judging by my sense of direction, climbing over the fence would be a shorter path back to the tabby house and possible help.

Very carefully, I hoisted myself up on top of the fence and swung my right leg over before lifting my left leg to follow. Then bracing myself on my arms, I let myself down into the grass on the other side of the fence.

I headed to the right in a slight diagonal, thinking I'd reach the far end of the paddock eventually and that the fence on that side would run relatively parallel to the oak alley. I kept my head down most of the way to watch where I put my feet, and used the hem of my shirt to wipe the sweat from my face, taking most of my makeup with it.

I'd walked about twenty yards when I heard an old, familiar sound. I stopped and stood motionless, then listened again, hoping it had been the heat and the throbbing of my knee that made me hear things that weren't there. But there it was again, the sound of chewing, of large, powerful jaws crunching on long grass.

Slowly I turned to my left and spotted a cherry bay gelding, its large expressive eyes regarding me with a wary gaze as it continued to chew. He was a large horse, about sixteen hands, with a red-brown body and black points. His black tail flicked away a fly as he considered the intruder.

I wanted to step back, to continue on my hunt for the fence and the drive, but my feet had developed their own mind and refused to move. I smelled the horse then:

sweat and grass and the heady odor of sun-heated horseflesh. The scent made me dizzy with remembering, my head swimming with the alarming thought that I might pass out. And then the horse turned and I stood riveted, staring at the vivid scar that bisected his flank, as stark and raw as my own.

I almost forgot my fear, distracted by the brutality of whatever had caused the animal's injury, and for a brief moment considered us kindred spirits, damaged yet somehow back among the living.

The horse lifted its head and nickered softly, then began to approach. "No!" I shouted, knowing I was being unreasonable and silly but his scent and the memories were colliding in my head, and nothing seemed irrational anymore.

"No!" I shouted again, my voice shrill, the edge of it tempting panic. I forced myself to move backward and managed to dislodge a foot, but my sandal caught on something solid and immobile protruding from the ground. My arms flailed as I tried desperately to regain my balance before falling into the sun-soaked grass. I lay still, frozen, just as I'd done in the grass as I waited for Fitz to slam into me, my broken body unable to roll away.

The horse startled, then continued its approach, his massive head appearing even larger from my supine position. I turned my head away as he nudged at my hip, nipping at the fabric of my pants. In the rational part of my mind that still functioned, I realized the horse was simply looking for a snack, but behind my closed eyelids all I could see was Fitz's body blocking the sun above me for that single moment that seemed to last a lifetime, and then the sudden, unbearable pain followed by blackness and my hope that I would never wake up again.

A low whistle came from the direction of where I thought the fence should be and then a man's voice called, "Here, boy. Come here, boy. I've got you some carrots."

I stayed where I was, mortified to be seen cowering like a frightened child. A shadow fell on my face and I turned my head, opening my eyes to see a tall man wearing riding boots and jeans, towering over me.

"Are you all right? Are you hurt?"

God. Knowing my only alternative was to lie still and play dead, I rose up on my elbows and squinted at my would-be rescuer, who had his arm extended toward me. With a moment's hesitation, I took it and allowed myself to be hoisted to my feet. I stared down at my mud-covered sandals and grass-stained shorts and saw myself as I must appear to the stranger's eyes. There'd been a time, long ago, when I'd been somebody, a person to admire. A world-class competitor. And now I wasn't sure who I was, but I knew it was none of those things I'd once been. I cringed from my rescuer's close scrutiny, knowing I'd come up short.

"I'm fine," I mumbled, brushing grass from my pants and trying to rub off some of the mud on my sandals in the tall grass. Furious at myself for being so stupid, I vented my anger on the nearest possible victim. I pointed an accusing finger at the cherry bay, who'd turned his attention back to eating grass. "You shouldn't allow your horse to roam freely like that. He or an innocent bystander could get hurt. Or is that how he got that scar on his side?"

I saw a flash of anger in the man's green eyes but it was quickly replaced by something that looked a lot like amusement.

"Not to disagree with a lady, but you climbed the fence, not him. So, basically, you're the one roaming freely and, I might add, trespassing on his property."

Embarrassment and ire filled me to capacity, leaving no room for apologies or silent mortification. Drawing back my shoulders, I met his laughing eyes. "Then I'll just remove myself from danger." Stiff with anger and carrying my bruised ego, I marched away in the direction I'd been heading when I'd been accosted by the horse.

I hadn't gone far before I heard him jogging up behind me, then felt him pulling me gently to a stop with a firm hand. "You're limping. You must be hurt."

I turned to glare at him, an angry retort on my lips, but paused. I could see his eyes clearly now and wondered how I'd missed it before: the darkness that hovered there that spoke of grief so fresh he hadn't yet learned how to hide it.

Looking away, I gently disengaged my arm, feeling blood rushing to my cheeks. "It's from an old accident. I'm fine." I began walking away again, conscious of my limp and feeling his eyes on me.

He called after me. "If you're trying to find the drive, you're going the wrong way."

Defeated and robbed of my noble exit, I turned toward him. He was trying very hard not to smile as he pointed me in another direction. As I began to walk away again, the man said, "If it makes you feel any better, that's the first friendly overture I've seen that horse make since I rescued him more than a month ago."

"It doesn't," I called back over my shoulder. "But thanks for trying." I considered for a moment asking him for help in extricating my car but quickly dismissed the idea. I had no desire to extend my humiliation by engaging him in more conversation and furthering our acquaintance.

I continued walking toward the fence without glancing back, and it wasn't until I was safely on the other side of the fence that I remembered the brief moment when I'd looked into the horse's eyes and seen the horrible scar, and felt for the first time in a long while that I was no longer alone in the world.

I ended up walking all the way back to the caretaker's cottage. My knee ached so much that I had to wrap it with ice and rest for a whole hour before finally calling Helen, who sent for a tow with apologies about the map. It had been drawn by Susan, she explained, when she'd first devised the idea of renting some of the outbuildings, but the road that I'd been on hadn't been in existence since the seventies when the golf course was built. We were both silent for a moment, wondering why Susan might have included a road that led to nowhere.

Setting my laptop on top of the pine

kitchen table, I flipped it open, having resigned myself to the fact that I'd have to wait until the next day to head to the library. I had a wireless card, so at least I could do preliminary Internet research on my grandparents' house as well as a search for any more news articles on the baby found in the Savannah River.

Still, my finger hesitated over the power button, my attention diverted to the scrapbook pages and tattered front cover that I'd placed in the corner of the table, an everpresent reminder of the real reason I was here. I'd had more than ample time to go through all the pages, but I resisted like a dieter contemplating fruitcake, desiring the sweetness but not sure if it would be worth the calories. I couldn't help but wonder if by continuing I'd be opening Pandora's box. But, I reasoned with myself, that box had been opened the moment the armoire had slid across the attic floor and exposed the hidden door.

After closing my laptop with a firm snap and sliding it away from me, I reached across the table, dragging the pages toward me before opening them up to the place I'd stopped the day before. I studied the drawing of the necklace again before flipping the page, staring at a sketch of the now familiar angel, and recalled that I hadn't seen an angel charm on the necklace in the box. And then I began to read.

March 29, 1929

I was right. My father did buy me a new mare for my birthday. She's a dun, with black zebra stripes on her legs and I named her Lola Grace. The Lola part was an inside joke for me, Lily, and Josie, but I'll call my beautiful horse just Grace. I always wanted a sister and that's the name I would have chosen, but I'll have to make do with using the name for my horse since Mama's been gone for so long and I don't think Papa has any plans to get married again.

We board Lola Grace at Asphodel, which is hard for me because I have to wait until somebody can take me there to ride. Papa is always seeing patients and can only take me on Sundays unless he's helping with a birthing, but most days it's Josie's older brother, Freddie. Their mama, Justine, has been taking care of the house and doing her best to raise me since my own mama passed, and seeing how Freddie is working at Asphodel while he's home from board-ing school in England for the summer, it seems to make sense.

Freddie didn't seem too happy with the arrangement at first until he learned that I could keep a secret. The first few times he drove me in Papa's old cart — now that he's got that fancy new automobile he doesn't use it anymore — Freddie took me directly to Asphodel Meadows. But then he started to make a few stops on his way, in neighborhoods my papa would have had a heart attack if he ever knew I'd been anywhere near them, to visit friends. I don't see how these people could be called friends. Firstly, they're all Negroes and Freddie's as white as I am although Justine and Josie are the color of my morning coffee with lots of milk. You can hardly tell they're black except there's plenty in this city who seem to make a big deal out of separating people and in their eyes Justine and Josie could never pass as white. But Freddie can, which is probably why he gets to go to school in England.

Anyway, he began to make these little visits to his friends on our way out to Asphodel, and sometimes he brings them things in bags or just papers and such. I haven't told Justine or Papa because I remember them telling

Freddie to drive me, and technically didn't say to take me there without stopping. And I somehow know that Freddie is testing me, and I don't want to disappoint. Freddie's grown into a real handsome young man and he's got beautiful manners that he must have learned in England and I guess it's natural for me to want to impress him.

Sometimes Josie comes with us and I've noticed that when she does Freddie takes us right to Asphodel. I guess because she's his little sister the rules are different. And maybe if she spilled the beans to their mother it would mean an end to his visits. So don't say anything, Josie, when you read this!

But I get to ride nearly every day and I've become a really good jumper. Mr. Harrington, Lily's father, said that if I got any better he might feel compelled to start the first female equestrian team for the Olympics. I know he's just teasing me because that will never happen, but I like to dream about it sometimes and I like the compliment just the same. I like being good at something, and when I'm on the back of Lola Grace, I feel as if I could do anything and the world is open to a million possibilities.

For the first charm I'm adding to Lola, I've chosen a horse for Lola Grace and all the horses at Asphodel for all the joy they bring us.

My eyes scanned to the bottom of the page. Two yellowed photographs, curled at the corners like a baby's finger, were glued to the paper. I leaned forward over the first one. I recognized the dun with the striped legs as Lola Grace. Astride her in breeches and tall boots was a girl with a long blond plait peeking out of her riding helmet. I recognized my grandmother but only from other pictures I'd seen of her. This girl had nothing in common with the grandmother I'd known. From her open-faced smile to the light in her laughing eyes, this girl was foreign to me.

She was laughing and looking down at the young man holding the reins. He was very tall and lean, with straight oiled hair parted on the side. His face was smooth and olive-skinned and I wondered if that was Freddie. He was smiling at the camera, but his eyes were looking up at the girl as if he were trying not to laugh, too.

The next portrait was of the same horse, but this was a different rider. I recognized Lillian with her straight, elegant nose that even as a very young girl made a person look twice at her. Her eyebrows were raised over an impish smile as if she'd just said something outrageous but was trying to pretend that she hadn't. The young man — Freddie — was also holding her reins, but he was closer to the horse and had his hand on her boot as if to make sure that the tiny rider wouldn't get hurt. And underneath the two pictures my grandmother had written *Best Friends Forever.*

A drop of moisture landed on the first picture and I wiped at it absently with the hem of my shirt. It wasn't until I'd closed the pages and shoved them away from me that I realized my cheeks were wet. I placed my hands over my eyes in surprise, until I remembered what it was that had made me cry. My grandmother had loved to ride and had her own horse named Lola Grace. And in my sixteen years atop the back of a horse, she had never mentioned it to me. And I had never thought to ask.

CHAPTER 9

Helen swayed in the golf cart as Odella took a turn, listening as Mardi's claws struggled to find purchase on the vinyl-covered backseat. Odella drove the golf cart like she did everything else: full speed ahead, using a straight line because it was the quickest, and not paying any attention at all to curves in the road.

Odella jerked to a stop in front of the caretaker's cottage, then came around to assist Helen from the cart and up the front porch steps to the door. Helen didn't need the help but she'd long since discovered that Odella's need to do for others stemmed from a questionable youth spent in places too far from home with people her family didn't approve. She'd once told Helen that she'd woken up one day next to her second common-law husband in a squatter's flat in Berkeley and decided it was time to go. Odella had returned to her roots in Georgia, finding Jesus and husband number three along the way and had been making amends for her misspent youth ever since.

It took Earlene a long time to finally answer the door, and when she did, she was out of breath. "Sorry. You're a bit early and I had to . . . clean up a bit." Mardi brushed past her and into the house.

"Get back here, boy," shouted Odella.

"He's fine," said Earlene. "I like dogs."

Helen listened to the frantic click of his paws as he searched from room to room. "He's looking for Susan. She used this house as her office space when it wasn't rented out and would bring Mardi with her."

"Poor thing." Earlene clicked her tongue. "My grandmother had a little dog. He adored her. And when she . . . went away, he missed her so much that he stopped eating." The door hinges squeaked as Earlene opened the door wider. "Would you like to come in? I'm not quite ready."

Helen felt Odella push her forward over the threshold, where Earlene took her arm. "Sorry we're so early. I can never be sure how long it's going to take to get somewhere when Odella drives. You remember Odella Pruitt, don't you? She's the real boss at Asphodel." Helen smiled in the older woman's

169

direction. "We'll be happy to wait until you're ready to go."

"Just for a minute. I need to run a brush through my hair and find some shoes."

Earlene led them into the sitting area at the front of the house and waited while Helen found a seat. Mardi came up to her and settled on the floor on her feet. "So what happened to your grandmother's dog?" Helen asked.

"He died. Less than a month after my grandmother left. And it was odd because . . ."

Helen felt Odella settle onto the couch next to her as she waited for Earlene to continue. "Because why?"

There was a long pause. "Because I hardly knew that she was gone." Her voice was soft, as if she hadn't intended for the other occupants in the room to hear her. "I'll be right back," she said, her voice recovered as her footsteps moved across the small braided rug and then to the hardwood floors that led to the single bedroom.

As soon as she was out of earshot, Helen turned to Odella. "What do you see?"

She could hear Odella rubbing her hands on her polyester slacks. "It's all as neat as a pin and only one place mat on the table, so we know she's at least been eating alone."

170

She paused, her tongue clicking against the roof of her mouth. "She's got one of them fold-up computers sitting on the kitchen table, but there's something else I can't figure out what it is. It looks like an old metal box."

Earlene called out from the bedroom. "I spilled toothpaste on my blouse, so I'm going to have to change it. It'll just take a minute."

"Take your time," Helen answered, then turned back to Odella. Lowering her voice, she said, "Don't be too intrusive, but could you go over and get a better look?"

She felt Odella leave the sofa, her tread light as she crossed the small room. "I can't believe the things you make me do for you on account of you being blind. And it's not 'cause I feel sorry for you, neither. You've got more hold of your faculties than most people I know with both eyes."

Helen, satisfied that Earlene wasn't finished changing, turned her face toward where she knew Odella was. "So what do you see?"

"Like I said, it's a metal box — a rectangle one like you see in the banks. You know, like a safety-deposit box. The lid's closed."

"Look inside, Odella. Quick."

"Lordy, Helen. If Miss Lillian finds out,

she's going to skin me alive. And I got to hurry — the corn bread has to go in the oven about now if we're going to eat at seven. You know how your grandmama gets when her supper's late."

"Hurry!" Helen hissed, the fear of being caught reminding her of the time she and Tucker had hidden in the trunk of their parents' car in the hopes that they might be brought along on one of their trips. They'd figured that after they were discovered at the airport it would be too late to turn back. But they hadn't even made it out of the drive because their mother had opened the trunk to place one more bag inside and discovered them sweating profusely and almost out of air. It didn't matter that she'd probably saved their lives by finding them when she did; their disappointment at being left behind seemed to them a much worse fate.

Odella paused for a moment. "It's a bunch of old scrapbook pages with just a ratty cover. Looks like something the cat dragged in." Something jangled against metal. "And there's a necklace in here, too. With a bunch of those little things you hang from a brace-let."

"You mean charms?"

"Yeah, those. Like that angel Miss Lillian

wears around her neck."

Helen grasped her hands into a fist, listening to Earlene opening the closet door in the bedroom. "Open the pages and read something."

Odella's sigh was accompanied by the sound of rustling pages. "There's a bunch of old pictures — they're all black-and-white. Mostly of some girls — and one of them looks like she might have been your grandmama from way back when. Lots of pictures of horses, too."

"But what does it *say?*"

Oblivious to Helen's urgency, Odella said, "Well, on the inside cover it says, 'This book is the property of Annabelle O'Hare, Lillian Harrington, and Josephine Montet. Unauthorized persons snooping inside this book will be shot.' " Odella snorted. "And there's a loose picture here of three girls — they're sitting on top of the fence in what looks like the north pasture. On the back it has those same names again and then some foreign language that I can't read."

"Can you sound it out?" Helen cocked her ear again in Earlene's direction, relieved to hear the water running in the bathroom.

Painfully, Odella sounded out the words with her South Georgia accent, brutalizing each one. By the time Odella had reached the fourth or fifth word, Helen sat back against the sofa cushion, recognizing Cicero's Latin words of wisdom. *Dum vita est, spes est.* They were the words her grandmother had taught her when a much younger Helen lay in her bed, sick with fever, on the first day she realized she could no longer see.

Helen heard the cover being slapped on top of the pages and then the faint metal sound of the box closing. She felt Odella's weight shift the sofa cushion at about the same time as she heard Earlene's footsteps approaching. Mardi let out a bark of warning just in case.

Earlene reentered the room, smelling of soap. "Sorry to keep you waiting."

Helen smiled as Odella helped her stand. "No problem at all. I just apologize for being so early." She turned to Odella. "Oh, and before I forget, we brought some more supplies — paper products and dishwashing soap — that I noticed you were low on when we stocked the refrigerator before you arrived. We left them out on the cart, so don't let us leave without us bringing them in. And I also wanted to tell you that you should give your weekly shopping list to Odella every Monday. She does a town run every Tuesday for groceries and she can pick up what you need then."

"Great, thank you. After this morning's incident I'm not in such a hurry to get back in my car. Odella, while you're helping Helen back to the cart, why don't I grab the bags and bring them in?"

"Sounds like a plan," Odella said as she took Helen's elbow, then led her out the door and down the porch.

While Earlene was putting the bags inside, Helen turned to Odella on the seat, still curious over the comment Odella had made earlier. "So if it's not my blindness, why is it that you think I can get you to do things you normally wouldn't?"

Odella grunted deep in her throat. "Because you're too much like your grandmother. It's not worth telling you no."

Helen smiled distractedly, her mind on something Earlene had told her in the cemetery. *You should talk to your grandmother now, before it's too late. Ask her to tell you her stories.* Her words had been nagging at her like poison ivy every since. Her grandmother's life had always been a taboo subject, one Helen had been warned about by her own mother. And now, as Helen thought about the scrapbook and the pictures of the three girls, she wondered if her grandmother's unwillingness to share her past had nothing to do with privacy, that the darkness Malily sought in her house mirrored something from her past.

Earlene returned and settled herself in the rear-facing seat of the golf cart next to Mardi. As they jostled side to side on the bumpy road, Helen thought of the scrapbook on the table that had her grandmother's name and picture on it, and why Malily's Latin words had reappeared in a place she least expected.

"Thanks for offering to bring me to dinner. I could have walked." I held on to the side of the cart, trying to press my teeth together so I wouldn't chip them. The movement didn't seem to bother the dog, whose large head was resting on my pink floral skirt, his nose making a wet spot on my thigh. With no place for my other hand, I let it rest on Mardi's neck.

Helen turned her head, her beautiful dark green eyes reflecting the golden sunset behind her, matching the color of the silk shantung dress she wore. On anyone else, the dress would have looked out of place on a golf cart. She smiled. "It's no problem. We had the supplies to bring to you anyway. But I have to confess to an ulterior motive, too."

I stiffened, and Helen raised a brow as if she sensed my wariness. "Really?" Even to my own ears, my voice was too casual.

"My brother, Tucker, will be joining us for dinner with his two girls, Sara and Lucy. If you wouldn't mind, please don't mention Susan. He hasn't . . . well, he doesn't talk about her. Especially in front of the girls."

I tried to hide my relief. "Thanks for letting me know."

Helen faced forward again and we rode the rest of the way in silence, as if to pay homage to the watchful oaks as we passed under their hovering branches, a canopy of old men protecting what was theirs.

Odella jerked to a stop in front of the front garden I'd noticed before. "If you don't mind, Miss Smith, could you take Helen inside? I got to run to the kitchen to stick my corn bread in the oven."

"Of course. Don't let me keep you."

I helped Helen out of the golf cart and put her hand on my arm. She held up a finger and we waited until Odella had disappeared around the corner. "Thank you, Earlene, but I'm fine. It makes Odella feel better if she's babying me so I let her. I don't have my cane, so if you'll just take me to the bottom step, I'm good to go. Unless you'd rather take the elevator inside?"

My chin seemed to jut out of its own volition, just like I remember doing whenever I was told I wasn't expected to win a ribbon at an event. "No," I said. "I'm fine with the stairs."

I tried to set a slow pace as we headed toward the steps but I found myself almost jogging to keep up with her long strides. She pulled away as soon as we reached the hand railing.

"I love your dress," I said as I executed a lopsided jog up the stairs behind her. We reached the landing and I was panting from the exertion, my knee beginning to complain. "I'm curious about how . . . well . . ." I stopped, realizing that I might be treading in sensitive territory.

"I shop by touch. If I like the way the material feels, I'll ask a salesperson or whoever I'm with to describe the color and design. But it has to feel good first." She headed up the last flight but went slower this time and I had a strong suspicion that she was doing it for me.

"Malily will be waiting in the parlor, where you saw her before. If we're lucky, she's already had a couple of drinks. And if Tucker's already there and he's playing bartender, definitely ask for a martini. He makes the best."

I nodded as I followed her into the darkened foyer and then down the dim hallway beyond the stairs to the room I remembered from before. When I entered I had the impression of a queen and her court. Lillian Harrington-Ross was seated in the same gilt chair she'd been in before, but on the floor flanking her were two blond girls, their hair the color of moonlight. They wore matching yellow sundresses and were each playing with a gold-and-diamond bangle bracelet. The younger girl was holding her small arm up to the light, watching the stones reflect the greedy ray of sun that had strayed into the room, the diamonds throwing drops of light onto the walls and furniture. The older girl simply stared at hers, as if willing it to do something more useful than just be beautiful. I noted Lillian's arm was bare at the same time I noticed the man standing by the open armoire.

I paused behind Helen in the doorway, wanting to back out of the room unnoticed, and suddenly aware that my skirt didn't completely hide the scars on my knee. I felt Helen pulling me forward and I inwardly groaned as she propelled me into the room. We greeted Lillian first before Helen introduced me to her nieces, Lucy and Sara, and then she turned toward the man.

"Tucker, I want you to meet Earlene Smith. She's the genealogist I was telling you about who's renting out the cottage for a few months. Earlene, this is my younger yet less good-looking brother, Dr. William Tecumseh Gibbons — otherwise known as Tucker around here."

His eyes held the same haunted expression I remembered from the horse pasture, but his lips were definitely twitching themselves into a smile. "We've met, actually, although I didn't catch her name before. She was making friends with the new horse." His lips broadened into a smile and his skin seemed strained from the effort.

Helen turned to me. "I thought you were afraid of horses."

I flushed with annoyance and mortification, remembering how I'd lain supine on the ground as the horse had searched my pockets for a treat. "I wasn't 'making friends.' It was after my car got stuck and I was trying to find my way back to the house to get help by crossing through the pasture. The horse . . . surprised me and I tripped."

"And Tucker didn't offer to help you?" Lillian asked, leaning forward, her fingers tucked tightly around a sherry glass.

Without meeting anyone's eyes, I said, "I didn't think to ask. My only thought at the time was to get away from the horse."

Helen raised two fingers to Tucker and he pulled out two martini glasses. He spoke as he mixed the drinks. "Although, as I told her at the time, she's the first person he's shown any interest in at all. Either he sensed your fear or . . ." He handed me my drink. "Or it was something else entirely. Maybe a familiarity with horses, even." He walked over to Helen and placed a drink in her hand. He returned to the armoire and picked up a double old-fashioned, the bottom filled with amber liquid.

I realized that everyone was looking at me, expecting an answer. I took a large gulp of my drink, my head already spinning. "I used to ride — a long time ago. But I fell off and I haven't had the need or desire to get back in a saddle again." I took another sip of my drink, alarmed that I was at the bottom of the glass already, and forced a smile. "Like every young girl's horse obsession, mine ended and I grew up."

The younger girl, Sara, had scooted over to sit by my feet. I was wondering what to do with my empty martini glass when I felt a small hand on the bare skin of my leg. "You've got a big boo-boo."

I looked down at her, wide crystal blue eyes turned up at me. Her forehead was creased with worry, her lower lip quivering. As much as I knew it would hurt, I squatted in front of her so that I would be at eye level. "It's an old boo-boo and it's all better now." I wondered how much I should tell her, knowing that because she was a young girl being raised around horses, I should leave out the part about how a large horse had caused my injury. Instead, I asked, "Have you seen *The Wizard of Oz*?"

Sara nodded emphatically.

"So you know the Tin Man. Well, the doctors put a piece of metal in my knee so that it would work better." I tapped on it. "See? Right as rain."

She continued to frown. "It must be rusted because you walk funny. Maybe you need some oil."

"That's enough, Sara," Tucker said as he approached and lifted Sara into his arms.

I stood, my knee stiff, and caught Tucker's gaze. "I'm sorry," he said quietly. "Children . . ."

"It's all right. She was just curious." I looked at Sara, who'd gone back to playing with her bracelet, and noticed how awkwardly her father held her, as if he didn't do it very often. He saw me looking and quickly set her down, her dress twisted and creased in the wrong way. Without thinking,

I bent down to straighten it. As my fingers sifted through the tulle and cotton, I had a flash of memory of my grandmother braiding my hair before a big event, her worn hands pressing down my jacket and brushing off any lint.

I stood, feeling dizzy, the memory fresh, the guilt heavy. I'd never remembered her at my events, but she must have been there. Who else would there have been to make sure my riding costume was beyond reproach?

"Are you all right?" Tucker's eyes had narrowed with concern.

I was spared from answering by Odella's appearance at the door. "Supper's waiting on the table. You'd best get at it before it gets cold."

Tucker moved to assist his grandmother out of her chair and lead her from the room as Helen called for Sara to come take her hand. That left the older girl, Lucy, and me. To my surprise, Lucy walked somberly over to me and slipped her hand into mine.

She spoke quietly, each word pronounced with care as if she were used to being misunderstood. "You can lean on me, if you need to. I don't mind. I think your knee must still hurt you and that's why you limp. Aunt Helen's blind and Mama was . . ."

183

She stopped, and I willed her to continue. "What I meant to say is that we're used to people with handicaps."

I stared down at this young girl, amazed at her astuteness and my own ignorance. Since the accident I'd never once thought of myself as handicapped — wounded and victim, sure, but never handicapped. For the first time I saw myself as others must, and the portrait made me cringe.

The dining room with its crimson walls and ornate ceiling was dimly lit, the candles on the table throwing shadows like draped lace. The blinds were closed on the four floor-to-ceiling windows, the enormous crystal chandelier and matching wall sconces that lined the walls losing the battle to encroach upon the darkness.

Tucker sat Lillian at one end of the table and then held the chairs one by one for the rest of us before taking his place at the other end. Odella had already set all of the serving pieces and utensils on the table and we began by serving ourselves before passing the food in a clockwise motion. Tucker was to my left and Lucy on my right. I'd thought she'd need some help with some of the heavier dishes, but she seemed determined to do it all herself without any assistance.

I watched as Tucker placed the food on

Helen's plate and then Sara's, cutting into small bitefuls everything on both plates before standing to pass the platters on to Lillian's end of the table.

I studied him surreptitiously from the corner of my eye, watching his serious expression as he sawed a knife into meat, saw his face relax as he addressed Helen, saw the slightly bewildered looks he gave to his daughters. It made me think of the dead Susan, and where she would have fit at the table, realizing with a start that I was most likely sitting in her seat. Maybe that was why he seemed to be avoiding looking at me altogether.

Helen turned to her grandmother. "Malily, it occurred to me while I was talking with Earlene the other day that you might be able to help with some of her research." She chewed thoughtfully on a forkful of ham. "She's working on a project for a friend, researching all the families in the area. Anyway, we were in the cemetery looking at Grandpa Charlie's obelisk and I realized that I really know nothing of your life here at Asphodel before you were married. Maybe if you could share some of that with her, maybe give her some of the names of people that were here at that time, that would probably be a big help."

Helen's sightless eyes rested on me for a moment, and although I knew she was blind, I could almost believe that not only could she see me, but she could see inside me, too. And I wondered if she realized how much she and Lucy were alike.

Lillian was on her second glass of wine and her eyes had taken on a faraway look. I figured that Helen had probably realized this and that was why she'd planned her first foray into her grandmother's past at the dining table.

Lillian's words were softly slurred, the ending consonants dropping off slightly as if they'd fallen down a short incline. "I was born here at Asphodel. Right up there in the bed I sleep in every night. I was probably conceived in that bed, too, but that wasn't ever a subject a properly brought-up young lady would ever ask her parents." A slight twitch lifted one side of her face in a gruesome smile.

She took another sip of her wine. "That was in nineteen nineteen, just a year before women won the right to vote and blacks couldn't despite the fifteenth amendment that said they should, and well-bred women were expected to have no bigger aspirations than to get married and have children." She paused, sifting through years of memories.

"I was an only child, although it wasn't for lack of trying. There are four graves in that cemetery of the brothers who didn't make it past their first year. I never knew my mother. She died when I was eight and before that she was too busy crying over her dead babies." She stared into her wine. "I suppose that's why I have no patience for people who can't move on."

Lillian stopped abruptly, her gaze flickering over Tucker, who'd gone very still. She drained her glass. "Doctors weren't sure whether it was the hard births or the grief that finally took her, but I always thought that she was relieved to go."

Lillian sat back in her chair, holding her empty glass close, and a dreamy look settled on her face as if she'd moved on to a different place, leaving us all behind. She closed her eyes. "It was a lovely time to be alive, to be young. It was just me and Father, and all of my lovely, lovely horses. I rode every day. Even in the rain or when it was too cold or too hot to do much of anything. All of those lovely horses," she said again, her words slurring.

"What about Grandpa Charlie? You've never told us how you met."

Lucy and Sara were dutifully eating a bit of everything from their plates, including their vegetables, although it looked like most of Sara's peas were rolling off her plate and onto the starched white linen tablecloth. Although she was sitting on several phone books, her chin was barely over the edge of the table, but still she persevered. She wore a look of determination and I wondered if she'd gotten that from Tucker or Susan.

Lillian picked up a piece of ham on her fork and considered it briefly before returning it to her plate. "My father introduced us. Charlie was an up-and-comer at the bank and Father thought we would be suitable for each other."

"And you fell in love?" Helen asked.

I glanced over at Helen to see if she'd meant it to sound so hopeful.

"Charles was the most beautiful dancer. He could do all the old dances and the new dances equally well. He'd take me to parties and we'd dance all night until I'd worn a hole in my dancing shoes."

Helen's empty gaze was focused on her plate and I wondered if she'd also realized that Lillian hadn't answered her question.

I cleared my throat. "Helen and I went to the family cemetery yesterday. His monument is very striking." I waited for her eyes to find me so I could gauge how much I could press on. Her eyes were filmy and unfocused, although her expression had lost none of its haughtiness. I continued. "In the back corner, near the large oak tree, is a small gravestone, marked only by an angel. Near the moonflower vine. I'm curious as to who might be buried there and wondered if you might know."

Her expression didn't change, but something flickered in her eyes as her gaze settled on me. "I'm afraid I don't. I've always assumed it was one of my little brothers. He could have been stillborn and never named." Carefully, she placed her wineglass on the table and picked up her fork, her hand shaking almost imperceptibly. "It was a long time ago, you understand. My memory isn't as good as it used to be." She speared a bite of roasted potato and lifted it to her mouth.

"What about any friends, Malily? Did you have any close girlhood friends?" Helen asked, her face turned toward her grandmother.

I stared at Helen, wondering how she'd known which question to ask. I turned to Lillian, and waited for her to answer.

She lifted a bite of food to her mouth and forced herself to swallow. Then she dropped her fork on the plate, the metal hitting the china and echoing in the still room as we all watched her. Slowly, her hand moved to her neck, where she wore her angel charm, identical to the one I'd remembered to remove before I came, and her ruined fingers grasped it.

"No," she said softly, and I watched as Helen stilled. "A few, perhaps. But no one in particular." Her thin chest rose and fell as if with heavy exertion, the angel charm winking at me in the candlelight.

I watched as Helen reached for her bread roll and Tucker slid the butter dish over to her, tapping it against her plate. She took the butter knife and I watched as she cut a perfect square of butter and placed it on her plate. Her voice was studiously nonchalant, as if she'd known Lillian's answer for the lie it was. "Are you still in contact with any of them?"

Helen faced me, her eyes meeting mine, and I had the uncanny feeling again that she could actually see me, could know why I held my breath as I waited for Lillian to speak again.

A sigh rolled out of Lillian's bony chest, a sigh that carried with it past years, and the lost hours gone without remark, but missed in retrospect. "They are all dead now. There's no one left who remembers . . . who remembers . . ." Her voice trailed off as her hand reached for her wineglass, then stilled when she realized it was empty.

"Who remembers what, Malily?" Tucker asked, his own utensils held aloft, suspended as we all waited for her to speak. A clock in the hallway chimed the hour. I counted eight chimes and considered how quickly the time had passed.

She stared into her empty glass, a soft smile on her face. "Him."

"Grandpa Charlie?" Tucker asked, his silverware now resting on the edge of his plate.

Lillian straightened in her chair and looked around as if realizing where she was. She shook her head as if trying to clear it. "No," she said. "I'm the only one who remembers. . . ."

I watched as Lillian focused her gaze on Sara, reached over, and stroked the soft skin on the back of her hand, the way a mother touches her baby's face. A cold chill crept up my spine, needles of apprehension teasing at my nape.

"Who remembers what?" Helen leaned toward her grandmother, her gaze turned toward the window, where the feeble light of the closing day glowed beyond the closed shutters.

Lillian's last words were barely audible, so quiet that I could almost believe that I hadn't heard them at all.

Lillian's face paled and Tucker stood, his chair skidding behind him. He rang a small bell that sat at the edge of her plate and took her hand. "I think this heat is getting to you, Malily. Odella's going to come take you to your room so you can lie down, all right?"

Odella appeared carrying a tray with coffee for the adults and ice cream for the children. She looked at me. "If you wouldn't mind taking care of this, I'll get Miss Lillian up to her room."

I nodded, watching with concern as Tucker helped Lillian stand, her hands shaking so badly that they couldn't hold her cane. Tucker watched as Odella took hold of Lillian's shoulders and gently guided her from the room.

All eyes were focused on me as I turned to the dessert tray and began pouring coffee, Lillian's words swimming in and out of my head like the tide, settling and disturbing sediment at the same time. *The truth,* she had said. And I remembered the way she'd touched Sara's hand, and the blue baby's sweater and blanket I'd found in my grandmother's house, how Lillian had lied about not having any particular childhood friends. But I'd heard her say *The truth.* And

I wondered if Lillian's truth could be the spray of light I needed to shine into the darkest corners of my own grandmother's past.

CHAPTER 10

"Aren't you having anything?" Helen asked, turning her face to Earlene. "I can't hear your cup against its saucer. Aren't you having any coffee?"

"No. I . . . I have trouble sleeping. I try not to drink caffeine too late in the day. Can I get you any sugar or cream?"

Helen shook her head. "No, thank you. I take a teaspoon of sugar but Tucker's already taken care of that for me." She reached over and patted his arm, not sure if she was reassuring herself or him.

"Will she be all right?"

Helen didn't have to ask who Earlene was talking about. "Malily's a tough old bird — and I don't mean that disrespectfully. She'd probably even agree. I think it would take a strong wind to blow her off her feet. Did she say anything that you might find useful for your research?"

There was a brief pause before Earlene

answered. "I'm not sure. I'll go home and make notes and then when I'm doing research something might come up that will reference something she said. Then I'll know, but not before."

Helen stirred her coffee thoughtfully. "Will you keep me posted on anything you find? I've always wanted to do what you're doing, digging into the past. There's something about not knowing your own history that's a bit bewildering."

Earlene's hands rubbed against the tablecloth, as if they were suddenly nervous at finding themselves with nothing else to do. "It's a bit like drifting in a boat on the ocean without an anchor." Her words were spoken quietly, as if she wasn't sure she wanted anyone else to hear them.

Helen sat back in her chair, feeling her brother watching her as she listened to the girls scraping the ice cream from their bowls. She felt an odd connection with this quiet, sad woman. Maybe it was because they were both essentially motherless, set adrift without their stories to guide them. Or maybe it was because Helen sensed that they were both traveling in a world that had been darkened by events they'd had no control over.

Helen leaned toward Earlene. "Before you

leave, I have something to give you that might help you with your research."

"Helen." Tucker's voice held a note of warning.

"Just some papers and family letters, Tuck. Everything else I gave to Malily when I cleaned up the cottage."

"I just don't want . . ." His voice faded, and she pictured him indicating Earlene.

"I know," she reassured him. "It'll be fine."

She felt her brother relax back into his chair, his breathing slowed. When he spoke again, his words were directed at their guest. "So you ride?"

"I used to." Earlene's voice held a note of wariness and Helen wondered if Tucker could hear it, too.

"She told us she fell off of her horse, remember, Daddy? That's why she doesn't ride anymore." Sara's voice was raised, but they'd all grown used to her conversations that sounded a lot like shouting contests. Helen supposed that was what happened when you were the youngest and had to fight to be heard. The little girl continued. "Malily always says that the best thing to do when you fall off is to get right back up again. 'Else you forget the reason you used to get up on the horse in the first place." Sara spoke with a mouth full of ice cream, but Helen didn't correct her. She was too interested in hearing what Earlene would say.

She could sense Earlene forcing a smile. "Yes, I suppose your grandmother is right." Glass clinked and Helen pictured Earlene taking a drink from her water glass. "But I . . . well, I guess I just figured I'd ridden long enough and that it was time to try something else."

"Like genealogy." Tucker's voice was devoid of recrimination, and held only surprise. Since his grandmother had put him in a saddle at the age of two, horses and riding had been constant themes in his life. Even through medical school, marriage and children, they remained as a sort of anchor to the man he strived to be regardless of where life tugged him.

"Like genealogy," Earlene answered, her words tight.

Lucy spoke, her clear, high-pitched voice belying the maturity of her words. "I think the scars on her knee are from falling off her horse, which means it was probably worse than just falling off. Maybe she had a good reason for quitting."

The quiet was deafening for a moment, Lucy's words silencing even her little sister.

Tucker finally spoke. "Or maybe it's a

good reason for getting on a horse again."

Helen heard Earlene's chair slide back on the rug. "I need to get going. Thank you so much for dinner. I can walk back to the cottage . . ."

"Don't be silly," Helen said as she pushed her own chair back. "The mosquitoes will have picked you up and spirited you away before you make it down the oak alley. Odella will most likely be with Malily for a while but I'm sure Tucker would be happy to drive you back." Without waiting for anyone to argue, she stood. "Tucker, since your nanny's off tonight and the girls are staying here, why don't you get the girls ready for bed while I take Earlene upstairs to give her those papers I talked about? Then you can drive Earlene home."

Neither one of them answered right away, and Helen couldn't decide who was more reluctant: Earlene, who couldn't wait to escape from having anybody scrutinize her life, or Tucker, who'd spent more time with his horses than his children since his wife's death.

Helen held out her arm. "Earlene, if you'll grab my elbow, I'll lead the way. I don't want to trip and hurt myself on the stairs." She hated using her blindness to extract sympathy, but she figured Earlene needed

198

her help as much as Tucker needed to spend time with his daughters so she did what she thought necessary.

She felt Earlene's cold fingers touch the bare skin on her arm before Helen led the way back to the grand staircase that curved up and around the foyer, hiding a rueful grin as she considered which one of them was more profoundly blind.

I hurried my pace to catch up with Helen, who didn't really seem to need my help. I was glad to be out of the dining room and eager to see what papers she had for me. As I'd been reading my grandmother's scrapbook pages, the whereabouts of Lily's and Josie's pages hovered in the back of my mind. From Helen's conversation with Tucker, I doubted Lillian's would be in there, but I was still hopeful that I'd find a reference to the scrapbook or necklace — anything that would give me something concrete so that I could finally approach Lillian.

For the first time in a very long time, I felt a small fire that felt a lot like longing sending sparks inside my chest, where my fearless heart had once beat. As we wound our way up the staircase, I thought back to what had first started it and realized that it was something Sara had said. *Malily always says that the best thing to do when you fall off is to get right back up again. 'Else you forget the reason you used to get up on the horse in the first place.* I remembered now where I'd heard it before. I'd been young, small enough to still be riding my first pony, Benny. I'd slid off of her backside because I wasn't paying attention, bruising my backside almost as much as my ego. It had been my grandmother's arms that had reached for me, pulling me up to stand while my grandfather looked on, his mouth turned down with disappointment. When she'd leaned toward me to brush the dust off of my collar, she'd told me why I needed to get back on.

That had been the first of only two times anybody ever had to remind me to get back in the saddle. I don't think that I'd ever thanked her for that, either. I'd taken her words of wisdom like I'd accepted her plates of fried chicken and corn bread — nourishment I needed but never noticed, forgotten as soon as the next challenge presented itself. And then I'd fallen from Fitz and I'd almost died. But my grandmother was in the nursing home by then, so there'd been nobody to tell me to get back on, and I quickly tried to forget the reason I used to get up on a horse in the first place.

Helen reached out her hand and let a finger slide down the wall as she began counting doorways, and I continued to analyze how my self-absorption had shifted almost imperceptibly. It was also something Tucker had said about me giving up riding horses for genealogy. His voice held the surprise of watching a starving man choose a glass of water over a four-course meal.

I'd met his eyes and seen none of the recrimination I'd expected. Instead, I recognized something familiar, and knew he understood how it was to feel incomplete unless you were in a saddle, how walking or running and even flying in a plane could never compete with the freedom and power you felt when you were riding into the wind on the back of a horse. It's the complex mix of vulnerability and bravado that makes a great horseman, and in Tucker Gibbons, I recognized the mind-set of the person I used to be. But I'd also noticed that he hadn't seen that person at all when he looked at me. It shook me at first. Shook me hard enough to start that little spark in my chest — enough to make me follow Helen upstairs instead of bolting out of the house as my instincts kept telling me to do.

Helen paused by the third door in the dim

hallway, then turned the knob and pushed open the door. She flipped on a switch and the room was bathed in bright lights from the ceiling and walls. Helen moved about the room, turning on table lamps. "Can you see all right?" she asked.

I wanted to laugh. I felt as if I were standing inside a crayon box, each wall surface brighter than the last. Her antique four-poster bed was draped with dark purple chiffon, contrasting with the fuchsia and lime green quilted duvet with matching toile shams and roll pillows. "I can see fine. In fact, I think I might need to put on my sunglasses."

Helen smiled as she made her way over to a Queen Anne lady's desk, which sat under an oval window on the side of the house I hadn't yet seen. "Malily helped me with it. I wanted colorful and she promised me that colorful is what I'd get."

I stood in the middle of the room admiring the way the lemon-colored rug thrown over the wood floor matched the painted ceiling. "I'd have to agree. It's really beautiful." I thought of the stern Lillian I'd just had dinner with, and I couldn't imagine her agreeing to create a room like this in her house. But she had done it for her blind granddaughter, and it made me wonder what other surprises lurked beneath the quietly refined facade of Lillian Harrington-Ross.

Helen pulled open the bottom drawer of the desk and lifted out a large three-ring binder that bulged with papers, their corners exploding from the confines of the cover. "After Susan died, Odella helped me gather her papers and put them in here. I'd read them if I could, but since I can't I guess I was just waiting for the right person to come along." She held it out to me. "I'm going to let you borrow these if you promise that you'll let me know if you find anything interesting."

I took the binder, its weight letting me think of possibilities. "I will — I promise." I clutched the binder to my chest. "But you mentioned something earlier — something about your grandmother's scrapbook?"

She straightened, and tilted her head to the side just like I'd seen Lucy do before she spoke. "Malily asked for it back, so I gave it to her. She said she didn't care about the rest of it, but she wanted the scrapbook. Actually, it's not even a scrapbook — it's just pages that have been torn out. I'm not sure where the rest of it is."

Her green eyes settled on me and I had to remind myself that she couldn't see me squirm. "Well, this should be a great boost to my research. Thank you. And I promise to give you a report of anything I find."

The door flew open and Mardi sauntered in, immediately zeroing in on Helen. She squatted down to scratch behind his ears. "I guess it's time for bed, hmm?" She turned her face in my direction. "He sleeps at the foot of my bed, guarding me. Don't think he'd do much to an intruder besides lick him to death, but I appreciate the thought." She straightened and yawned. "Excuse me. I guess I'm more tired than I thought." She yawned again as if to accentuate her point. "Tucker is probably still with the girls. If you take a right out of my room and go to the end of the hallway, their door is the last one on the left." She grinned up at me. "Since they're here so much, Malily allowed me to design a room for them — I went a little wild with the colors in there, too, but the girls seem to enjoy it. Just stick your head in and let Tucker know that you're ready to leave. Unless you'd feel more comfortable if I took you myself."

I resisted the temptation to take her up on her offer. "No, that's all right. I'm sure I can find it," I said, wondering briefly if anybody would notice if I just let myself out of the house and made my own way home.

As if reading my thoughts, Helen said, "Tucker would take the cart back to the tabby house anyway, so he might as well drop you off, too. And I'd feel better knowing you made it back safely."

I felt my way down the dim hallway, avoiding antique tables with vases filled with fragrant flowers and looking for a light switch. I followed the thin glow of light from under a door and stood outside for a moment, listening to Sara's voice.

I tapped on the door and pushed it open further, then peered inside. Sara and Lucy had matching pink lace-topped canopy beds but both girls were propped up on large pillows on one of them, sharing a book while Lucy read out loud. Tucker sat across the room in a stuffed rocking chair, his elbows on his knees and his fingers steepled as he silently regarded his daughters.

I saw the same bewildered expression that I'd seen at dinner, like that of a man meeting a stranger but recognizing something oddly familiar about them. No one looked up as I stood there and I had just decided to back out quietly and find my own way home when Sara looked at me and smiled.

"Hello, Miss Earlene. Did you come to tuck us in and say good night?"

Her smile was infectious and I smiled

back. "Yes, among other things." I set the notebook down outside the door and entered the room. The walls were painted a faint lavender, matching the lavender shag rug on the floor, and at the top near the ceiling cornice were handpainted nursery rhymes in gold sparkling paint. Helen's artistic spirit could be seen everywhere, including the cobalt blue rocking chair shaped like a crown that Tucker sat in.

Tucker stood as I entered. "Are you ready to go home?"

"Yes, if it doesn't inconvenience you at all." I had trouble meeting his eyes, remembering what I'd thought when I'd first seen him, how fresh his grief was. Being near him felt like an intrusion, as if his dead wife was in the room and I'd interrupted them in conversation.

"Not at all. Let me tuck in the girls and I'll be ready."

Sara slid from the bed, her white cotton nightgown brushing the floor as she ran to me. "I want Miss Earlene to tuck me in."

I reached down to pick her up, managing not to wince as my knee protested at the sudden weight. "I've never done it before, but you can teach me, all right?"

I carried Sara over to the other bed and set her down on the side of it.

"It's easy. I taught Emily, too, and she does everything just like Mama did. We've been teaching Daddy, too."

I glanced over at Tucker, who hadn't moved from his spot but stood watching Sara and me closely, his hands tucked into his pockets.

"Okay," I said, turning back to the little girl. "What do I do first?"

She lay down on her back, her head on the lace-covered pillow. "You tuck the sheets all the way around me so that they're really, really tight. Like a mummy, except you leave my arms outside."

She lifted her arms over her head and I did as she asked, not able to resist a quick tickle under her arm. She giggled. "Mama used to do that, too."

I stilled, staring down at her. *Mine did, too,* I wanted to tell her. *And so did my grandmother.* It must have been when I was very young, before I'd grown too wild and my ambitions too elevated for me to take much notice of my grandmother's quiet presence in my life.

"What's next?" I asked quietly, watching her pale blue eyes that were so different from her father's.

She pursed her lips for a moment as if she were thinking. "I say my prayers. Then you kiss me on the forehead and turn off the light."

I sat down on the edge of the bed and folded my hands. "I'm ready."

Sara clenched her eyes shut. "God bless Daddy, and Malily, and Lucy, and me, and Odella." She opened her eye and looked at me for a moment before shutting it tightly again. "And Miss Earlene. God bless Mardi, and all of the horses, especially the mean one with the scar on his side. Please help Daddy fix him, too, so that he's all better and doesn't remember any of the bad stuff that happened to him before he came here." She turned her head to face her sister, who was lying quietly on her side, watching us. "Did I forget anybody, Lucy?"

Lucy nodded her head solemnly and I heard Tucker let out a small breath. "You forgot Mama."

"Oh, yes," said Sara, squeezing her eyes shut again. "God bless Mama. Please help her find what she's looking for."

A heavy silence descended on the room and I was glad my head was bowed so I wouldn't have to look at Tucker and he wouldn't have to see my face as I tried to figure out what Sara meant.

"Amen," Lucy said softly.

I stood and smoothed down Sara's hair,

then leaned down and kissed her softly on her forehead. I waited for Tucker to approach, but when he didn't, I moved to Lucy's bed. "Can I tuck you in, too?"

She nodded, her large eyes never leaving my face. I tucked her in like I'd done for her sister but without the tickling, and then, after hesitating only a moment, I kissed her forehead. "Good night, Lucy." I started to move away but paused, remembering something else I'd long since forgotten. "Sweet dreams," I added and watched as Lucy's solemn face broke into a wide grin, the first one I'd seen.

"Mama used to say that to us. It works, too. I always have good dreams when somebody says that."

I smoothed her blond hair away from her face. "My mother used to say that to me, too, when I was a little girl."

Her face was serious again. "She doesn't say that to you anymore?"

I considered what to tell her and then decided on the truth. "My mother died when I was six years old. That was a long time ago and I think I'd forgotten about her telling me sweet dreams until tonight. So thank you for helping me to remember. It's a nice memory to keep."

"You're welcome. Good night, Miss Earlene."

"Good night," I said again, and watched as Tucker moved to the side of each bed, bending stiffly to kiss a forehead and say his own good nights before following me out into the hallway.

He waited as I bent down to retrieve the notebook. "Can I carry that for you?"

It was going to make walking more difficult, but I knew how he felt about the book and its contents and who had last seen them and I couldn't bring myself to ask for his help. "No, but thank you. I'm fine."

We walked in awkward silence down the hall but I voiced my surprise when we passed the staircase and continued walking to the other end of the long hallway.

"Elevator," he said, as we stood in front of what looked like another bedroom door, but this one had two buttons on a panel beside it.

I nodded my acknowledgment, secretly grateful that he wouldn't have to witness my clumsiness climbing down a set of stairs while holding the heavy notebook. We descended in silence, both of us staring at the closed door. The elevator smelled of new carpet and the air was filled with all the words that I couldn't say: how sorry I was about his wife; how precious his two daughters were and how they would all get used to the idea of living without their mother; and how I hadn't always been a crippled genealogist but that I'd once been an equestrian champion with dreams of winning Olympic gold.

Instead, I waited in silence for the doors to open, clutching the bulging notebook as I stepped out into the dimly lit marble foyer.

"This way," he said, indicating the back of the house. "Odella always leaves the cart by the kitchen entrance." He pushed on a piece of wall paneling in the dining room, which revealed a hidden door and I followed him into the kitchen, which smelled like dish detergent and lemons and reminded me of my grandmother and the way she'd taken such pride in her kitchen. I stopped in front of the island, staring above at a pot rack covered in gleaming stainless-steel pots and felt a stab of nostalgia for the woman who'd cooked for me all of those years but whom I barely remembered.

"This way," Tucker said again as he held open the screen door that led outside.

I stood on the brick steps, and inhaled sharply. A mixed bouquet of flower scents wafted toward me like a spritz of perfume, and I turned to Tucker to see if he'd smelled it, too.

He'd paused on the bottom step, his face illuminated by an outdoor gaslight. He had the same half-amused expression he'd worn the first time he'd seen me, flat on my back in the middle of the horse paddock. "It's Malily's garden for the blind."

I joined him on the bottom step. "Her what?"

"She planted it for Helen. It's full of the most fragrant flowers in existence so that you don't have to have sight to enjoy it. It's Helen's favorite place in the world."

"I can see why," I said, closing my eyes as I breathed in deeply.

"You should come by in the daylight to see it. It's almost as beautiful as it smells."

"I will," I said, and moved off the steps. I hadn't gone very far before I realized that Tucker wasn't behind me. "Is something wrong?"

He stood staring at me for a long moment before coming toward me. "No. I was just thinking." He stopped in front of me, his back to the gaslight and his face in shadow. "Lucy and Sara want to learn how to ride, but I don't really have the time or the patience to teach them myself. I've tried to hire someone, but I can't find anybody who wants to come all the way out here."

I listened to the thick air stir itself enough to push a wind chime, to press the scent of moonflowers against my skin. "Like I said, I don't ride anymore," I said, squeezing the book tighter against my chest.

"I'm not asking you to. I just need somebody who has experience and knowledge to teach my daughters the rudiments of riding. That's all they need for now."

I shuddered, but at the same time felt the heat of the old flame lick at my chest again. "I don't . . . I mean, I've never taught anyone before. I wouldn't know where to start."

"But I'm assuming you were an advanced rider, correct? To sustain the kind of injury that you have, you must have had a serious fall. Not from a cross rail, in other words."

I searched for his eyes in the shadows, but saw only the darkness. "I don't like horses anymore. I haven't had anything to do with them for a very long time."

I felt him watching me closely. "If only it were really that easy to stop. Once horses get into your blood, there's no amount of bloodletting that will make it go away." Without waiting for me to respond, he began walking toward the golf cart, then stopped by the passenger side until I caught

213

up to him. He took the book and helped me sit before placing it in my lap. He didn't speak again until we'd gone around the house and were facing the alley of oaks. They looked different at night, altered by the settling darkness. They wore the shadows like cloaks, their ancient knobs and limbs trembling slightly with impotent anger, hovering close over the alley as we began to pass through it.

A high-pitched whistle pierced the night, a lingering song whose words were lost in the black branches and Spanish moss outlined against the sky. I clutched at Tucker's sleeve without being aware of it. "What is that?"

"It's the oak trees," he said, slowing the cart. "The breeze off the river at night stirs them up." He tilted his head as if to hear it better. "They say that it started after they changed the course of the river and that when the wind blows it reminds them of the time their brothers were cut down and they shout out their grief."

I let my hand drop. "What do you think it is?"

He watched me for a moment before he answered. "I think that when they dammed the river it changed the way the wind hits the land, which is why they started whistling after the alley was carved in half. It's the only explanation that really works. I just can't imagine that anything could grieve for that long." He hit the pedal hard with his foot, causing the golf cart to jerk forward.

We didn't speak again until we'd reached the cottage. He helped me out and walked me to the door. He said good night but hesitated. Finally, he said, "Would you at least think about it?"

I didn't have to ask him what he was talking about any more than I had to think about why I hadn't already told him no.

"I wouldn't ask you to get on a horse if you didn't want to. Just supervise the girls. And it's only temporary since you're leaving in a few months. It's just . . ." He raked his hands through his hair and I remembered what he'd said in the cart. *I just can't imagine that anything could grieve for that long.*

"After their mother died, I promised them that I would teach them. It's different between us now . . . without their mother being here. I'm not sure how to go about it. But I thought if they could learn to ride . . ." His voice drifted off and he turned as if to leave. "Never mind."

I pulled him back. "I understand," I said, knowing more than most that this one thing in common could be what they needed. And I understood, too, that the grieving time wasn't determined by the hours in a day but by something else I didn't yet have a name for. But my own grieving time for the life I had once thought to have had come to an end. Like closing a casket or burying a box, I'd make it go away. Probably not forever, but hopefully long enough that I could find something else to look forward to.

"I'll help you," I said. "I won't be getting back on a horse, but I can help you teach the girls to ride."

His teeth beneath his smile showed white in the porch light. "Thank you, Earlene. Thank you." He slapped at something on the back of his neck. "Well, there's a lot to do then before we can get started. I'll have their nanny, Emily, call you tomorrow to discuss their schedule. And I'll call after I check out a few horse auctions for some ponies. We can discuss money, too, since I don't expect you to do it for free."

"No, please. I don't need to be paid. I'd like to do it. I like Sara and Lucy and I think we'll have fun together. And I think I might need this as much as they do."

He was silent for a moment. "If you're sure. And if you'll let me know if you change your mind." He slapped at his neck again. "I'd better be going before these damn mosquitoes eat me alive. Thanks again, Earlene. I really can't thank you enough."

"You're welcome," I said and watched him climb back into the golf cart. "And thank you," I said softly as I watched him drive away, listening again for the whistling oaks, and wondering how long it would be before they realized that they had grieved enough.

CHAPTER 11

Lillian sat on the bench listening to the splash of water from the fountain in what she always considered to be Helen's garden, her face shaded by the large brim of her straw hat. The morning sun was hot, but not yet hot enough to have evaporated the morning dew that clung to the closed marble petals of the moonflowers that dangled from the stone fountain.

She sensed the girl's presence before she spotted her by the garden gate, hovering there as if unsure she should proceed now that she realized she wasn't alone. Their new tenant was past girlhood, Lillian knew, but there was something so vulnerable and fragile in Earlene's eyes, and in the way that she stood with her shoulders down, that reminded Lillian of her motherless great-granddaughters. It was as though she'd found life disappointing and had managed to retreat to the point in her life where the burdens of growing up had not yet found her.

From the corner of her eye, she saw Earlene turn from the gate as if to leave.

"Would you like to join me?" Lillian called out. She wasn't sure why. She'd come to the garden to be alone. Maybe it was because Earlene had needed to be alone, too, and had chosen Helen's garden. Most people would have chosen to stay in bed at this early hour, wrestling with jumbled thoughts behind closed blinds. But Earlene had sought the garden, and the fragrant blooms that Lillian had once been told by an old friend represented the hand of God on earth.

"Only if I'm not intruding."

Lillian moved over on the bench as an invitation for Earlene to sit, then tilted back her head so her hat brim wouldn't obscure the view. "Not at all. My gardens have always been meant for sharing."

Lillian studied the younger woman as she approached, her limp less pronounced in the flowing calf-length skirt she wore. She was very pretty, Lillian thought, and could be prettier with more attention to cosmetics and maybe a softer hairstyle other than the low ponytail she always wore. But her skin was smooth and fine, her delicate eyebrows giving her face an almost angelic quality. It was her eyes, though, that commanded attention. They were light brown and outlined with long, dark lashes and stared out at the world like those of a wounded animal. But there was something more, too — a light that simmered beneath her defeatist attitude, but a light nevertheless. Lillian couldn't help but compare Earlene to the damaged horses Tucker rescued, and wondered if she'd be like the ones that somehow managed to regain their spirit.

Earlene sat and Lillian continued to stare, too tempted to get a close-up view to care about politeness. The young woman seemed so familiar to her, reminding her of someone she couldn't yet place. But maybe it was that familiarity that had made Lillian pat the seat next to her, to want to share this corner of her garden with a stranger.

Earlene gave her a tentative smile. "When I left the house last night, I smelled the garden and Tucker invited me to come see it in the daylight. I don't think I've ever smelled anything quite like it, except maybe for the garden at my house in Savannah. I recognized the gardenias. And the moonflowers."

Earlene cupped her hands, one inside the other, and rested them on her skirt. Lillian studied them, the neatly clipped nails and the fading calluses on the outside of her ring fingers. Lillian smiled to herself. Yes, it was true you could stop riding horses. But there would always be something left behind to remind you of what it was like.

Lillian smiled. "Not many people recognize the scent of the moonflowers when there are gardenias nearby. Gardenias are like the bullies of the garden, always muscling out the scents of the other flowers."

Earlene leaned forward and touched the folded-up moonflower bloom. "But these are my favorite. I think I'd recognize their scent anywhere."

"Your favorite? But they only bloom at night and during the day they look like wet tissue paper." Lillian's voice sounded sharper than she'd wanted it to. But she'd always considered the moonflower a sentimental bloom, favored by those who took a childish delight in surprises. Annabelle had been like that, and she'd learned the hard way that it was best to take things at face value. Moonflowers had been Annabelle's favorite flower, too.

Earlene's shoulders went back in a defensive gesture at odds with the placid demeanor she normally showed the world. "True. But I like to think of them as courageous flowers. I mean, how many people would keep a flower in their garden that looked like this if they didn't know what happens to them at night? It's like the flowers like the risk of being yanked out of a garden, holding on to the thrill that some lucky gardener will discover them at night."

Despite herself, Lillian grinned. "That's certainly one way to put it." She ducked her head, hiding her eyes under the brim of her hat. "I used to have a friend who gave the flowers personalities, too. It used to annoy me."

She looked up to see Earlene watching her steadily. "Was she a good friend?"

"The very best. She was like a sister to me."

"Are you still friends?"

Lillian shook her head. "She died recently. But we'd had a falling-out a long time ago, so we hadn't kept in touch. It was a . . . misunderstanding."

Earlene was silent for a moment, staring at the drooping moonflowers, their glorious blooms hidden until nightfall. "Do you regret not mending the misunderstanding before she died?"

Lillian closed her eyes, the heady mixture of the gardenias and ginger lilies making her feel faint. If she'd ever allowed herself to feel regret, it would have left her paralyzed — afraid and unable to move forward. No, regret was an indulgence she wouldn't allow.

"I don't believe in regret. I've always thought that regret is as useful as trying to stop a flooding river with your hands. It'll keep you busy, but you'll still drown." Lillian sat back, letting her ramrod-straight spine touch the sun-heated back of the bench. "I've always thought that regret was just another word for fear, and I've got no patience for that, either."

Lillian felt Earlene bristle next to her. She hadn't meant to alienate another person, although it had become apparent to her recently that she'd become incredibly good at it. She supposed old age really did have its perks, after all. But not Earlene. Earlene was a mystery Lillian needed to figure out. And she loved Lillian's garden, especially the silly moonflowers.

Earlene clasped her hands tightly together. "I think you're wrong. I think regret is a way to atone for past sins."

"Nonsense. Go plant a tree or adopt a puppy if you want atonement. But regret is just another way of saying 'I quit.'"

Earlene turned to Lillian, her brows drawn together and perspiration dotting her nose.

"Then you must have led a very boring life with little to regret."

Her earnestness and fire surprised Lillian; she'd been wondering if what she thought was glimpses of personality hiding behind the wounded victim persona was just in her imagination, and it was almost gratifying to see that it really did exist. But her words brought memories back to her — memories of Annabelle, and Josie, and Charlie. And Freddie. The grief that always seemed to float around the periphery of her vision shimmered for a moment, tightening around her heart until she thought she couldn't breathe. She pressed her fingers around the angel charm and let it work its soothing magic.

"No," she said softly, facing Earlene to look her in the eyes. "Quite the opposite, actually. I just choose to live my life in the present."

Earlene's mouth formed a perfect "o" of indignation. They stared at each other for a long time before Earlene stood. "I've intruded on your morning long enough and I need to get to work."

"Oh, don't leave in a huff. Why don't you sit back down so we can agree to disagree for now, and we can talk about my beautiful flowers? Maybe you can tell me more about why you like the moonflowers. Who knows? Maybe I'll find a reason to like them."

"I doubt it," Earlene said, almost out of hearing. But she sat down anyway, her chin jutting out with a mixture of stubbornness and indignation.

Lillian ducked her head, hiding her face under the brim of her hat so Earlene couldn't see her smile.

I sat on the bench next to Lillian in the garden for a long time as we talked about the merits of each of the flowering blooms, all placed according to their scent and color scheme to create a feast for all the senses. Lillian appeared to enjoy argument, always playing devil's advocate when I'd question her as to why she didn't use a particular plant and chose another one instead.

"Because I learned from a gardening master. The friend I was telling you about before. When I was about thirteen I got very sick and couldn't leave my house for a long time. As I was slowly getting better, she dragged me out of my bed and warm blankets and brought me out here to where the gardeners had a boring English boxwood garden. She helped me recuperate by refocusing my attention on getting things to grow, and showing me how to plan and choose. I don't know if it was the distraction or fresh air that made me better, but my friend had taught me an important lesson."

I knew who she was talking about, of course, and it was almost like sharing a memory. The first day I'd come to live with my grandparents after my parents died, my grandmother took me out to her garden. I'd wanted hugs and sympathy, but my grandmother instead gave me lessons about the life-giving properties of the soil and how to coax living things to erupt from the dark earth, sprouting life and color and scent where nothing had been before.

Most of the time we'd spent together in those first fragile months had been spent in her garden. I'd resented it at first, wanting to be allowed to retreat into my grief. It had taken me a long time to realize that by placing a beloved rose clipping in my hand and telling me to plant it, my grandmother had given me the deepest part of her heart. But then my grandfather put me on the back of a horse and I quickly forgot my grandmother's gentle teachings as I began my pursuit of invincibility.

I found myself searching Lillian's face, wanting to be recognized. "What was the lesson your friend taught you?"

Lillian looked at me with familiarity and for a moment I thought she did know who I was. But then I realized that she was seeing her childhood friend again, and maybe even recognizing a part of me that reminded her of Annabelle.

"That there are no troubles in life that can't be sorted through or solved by spending time in your garden. And, for the most part, I've come to believe she was right."

I thought back to the barrenness of my grandmother's garden at the Savannah house and felt a wave of shame and ingratitude overcome me. I couldn't blame its neglect on my grandfather; Annabelle had chosen me to spend time with in her garden, after all.

I focused on the sun flare roses that bordered the outer edges of the garden's brick paths, like yellow lights marking a stage. I looked down at my once-capable hands — hands that had done nothing recently but flip through old books and tap on computer keyboards. Maybe if I'd turned to my grandmother's garden instead, I would have found the answers I was still looking for.

"I just might have to agree with you on that one, Miss Lillian, if only because I was once told the same thing."

I felt her staring at me, but I refused to meet her gaze, afraid to give too much away. "My aunt had a garden in her Savannah house — the house I grew up in. I've allowed it to go to weed. But being here, it reminds me of how much I used to enjoy it." I looked up at her, blinking into the sun. "I was thinking, maybe, if you didn't mind, that I might be able to help out in your garden. It seems a lot for just one person. I won't change anything, unless you want me to. Just tend it."

A soft smile lit the old woman's face. "I'd like that, Earlene. I'd like that very much. I can't do much garden tending anymore because of my arthritis and I was just sitting here wondering if I should hire somebody or let it go to weed. But here you are, and it looks like you could use some dirt under your fingernails."

Opening my hands, I saw the clean fingernails and the fading calluses that wouldn't go away fast enough. "I'm way out of practice. I'll probably have lots of questions."

Lillian waved a dismissive hand. "Nonsense. It's like riding a bicycle. But I'm here every morning at seven o'clock if you think you need instruction."

I smiled to myself, remembering the

imperious younger Lillian in my grand-mother's scrapbook and wondered if there had ever been a time when she hadn't been able to get her own way. "Fine. I'm an early riser, too, so it shouldn't be too hard to manage."

"And if there's nothing to do in the garden, you can just sit here next to me and we can argue some more about the moon-flowers or why I chose Confederate jasmine over honeysuckle for the back wall trellis."

My response was interrupted by the shutting of the garden gate. Odella, wearing a man's camouflage fishing cap to block the sun from her face, marched down the path carrying what appeared to be an envelope.

"Sorry to bother you two, but when I poked my nose out the kitchen window to shake out a dust rag, I saw that you were out here and wanted to save me a trip to the cottage." She held out the envelope to me. "It's a letter addressed to you. I would have given it to you last night but it was stuck between my Precious Moments and Williams-Sonoma catalogs, so I didn't see it until this morning."

I hesitated a moment before reaching out my hand. "Thanks. I appreciate it." I glanced down at the return address: Morton, Morton & Baker, Savannah. I flipped it over in my lap so Lillian couldn't see it.

Odella turned to Lillian. "And you, Miss Lillian, have been out in this sun far too long. I'm going to bring you inside and set you next to an air conditioner so you can cool off."

I noticed with alarm Lillian's flushed cheeks and felt a stab of guilt. "I'm sorry — I should have known better. Let me help you get her in the house."

Lillian waved a hand. "I'm not an invalid yet. I can manage on my own, I assure you. And I'm only going inside because I'm thirsty and would like some lemonade with a little touch of something stronger to wake me up. Not because I'm too old and delicate to be in this heat. In my day, I used to ride horses and jump fences without a helmet. If that didn't kill me, then I doubt the sun will."

She faced me. "I'll see you tomorrow morning." Then, using her cane to stand, she allowed Odella to lead her from the garden.

I waited until the gate shut behind them before opening the letter. As I'd suspected, it was from George. Although initially disapproving of me being at Asphodel Meadows at all, he seemed to have embraced the covertness of my presence by putting the name Earlene Smith in block letters on the outside of the envelope as well as in the address inside the letter. When I'd told him about the torn scrapbook pages and the newspaper clipping, he'd seemed almost eager to help me with my research. I hadn't really expected anything from him so it was with curiosity that I opened the letter and began to read.

Dear Earlene,

I hope you are doing well and have found at least some of the information you were seeking. I'm still not exactly clear why you need to be there as you can see from the rest of this letter that there is plenty to research right here in Savannah. As I'm sure you are already aware, there was a suicide a little over a year ago at Asphodel Meadows. I'm not implying that you're in any kind of danger, but thought you should be aware that that sort of thing goes on there.

I lifted my gaze from the letter for a moment, picturing George in his seersucker suit dictating this letter to his secretary without even pausing to think about how ludicrous he sounded, as if suicide were a communicable disease. I thought about writing him back to mention the borderline alcoholic doyenne of the estate, the blind daughter with a penchant for colors, the two little girls who were wise beyond their years, or their father whose odd mixture of aloofness and caring I found more attractive than I wanted to admit. Instead, I bent my head back to the letter and continued to read.

Per your request, I've done a little research on your grandparents' house on Monterey Square. As you probably already know, the house was built in 1858, two years after the square was established, by your great-great-great-grandfather on your mother's side. He was a successful doctor, as were the oldest sons of the following generation up to and including your grandmother's father, Leo O'Hare.

I was able to find the original builder's blueprints in the historical archives and found that the attic was originally designed as one large room, as we had thought. But this is where it gets interesting. My mother's second cousin on her father's side is a bit of an amateur historian, so I figured I'd ask her if she knew anything about the attic room. She recalls reading various accounts in unrelated research about families keeping less-than-perfect children in attic rooms to save the family from the disgrace of admitting to having given birth to an imperfect offspring.

There had been a kitchen addition in the early 1870s and the blueprints still showed a single attic room, so I knew to focus on records past 1870. I went back to the archives to find the family records and discovered a Thaddeus and Mary O'Hare, married in 1878, and the birth certificates of three children born between 1881 and 1900 — the oldest being your great-grandfather, Leo. I took the liberty of using the house key that you entrusted me with, and went into your grandfather's study, where I knew the old family Bible is kept. Your grandfather showed it to me once when I was on a business visit with my grandfather and I expressed an interest in the old book. I must say that I deserve a little pat on the back for this insight on my part, and I have to admit that it gave me a thrill to discover that I have a little bit of a detective lurking in me.

I shook the letter in frustration and hastily skimmed the rest of the paragraph dealing with George's brilliance and skipped to the next sentence.

I found Thaddeus and Mary, with their birth and death dates, along with their children — except in the Bible there were four children listed, the third one, a girl named Margaret Louise, having been born in 1898 but with no death date. There are no public records to indicate that a Margaret Louise O'Hare ever existed. I think my next visit will be to check burial records from 1898 on at Bonaventure and other local cemeteries. I'll let you know what I discover.

I've enclosed the copy I made of the inside of your family Bible — which is why I'm sending this as a letter instead of an e-mail — so you can add it to your stack of research in case it means something later on.

I do worry about you being alone right now, but when I spoke with my grandfather earlier this week and told him that you were at Asphodel Meadows, he told me that it would be good for you, which made me feel better. Please don't hesitate to call me if you need anything — personally or professionally. You know I am here for you.

I will get back to my sleuthing as soon as I'm done with a couple of legal briefs I'm working on. I will be in touch as soon as I discover anything new. In the meantime, remember to eat well and to do your exercises for your knee.

Very truly yours,
George Baker

I folded the letter and shoved it back into the envelope. Regardless of how interesting George's discoveries were, I couldn't help but feel disappointed. Margaret Louise was born in 1898, eighteen years before my grandmother had been born. And she'd been a girl. I realized that the blue blanket I'd found in the secret room could have swaddled a baby of either sex, but my discovery of the blue sweater in my grandmother's trunk had me convinced that I should be looking for a baby boy. And, even though I hadn't found any evidence to show that they could be related, there was still the newspaper article about the discovery of a male infant found in the Savannah River.

I stuck the letter in the pocket of my skirt, then left the garden, eager to return to the cottage and the binder Helen had given me. I'd begun to sort through it the night before, finding it mostly to be business papers and shopping lists with a few surprisingly sterile letters between a newly married Charlie and Lillian. Disappointed, I had fallen asleep on the sofa, the papers scattered around me. I hoped that with a clearer head this morning I'd be able to at least document the contents of the binder and even organize them in some meaningful way before returning it to Helen.

I walked to the circular drive in front of the house, and stood between the front garden and the sundial I'd passed several times but hadn't yet approached. It sat on a stone pedestal at the "v" that pointed toward the oak alley, its bronze face darkened by time and weather. I shaded my eyes and peered at the inscription that had been carved along the edge of the dial. *Tempus fugit, non autem memoria.* I knew the first part meant time flies, but I wasn't sure about the rest of it, although I had once known it. I committed it to memory so I could check online once I got back to the cottage.

I began to walk down the alley, apprehension scuttling up and down my spine as I remembered the previous night and the eerie whistling. By light of day the trees didn't appear quite as ominous, but I still couldn't shake the feeling that I was being watched as I passed under the arch created by the first two oaks.

The sound of a man's voice and the unmistakable beat of horse's hooves against hardened dirt made me stop. I looked around and realized the sound came from the far side of the house, where the oval window in Helen's bedroom must look out. I heard the man's voice again and recognized it as Tucker's. I wanted to continue walking, but something held me back. I remembered how he'd looked the previous night when he asked me to teach his daughters to ride, and how much it must have cost him to ask. He didn't strike me as the sort of person who asked for help very often, and I realized how much he must love his daughters to even try.

Slowly, I turned around and headed toward the sound of hooves until I emerged from the shadow of the house and found myself facing an equestrian's dream. The land sloped downward away from the house where green pastures bled out into the horizon as far as I could see, separated by the elegant lines of white picket fences. Horses dotted the fields, their necks bowed down to the grass, their tails batting peacefully. The stables, appearing almost as large as the house, sat in the near distance below a rise, which is why I hadn't seen it when I passed through the garden gate.

Nearer the house was the lunge ring, where Tucker now stood with his whip, coaxing the scarred horse around the circle, speaking quietly to the animal in a language I had once understood. I stopped outside the ring not touching the fence, and watched the horse and the man, each focused on the other, each seeing what the other was willing to give and to take. The whip never touched the horse, yet the horse responded, knowing what was expected as if he'd done this before. But he wasn't doing it willingly, fighting Tucker with each gait, making me wonder what had been done to him before he'd come to Asphodel Meadows.

They came to a stop as soon as Tucker saw me. "Good morning," he said, removing the lunge line from the horse's halter and attaching a lead rope. I took a step back as Tucker led the horse to the fence, both of them regarding me intently.

"Good morning." I forced the words past my constricted throat. The horse stood directly in front of me, calmly appraising me as his tail twitched behind him. He was thin, but his conformation was good, his legs long. *I bet you can really fly,* I thought before I could stop myself.

The horse nickered softly, startling me so that I took another step back. Tucker's smile wasn't mocking but meant for comfort. "He thinks you're the treat lady. Do you want to give him an apple?"

Before I could refuse, he'd stuck his hand between the fence slats and pulled out an apple from a duffel bag near my feet. He handed it to me without bringing it back to his side of the fence, then stayed in the awkward position and I knew he would remain there if I didn't take the stupid apple.

"Just keep your fingers flat and he'll do the rest."

I looked at Tucker with annoyance. "I know that. It's not like I've never fed an apple to a horse before."

His smile broadened and I knew he was goading me on, making me feel like a horse in the lunge ring, and I had to resist the urge to throw the apple at him and stalk away with righteous indignation. But I held the apple with the fence between us, and I reminded myself that I had once hurdled five-foot jumps on a horse. Surely I could feed a single apple to one.

The horse stretched his neck over the fence, but the apple was still out of reach.

"If you're too afraid, let me have the apple

and I'll do it."

It was like Tucker knew just the right words to say. Without looking in his direction, I took a deep breath and stepped forward with the apple in my palm, my fingers flat. The horse took half of the apple in one bite, his soft velvety lips brushing my skin and bringing back all the memories of doing this exact thing so many times. Apple juice ran down my fingers as I watched the powerful jaws chomp until there was nothing left. He pawed the ground with his front hoof, giving me a look that suggested he wanted more.

"Where did you find him?" I asked. The horse had turned and I found myself staring at his scars.

"At an auction in Columbia. I always look for the one horse nobody else wants. If I hadn't taken him, he would have been sent to the slaughterhouse."

I shuddered, not wanting to think about what happened to all the other horses nobody wanted. "But do you know where he came from before that? What his name was?"

Tucker shook his head and gave the horse's neck a solid pat. "He was found abandoned in a dirt paddock with barely any grass and no signs of hay or feed. A filthy bucket with rainwater was all he had to drink."

I stared at the large animal, feeling again that the two of us had more in common than just our physical scars. "He's a great horse. Anybody can see that, regardless of his scars. I can't believe that nobody wanted him." The horse stretched out his head again, wanting me to scratch his head but I held back. I didn't want to touch the soft coat under my fingertips, was afraid to feel a nudge of affection from the large head. "So, you do that a lot? Rescue horses, I mean."

He shrugged and looked away for a moment. "I haven't always. It's just something that I sort of fell into. About two years ago I went on hiatus from my medical practice in Savannah to come here. My wife . . . Susan . . . she was ill and I figured we could all use a change of scenery. I thought being around horses would be good for her." He shook his head. "She was afraid, though. Wouldn't go near them.

"Anyway, our stable manager, Andi, mentioned to me that while she'd been at auction, she'd looked at a horse she thought we should consider. He was undernourished, but showed no signs of lameness, and his temperament, considering what he'd been

241

through, was something we could handle. I went to see the horse, knew what the alternative would be if I didn't take him, and that's how it started. I rehabilitate them and then either sell them or find a good home for them, depending on the situation."

The horse shook his head again and shifted his feet with impatience at having to stand still for so long. I looked into his large almond-shaped eyes and I had the oddest feeling that we were both thinking the same thing. *You want to fly.* The words were so amplified in my head that for a moment I thought I'd spoken them aloud.

Instead, I asked, "Have you named him yet?"

Tucker didn't say anything, and when I looked at him, I saw that he was watching me closely, a small smile on his lips. "No. I usually don't since I don't intend on keeping them. But for this one, well, I'm willing to make an exception."

He was still smiling at me as if waiting for me to get the punch line of a joke.

"Why are you looking me like that?"

His smile fell and he was serious again, wearing the wounded look I'd begun to be familiar with. "Because I can't imagine what it would be like to never ride a horse again.

And because I think you want to name this horse."

I wanted to deny it, and tell him that it wasn't so hard to walk away from a sport that had crushed more than just bones. But I'd always been a horrible liar, and I couldn't forget the way the horse had shown his impatience, had made me aware that he wanted to fly. "I'd call him Captain Wentworth," I said, jutting out my chin and crossing my arms over my chest.

Tucker's smile was back. "Ah, a Jane Austen fan. You and Helen have a lot in common."

"I'll take that as a compliment."

"You should." Turning back to the horse, he said, "So, Captain Wentworth it is. Captain, for short. Although I think Andi would have preferred something like Bruiser or Killer. He broke her nose when she was loading him into the trailer to get him here." He rubbed the horse's neck. "But I think Captain Wentworth is better. I'll let everyone know. Maybe even get a nameplate for his stall."

I pushed back the wave of excitement I felt, knowing it really had nothing to do with me. "Good," I said. "He deserves it."

He was watching me closely and I felt myself blush under his gaze. "I think you need to ride again."

His words, spoken so softly, felt like splintering bones and I was lying on the ground again, waiting for the blackness. I stared at Tucker, speechless, then looked back at Captain Wentworth, his tail moving in a languid rhythm, teasing me with old memories that weren't all bad. I looked into the horse's eye again. *Let's fly; let's fly high together.* My breath quickened as I imagined the rush of wind on my face and the exhilaration of landing a jump, could almost hear the roar of a crowd. *Oh, God.*

I stared at him for a long moment, a horrible realization settling on me like ash. I felt sick, the ugliness of my thoughts making my stomach churn. I turned on my heel, walking blindly in the direction I'd come, knowing I couldn't stay without blurting out what I'd only just come to understand.

In the face of disappointment I'd done the one thing I'd always despised about lesser riders; I'd given into my fears, surrendered in the face of my own mortality. And it was anger at myself that propelled me away from Tucker and from confessing what I'd just seen with startling clarity as I'd faced the newly named Captain Wentworth over the fence and felt his desire to fly: I wasn't afraid of horses at all. What I feared the most was getting back into a saddle and discovering I wasn't a champion any longer, that I had instead become nothing more than ordinary.

"I'm not one of your horses who needs rescuing," I shouted over my shoulder without slowing down. He didn't say anything but I knew he was watching until I'd turned the corner of the house.

I paused in the drive, putting my hands on my knees until I could catch my breath. I stood again in front of the sundial and the words suddenly formed meaning. *Time flies, but not memories.*

I gulped in the hot, humid air, my heart beating fast and my knee throbbing. But none of those things could take my breath away as quickly as my newfound knowledge had, or my sudden desperate need to prove myself wrong.

CHAPTER 12

Helen knocked on her grandmother's sitting room door and then entered. "Are you done resting?"

Lillian's voice was tinged with exhaustion. "It's a hopeless cause. I don't know why I bother. My back and my hands would rather keep me awake and restless."

Helen moved to where she knew her grandmother's chaise longue sat near the window. She felt for a nearby sofa and sat down, sensing by the lack of warmth hitting her skin that the plantation shutters were closed tight. "Can I get you your medicine?"

Lillian let out an uncharacteristic snort. "All they do is make me groggy and stupid and Odella says I can't have anything to drink when I take one, so what's the point? I'm miserable whether I take them or not, but if I don't I can at least find a little relief with my wine."

"I'm sorry," Helen said, and meant it.

Despite Lillian's outwardly cool demeanor and her strict code of acceptable behavior, she'd essentially been the only mother Helen had ever known. Although Lillian had never been demonstrative, Helen had always felt loved by her grandmother. And it had been Lillian, and not Helen's own mother, who'd slept in a cot in her bedroom when she'd been sick with fever, and had held her hand when her sight had gone to let her know that even though it was dark, she wasn't alone.

Helen sat back in the sofa, her arm brushing papers, and felt one slide to the floor and land on her foot. Leaning over, she picked it up and handed it to her grandmother. "Sorry, Malily — I knocked this off of your stack of papers. I don't want to replace it in the wrong spot."

Lillian didn't say anything, nor did she take the paper Helen held. "Malily? Are you all right?"

Lillian's voice sounded strong but distant when she spoke, and Helen pictured her looking out the other way, toward the shuttered window. "I sat in the garden for a spell this morning with Earlene. We talked about the merits of moonflowers among other things. And all that talk about my garden reminded me of an old friend of mine who taught me everything I know about gardening. Made me nostalgic enough that I pulled out my scrapbook pages from when I was younger. The ones I'd given to Susan."

Helen withdrew her arm but held on to the page in her hand, a question already forming in her head. "What happened to the cover? And the spine?"

Malily gave a throaty chuckle. "Well, that's part of the story right there. There were three of us, you see. Three friends and one scrapbook we shared. When we . . . parted company, we each took our pages."

Helen placed the single page on her lap and smiled to herself, recalling the pages Odella had seen on Earlene's kitchen table. "You never told me any of this before."

She heard the cushions sigh as Lillian moved on the chaise. "No, I haven't. I always thought that I should share it with your mother first, but I don't think that's going to happen now."

Helen jerked her head with surprise as she felt the old woman's hands clutching at hers. She grasped them, feeling the papery skin, the misshapen joints, and for the first time saw her grandmother as an old woman instead of the heroine of Helen's childhood.

Malily continued. "I thought that by giving these pages to Susan along with all the other family papers, she could prepare the story in logical sequence, even make it easier to understand how all the pieces fit together. But I didn't realize how . . . fragile Susan was. It was a mistake."

Helen clutched her grandmother's hands tighter. "None of us understood what was going on in Susan's head, not even Tucker. She seemed so upbeat and excited about being our family's official chronicler. No one expected her . . ." Helen stopped for a moment. "What Susan did was her own doing. None of it was your fault."

Lillian disengaged her hands. "You need to reserve your judgment, Helen." She heard the throaty laugh again before her grandmother spoke. "I should have known that Annabelle would always have the last word." A heavy sigh filled the room like damp fog and then everything was quiet. Helen thought for a moment that her grandmother had fallen asleep and then Malily spoke again.

"The scrapbook was Annabelle's idea. She used to say that it was our duty as women to pass on our stories to our daughters. But I don't think she had any more success with that than I did."

"But there's still time, Malily. And you've got me."

"Not too much time, Helen, which is why I think Annabelle's words won't leave me alone. And I do have you, don't I? You've never been one to rush to judgment, unlike your mother."

Helen lifted her head. "I'm a good listener. Maybe you can tell me your story. And I can tell my mother when she's ready to hear it."

"She already knows parts of it. I shared it with her too soon, I think. But she was almost transfixed by the angel charm I've always worn — that's part of the story, you see. And I thought that if I told her the story of the necklace, she'd want to learn the rest. And she did — to a point. She asked me to stop before I'd reached the end, so I did."

"Is that why she left? Because she didn't want to hear the rest?"

She heard her grandmother swallow. "There are many reasons why your mother left, Helen — and none of them have anything to do with you or Tucker. I think mostly it was because she couldn't live with someone who'd never confused guilt with regret."

Helen smiled softly, turning her face toward her grandmother. "Like that story you used to tell us as children — about the boy who gets caught stealing candy and feels guilt over breaking the law but doesn't regret trying. I always got the impression that you didn't think the little boy was all bad. That he learned his lesson and wasn't going to do it again, but that he should have been proud to have had the courage to at least try."

Lillian's voice held the hint of a smile. "You and Tucker both understood that, but your mother couldn't. Or wouldn't. We all know that stealing is bad. But what if the little boy was stealing to feed his starving family? Does that make him bad? Or just his actions? And does the end justify the means? Your mother's been traipsing all over the world ever since, trying to find the right answer. The one truth."

Helen cupped her chin in her palms as she leaned forward, her elbows braced on her legs. "But there isn't just one."

"And there you go," said Lillian triumphantly. "But some people live their lives as if there could only be one right answer. Life would be easier that way, I imagine. But it wouldn't be better."

Helen closed her eyes and tried to picture her mother, but found she no longer could. "Then tell me. Tell me your story." She reached her hand behind her where the loose pages lay on the sofa. "Read these to me so I can understand. And maybe one day I'll be able to explain it to my mother. Or my daughters."

Lillian was quiet for a long time, her breathing slow and steady. Helen didn't move, knowing she hadn't fallen asleep but was searching for an answer. But it brought back memories of the first time her mother had gone away, when her mother was packing her clothes into a suitcase. Despite her mother's insisting that her leaving had nothing to do with Helen, Helen hadn't been convinced. Her answer had haunted Helen for a very long time. *Some things are best kept tucked inside yellowed newspapers in the attic of our memories.* And then her mother had gone back to her packing, promising to be back soon, and that next time she would take Helen and her brother with them. But the next time Helen had been blind and Tucker wouldn't leave her.

Lillian's voice brought Helen back to the present. "I suppose it's time, then." Helen felt her grandmother take the paper from her lap. Then she took a deep breath, and after a brief pause, she began to tell her story.

"There were three of us: Josephine Montet, Annabelle O'Hare, and me. We weren't friends at first. Josie and Annabelle were —

Josie's mother worked for Dr. O'Hare and Josie lived in the housekeeper's room with her mother and they'd known each other since they were small — and they were only two years apart in age. I was a year younger than Josie — three years younger than Annabelle — but I was allowed to tag along most of the time when my father and Dr. O'Hare had business together and they pretty much ignored me. Until we bought the necklace."

She explained to Helen how they'd seen the necklace in the store window and had purchased it together, making a pact to share it and record in a scrapbook what they did while they had the necklace. And then they would add a charm to the necklace that they had named Lola.

Helen sat up. "That's where your angel charm comes from — the one you used to always wear around your neck on a chain."

"And still do." Malily's voice was tired. "This is the only charm with a duplicate because we all bought one when we started. It's all I have left of the necklace."

Helen opened her mouth, ready to tell Malily about the necklace Odella had seen in Earlene's cottage, but stopped. It had become obvious to her that Malily wasn't the only one hiding secrets. But Helen needed to find out more, and she knew that neither woman would be forthcoming if they suspected Helen knew more than they were willing to tell her.

Malily continued. "We each had the book for four months during the year, then passed it on to the next person. That meant we had to chronicle the most important part of our lives for the past year. We kept it for ten years — and we were supposed to have one entry for each of those years. But I hated to write — so I didn't always do it, which made Annabelle mad. But I always added a charm — sometimes more than one, which also made Annabelle mad. She was always about following the rules." She was silent for a moment. "When we had our . . . falling-out, we destroyed the scrapbook, each taking our own pages. Josie took hers up to New York with her, Annabelle kept hers, and then mine are here. I've somehow misplaced my earliest pages, so mine don't start until nineteen thirty-two when I was thirteen. But that's really where my story starts, anyway."

Lillian paused and Helen waited, afraid to move or say anything in case her grandmother changed her mind. Finally, Malily said, "Would you please get me a glass of water? The pitcher and a glass are on the table by my bed. While you do that, I'll gather up the pages and decide on the best place to start."

Helen moved with methodic slowness, not wanting to spill the water or trip and make her task take longer than she wanted. She crossed the room, counting her footsteps as she'd done since childhood and stopped in front of the chaise. After her grandmother took the glass from her, Helen sat back on the sofa and made herself comfortable, prepared to listen for as long as her grandmother was willing to talk. And then Malily began to read.

May 10, 1932

I've been sick for two weeks. My head aches and my stomach aches and even my teeth ache. I pretty much hurt all over and I've got a bad fever. I heard the doctor say the word influenza and my papa took him out of the room so fast I could almost think that he hadn't even been here! But I am feeling a little better today, so I thought I'd write in this scrapbook if only because I know Annabelle will check to see if I did it when it's her turn.

It's boring lying up here in my room by myself. Nobody's allowed to visit me and I can't even think about riding. Papa said if he caught me near the stables he'd sell my mare, Cimarron. I know he's not serious, of course, but I won't go near Cimarron. I feel too weak to even think about climbing up on her back again.

May 15, 1932

I feel much better now but Papa refuses to let me leave my bed. All of this lying about has made me so weak I can barely stand. I miss my horse so much — I'm wondering if she'll even recognize me when we're finally together again.

I'm still not allowed to have visitors, but Annabelle came today with her father. Dr. O'Hare convinced Papa that I needed a companion to help me convalesce and that I was no longer contagious. Of course I knew it was Annabelle's idea — she always has big ideas — and when her father left her for a long stay, I thought we'd spend the time together in my room with her fetching water for me and fluffing my pillows as I got better.

My excitement didn't last long because as soon as her father left, she yanked me out of my bed and forced me down to the English boxwood garden that my mother had installed. Annabelle said it was uninspired and that she was going to teach me how to garden. She actually gave me a little shovel and made me dig holes in the dirt. I told her I was too weak from being sick, so she said I could sit while I dug.

I think the garden now looks the same — but now the ground cover is gone and there're just holes with seeds all over the place. Annabelle says that's part of the garden's secret: that with love and patience we'll be rewarded with a little piece of heaven here on earth. To give me some encouragement, she's going to bring cuttings (whatever that is!) with her the next time she comes.

We worked the entire time and maybe it was spending time outdoors or the actual physical work, but I did feel better by the time Annabelle left. She said that there are no troubles in life that can't be sorted out or solved by spending time in a garden. I didn't admit this to her, but I think I'm looking forward to finding out if this is true.

Lillian stopped reading and Helen smiled. "That was nineteen thirty-two so you were thirteen years old. That's the same age I was when you first dragged me kicking and screaming into the garden shed and gave me a trowel." She leaned forward. "I guess that means you found out that what Annabelle told you was true."

"Yes, I guess I did. And I tried to teach your mother, too, but she wasn't as good a pupil as you were. You were both unwilling in the beginning, but you seemed to understand very early on the magic of it all. I don't believe your mother ever did."

Helen closed her eyes for a moment, remembering the flowers of her first garden, the thrill she'd felt at creating such beautiful life from seed, dirt, and water. She opened them again. "Can you read more?"

She listened as Lillian rustled pages. "I'm embarrassed to say that I didn't write anything for a while — my next entry doesn't happen until four years later when I was seventeen. I don't suppose I thought those other years were worthy of recording, and I still think I was right. The awkward adolescent years were difficult to live with while I was going through them. I can't imagine that I'd want to relive them in the pages of a scrapbook."

"I wish you had. I'd like to hear them."

"Yes, well, maybe you'll find this next

entry makes up for the lack of earlier pages. My seventeenth year was full of excitement." With a brief pause, Lillian began to read.

June 4, 1936

Tonight is my come-out party. Because of the "financial troubles" Papa is always talking about these days, I won't be having the ball at the Oglethorpe Club like he always talked about. Instead, we are having a formal dinner dance right here at Asphodel Meadows with a guest list of only one hundred. I told him not to bother, that the heat will be atrocious even with all the windows thrown open in the ballroom and dining room. And besides, I don't need a come-out ball. I've already met the man I want to marry, so exposing me to the marriage market is rather moot. Nevertheless, the announcement of my debut was made in the paper on Mother's Day and I will be expected at various entertainments up until New Year's Eve, when I will be officially declared "out" in Savannah society and officially marriageable. I only wish that I could be as excited as Papa is.

When Annabelle learned that I was going to make my debut (she's three years older than me but her papa is getting paid in chickens and eggs these days and couldn't afford a debut season — which was fine with her because, in her words, with the state of the world she had bigger fish to fry right now than finding a husband), she snuck me a copy of *The Hardboiled Virgin* by Frances Newman. It's a book that pokes fun at debutantes and Papa would horsewhip me if he knew I'd read it, and would make sure I never saw Annabelle again, but I laughed and laughed while I read it as I recognized me and my fellow debs.

Annabelle helped me select my signature flowers, which I will be wearing on my wrist and which will decorate all the tables. She chose calla lilies because of my name and because they symbolize regalness — which made me laugh, but they are such beautiful flowers. Then she chose gladiolus, which represents strength of character. Papa thought pink and white would be appropriate choices, but Annabelle and I also included bright purple to the order to make a statement. She's brilliant with flowers, and I've been eagerly learning everything she knows so that one day, when I'm an old matron with twenty grandchildren at my feet, I can work my own garden and be admired all over Georgia for the beauty of my flowers.

Gladiolus is the flower I would have chosen for Annabelle if our roles had been reversed. She has become her father's helper as he services the poor, regardless of the color of their skin. He has made many enemies of his own kind for this, and I know it will forever hurt Annabelle's chances of making a good marriage, but she wouldn't have it any other way. She talks about the inequalities in our society — much of which she's learned from Freddie, I'm afraid — but she makes actions out of her words. I've only had to lie for her once — when she was late coming back from a meeting with Freddie — and I did it so well that I think that's what she meant by strength of character. I didn't have the courage to tell her that I lied for Freddie, whose punishment would have been much more severe than a father's disapproval. I've seen Papa going to his "political meetings," which always seem to coincide with a lynching, and my blood runs cold thinking about the trouble Freddie could cause for not only himself but for Josie and Justine.

My dress is rather lovely, although it was sewn by a local seamstress instead of coming from Paris like Papa had always promised. It's all satin and lace with a huge bow that ties in the back, and it makes me look like a child. But I am no longer a child, no matter how Papa regards me. Being in love has made me a woman and I know there is no turning back now.

Lillian stopped reading, and Helen didn't say anything at first, unwilling to break the spell. Her head was filled with images of the ball, of men in black tuxes and Lillian all in white. And white and pink flowers overshadowed by glorious purple gladiolus. "Who was Freddie?"

"Josie's brother. He worked in the stables here for a time. Annabelle practically grew up with him and Josie." Lillian took a sip of her water. "It's funny how I can barely remember yesterday, but I recall every single thing about that evening. I remember the feel of Charlie's tux under my cheek and the way Papa's cologne smelled. I remember being incredibly happy, even though Annabelle wasn't there. It was . . . magical."

"Are there any photographs?"

"Just one. We had a newspaper photographer there, of course, so that my picture would appear in the society pages. He gave me one of the photographs they didn't use and I put it in the scrapbook. It's of Charlie and me, at the dance. He was such a good dancer! My papa had hired an orchestra of local musicians and they played everything I asked them to. And Josie was there to sing — she had the voice of an angel — and even though I wasn't allowed to talk to her socially, she sang all of my favorites. There were other boys there at the dance, but I don't remember a single one. I just remember dancing with Charlie for most of the night. Dancing with him was magical. It made me feel breathless; he made me feel like I'd found a little piece of extraordinary."

Helen smiled, an ache in her heart. "So you knew from early on that you wanted to marry Grandpa Charlie?"

Lillian didn't answer right away, and Helen listened closely, almost hearing her grandmother searching for the right words.

"Do we ever know what we really want? It was so long ago and I was so young; I believe that what I wanted and what I felt about things changed almost daily."

Helen listened to the rustle of paper, hoping it meant that her grandmother would continue reading. Instead, Malily said, "I'm suddenly very tired. I think I'm going to try to take a little nap before lunch. Could you please go tell Odella to come get me in an hour?"

Helen tried to hide the disappointment in her voice. "Sure. We can read more later when you're rested." She stood and took her grandmother's hand, surprised that it no longer felt like the smooth debutante's hand of her imagination, then leaned over to kiss the soft cheek. "I'll see you at lunch."

She'd made it to the door before she remembered the question that had been lurking in her mind as she'd listened to her grandmother's story. "What charms did you add to the necklace?"

Lillian's voice sounded tired, but Helen heard the lightness there, too. "I added three. I was never one who accepted limitations." Helen imagined her grandmother smiling, recalling the girl she'd once been. "I added a woman's shoe, because I'd felt like Cinderella at my debutante ball, and a lily."

"And the third?"

"A heart."

"For Grandpa Charlie?"

Her grandmother paused just for a moment. "For my first love."

Helen smiled. "Have a good rest." She opened the door and stepped out into the hallway, nearly tripping over Mardi, who'd been lying across the doorway, waiting for her. She hummed a waltz to herself, imagining she wore lace and satin, with high-heeled dancing shoes, and she'd almost reached the stairway before it occurred to her that her grandmother hadn't really answered her question.

I found the covered ring behind the stables, with Lucy and Sara already waiting for me. They wore brand-new riding gear, complete with riding crops, clean breeches, and shiny new paddock boots. Braided pigtails with bows on the ends poked out underneath black velvet riding hats.

As I approached, I could see their faces more clearly. Sara's eyes were wide and apprehensive, and her bottom lip was red from being squeezed between her teeth. The look was familiar to me, as it filled the beginner classes at most of the horse shows I attended. My grandfather told me I had not once shown fear regardless of how big the horse, but it was common to see a tiny girl literally shaking in her boots the first time she was made to stand next to a horse and contemplate mounting it.

Lucy, however, was different. Her eyes were also wide with apprehension, but a certain light in her eyes and the way she stood showed more anticipation than anything. She looked to me like a girl bent on proving a point — yet another look I'd been overly familiar with.

For a moment, I stood watching and allowed myself to feel a small tremor of excitement, although I wasn't sure if it was for the girls or for myself. A woman I hadn't noticed before pushed away from the side rail and approached, her hand extended toward me.

"I'm Emily Kent, the girls' nanny. You must be Earlene Smith, the horsewoman extraordinaire."

The woman was very young, very pretty, and very blond with a wide, open smile and warm manner. I couldn't help but smile back as I shook her hand. "I wouldn't go that far, but I am here to give Lucy and Sara a riding lesson."

Sara ran over to Emily and wrapped her arms around one of her legs. "We're going to be e-ques-tree-ans," she shouted, hopping up and down.

Emily reached down and scooped up the little girl, mindless of the dirt on her pants from Sara's boots. "That's right. Tell Miss

Earlene that we've been reading about the different types of riding costumes, and the different kinds of horses and saddles."

Sara nodded exuberantly. "We went to the library and got lots of books. Then Miss Emily took us shopping and we bought all these new riding clothes."

"I can see that," I said, unable to resist tugging on one of her pigtails. "There's only one thing missing, though," I said, looking pointedly at the otherwise empty ring.

Emily set Sara on her feet again. "Oh, you noticed that, did you?" She grinned. "Tucker's bringing the ponies up from the stable — he'll be here in just a minute. A friend of his is allowing him to borrow two of their school ponies until Tucker can determine if the girls even like riding. And if they seem to want to continue, he'll take them shopping for their own ponies."

Lucy, who'd remained silently watching us the whole time, walked slowly up to us and turned her dark eyes up to me. "I'm going to be a very good rider."

I met her solemn gaze, recognizing the courage it had taken for this small, serious girl to tell me that, as well as something that reminded me of a younger version of myself. "And that's the attitude you'll need if you want to be. When I competed, there wasn't a single competitor out there who thought they weren't any good. Those with doubts had already dropped out."

She nodded her head, satisfied with my answer.

"Do you still ride competitively?"

Emily's question caught me by surprise and it took me a moment to answer. "No. I had an accident, so I don't ride anymore."

She nodded again, her lips pursed in thought. "I'm not trying to offend you, but I noticed you limping — I'm assuming from the accident."

Sara saved me from answering. "She got really big boo-boos on her knee and that's why she walks funny."

"Sara!" Both Lucy and Emily spoke together in the same admonishing tone.

"It's all right," I said. "She's right. I do walk funny and it is because of my scars." I was beginning to find it easier the more I talked about it. As long as the questions didn't go any further.

"Are you still doing physical therapy?"

I looked at Emily's innocent expression and wondered if George had found a way to contact her so that she could harass me in his absence. "I did at first, but I didn't seem to be getting anywhere so I just . . . stopped." I didn't see the need to explain that I'd also stopped doing everything else at the same time so it made it easier to no longer notice that I couldn't walk without a limp.

"I'm not trying to be nosy. It's just that I'm going to school at night to become a physical therapist, so I was curious about your type of injury and what sort of treatment you were given."

I was about to ask her if she knew George Baker, but was thankfully interrupted by the appearance of Tucker leading two very small ponies, one even smaller and plumper than the first.

Tucker stopped in front of the girls, a pony on either side of him. "I tried to gift-wrap them, but Oreo here didn't want to get in the box." He sent them a shy smile.

"Silly Daddy," Sara said as she moved to stand in front of Tucker, keeping a distance between her and the animals. "Which one's Oreo?"

Lucy rolled her eyes. "It's the black-and-white spotted one, stupid. Who would name a white pony Oreo?"

Emily glanced at Tucker before speaking to Lucy. "Lucy, you know you're not supposed to call your sister names. Please apologize."

After a frown and a heavy sigh, Lucy

apologized, her voice even managing to sound sincere.

"I want Oreo," Sara announced.

"That's a good thing," Tucker said. "Because that's the one I thought would be perfect for you."

I stepped forward. "Which one of you would like to go first?"

Sara pointed to her sister. "Lucy."

I looked at Lucy, and when she nodded, I took the reins of the larger pony from Tucker and led him to the mounting block. Small, slow, and placid, he was the perfect horse for a first timer. It was also the perfect horse for me. I patted his neck before tightening his girth and checking the bridle. My fingers ran the irons down the leathers in motions I didn't even have to think about — movements that were as much a part of me as breathing.

I turned to Lucy. "You ready?"

She nodded and approached the mounting block.

"Have you ever ridden before?"

Lucy glanced over at her father for a moment as if seeking his approval. "A few times, with Malily — until Mama found out and told us to stop. She didn't think it was . . . safe or something. Sara was too little, so it was just me. Malily doesn't ride anymore, but she told me what to do and we stayed inside the ring the whole time. But we didn't use saddles or anything."

"Oh, so you've ridden bareback. That's a really great way to get a feel for a horse's different gaits. We'll be doing it a bit, too — especially at first. Right now I just want to get you comfortable on your mount and with your saddle. Do you need help getting on or do you think you can do it yourself?"

Tucker gave Oreo's reins to Emily to hold and moved next to Lucy. "I can lift you on the first time if you'd like."

For a moment, I thought Lucy would say yes. But then she looked back at the pony and I watched as she set her jaw. "No. I want to do it myself."

I showed her where to put her hands on the pommel and then held the reins while I watched her slip her left boot into the stirrup and hoist herself into the saddle. The pony took a step to the side and for a moment it looked as if she might lose her balance and fall back to the mounting block. Tucker made a move to step forward but I held him back with my hand.

Biting her lip, Lucy held on to the pommel and slid her right leg over the pony so that she was sitting astride.

"Great job," I said, patting the pony's

flank and then handing the reins to Tucker so I could finish adjusting the stirrups for Lucy. "How does it feel?"

Her smile made me want to look away, reminding me too much of what it felt like to sit astride a horse. "Like I'm twelve feet tall." She smiled even brighter. "Like I have four legs instead of two." Her eyes closed, her expression dreamlike. "And I can run faster and jump higher than anybody."

Something seemed to tighten around my heart. *Yes. I know.*

Lucy leaned down and gave a tentative pat on the pony's neck. "What's his name?"

Tucker rubbed the pony's nose. "You know, I forgot to ask my friend. But I don't think it would hurt if you wanted to call him something different for now, if you'd like."

Lucy nodded, her face solemn again. She turned to me. "Do you remember the name of your first pony?"

"Oh, yes. Her full name was Elizabeth Bennett but I called her Benny for short." I glanced over at Tucker, who was shaking his head and trying to hide a smile. "I had a babysitter at the time who was obsessed with Jane Austen and her books and she helped me name her."

Lucy looked thoughtful for a moment.

"I'd like to call my pony Benny for now."

Tucker gave Lucy a tentative pat on her leg before removing his hand. "Then that's what he'll be. Just don't let him know that he's named after a girl."

I put the reins in Lucy's hands. "Keep your thumbs up and your hands low and steady. I'm going to have your father lead you around the ring while I get Sara onto her pony."

For the first time since meeting her, I saw a rebellious look cross her face. "I don't need Daddy to hold on. I can do it myself."

I placed my hands over hers. "I know that, but it's also important that we start slowly. I want Benny to get used to you and you to get used to Benny. He seems gentle and sweet, but I'd feel better knowing that your father is close by just in case. I promise you'll be riding by yourself before you know it."

"But I want to go fast." She bit her bottom lip again, as if punishing herself for having spoken out loud.

I know, I wanted to say, recalling the solid feel of saddle and horse beneath me, the power and joy of racing the wind, the temporary illusion of invincibility.

Before I could respond, Tucker turned to her. "Miss Earlene is right. You always need to learn to walk before you run." He wiped dust from Lucy's boot. "Would you rather Miss Earlene walked you around first instead of me?"

I think we both held our breath as we waited for her answer.

Lucy focused on her hands in her brand-new riding gloves. She shook her head. "No, Daddy. I want you to."

I saw the relief on Tucker's face before facing Sara, who had moved so far back that she was now pressed against the fence, as far away from the ponies as possible.

"Are you ready, Sara?"

Avoiding looking at anybody, she vigorously shook her head, her pigtails flying.

Slowly, I approached her and knelt in the dust, oblivious to my pants or my knee. I put my hands on her shoulders and looked her in the eyes. "It's okay to be a little scared the first time. Most people are." I didn't tell her that I'd been scared, too, because I sensed that she'd know I was lying.

Then I remembered the second and last time my grandmother had to tell me to get back in the saddle — an incident that I'd nearly forgotten if only because I'd barely listened to her at the time. I was about eleven or twelve years old, unbeatable, it seemed, in my quest to be the best. I'd long since grown used to relegating my quiet grandmother to the background, a background she seemed to crave or at least had grown used to. So I'd been surprised that after I'd taken a fall and sprained my wrist, she told me to get back on, just as she'd told me the time I fell off my first pony, Benny. That I could do it despite my grandfather's doubts and insistence that I withdraw. I'd won first place in that competition, and the trophy was somewhere in the attic of my grandparents' Savannah house.

I looked Sara in the eye and repeated from memory, "The only way to get beyond something difficult is to put it behind you." I thought for a moment, trying to phrase it in words she might understand better. "It's like eating your vegetables so you can have dessert. The sooner you finish the broccoli, the sooner you get to eat your ice cream."

Her brows furrowed in confusion. "But I like broccoli."

Tucker coughed and Emily looked away, hiding her smile.

"Then imagine that you didn't. What's the fastest way to get that ice cream?"

"To eat my broccoli."

"That's right." I squeezed her hands.

"Sara, do you really want to ride Oreo today?"

Slowly, she nodded.

"And what's the best way to do that?"

She looked up at me and then over at the pony. "Get up in the saddle?"

"Right. And once you're up there, how do you think you'll feel?"

Sara thought for a moment. "Like I'm riding a horse."

"Exactly. And you do know that your daddy, Emily, and I won't let you get hurt, right?"

Her wide eyes swiveled back from the pony to regard me. "But you got hurt."

I remained where I was without blinking, ignoring the pain in my knee from kneeling so long. "But that was my fault, not the horse's. He did everything right. I was the one who lost my concentration, even though it was only for one second. My horse depended on me to tell him what to do, and I failed him and myself because of that mistake. But I'm here to teach you how not to let that happen. So, see — you're already one step ahead of me."

"But what if I fall off?"

I leaned forward, recalling the rest of what my grandmother had told me. "Then you get back in the saddle before you forget the reason you got up on a horse in the first place."

I stood, almost groaning with relief when I straightened my knee. I held out my hand and she took it. "So are you ready?"

Sara gave a firm nod and allowed me to lead her to the mounting block, where Emily had already moved Oreo into position. I put my hands on her narrow hips. "Oreo's a bit on the plump side, so you're not going to have any trouble staying on her. I'm going to lift you into the saddle, all right? Otherwise, you might hurt her feelings when you can't fit your right leg over her back because she's been enjoying the grass a little too much."

Sara giggled as I lifted her and placed her in the saddle. I held on tightly until I was assured that she had a firm grasp on the reins. "How do you feel?" I asked.

"Like I'm on a horse," she said matter-of-factly.

"Great. Then we're on the same page." I showed her how to hold the reins, then took the lead rope from Emily. I turned back to Tucker. "Let's just walk them around the ring a few times and then let them practice getting on and off their ponies. That should be enough for their first lesson."

"Can we at least walk fast?" Lucy asked,

kicking her heels into Benny's flank.

I watched as Tucker struggled not to smile. "After you show me you can keep your seat while we're going slowly. Then we can up the pace. But not before."

She looked at her father without smiling. "I'd much rather go fast."

Tucker returned her gaze. "We can't always get what we want."

Lucy touched the pony's mane with one hand. "I know that, Daddy." Her voice carried with it more hurt than I thought an eight-year-old could know.

I looked away, unable to look at Tucker's face and tugged on Oreo's reins, clicking my tongue. "Let's go. And try to remember to keep your heels down and your toes up." Slowly, Oreo began to amble, followed and eventually surpassed by the more spritely Benny.

After an hour, we stopped. Emily took the girls home to change into swimsuits before going to swim in the pond, and the stable manager, Andi, with her nose still bandaged from her encounter with Captain Wentworth, appeared to take the ponies back to the barn, leaving just Tucker and me. I felt awkward being alone with him, remembering my outburst from the previous day as well as Lucy's pervading silence during the entire lesson. There was a tension between Lucy and her father that I couldn't discern, something that went a lot deeper than childish disappointments. I had no interest in becoming involved; I'd be leaving at the end of the summer and had no business delving into problems that had nothing to do with me.

But then I remembered what Lucy had said when she was on the pony, how she wanted to run, and to run fast. I was lost then, of course. I had found a kindred spirit, not one I could easily leave behind. And Tucker, too. He carried his regret like a suitcase, a barrier between him and everyone else, including his daughters. *Regret is as useful as trying to stop a flooding river with your hands. It'll keep you busy, but you'll still drown.* I recalled Lillian's words, and wondered if she'd ever shared them with Tucker.

His eyes were warm but still guarded as he approached me. "Thank you, Earlene. The girls really respond to you. I can't tell you how much this means to me."

He stood close, close enough that I could smell the peculiarly enticing scent of citrus cologne, male sweat and horse. An understanding seemed to hover between us — an understanding of kept secrets mingling with the desire to be set free from them. I looked

279

away, uncomfortable.

Tucker continued. "I can tell you really know horses and riders. And that you must have once been a pretty amazing equestrian."

I made a great show out of wiping dirt from my hands as I weighed my answer. Finally, I looked up at him, unable to resist parting with a piece of truth. "I was pretty good, I guess."

His eyes narrowed. "You must not have spent a lot of time on the circuit or I'd recognize your name."

I swallowed hard, forcing down my pride. "It was just a hobby for me. Never really expected anything to come out of it, so I just did it for fun."

He nodded slowly, his eyes not giving anything away. Finally, he broke his gaze and turned toward where the girls had gone with Emily. "I'd like you to keep me posted on their progress."

Surprised, I asked, "Won't you be here? I've worked it out with Emily that their lesson will be every day at ten o'clock. I was hoping that with a regular schedule you might be able to be here."

He looked down at his dust-covered boots, and shook his head. "No. I think it's better if I don't."

I pictured Lucy's face and her expression of pure joy when she'd first mounted the horse. A small fissure of anger erupted inside of me. "Because you don't think they'll be good enough? Or because their small attempts now aren't big enough to warrant your attention?"

His jaw ticked as he turned to me, his anger matching my own. "You have no idea . . ." He stopped, shook his head, then looked away toward the house. It didn't occur to me until later that beyond the house lay the cemetery, and his wife, buried outside the consecrated ground.

Ignoring his cues to stop, I continued. "Sara was so happy and confident with herself as she sat on top of her pony. Surely you saw that. And Lucy — she's really got it. The confidence, the seat, the ease in the saddle. It will take a great trainer to make sure she walks before she runs — but look out world when she's ready to run. Didn't you see that? Don't you care? Because more than their own abilities, they need somebody who loves them to tell them how wonderful they are. Without that, nothing they do will seem to matter as much."

I realized I was almost crying, and that the words I was saying were words I'd rehearsed for years. Words I'd always intended to tell my grandfather, whose love for me seemed to be hinged on how well I performed. It had driven me to succeed, but when I'd failed that final time, I'd found I'd had nothing to fall back on. And the woman who could have convinced me to get back in the saddle had long since been gone from my life, her role in my success unnoticed and forgotten until it was too late.

His eyes softened as he looked back at me. "Don't you think I know that? They're my children, and I want only the best for them — whatever they decide that's going to be. But Susan . . . she made me promise that they wouldn't ride if for no other reason than that she couldn't and she saw it as something that would take them away from her. And now that she's gone . . ."

I swallowed back my anger, remembering the huge loss this man had suffered and felt ashamed. "You must have loved her very much."

He looked startled as he stared at me for a moment. Then he laughed, a bitter, choking sound that made me take a step back. "No. I never loved her enough. She killed herself because I couldn't love her enough." His voice diminished to an almost whisper as he finished speaking.

A stricken look crossed his face as if he

was just realizing who he was talking to and that he'd said too much. He took a step back. "I'm sorry. I shouldn't have said that." He wiped his hands over his face. "I've got to get back to work. Thanks again." He began to walk away, his long strides covering ground quickly. He'd made it out of the ring before he turned back around. "Malily asked me to tell you that she expects you for dinner again tonight. Seven o'clock as usual. Don't be late."

"Yes, I can make it," I said, although I realized it hadn't been a question.

He nodded and continued his walk back to the stables. I remained where I was, mulling over our conversation, his words haunting me. *I never loved her enough.*

I limped out of the ring, closing the gate behind me with a solid click before finding my way back to the alley of oaks, their moss-covered limbs and leaves silent in the bright light of day as if in mourning for a woman whose husband hadn't loved her enough.

CHAPTER 13

Odella stood behind Lillian at her dressing table, squinting at the hook clasp on the back of Lillian's blouse. "I swear I'm blind as a bat when it comes to seeing small things anymore. Are you sure this hook matters?"

Lillian raised an eyebrow. "It's all in the details, Odella. That's the problem with society these days. Nobody cares about the details anymore. Women going about wearing less than what I used to wear at the beach, without hats or gloves or anything that marks them as ladies. It wasn't like that in my day. A lady dressed like a lady and was treated as such."

Odella snorted, putting a hand on her hip. "So you want me to keep trying with this hook, then?"

Lillian didn't answer, but continued to look pointedly at her with the raised eyebrow. After more struggling, Odella eventually announced success and helped Lillian stand. As she straightened, something slid off of her lap, landing with a small thud on the Aubusson rug.

"What's this?" Odella bent to retrieve the picture frame that had landed facedown.

Lillian reached for it. "I forgot I was looking at that. It's been in my drawer for so long that I forgot it was there. But I was sharing my scrapbook with Helen earlier and that reminded me."

Odella placed the frame in Lillian's hand and she looked down at it, the image fuzzy even with her glasses, not that it mattered. She'd long since memorized every detail of the old photograph, could even recall the conversations and the perfume she'd worn. It had been taken the night of her come-out party, using Josie's Brownie camera that Dr. O'Hare had given her for her seventeenth birthday. It had been right after Annabelle had finished with the flowers and was getting ready to leave. Lillian remembered feeling guilty that Annabelle hadn't been invited, and insisted on including her in the photograph.

Odella looked down at the picture. "I recognize you in the middle, but who are the other two?"

Lillian smiled, remembering, and pointed

to the woman on her left. "That's Josephine Montet. She was a good friend of mine."

"Holy heck — *The* Josephine Montet? The world-famous jazz singer whose records I still own even though I no longer own a record player? You know her?"

"Knew her," Lillian corrected, moving a gnarled finger over the image of the beautiful young woman with the coffee skin and heavenly voice. "She sang at my come-out party."

Lillian pulled the frame closer to see it better, noticing that Josie wore the charm necklace, even though it had been Lillian's turn. Not wanting her father to see it, she'd given it to Josie to wear so that Lola could share in the festivities. Lillian smiled, recalling the small musical note she'd added to Lola to remember how Josie's voice had filled the ballroom, and made the night sparkle.

Odella straightened. "So who was the third friend?"

"Annabelle O'Hare. Josie's mother worked for her father, Dr. O'Hare." Lillian squeezed the metal frame, as if the action would somehow bring them all back to that moment when life stretched before them, a road of shimmering possibilities. "We were thick as thieves." Lillian grinned at the

286

memory.

"Who's the man?" Odella pointed to the tall man with the straw hat and striped jacket.

"That's Freddie Montet, Josie's brother."

Odella whistled. "He's what the kids today would call 'hot.' But are he and Josie really related? He could sure pass for white."

"And he did. He even attended university in England, and did very well. That summer, he told me that he'd run out of funds and that he was going to work with the horses at Asphodel like he'd been doing during his school breaks to earn enough money to return."

Odella tucked her chin into her neck. "But who paid for the rest of it? I can't imagine he would have earned much working for your daddy during the Depression."

Lillian blinked at her image in the mirror. "I've asked myself that a dozen times. To be honest, when I was young it never occurred to me to question it. It was only in my adult life that I began to wonder. His mother was the housekeeper in a doctor's household and his father was never in the picture. I suppose he could have borrowed funds from the doctor — but I always thought that would have been a lot more forward-thinking for the times back then than it would be now."

Lillian leaned forward and placed the frame on her dressing table. "Not that it matters anymore. Freddie's been dead for a long time. Before I married my Charlie and that was almost seventy years ago."

"That's a shame," Odella said as she held on to Lillian's elbow until the older woman had grabbed her cane. "A real shame."

By the time they'd reached the dining room, Lillian was exhausted. The memories pressed down on her, as heavy as the layer of years, making her stumble. She turned to Odella to ask her to take her back to her room, but her eyes settled on Earlene instead.

Earlene stood behind her chair in conversation with Helen, across the table. She was angled slightly, so that her back was partially turned to Tucker in a not-so-subtle gesture. Tonight she had her hair pulled back, showing her profile, and her long elegant neck. And, despite the shoulders that Earlene seemed to force into a rounded position, she held her head regally, as if she'd once been used to being looked upon with admiration and hadn't quite learned how to hide it completely.

But there was something else that drew Lillian into the room toward her seat at the head of the table. It was the feeling of familiarity she felt with Earlene, of having found a friend. It was odd, considering their age difference, but maybe a love for flowers and horses was the great equalizer — the ties that bound the generations together like smocking on a dress.

Lillian's ruminations were interrupted by Tucker as he came to her side to escort her to the table while Odella returned to the kitchen. He kissed her on the cheek and cupped her elbow in his hand. "I'm sorry we missed you for cocktails, but I made your favorite and it's waiting by your plate."

He pulled out her chair and seated her before returning to his chair and waiting for everyone else to sit before joining them. Conversation was light while they passed the dishes that Odella had brought in, and Lillian carefully watched the skittishness between Tucker and Earlene, like two magnets of the same pole.

Lillian turned to Tucker. "Where are Lucy and Sara?"

Tucker wiped his mouth with a cloth napkin. "They were exhausted from horseback riding and from swimming in the pond for most of the afternoon. Emily's making them grilled-cheese sandwiches and tomato soup and putting them to bed early. She didn't have classes tonight and offered to stay."

"Are they here or at your house?" Lillian took a long sip of her cocktail but even that wasn't taking the edge off her impatience with her grandson. To outsiders it would appear that his cup of grief was bottomless, and maybe that was true. But she'd seen Tucker's face when they'd pulled Susan from the river, and the look of relief that had initially crossed it. The grief had come later, but Lillian had never been completely convinced it had been grief over Susan's death.

Tucker set down his glass of wine. "They're here. Emily is off at nine and I . . . have plans for later tonight. I didn't think they should be left alone at the tabby house."

"No," said Lillian tightly, "I don't imagine they should be."

They ate in silence for a while, the clink of silver against fine china the only sounds. Lillian kept stealing glances at Helen, who seemed unusually restless. Her fingers played with the unused utensils, flipping them over and dropping them on the table-cloth.

Finally, Helen's fingers stilled and she leaned across the table toward Earlene.

"How is your research coming along?"

Earlene took her time chewing her food and washing it down with wine, as if buying time to figure out an answer. "Very well, actually. Thank you. I've finished going through Miss Lillian's papers and those have been very helpful in gathering the names of people who would have been in the area in the earlier part of the last century." She turned to Lillian. "The plantation business records have been particularly interesting, and make a good illustration of the business decline during the Great Depression. I noticed that by nineteen thirty-seven your father had sold about thirty of his horses and was down to one stable hand. That must have been hard for you."

Lillian took a large sip of wine, sensing Helen's interest. She raised her eyebrow, hoping to convey uninterest and a real desire to steer the conversation away from where she was afraid it might lead. "One's lack of funds is generally considered to be a difficult thing. Losing one's favorite horse to the highest bidder would be another one."

Helen tilted her head, her brow wrinkled. "The remaining stable hand would have been Freddie, right, Malily?"

Lillian dabbed at the corners of her mouth

with her napkin, nostalgia tugging her backwards. Her gaze found Earlene. "Yes. Probably because Papa didn't have to pay him the same wages he'd been paying the Irishmen. Were there any accounting records of my come-out ball? I was discussing that with Helen just this morning."

"Yes, actually, there were. For the wine, and the flowers, and your dress. It must have been a beautiful evening. The guest list was there, too, but I didn't see your gardening friend — Annabelle."

Lillian slowly chewed a forkful of food, but didn't taste anything. "I suppose I'll have to admit to a little spite. I believed at the time that she and I had romantic aspirations about the same man, and I didn't welcome the competition." She took another sip of her wine. "Besides, Annabelle was busy crusading against public ills and wouldn't have come anyway."

"But she helped with the flowers," Helen added.

"Yes, she did do that," Lillian answered, once again smelling the calla lilies and the gladiolus, and feeling the warmth of Charlie's hand on the small of her back. Exhausted again, Lillian leaned back in her chair and regarded the other table occupants through half-closed eyes, her attention grabbed by Earlene, whose hand had slipped into the collar of her blouse, her fingers moving around the circumference of her neck as if she were searching for something.

Lillian shifted her attention to Tucker, giving in to a fit of restlessness brought on by her memories of Annabelle that clung to her like a too-tight riding jacket. She placed her forearms on the table and leaned toward him. "Tucker, remember how you used to describe people and things to Helen so she could picture them in her head? It just occurred to me that Earlene has been here for over a week, and shared our dining table twice, but Helen has no idea what she looks like. Why don't you describe Earlene to help Helen out?"

She wasn't sure who looked more uncomfortable: Tucker or Earlene. Both looked as if they wanted to flee from the room and Earlene even had the knee-jerk reaction of sliding her chair back. But the tension in the room helped ease the ache around Lillian's tired heart and bones, a diversion that made her look forward to something again.

Helen, despite her skill at determining people's emotions, seemed more intent on joining Lillian in her game than sparing Tucker's or Earlene's feelings. She clasped her hands together and Lillian was afraid for a moment that she would actually clap. "Yes, please. But first, let me describe you the way that I see you and then Tucker can tell me if I'm right or wrong."

Earlene looked down at her plate, a small flush coloring her cheeks. She took a deep breath, then glanced up at Helen and managed a small smile. "All right, I'm game. Go ahead."

Helen closed her eyes, her long, elegant nails, tipped with her signature scarlet red nail polish, splayed on the white tablecloth. "If I make any mistakes, my only excuse will be that once I discovered that you were a horsewoman, all of my assumptions about you were clouded by the way I think a horsewoman should look." She drummed her fingers on the table and took a deep breath. "Your voice is very soft, which makes me think that you're petite — maybe five foot three or less. Your hair is very straight, and you wear it in a low ponytail, not because you particularly like it that way, but because that's the way you've been wearing it since you were a little girl and needed to fix your hair so that it stayed beneath a riding helmet." She smiled in Earlene's direction. "How am I doing?"

"Keep going," Earlene said, her eyes on

Helen and her face closed.

"I think your hair is dark blond. When you're in the sun it lightens up, but since you're a genealogist I don't think you're in the sun that much anymore, so it's dark. And I picture your eyes being blue or gray — something that goes with blond hair, although that's just a guess." Helen puckered her lips for a moment before continuing. "I think you're very slender. I determined that by listening to you walk. When you limp, it doesn't seem as if you're throwing that much weight around, so I figured you probably don't weigh more than a hundred and five pounds or so." She held up her hand in Lillian's direction. "I'm blind, remember, which means that I can freely discuss other people's handicaps so you don't need to say anything."

Helen winked at Earlene. "I also noticed that you don't like standing too close to people. Like you have an invisible barrier that prevents people from getting too near you. Like Tucker. Although he didn't used to be that way." She paused for a moment, as if realizing that she'd just spoken aloud, then turned her head in Tucker's direction. "It's your turn now. How did I do?"

Tucker was looking at Lillian, his eyes narrowed, recognizing her enjoyment in the proceedings but not begrudging her the rare pleasure, either. He placed his napkin beside his plate and faced Earlene, staring at her for a few moments before speaking. "Very good, Helen. You got most of it right. Her hair is what I call light brown but what I've heard referred to as 'dirty blond.' I imagine it will lighten up some if she stays in the sun long enough. Maybe I'll have her give the girls lessons in the outdoor ring." He gave Earlene a half smile, but Lillian wasn't certain whom he was trying to reassure.

"Her eyes are actually light brown, almost gold when the light hits them. They tilt a bit at the corners when she smiles, although she doesn't do that very often." He took a sip from his wineglass before continuing. "I have noticed that she likes to keep her distance from others, but that's to be expected. We're strangers to her still. She hasn't discovered all of our demons yet — not all of them, anyway. And she sure as hell hasn't let any of hers out of the bag, either."

Lillian shot him a look of warning. He pushed his almost-full wineglass away from him before sliding his chair back so that he could fully face Earlene. Her face was still flushed, her skin glowing in the candlelight.

"But you're wrong about her height. She's

more like five foot six, but she has this habit of rounding her shoulders, which makes her look smaller. It's like she's trying not to be noticed, but it doesn't matter. There's something about the way she carries herself that makes her stand out anyway. It's like she's used to leading a parade or something, and that even without the parade behind her, she can't help but walk as if she were still up front."

Tucker leaned back in his chair, as if he were enjoying not being the center of Lillian's scrutiny for an evening. He continued. "Oh, and forget what you said about her soft voice. That's her 'inside voice,' to borrow an expression from the girls. You should have heard Earlene this morning in the ring. She was downright authoritative, although I can't say for sure that she really ever raised her voice. I think it had more to do with the confidence she felt about what she was saying; she knew her stuff and she wasn't afraid to let everybody know it."

Earlene's eyes were focused near her plate, her hands folded tightly in a fist that rested on the table's edge. Lillian began to open her mouth to tell Tucker that he'd said enough, but she stopped. Tucker had never been cruel. Even as a young boy, when little brothers were expected to torment their

297

older sisters, he and Helen had been more like best friends, inseparable long before Helen lost her sight. She watched as Tucker's face softened, almost visibly backing off. It seemed to Lillian that he had recognized something in Earlene that reminded him of himself — another person recently and profoundly blinded, bumping into the world around them as they tried to find their way in new surroundings.

When he next spoke, his voice was soft. "She's very beautiful, Helen, although I don't think she realizes it. And maybe that's an assumption on my part, too, because I also think of her as a horsewoman. As you know, most horsewomen are so into their horses that they don't take a lot of time looking at themselves in a mirror." Tucker gave his trademark half smile, which most women swooned over, but Earlene, who was still focused on her plate, didn't notice.

"She appears to be delicate, but I'm not fooled. I've seen her work with horses, and they didn't think she was delicate either."

Tucker paused and Earlene looked up to meet his gaze. "Are you finished? I think Helen has a pretty good idea of what I look like now, thank you." Earlene had released her fists and her hand went back to her collar, her fingers surreptitiously slipping inside, searching.

"Is there something wrong?" Tucker leaned forward, his eyes wary.

Earlene nodded, a frown between her eyes. "My necklace . . . I can't find it. I wear it almost all the time, and I'm pretty sure I had it on when I arrived." She stood and shook her blouse, but nothing fell out of the bottom. Her voice rose in pitch. "It's gone." She began looking around her chair on the floor, her movements jerky. "It must be around here somewhere."

Tucker stood, too, and touched her gently on the arm. "Don't worry. We'll find it. I'll tell Odella so that when she vacuums in here tomorrow she can look for it."

Inexplicably, Earlene's gaze met Lillian's for a moment before she quickly looked away. "But I really want to find it now."

"Is it valuable?" Helen asked as she stood, too.

Earlene shook her head. "Only to me. It's sort of a family heirloom."

Helen slipped off her high-heeled shoes and began rubbing her bare feet in an arc on the rug. "What does it look like?"

Earlene's skin had gone from flushed to nearly white. "It's . . . it's a gold chain. With a little ornament hanging from it."

Tucker had also begun searching, moving

back his chair and peering under the table. "What kind of an ornament?"

Lillian watched as Earlene swallowed. "A gold figure. Of a woman."

"Like a doll?" Helen stopped moving her feet and faced Earlene.

"Yes. Something like that."

Seeming satisfied with her answer, Helen and Tucker continued to look, Tucker going as far as into the hallway to see if it had fallen off there.

He returned, shaking his head. "Didn't see it, but don't worry, it'll show up. I'll tell the girls and Emily to be on the lookout for it, too." He stood back from Earlene, whose hand lay clutched at her neck while her other hand rested on the table as if for support, watching her as he had once watched Susan, waiting for an outburst or a complete meltdown.

Lillian stood, defusing the tension. "Let's all go into the parlor and Odella can serve us coffee in there. I promise you that we'll find it, Earlene." She moved to Earlene's side and slid her hand into the crook of Earlene's arm without asking first. As Earlene led her from the dining room, Lillian squeezed her arm hard, hard enough to hurt, and was rewarded with an angry and surprised look from Earlene. *Good,* thought

Lillian. *She's not like Susan, after all.* It wasn't until they'd reached the parlor that Lillian thought to wonder why Earlene could have been so panicked over the loss of a simple necklace.

I barely followed the conversation following dinner, being too worried about finding my angel charm. The chain I'd been using was old and the clasp must have broken and I berated myself for not having purchased a new chain.

Unable to contain my restlessness and eager to return home to see if the charm might have fallen off there, I waited for a lull in the conversation and stood to excuse myself. I'd driven my car to the house, not willing to take another open-cart ride under the old oaks at night again, so I was disappointed when Tucker stood, too, and told me that he would walk me out. I didn't want company, especially his. *There's something about the way she carries herself that makes her stand out anyway. It's like she's used to leading a parade or something, and that even without the parade behind her, she can't help but walk as if she were still up front.*

At first I thought he'd discovered my secret, and then quickly dismissed the idea. I had no doubt that I'd be heading back to

301

Savannah with a hastily packed trunk and a car full of unanswered questions if that had been the case. But while I'd been sitting at the table and listening to Tucker describe me to Helen, the repercussions of what would happen when my deception became known had become illuminated in my mind. I'd always been headstrong, always leaping before I looked, and this plan had been no exception. My only excuse was that it had given me a reason to get up in the morning for the first time in over six years. I think George had known it, too, or he would never have allowed me to do something so stupid. I'd have to figure something out — something that would salvage my relationship with the family I had grown to like; and I hoped that the lost angel charm wouldn't force my hand before I was ready.

I said my good nights before preceding Tucker to the front door. He opened it for me and then surprised me by following me outside into the humid summer night air that lay as thick on our skins as marsh mud.

"I'm heading to the stables to check on Captain Wentworth. Thought maybe you'd like to come." His words weren't warm or inviting, but he sounded sincere.

I nodded, my reason for agreeing unclear even to me. "Sure," I said, then turned with him and began to walk in the direction of the stables. "Do you always tuck your horses in at night? I thought Andi Winkle was your stable manager."

"She is, and she does a great job. But sometimes we get a horse who was so abused that they need a little help before they can trust humans again. Those are the ones I give a little extra TLC to. And Captain Wentworth — well, he always gets a bit nervous when we leave him in the stall, so I make it a practice to check on him a few times to let him know that nobody's forgotten him."

We walked the rest of the way in silence, watching as the sun dipped lower in the horizon, filling the pastures and marshes with golden light before slowly stealing all the color, wrapping them up with night.

I wanted to ask him why he'd taken leave from his medical practice and moved to his grandmother's farm, and why he rescued horses now instead. But I knew that the answer lay close to his grief, an uneasy alliance and unreliable bedfellow, so I remained silent, not willing to spoil the peaceful night.

As we approached the barn a horse whinnied, calling out to us, and I looked at Tucker. "Is that Captain Wentworth? He must know you're coming."

Tucker slid a sidelong glance at me as he paused to let me enter the barn first. "That's actually the first time he's done that. I would think he probably recognized your footsteps because they're so different from everybody else's."

I bit back my defensive remark and instead concentrated on its implications as we approached the first stall. Captain Wentworth watched warily as we approached, and when I drew near he stretched his head toward me, but when I reached my hand up to pat his nose, he jerked back.

Before I could lower my hand again, Tucker grabbed my wrist. "Keep holding it up so he can see your hand's empty."

I nodded to show I understood and his hand fell away. Tentatively, Captain Wentworth stuck his head out again and I reached for him, my hand resting on his long nose as he stood still for me, allowing me to pet him. Sensing his trust in me, I stepped closer and he allowed me to pat his powerful neck and scratch him around the ears like a big dog, just the way my horse Fitz had liked.

"Have you ridden him, yet?" I asked, as Captain Wentworth began nuzzling around my shirt, stretching downward to reach my pockets in search of a treat.

"No. He's not ready. I don't know how he'd handle a rider right now. Besides, his hooves are still healing. He had some nasty infections when I first got him. Took a while before we could get close enough to shave off the overgrown hooves because they must have been hurting him something bad. Maybe in another week or so we can try putting a rider on him. We'll need a pretty experienced rider for that, though."

I didn't look up at him, feeling his full gaze on me. "It's a good thing you're an experienced rider, then."

Tucker had picked off a single straw from a stack of clean hay as we'd passed it, and begun chewing on an end. "Yeah, I guess so. Although he tends to prefer women." He pretended to think for a minute. "With her gumption and your training, maybe Lucy will be ready to ride him in a week or so. She'll certainly think so." His face erupted into a wide grin, and my heart squeezed a little as he spoke about his daughter with such pride.

I pictured the diminutive Lucy demanding to ride the huge horse and couldn't help smiling, too. "Yeah, I can picture it."

Captain Wentworth nuzzled my side again, continuing his search for something good to eat. I felt comfortable and at ease, something I hadn't expected, and I wasn't sure if it was the proximity of the horse who reminded me of my old self, or the man who stood next to me. His own vulnerability made me feel strong again, and when I looked at him, I saw the man who could heal damaged horses and had once loved playing pranks on his family but who had been afraid of thunderstorms.

Captain Wentworth bumped me with his nose and I stumbled backward, caught by surprise. I grabbed his neck to keep my balance, pressing my face in against him and smelling the old familiar horse scent — the same scent that still made me wary, though I was no longer afraid of it. I had left that fear behind as I'd stood outside the lunge ring watching Tucker and Captain Wentworth, replaced now with something more like apprehension and a different kind of fear altogether. But as long as I remained on the ground, my fear of failure was as elusive as a moonflower bloom at dawn.

"Hey, boy," I said, rubbing his nose, "what's wrong? Why the long face?"

Tucker snorted. "That's the oldest joke in the book."

I turned to him, trying to keep a straight face. "Then why are you laughing?"

We laughed together for a few minutes

until we both seemed to realize where we were and whom we were with. Our smiles gradually faded as we stared at each other. Tucker finally broke the silence. "You really should laugh more, you know. You're beautiful when you do."

Embarrassed, I turned back to Captain Wentworth and fumbled for something to say. "My grandmother told that joke to me when we bought my first horse. It was sort of an ongoing joke for a long time." *Until her presence at events became superfluous and all that remained was my desire to be the best.* Quietly, I added, "I'd almost forgotten it until now."

I gave Captain Wentworth a final pat and stepped back. "Good night, big guy. We'll see you tomorrow. And I promise to bring a treat."

We walked past the other stalls, including those of the new ponies, giving a pat to whoever stuck out a nose, exiting the building on the opposite side. Full dark had fallen, leaving a moonless sky scattered with stars and gathering clouds. Tucker held out his arm. "The path can be rough going at night. It might be best if you held on."

I wanted to refuse, to ignore my stiff knee if only for one beautiful night and pretend I was the woman with two good legs who everybody believed was headed for great things. I grabbed his elbow and held on, grudgingly thankful.

When we reached my car, he held the door open for me as I got in, then stood back, his hands in his pockets.

"You don't have to watch me leave, Tucker. I know the way."

"I know that. I'm just . . . contemplating."

His tone, usually so remote, welcomed me in this time, as if he wanted me to question him. As if our sharing of laughter over a bad joke had breached a small portion of the wall between us. "Contemplating what?"

His eyes were focused over the top of my car toward the alley of towering oaks. The night was still, the trees keeping quiet. "Whether or not I should go out tonight or stay at home and read a story to my little girls."

The roll of emotional adviser was a new one to me. Before I'd come to Asphodel, I'd always considered myself to be the most damaged person I knew. My scars were deep, but I was beginning to learn that they weren't as permanent as I'd once believed, and many of them were self-inflicted. But the loss of a wife and mother was forever, regardless of the circumstances. I got out of the car and stood in front of him. "I know

I'm still pretty much a stranger to you, and you probably weren't even asking a question you expected me to answer, but I don't feel right driving away without trying to answer you anyway." I took a quick breath, waiting for him to stop me before I could continue. When he didn't move, I said, "It would seem to me that Sara and Lucy would benefit more having you here."

"You think so?" As if remembering that I was there, he shifted his eyes from the trees to me, dark pools of shadow backlit from the lights of the house. "Their mother certainly didn't benefit from my presence." He seemed to consider his next words for a moment. "She thought she would be better off dead than living with me."

I touched his arm, his skin cool and clammy. "You told me that you didn't love Susan enough. But what about your daughters? Do you feel the same about them?" I waited for him to answer, not completely sure what he would say.

"I love them more than enough. More than I ever thought possible," he said softly. "But what if Susan was right? That they're all better off without me?"

I felt his hurt while I grappled with my own shame. Had that been the reason my grandmother had retreated from my life?

From reading her scrapbook and listening to Lillian's stories of their childhood, I had learned that Annabelle O'Hare had once been a strong-minded, independent woman. Had my own selfishness driven her to recede into the shadows? Or had something else happened first, and I'd simply been the catalyst to finish the job?

I leaned toward him. "My grandmother gave me something with a Latin verse on it that means 'Be patient and strong; someday this pain will be useful to you.' She was also the person who used to tell me to get back on the horse whenever I fell. It took me a long time to realize that they mean the same thing. And she was probably right on both counts."

I felt his warm breath on my face as we continued to stare at each other in the dim light. The wind had begun to pick up, the restless oaks behind us beginning their odd whistling as if summoning a storm.

"It's always a lot easier to give advice than it is to take it, isn't it?"

I pulled back, stung. "I'm sorry. I shouldn't have said anything," I said, stumbling toward my car, feeling suddenly embarrassed about my limp. I slid into the car behind the wheel and slammed the door. My chest rose and fell with indignation, even as the realization bloomed that he was right, and that I was angrier with myself than with him.

I thought back on the last six years during which I'd wallowed in my own misery while my grandmother was left alone. How many days had that been? How many hours and minutes had I let pass between us like wind through leaves, not even bothering to look up and see how they glistened when they moved? Without reaching out to the one person who held all the answers long before I ever thought to ask the questions.

Keeping my eyes focused on the swaying moss in the trees, I said, "Just don't let Susan be right. You're here, and she's gone. And those two little girls are upstairs now." I didn't wait for him to answer. Instead I turned the key in the ignition and pulled away from the house and into the whistling oaks just as the first drops of rain began to fall.

CHAPTER 14

Lillian sat on her garden bench, feeling more tired than she remembered being in a long time. But the garden nourished her, the ninety-year-old magnolias that stood inside of the brick garden wall reminding her of all that they had witnessed since her mother had planted them as seedlings. Despite the turmoil in her own life, the garden had been her constant, a friend who gave her companionship without stealing her solitude. Or making her question the paths she'd walked, or causing her to look back at the road not taken as if it were still an option.

A heavy storm had passed through the night, keeping Lillian awake with her fear and her memories, but it had cleansed the air, leaving behind a cooler temperature and shining crystals of raindrops on her beloved flowers, raising blooms of rain lilies into clumps of star-pointed white flowers earlier in the season than they usually appeared. The leaves of the magnolia shimmered, waving their copper-backed leaves at her in the soft morning breeze. *The garden is the soul of the house,* her mother had told her as she'd knelt next to a young Lillian and explained how to plant an ugly jonquil bulb, promising her that the resulting spring bloom would be worth the work.

Lillian tilted her face back to let the sun warm her, remembering how she'd once planned to share the secrets of her garden with her own daughter, and how Margaret had never liked to come here, had told her that the magnolia frightened her, that the array of colors and scents made her head ache. There was Helen, of course; Helen adored the garden and the work involved, despite her limitations. But even Lillian had to admit that it wasn't the same, and that the hours she'd spent in the garden with Earlene Smith in the last month had been the most satisfying hours she'd spent in anyone's company in a very long time. Earlene understood the garden, the annual cycle of colors from brilliant summer, to green fall and brown winter, to the rebirth of the garden in springtime. She spoke of it as if speaking of her own heart, of how the changes echoed her life. And Lillian saw how Earlene seemed to linger in winter, holding back, waiting for spring.

A noise at the gate caught her attention and she turned around, expecting to find Earlene. She came often, although not every morning, deadheading blooms and plucking errant weeds. She'd even remulched the beds with pine straw, annoying Lillian at first because she hadn't asked for permission, and then making her smile because she'd seen it needed to be done and had taken care of it. Just as Lillian would have done.

Tucker came through the gate, looking thoughtful but less drawn than Lillian was used to him being. She knew from Helen that he hadn't been going out at night as much so he must be getting more sleep. But it was more than that. She'd like to think it was the time he'd begun to spend with the girls — awkward hours spent reading to them or watching them swim in the pond. He still didn't attend their riding lessons, but received frequent updates from Earlene. It was an uneasy alliance she'd seen between Tucker and Earlene, like two bloodhounds searching for the same elusive fox, and she wondered if they had also noticed that their unease with each other was because they were so much alike.

"Good morning, Malily. You're up early."
He leaned over and gave his grandmother a
kiss on her cheek. He smelled of the outdoors and of horse and she knew he'd
already been riding.

"I didn't sleep, if that's the same as being
up early." She rubbed her knuckles, the
dampness seeping into the old bones.

"Storm keep you up?"

"Partly," Lillian said.

Tucker raised an eyebrow in question and
Lillian looked into the eyes that reminded
her of Charlie's. "Remember earlier this
year when I received that letter from Piper
Mills — the granddaughter of an old friend
of mine?"

Tucker nodded. "I do. I actually read her
name recently in *Today's Equestrian* —
something about how some newcomer was
going to try and break a record Piper still
holds although she hasn't competed in more
than six years. The anniversary of her last
event is this month, so there's a lot of buzz
right now."

Lillian closed her eyes and smelled the
scents of her garden, breathing in the
peacefulness and rest that eluded her at
night. "I was thinking that I shouldn't have
told her no. That I should have invited her
here to talk about Annabelle."

She felt Tucker stiffen beside her. "I don't see why. Whenever I hear Annabelle's name mentioned, it's always associated with something bad. Twelve years ago when you received the letter from Annabelle's husband saying that he'd put his wife in a nursing home, you . . . changed. Not that the outside world could see it, but I could. You walked slower, you seemed more aware of your own frailties. And then Susan . . ." He stopped for a moment. "I know her . . . relapse had more to do with her own mental state than anything else, but she became obsessed with the story of your friendship with Annabelle. I just find it hard to believe that you'd want to revisit any of it."

"I'm getting old, Tuck. And I'm not going to live forever. I suppose it's natural for the elderly to look back on their lives and see if there's something that needs to be put right. To undo damage."

He looked intently at his grandmother. "Damage?"

Lillian shook her head. "I . . . lied to Annabelle about something. Something important and she died never knowing the truth. And since reading Piper's letter, I've come to think that maybe it's not too late. That by telling her granddaughter I can make amends to Annabelle."

Tucker was staring at the moonflowers, their blooms tucked tightly inside themselves, the droplets of rain like tears. "Did Susan know about it? This . . . lie?"

"She might have. I'd written an apology to Annabelle that I never sent but kept hidden. Susan might have seen me access it once, but I never thought she'd pry. But when Susan died in the river, I suspected she might have."

"What do you mean?"

She looked into Tucker's face, seeing the devastation again, and knew she couldn't tell him. Not now. Glancing away, she said, "It was just very emotional — you know how girls are. I think that's why I kept it from her, knowing that even though Susan seemed fine, that maybe it would be too much for her to handle.

"I never gave her my scrapbook — she took it, remember. I thought she'd be content with all the rest of my stories, and my papers. She seemed so happy to have something to make her feel useful. She told me she didn't need the pills anymore because she was feeling so good. Maybe she did that on purpose so I wouldn't pay that much attention to what she was doing. So when she found the letter from Annabelle's husband and was determined to find out more, I didn't know to stop her."

His voice was hard. "None of this is new to me, Malily. Except for whatever you lied about to Annabelle. Maybe if you just told me the rest of your story, I could contact Piper Mills and tell her myself. That might satisfy her and then you can stop worrying about something that happened years ago that doesn't matter anymore."

Lillian faced her grandson and sighed. He was male, and destined to think of history as only battles fought and won. He could never understand. "I need to tell her myself, Tucker. I think we need to contact her again."

Tucker stood, then reached over to shake the moonflowers, their drops raining on the brick walkway. "What about Helen? She told me you've been sharing your scrapbook with her. Isn't that enough?"

Feeling agitated, Lillian stood, leaning heavily on her cane. "No. No, it isn't. Helen doesn't need any life lessons from me; she's never once looked back on her past and wished she'd done something differently." She shook her head. "I need to tell Annabelle's granddaughter. I need Annabelle's forgiveness."

"She's dead, Malily. It's too late."

His eyes were dark with terror and pain

318

and Lillian wished she could make it go away with a kiss as she'd done when he was small. She knew he wasn't referring just to Annabelle, but that the ghost of his wife's suicide lingered near him still, his guilt and regret unwilling to let her remain buried.

She touched his arm. "Until you bury me, it won't be too late. 'Where there is life, there is hope,' remember?"

He shook his head. "I think you're making a mistake, but if you want me to contact her, I will."

She looked into his face and saw the boy he'd once been: the wild, reckless boy full of mischief and practical jokes. Lillian refused to believe that the boy was gone forever, hidden inside this sad shell of a man. Her lasting hope was that the revelation of her secrets would set all of them free — free from lives spent looking backward and wrestling with past mistakes.

Lillian stood on her toes and reached up to kiss him on his cheek. "Yes, I'd like you to."

He put his hands on her shoulders and she looked up into his eyes, feeling much shorter than she remembered. Had he always been so tall? Or was she just shrinking? Becoming smaller and smaller until she would simply cease to exist? Perhaps that was what death would be like for her: a crumbling into dust, where pride and old wounds didn't matter anymore.

A corner of his mouth lifted before he spoke and Lillian caught a glimpse of the old Tucker. "You're really a big bully, you know. Always managing to get your own way. I don't fall for this old-lady act at all. I never have."

She smiled back, relieved to see his smile again. "I know. You're much too smart for that. You got that from me."

He grinned again, revealing his elusive dimple and her heart didn't seem to ache as much. Shoving his hands in his pockets, he said, "I've got to go to the stables, see if today is the day Captain Wentworth is ready for a rider."

"Captain Wentworth?"

Tucker dug the tip of his boot into a crack in the brick walk. "The new rescue horse. I let Earlene name him. After the Jane Austen character. I figured we wouldn't be keeping him, so it didn't matter."

Lillian watched him closely. "So what do you think of this Earlene?"

He grew still for a moment, his eyes focused on the coppery waves of the magnolia leaves. "I can't really put a finger on it, but there seems to be something . . . missing. I mean, where are her family and friends? She doesn't talk about her past at all, and is here to study somebody else's life. She reminds me of a college buddy of mine who had lost a leg in a hunting accident. He acted shell-shocked, barely able to focus on what was going on around him, sort of living those last moments before the bullet hit him again and again. Like he was afraid to move forward in life in case something like that happened again."

She didn't say anything, wondering if he realized how much he'd just described himself.

"What about you, Malily? What do you think?"

Lillian sat back down on the bench and stretched out her legs, willing the aching in her feet to stop. "She loves my garden."

Tucker nodded, understanding as she knew he would. "I'll see you at supper."

She raised an eyebrow, but didn't risk saying anything in case he changed his mind. She watched as he walked back toward the garden gate, stopping once to pick up something from the brick path. He turned it over in his hand and studied it for a moment, then pocketed it before snapping the latch closed behind him.

■ ■ ■ ■

I sat in the kitchen of the cottage, the air cool enough to leave the windows open. A breeze stirred the scrapbook pages in front of me on the table, the paper rustling with impatience. I'd put the scrapbook aside to go through Lillian's papers, knowing already that I'd find nothing I needed in them. What I needed was Lillian's scrapbook pages to read alongside Annabelle's, but I knew Lillian wouldn't part with them, especially to a stranger.

Dutifully, I'd taken notes on everything I'd seen in Lillian's papers, and when Tucker had sent over a family tree — via Helen — that Susan had made, I'd plugged everything into my genealogy software if only because it gave me something to do while I waited for the answers I sought to come find me.

The blue knit sweater and baby blanket lay on the table next to the scrapbook as a reminder of why I was here. I felt the softness of the sweater again and raised it to my nose, still smelling the mothballs and dust. I was no closer to discovering who had owned these two things, or who had lived in the hidden attic room of my grandparents' house than when I'd first arrived. But somehow I didn't feel as despondent as I should have.

I gave the girls riding lessons four times a week — up from the proposed twice-a-week schedule because Lucy had asked and because I really wanted to. She was good — really good — with the confidence and ease of a much older rider. But she also had a hint of recklessness and fearlessness that made me outwardly scold her. Secretly, though, I applauded her sturdy little character, knowing she had what it took to be a solid competitor when the time came. Sara made me laugh with her plodding pony and Lucy made me remember what it had been like to be fearless. Through them, I found myself easing my way into days in which I didn't dread getting up in the morning.

I stared at the scrapbook bundle for a long moment before opening it up and finding the place where I last stopped. Most of the entries I'd read so far were filled with the mundane aspects of my grandmother's adolescent life: outings with Lillian and Josie, horseback riding on Lola Grace at Asphodel, and more mentions of Freddie. She never wrote about any romantic feelings toward him, but the sheer number of times his name was mentioned made me wonder.

With the sweater and blanket cuddled in my lap like a small child, I began to read:

May 30, 1934

I was supposed to give this book and Lola to Lily back in March, but I don't seem to have as much time to visit Asphodel — or to write in this book. But I get sore at Lillian for saying she's too busy to write in it, so I can't slack off, too, or she'll become Miss Know-it-all.

At least I know I'm spending my time constructively. Now that I'm eighteen, my father says I'm old enough to help him on some of his doctor visits, especially if the patient is a woman. He said that a lot of women, especially in childbirth, seem to relax more in the presence of another female. I don't do much but hold hands and give to Papa whatever he asks for, but I don't get tired of it. There's something about bringing life into the world or helping to alleviate the suffering of those already here that never tires me. Papa said that there will be a day when there are just as many women doctors as men, but I can't see that happening.

Today Papa went to help a woman who

seemed not much older than me deliver her fourth child. Since no one else was present, I kept the younger children out of the way, playing with them and feeding them lunch with whatever scraps I could find in the kitchen. The oldest boy had a stick he pretended was a machine gun like the ones Bonnie and Clyde used to rob all of those banks. Everybody's talking about them now because of how they were killed last week in Louisiana. I saw a picture of their car, with all those bullet holes in it, and I couldn't help but wonder if all that excitement and passion in their lives could have been worth ending that way.

Papa also taught me to drive his Ford. It was scary at first, but now I love it and I do think I'm a better driver than he is (although I could never tell him because it would hurt his feelings). Papa said that now I'm all grown-up and taking on new responsibilities, I should start thinking about a husband and family. I didn't answer him. I think it's because the first thought I had was, Why I would want to settle down so soon after finding my freedom for the first time?

I'm putting a picture in the scrapbook of me behind the wheel of Papa's car.

Paul Morton, the thirteen-year-old son of Papa's lawyer, took the picture of me and gave it to me as a gift. Papa said the boy is sweet on me and I laughed because he's still just a child.

P.S. I'm adding a charm of a Model T to Lola.

I sat up at the mention of Paul Morton's name. He had said he'd known my grandmother, but that was all. I smiled to myself, thinking of old Mr. Morton as a young boy with a secret crush on a girl five years older than himself and wondering why he hadn't mentioned it to me.

I turned back to the scrapbook pages and continued to read. I skimmed over the entry from 1935, a simple laundry list of Annabelle's household chores and her duties with her father, quickly turning the page in the hope that her next entry might be more interesting. I wasn't disappointed.

January 15, 1936
Tonight is a night of celebration. Thurgood Marshall, a lawyer for the NAACP, has successfully won his case to admit a black student into the University of Maryland Law School. Freddie told me it would happen and he's so persuasive

that I think that even I believed it a little. But now it's fact, and the course of public education in this country is bound to change.

Papa said that there might be trouble brewing in the streets tonight and that I should stay home. I didn't want him to worry, so Josie and I snuck out of my window with Freddie's help and we went to an establishment on West Bay Street that I knew Papa wouldn't approve of, regardless of his liberal views of society. I was the only white woman, but I felt safe and protected by Freddie, who commands a great deal of respect wherever he goes. I had my first taste of whiskey (Papa definitely wouldn't approve!) and I almost swooned, which made Freddie laugh and that alone was worth the embarrassment of being such an ingenue. He doesn't laugh a lot, and it always makes the world a whole lot brighter when he does.

Josie ended up singing on the bar where some of Freddie's friends had lifted her and I was amazed again at what a presence she had and what an incredibly beautiful voice. She's been talking a lot about moving to a northern city, where there are more opportunities for women of color. I love her like a sister, but I can't be selfish and demand she stay with me. She tells me that she's not serious, that even the famed Josephine Baker was called a "Negro wench" in the <u>New York Times,</u> and she would starve or worse if she left Savannah. But I think she should follow her dreams, wherever they might lead. I confided in her something I've never told anyone: that I want to be a doctor like my father. I have no idea how I'll accomplish getting into medical school, but if Josie has the courage to pursue her singing, maybe I can do this, too.

I spend a little bit of every day in my garden. Josie's mother, Justine, has officially handed it over to me, putting me in charge of the herbs and vegetables that she uses in the kitchen in addition to my beautiful blooms. She says I have a way with flowers, that all I have to do is touch dry earth and something beautiful springs from it and that my mother was the same way. It makes me feel close to the mother I barely knew, imagining her working by my side as I dig holes for bulbs or tie back vines that have become unruly. Justine told me that my mother liked her garden a little wild, so I've let a section of lantana go without pruning, and I like the way it makes its way to the back porch — like a reminder that even flowers have their own wild nature if left to themselves. My garden is a bit like my soul, I think; its blooms like refreshing rain to my spirit. I'll take a few rose clippings to Lillian next time I see her as a sort of peace offering for her own garden, a permanent tie between us and the gardens of our hearts.

I haven't been up to Asphodel Meadows in over a month. Lillian hasn't written or called — she says she doesn't have time because she's too busy with her social life and her horses. I know there's something else, but she won't admit to it. It doesn't matter — she's the sister of my heart and I forgive her for everything. Always.

Her new horses aren't the pure breeds she was used to, but instead horses whose owners have abandoned them because they could barely feed themselves, let alone an animal. She's acquired four so far and her father says that feeding them will bring them all to ruin, but Lillian's being allowed to keep them.

Freddie is still working at Asphodel

and says he'll take me this weekend to see Lillian and to ride. It's been so long and I wonder if my restlessness is because I haven't ridden Lola Grace in so long, or if it's because of something else I feel shimmering on my horizon. Maybe when I'm at Asphodel with Lillian, Josie, and Freddie this feeling will go away as I sink back into the comfort of how it was when we were younger. But I'm afraid something has changed for all of us; maybe it's just because we're older now. Or maybe it's something else entirely.

I wore Lola to the celebration party, and the charm I added was a dove, which symbolizes peace — a hopeful symbol that all Americans seeking education shouldn't be denied. And that the rumblings of war in Europe that Papa is always grumbling about won't touch us here.

Yet when I turn off my light at night, the restlessness returns like a persistent insect, pecking at me until I finally manage to fall asleep.

I stared at the picture of my grandmother standing in front of an old black sedan next to an older man I imagined to be her father.

She was holding a large black doctor's bag and smiling a secret smile that made me think of her dream to be a doctor.

I pushed the scrapbook pages away from me, their splayed position like that of a dead bird, then gathered the blanket and sweater in my hands, burying my face in their softness. *My grandmother had wanted to be a doctor.* I felt as if I stood before a locked room and I couldn't shake the impression that Lillian held the key high above my head, where I couldn't quite reach it.

And yet I felt no compunction to continue reading. I was like a person stumbling down a hill trying to stop my descent, knowing that reaching the bottom would hurt. I knew how my grandmother's story ended; but I didn't know the part in between that had turned an independent-minded young woman who loved horses and wanted to be a doctor into the thin shade of a person I had known. There was a large part of me that didn't want to know the truth, didn't want to see the part of her that might be a part of me, too.

Frustrated, I slid my chair back and stood. After circling the living room and kitchen several times, I left the cottage, not really sure where I was heading.

■ ■ ■ ■

Helen sat on the ledge at the bottom of the obelisk and took another drag from her cigarette. She'd taken to smoking in places where the children couldn't find her, their disapproval taking all of the fun out of smoking. Mardi crouched beside her as if making sure she wouldn't slip off the narrow ledge while her heels sank into the soft earth around her grandfather's grave.

The canvas she'd been working on sat tucked behind the obelisk, out of the sun. She'd been painting Earlene, using Tucker's description, seeing her clearly now in her mind and hoping she'd managed to at least convey part of it onto canvas. She wasn't sure if she was done, and would wait a while before calling Tucker to come and retrieve her and her paints.

Helen heard the approaching uneven footsteps before Mardi sat up at attention and let out a bark of warning. "Earlene?"

The sound of crunching leaves became louder. "Is my limp really that bad?" Earlene's voice sounded more amused than annoyed.

"Just distinctive," Helen assured her. "You know, maybe you should talk to Emily about exercises you could be doing that might lessen your limp. She's studying to be a physical therapist."

Earlene's footsteps stopped abruptly in front of Helen. "I don't need fixing."

Helen smiled, then took another drag from her cigarette. "Oh, we all need fixing."

Earlene leaned against the ledge. "You shouldn't smoke; it's really bad for you."

"I was blinded by measles as a child. I figure lightning has already struck me once — it's not going to strike me again."

Silence fell on the cemetery, the only sound that of the wind in the trees and a small sigh from Earlene.

"I used to think the same thing. When my parents died I thought I'd already lived through the worst thing that could happen to me. But I was wrong."

"You had your accident on the horse."

"Yes."

"And now you think fate's gunning for you, waiting to trip you up again." Helen took a long drag from her cigarette, waiting for her words to sink in. "I don't believe life works that way. Helps me to get out of bed each morning, knowing that I've got more to look forward to than dread."

Helen took another drag. "But yes, I know that smoking's bad for me. The girls keep telling me that and eventually I'll quit. I'm just enjoying it too much right now." Helen blew out smoke away from Earlene. "How's your research going?"

"Frustrating. The more I find out, the more I don't know. I know all the puzzle pieces fit together, but I just can't see how."

"Like they're all white pieces with no picture to show you how they fit."

There was a short pause before Earlene answered, "Exactly."

"Was the family tree Susan made helpful to you at all?" She heard a squirrel run through leaves a second before Mardi bolted from her side.

Earlene's words sounded measured. "Not yet. I plugged all the names and dates into my software, so at least I've got them for reference. I also found the burial records for all of the plots in this cemetery, and I was able cross-reference each grave with a name on the chart. Except for one. The small angel marker in the corner without any inscription. There's nobody in the Harrington-Ross family tree who's not accounted for. I'm beginning to think it's not a marker at all."

Mardi returned to Helen's side and bumped his head against her leg. She reached down and took the stick from his mouth and threw it in the direction of the small angel, listening as the dog raced toward it.

"Oh, there's definitely something buried beneath it."

She felt Earlene looking at her. "How do you know?"

Helen gave a small laugh. "I'm almost too ashamed to tell you, but I figure it was long ago enough that I can blame it on my youth. But once, when Tucker and I were still kids and full of mischief, we wanted to find out what was under that little angel. I guess we were curious because there wasn't a name or anything on it like the rest of the markers in the cemetery. We made a bet — I thought it would be dog bones but Tucker thought there was buried pirate treasure. So we each took a shovel from the gardening shed and began digging."

Helen pictured Earlene holding her breath. "And what did you find?"

Helen rolled the cigarette between her fingers, remembering the smell of damp earth and rotting leaves. "It was some kind of cloth — Tucker thought it might be a rotting blanket, but it was hard to tell because it looked like it had been there for a long time. I guess we were both spooked because we didn't stick around to find out more. We dropped the shovels and ran away screaming. Our mama caught up with us and she was so angry over what we'd done that I thought she might knock us into next week."

"So what happened?"

"She made us swear that we'd never desecrate a grave again and then she marched us over to the groundskeeper and we had to help him refill the hole and replace the grass. I think it was almost a year before either one of us stepped foot in the cemetery again."

Earlene's voice sounded distant, as if she'd turned her head away to face the lonely angel marker in the corner of the cemetery. "Did you ever ask Malily or your mother about it?"

Helen thought back for a moment, remembering. "My mother didn't know anything about it, and made it clear she had no interest in knowing. She was all about saving the world, oblivious to what needed saving in her own backyard. But Malily — well, I did ask her once."

"And what did she say?" Earlene was facing her again, the soft scent of her perfume bridging the space between then.

"That she didn't know. But I think she was lying." She turned her face up to Earlene. "I've found flowers on it, and always in the late summertime. Like there's an anniversary being remembered."

"Interesting," Earlene said slowly. "I suppose I'll have to dig a little deeper in the archives. But I don't think I could be persuaded to dig up a grave."

Helen recognized Earlene's attempt to lighten the conversation and smiled in response. "Have you found out anything else that's interesting?"

"The only other thing that really struck me was that your uncle was born nine months to the day after your grandparents' wedding."

Helen smiled to herself. "Are you suggesting my grandmother was less than pure on her wedding night?"

"Or just really fertile." Earlene shifted her position on the ledge. "Do you remember your grandfather Charlie? And his relationship with Lillian?"

Helen jerked her head in Earlene's direction. "Your friend — what was her name, Lola? — needs that kind of information?"

"My friend . . . ? Oh, no . . . I'm just curious, that's all. I'm sorry if I'm getting too personal."

"Don't worry about it. Digging up information is probably just an occupational hazard for you. And I don't mind answering. I'll admit that it's been refreshing to have you here at Asphodel and to have someone to talk to about things not related to horses or flowers."

Helen took a long draw on her cigarette. "But in answer to your question, yes, I knew my grandpa Charlie. I was twenty when he died. He really loved Malily. And I'm pretty sure she loved him, too. Still . . ."

"What?"

Helen listened as Mardi began to prowl the perimeter of the fence, scattering squirrels and leaves as he approached. "My grandmother has finally decided to share her girlhood scrapbook with me. One of the parts she read to me is when she's seventeen years old and her father is throwing her a come-out ball. She mentions my grandfather being a great dancer and dancing with him. She wrote that her father was wasting his time throwing her a ball to find a husband because she'd already fallen in love."

"With your grandfather."

Helen nodded. "Of course. Although she never said it, that's what I was led to believe from everything else she wrote."

Earlene stood, her feet soft against the pine needles and leaves that lay scattered on the ground, like accessories for the dead.

"Did you ask her to clarify?"

Helen laughed. "In case you hadn't noticed, my grandmother isn't the sort of person who likes being questioned about anything. She charts her course and plows right on through, oblivious to who she might accidentally roll over, and don't ask her to make any apologies or explain herself. She claims that she's survived the Depression, a World War, and the loss of a husband and child, and she's doing just fine, thank you very much. I was just so happy to be asked to share her scrapbook that I didn't really want to say anything."

Helen held up her hand. "Don't get me wrong. I love my grandmother. I've never doubted that she loves me, and I owe her a great deal. She's the one who's made sure I have as normal a life as possible and don't feel sorry for myself. She planted that garden for me and painted my bedroom exactly as I wanted it. But still . . ." She paused, not sure what she wanted to say next.

"But still . . . ?"

Helen thought of the portrait she'd made of Earlene, of a woman with large eyes who always seemed to be searching for something that was just beyond her grasp, like a fistful of wind. Helen had left the back-

339

ground blank, unsure of what setting to place Earlene in. But from what she already knew about Earlene, she wouldn't place her inside at a desk poring over somebody else's family tree. The Earlene she wanted to know was the girl who'd been brave enough to risk whatever it was that had caused the scars on her knees. The type of girl Helen had once imagined herself to be.

She took a deep breath, deciding to share confidences, hoping Earlene would give some of herself away, too. "I don't feel as if I really know her. There's a huge part of her life I know nothing about. And I'm pretty sure it was intentional. Until now." Helen smashed the end of her cigarette into the stone base, then left the stub on the ledge. "She received news a few months ago that an old friend had died. Even though she hadn't seen this friend in a very long time, it seemed to make her face her own mortality. Like she could suddenly count the hours she had left. And those she hadn't used."

Earlene took a few deliberate breaths. "Your grandmother's friend — that would be Annabelle, right? Is she in your grandmother's scrapbook?"

Helen nodded. "Yes. Quite a bit."

Earlene was silent for a moment. "I'd like to see her scrapbook. Do you think she'd let me?"

Helen shook her head. "No, she wouldn't. My grandmother has only chosen to share it with my mother and Susan and now me. I think there's something in her past that conflicts with her idea of who she believes herself to be — the persona she's built around herself. She's already failed twice in her attempt to receive validation. And I think the only reason why she's chosen me now is because she knows her time is short and there's no one else."

Earlene sat back down on the ledge. Softly, she said, "That's not true." After a brief pause, she added, "Annabelle was my grandmother."

Ah. "Well, that certainly explains a lot."

"What do you mean?"

"Odella and I found scrapbook pages and a necklace in a box on your kitchen table along with pictures of Malily. We figured there had to be a connection."

Earlene jerked herself up to a standing position, blocking the sun that filtered through the pine trees on Helen's face. "You were snooping?"

"Only a little. They were left out in plain view. But apparently I'm not the only one with a little secret, Earlene. And that's not your real name, is it?"

341

Earlene let out a puff of air that could have been a laugh or just relief. "Actually, it is. But I've always gone by my nickname, Piper. But my last name is Mills."

"It suits you better. And I recognize the name, of course. You're pretty famous in equestrian circles."

"Yes, well, not anymore." There was a short pause. "As good as it feels to have finally confessed to someone, I know how stupid I must appear to you right now. My only defense is that I needed to talk to your grandmother to find out about mine. And when I sent letters here, your brother answered that she was too ill and didn't remember my grandmother at all. And I knew that wasn't true."

Helen tried to find the personal affront and anger she probably should be feeling at being deceived. Instead she had the oddest compulsion to clap Piper on the back for her creativity, and felt vindication that she'd known all along that there was more to Earlene Smith than family trees and dusty libraries. "So you decided to come here under false pretenses to find out what you could."

"That sounds awful, I know, but I didn't do it to deceive. I did it because I didn't stop long enough to think of another way."

Mardi brought the stick back but Helen patted him on the head, letting him know the game was over. She remembered how she'd felt sitting in her grandmother's room while Malily read from her scrapbook — of the way her heart ached at the bridge of words that connected her grandmother's life with her own. "Why is digging up your grandmother's past so important to you now?"

Piper's voice was muffled, and Helen pictured her with her hands over her face, like a person bent in prayer. "My grandmother and I never had a close relationship. She seemed content to hide in her garden while I seemed hell-bent on seeing how close I could come to killing myself on the back of a horse. It was different when I was small, when I first went to live with my grandparents. She taught me about her garden, how to make things grow. But then I discovered horses and I couldn't reconcile myself to the fact that my grandmother was content to remain in the background, never once tempted to risk the heat to touch the sun, as my trainer used to tell me. It seemed her life was pointless and I wanted nothing to do with her."

Helen could hear the wedge in Piper's throat, the dam that was holding back the tears long enough so she could make her case. Gently, Helen asked, "So what changed?"

"After both of my grandparents died, I discovered a box my grandfather had asked me to help him bury years ago when my grandmother was put in a nursing home for Alzheimer's. It contained portions of a scrapbook, a necklace with a lot of charms dangling from it and . . . and a newspaper clipping. About the discovery of a black infant boy in the Savannah River."

A sticky breeze stirred the leaves on the ground, sending a chill down Helen's spine. "Any idea who the child was, or why the article would be with your grandmother's things?"

"None. And there's more. I discovered a secret room in the attic of my grandparents' Savannah house. In it was a baby's bassinet with a blue hand-knit blanket."

Again, Helen felt a chill, the kind that Malily used to tell her meant somebody was walking over her grave. "And all of that proved to you that your grandmother had a life before you met her — maybe even a bigger life than your own. And that you wasted all of those hours while she was in your life."

"Yes. It made me angry — at myself. Since my accident, I'd been living exactly as I thought my grandmother had — wandering around that big house, waiting for something to happen to me. I think that's why I chose such a drastic plan. It was almost refreshing to discover that the competitive rider in me hadn't completely disappeared. The risk taker was still there and I was so relieved I didn't stop to think how stupid the idea was. Or of the long-range implications."

"Like what would happen when we found out you'd lied to us — as you undoubtedly were aware would happen." When Piper didn't respond, Helen continued. "So how did you end up here?"

"After my grandfather died, his lawyer brought me unopened letters that my grandmother had written to Lillian. They were all returned, unopened. In it, she asked for Lillian's forgiveness for something she'd done."

Helen rubbed her hands over her arms, feeling cold despite the afternoon heat. "And you have no idea what."

"No. And I'm not completely convinced that I want to know. I think that's why I haven't finished going through her scrapbook. I'm not sure I'm not going to wish I'd never found it. Like I'm about to open Pandora's box."

Helen stiffened. *Pandora's box.* "That's

what my mother said when she caught Tucker and me digging up graves. Strange, isn't it?"

"Yes, it is."

Helen felt Piper watching her, measuring her words like sifting flour for a cake. "What are you going to do now? Are you going to tell your grandmother? And Tucker?"

Helen stood, her hand resting on the obelisk. "It's not for me to tell them. If you're going to salvage any of this, and solicit Malily's help, you're going to need to tell her — and soon. She's very bright and it wouldn't surprise me if she's close to figuring it out on her own. As for Tucker." Helen shook her head. "He's going to be pretty pissed. But I think he'll come around — as soon as he realizes who he's got teaching his daughters how to ride.

"But I would like to see your grandmother's scrapbook. And that newspaper article. But not before you've resolved everything and managed to talk Malily into letting you stay. Then we can compare notes."

She felt Piper's hand on her arm. "Thank you. You've been a lot more understanding than I deserve. I'll tell them — just as soon as I can figure out the best way to do it."

"Don't wait too long. That'll only make it worse."

"I won't. Promise." Piper squeezed Helen's hand gently. "I've got the girls' riding lesson now. Can I walk you back to the house?"

"No, but thanks. I'm almost done here and Tucker's waiting for me to call him so he can come get me."

"Great. Then I'll see you at supper again. Your grandmother invited me."

Helen raised an eyebrow. "Again? It's surprising. She usually doesn't take to strangers. Unless you don't feel like a stranger to her."

"I almost think it would be easier if she came right out and said something, but don't worry. I won't wait for it."

They said their good-byes, and as soon as Piper's footsteps disappeared into the woods, Helen returned to her canvas, finally knowing what she needed to finish it. She picked up her brush and counted over to where she knew red was on her palette and began to paint. She didn't once consider painting Piper in an equestrian setting, with horses and a stable or simply green pasture. Instead she filled the background with flowers from Malily's garden, in a tribute to all

of those who could see but insisted on being blind.

CHAPTER 15

I'm dreaming the same dream again, everything even more vivid than before. This time
I hear the announcement of my name and
event, but the voice is long and slow, as if
speaking underwater. Fitz shifts his feet, a
tremble of anticipation lifting his head.
Silently, I visualize the course I was allowed
to walk earlier, feeling Fitz move beneath
me as if he can see it, too. The air hums
around us with hope and possibilities and I
smile to myself in the dream, feeling Fitz's
power and confidence flowing into me.

But then my view shifts and I'm standing
next to my grandmother behind the spectator ropes, and everyone else seems to fade
away around us as I turn to her. She isn't
looking at me but down at her hands. I follow her gaze and recognize the scrapbook,
but it's still intact, without torn or missing
pages, and spread open as if she's in the
middle of looking at it.

I lean over and whisper in her ear, "I didn't know that you loved horses. Or that you wanted to be a doctor. You never told me."

She looks up at me and I see that her eyes are brown like mine, and it makes me want to cry because I hadn't remembered that either. She smiles at me with the same smile she used after I'd dug up the back corner of her garden when I was seven and planted moonflower seeds because she'd told me that they were her favorites. "You never asked," she says, her mouth not moving. I feel her cold hand on my arm; then she slowly leans forward and I shiver, frozen in place and unable to pull back. Her breath is icy on my cheek as she whispers, "But I'm glad you're asking now." And then she presses something into the palm of my hand, the gold wings of the angel pricking my skin and I know what it is before I look down and see my lost angel charm.

And then I'm back on Fitz and we're approaching the flower basket, but this time I'm pulling him up, trying to get him to go around the enormous basket, because I know what is going to happen. But I'm crying because I can't stop him from taking that jump any more than I can bring my grandmother back to life and ask for a second chance.

"Earlene? Earlene, are you okay?" A warm hand touched my bare arm.

I struck out, disoriented, still feeling the weight of disappointment pinning me to the dusty ground. And for some reason I thought George Baker was there because he was calling me by that ridiculous name. "Don't call me that — it's not my name!" I opened my eyes, surprised to find myself leaning against the outside of the garden wall at Asphodel Meadows, shaded by the old limbs of the magnolia, and facing the stables and the riding ring.

"Excuse me?"

I blinked and looked up into a pair of dark green eyes that looked vaguely familiar. I quickly slid up the wall to a standing position, light-headed from the sudden movement. Holding on to the wall with one hand, I shook my head to clear it. "God, sorry — I must have been dreaming."

Tucker nodded slowly. "Do you need to sit down again? You're looking a little unsteady."

Without answering, I let myself slide back down the wall, my legs stretched out in front of me. "I was just sitting here in the shade, resting for a moment while I waited for the girls. I guess I fell asleep."

He sat down on the grass beside me, his long legs crossed at the ankles. "I was looking for you to tell you that the girls are going to be a little late. We were swimming in the pond and lost track of the time."

I noticed his hair was still dry, and I looked away trying to hide my disappointment, the shadow of my dream still hanging over me. "One of these days you're going to have to step off the sidelines and into their lives, you know."

Glancing up at the magnolia leaves, he grimaced. "So what makes you such the expert on little girls?"

"Because I used to be one. Barbies, bows, horses, and more horses."

His smile was genuine, his face relaxed. "Sounds like my girls — although Lucy in particular. Sara loves to ride, but she loves the horse primarily. For Lucy, she loves the horse, but it's the challenge of communicating with the horse that she really loves. She says she's ready for trot poles."

I sat up straighter. "She's only been riding a month, Tucker. I agree that she's good and confident, but we shouldn't push her."

"I'm not pushing her. I think she's ready and she wants to try. I've already made a few phone calls to find a nice, gentle mare for her. Give her a taste of what it's like to

352

ride a real horse."

"But what about Sara? How will she feel if Lucy gets the new horse and she still has her pony?"

"Sara's told me that she never wants another horse, no matter how big she gets. She loves Oreo."

I bit my lip, knowing that was exactly what Sara would have said. "Still, I think it's too early for Lucy."

Tucker leaned toward me, his eyes searching. "Don't you remember what it's like? That one passion that overshadows everything else in your life? The kind that makes you want to jump out of bed in the morning. Has it been so long that you don't remember?"

I felt my chest rise and fall, as if someone else had blown air into me, forcing me to breathe. *Yes,* I wanted to shout. *Yes, I remember.* Instead, I said, "We all have limitations. Her age and size are two of them. Her inexperience is a third. She shouldn't be pushed to do more than she's capable of."

"Were you pushed too hard, Earlene? Is that how you hurt yourself and made you never want to ride again? Is that why you're so adamant that I keep Lucy on a pony?"

I turned to him with anger, not registering that I saw no belligerence in his eyes, only a need to understand. "I was pushed — but only because I wanted to be. Because I wanted to be the best there was, and the only way to do that was to get pushed hard enough until I learned how to push myself."

"And did that make you the best?"

I was shaking, remembering it all. I could taste the sweat and the anticipation of victory. But I couldn't tell him the truth. Not yet. "I wanted to be. I tried to be. In the house I grew up in, in Savannah, my uncle left an entire wall blank so that he'd have a place to hang my Olympic gold medals when I won them." I flushed at the memory, remembering my grandfather's look of pride and the way my grandmother had looked away, then left the room. I'd heard the back door close shortly after that, and I'd known she'd retreated to her garden.

"You need to get back on a horse again, Earlene. You're not afraid of horses, I see that now. And you and Captain Wentworth have a mutual fan club. He's definitely ready to ride again, but needs an experienced rider. I think he's just been waiting for you."

I struggled with warring emotions, remembering what Helen had told me, about how Tucker had once dug up a grave looking for pirate treasure, and I thought I saw a glimmer of that boy now. He was a doctor by profession, in search of healing others, yet unable or unwilling to see that his own wounds remained unbandaged.

I shook my head, not even sure if I understood my reluctance enough to explain it to someone else. Or maybe I was just too ashamed of the real reason I suspected I couldn't do it. I felt my anger at myself and quickly turned it on him. "Stop pressuring me. I'm in a lot of pain with my back and my knee, which precludes my riding. I have pins holding my knee and leg together, if that draws a clearer picture for you."

He didn't look away, and his eyes reminded me of Helen's and her ability to see behind the words, and I knew I hadn't fooled him at all. "I'm a doctor. I know about these things. I also know that there are exercises you can do to strengthen muscles to lessen the pain and increase your flexibility. Emily can probably help you, if you just ask."

I stood, wondering if there was a mass conspiracy going on. "I've heard, thank you. I tried exercises in the beginning and they didn't help. But if it will get everybody off of my back, then I will, okay? But I'm never getting back on a horse. Not ever, so you can stop asking."

He stood, too, and smiled a brilliant smile, surprising me. "We'll see. In the meantime, I'll tell Lucy that she'll have to wait to ride Captain Wentworth until after you've broken him in. That was her idea, by the way, and not mine."

The image of Lucy negotiating to ride Captain Wentworth made me want to laugh, but I managed an inelegant snort instead.

"My Lucy has a sense of humor."

My Lucy. I wondered if he was aware he'd said that. "She comes by it honestly at least," I said.

"What do you mean?"

"Your name's William Tecumseh Gibbons. Obviously, somebody in your family would have to have a sense of humor to name you after the Yankee general most Savannah residents still refer to as Satan. It's sort of like naming the British heir apparent 'Napoleon' or something."

He pulled out a few tall blades of grass and pressed them between his fingers. "My mother named me. I don't know if it was because she had a sense of humor or because she wanted to piss off my grandmother. Not that it mattered. My grandmother called me Tucker the first time she saw me and that's what it's been ever since."

He turned his gaze to me again. "My wife

— Susan — called me William. She thought that using a nickname was a sort of deception. As if it gave me license to pretend to be someone else."

I tasted the roof of my mouth, my tongue suddenly too thick to speak. I wanted to tell him then who I was, but I thought about how I'd told him about my Olympic dreams and how he hadn't laughed, and how he'd stayed with his daughters the night under the oaks when I'd told him he should be with them. I liked William Tecumseh Gibbons, and I liked that his nickname was Tucker and I knew that whatever relationship we'd forged over the last month would be over the minute he learned that I was Piper Mills and that I'd been lying to him from the first moment we met.

I knew I should probably steer the conversation in another direction, but I couldn't help myself. I couldn't forget the grave that rested in unconsecrated ground outside of the family cemetery, or not be curious about the mother who'd abandoned Lucy and Sara. "How did you introduce yourself to her when you first met?"

He didn't answer right away. "I didn't, actually. She was a . . . patient of my medical school mentor, a psychiatrist. He's actually my partner now. But I met her in his office."

I looked at him in surprise. "She was his patient?"

"I didn't know at the time — patient confidentiality and all that — but she was seeing him for several things, mostly severe depression and a substance-abuse problem she'd struggled with since adolescence. She'd been in and out of rehab since she was a teenager, trying to cope with the fallout from a dysfunctional childhood. She was responding well to therapy, so when I met her, I didn't . . ." He closed his mouth, seeming to struggle between loyalty and honesty. "I didn't realize how emotionally unstable she was until we got engaged during my second year of medical school."

"And you didn't break it off?"

He looked away. "She found out she was pregnant and wanted the baby. I couldn't let her have the baby on her own. It was my child, too. And at least if I were with her, I could keep her healthy if not for her sake, then for the baby's."

"Lucy?"

He nodded.

I was silent for a moment. "How did she handle motherhood?"

"After Lucy was born, she went back on

her antidepressants. She seemed to be herself again, and I thought we could still make a go out of our marriage now that we were parents."

"But that didn't happen."

Tucker shook his head. "Susan became more and more dependent on me, almost as if I were a substitute for her drugs. And if I didn't give her the attention she needed, she'd stay in her room for days until I could find a way to get her to forgive me." He flattened his hands against the garden wall, studying his callused fingers. "I knew she had serious issues dating back to her childhood. The details she gave me were sketchy, but enough for me to agree with her choice to cut off all contact with her family. But there were demons she fought every day. Shortly after Lucy was born, Susan started stealing prescription drugs from my medical office. We didn't notice at first because she was just taking samples, but we eventually caught on and I knew immediately who it was. She went to rehab — again — and it seemed to help."

His eyes held the haunted look I remembered from the first time I'd seen him, and I wanted to look away. "So things got better then?"

"For a while. But then she got pregnant

with Sara. I shouldn't have allowed that to happen. . . ." He shrugged. "And it was different this time after Sara. Her old antidepressants weren't working and it took us a while to find one that did. When Sara was three, I took a leave of absence from my practice and moved us to Asphodel in the hopes that a change of scenery would help, and to get her away from her drug sources. She was too busy self-medicating for us to figure out something that might help, and taking her away was pretty much a last resort."

He smoothed the dark hair from his forehead with both hands. "Then I thought we had the answer to all of our prayers when Susan got on this genealogy kick and seemed to have found a purpose for her life. Maybe she was pretending that the lives she was discovering were her own, in some warped way of erasing her own past. I didn't bother to analyze it. She was happy and excited for the first time since we got married. And then it sort of . . . fell apart about a year and a half ago."

"What happened?" I asked, watching as he stooped to pick up another handful of grass before disintegrating the blades between his fingers.

"I'm not really sure. She'd been after Malily to give her access to all of her papers. Malily told her that some things were meant to remain private, but that didn't stop Susan. She apparently went snooping in Malily's room when my grandmother was out of town at a horse event, and found something. I believe Malily discovered it was missing and got it back because I never found out what it was. But it was enough to send Susan into a tailspin."

"Did you ever ask Malily what it was?"

"Yes, and she told me it was just a letter she'd written to a friend but never sent. But that with Susan's mind being the way it was, she read things into it. Malily thought that Susan had somehow become so absorbed in my grandmother's story that she was sort of reliving it — the good and the bad. Maybe there were parts that reminded Susan of her own childhood." He dropped the shredded grass back to the ground. "I guess I'll never know for sure. She drowned herself a week later. She simply . . . walked into the river. I've never been able to figure that one out. We had the pond here, after all. But she chose the river."

A letter to a friend. The words hung in the air between us, and I had to keep myself from asking more.

He looked at me, as if just now realizing I

was there. "I'm sorry. I don't know why I'm telling you all this."

I thought for a moment, realizing how since my accident even strangers on park benches or in grocery store lines seemed to want to confide in me. I almost smiled, the reason why so clear to me now. "Don't worry. It happens a lot. I think it's because people see that I'm damaged, so they think I'll understand their problems more than their spouses or friends. Like I have an inside track to figuring out problems because mine are undoubtedly greater than theirs."

He regarded me and I could see him struggling with the correct response. "It doesn't have to be that way, you know. Maybe you're using your injury as an excuse. As long as your knee is stiff and painful, you have a reason for not trying. You don't have to jump again, Earlene. Nobody's asking you to. But wouldn't it be nice to ride again — just for fun?"

I almost told him then that I was Piper Mills and that it had never occurred to me to just simply ride for fun. I was a competitor. I wasn't a mountain climber who climbed a mountain just because it was there. I rode horses because I was good at it, because at one time I'd had a shot at being the best at it. I rode because there was something inside of me that wanted to be something other than ordinary.

Instead, I looked up at the copper and green magnolia leaves, how still they were as they waited for the next breeze to move them. "And because you're a doctor you think it's your job to heal everyone. But not everyone needs or wants healing, you know."

I felt him watching me and I wanted to look into his marsh green eyes because I could always see a pain there that matched my own, but I didn't. Because every time I did look at him I felt something else, too, something I wasn't ready to explore. Two damaged people did not make a whole.

"Everyone needs healing," he said softly.

Without waiting for me to respond, he said, "Before I forget, I think I found the necklace you were looking for." He reached into his pocket and pulled out my angel charm, the chain dangling from his hand like an unanswered question. "It's odd, because Malily has one identical to it — so much so that I would have thought it was hers if I hadn't seen her wearing it right before I found this on the garden path."

The words sprang to my lips before I could pull them back. "I think angel charms were like mood rings to our grandmothers'

generation. A lot of women their age probably had one."

"With the same inscription?" He pulled
his eyebrows together in question.

"Yeah. Latin must have been the 'in' thing
back then."

"Must have been," he said, smiling, making me feel worse. "I hope you don't mind,
but I fixed the chain."

"Thank you," I managed, and before I
could say anything else, he'd placed the
necklace around my neck, fastening the
chain while I held up my hair. Our eyes met,
and I knew that if I didn't speak up now,
I'd have no defense later when the truth
inevitably found its way to the surface.

"I need to tell you something. . . ."

My words were cut short by the appearance of Lucy, who came running around
the corner of the garden wall. She was
dressed and ready for her riding lesson,
holding the fluorescent purple crop I'd
purchased for her on a whim at a local tack
shop. "Where's Sara? We're supposed to
have our lesson now, but she's not in her
room and she's not at the ring, either. And
her riding clothes are still on her bed. I
don't want us to be late because then my
lesson will be shorter."

"Where did you see her last?" Tucker

asked, his voice firm but gentle.

"In the kitchen with Odella. Odella was making us pimento cheese sandwiches because that's Sara's favorite. And then we were supposed to go upstairs to get changed out of our swimsuits. I left first because Sara's a slowpoke and hadn't finished hers yet."

"Did you look in the kitchen?"

Lucy shook her head. "No, because she was supposed to be done."

As if an afterthought, Tucker gently tugged on one of her braided and bowed pigtails, causing Lucy to lean toward him. "She's probably still in there, listening to some long-winded story of Odella's. I'll go find her and hurry her up. Meanwhile, you and Miss Earlene can get started with your lesson."

I watched as he walked away, swallowing my confession until I could find him alone again. I turned to Lucy. "We're going to work on a couple of new things while we're waiting for Sara. I'm going to teach you something today called 'two-point' — do you know what that is?"

Lucy nodded eagerly. "It's to learn how to jump, isn't it?"

"Not necessarily," I said cautiously. "It will strengthen your quads — those are your thigh muscles — and teach you proper positioning, which you need for all riding, including jumping."

"Oh." She sounded disappointed. "And then how much longer before I'm jumping?" Her dark brown eyes looked up at me eagerly. "I think Daddy wants me to be a really good jumper."

I stopped walking and squatted in front of her. "Lucy, if you want to be a good jumper, you have to want to do it — nobody else. It's always great to have somebody you love supporting you in the sidelines. But when it's just you, your horse, and a five-foot jump, there's no room for anybody else, okay?"

Her eyes darkened, her face serious. "I want to be the best. It's been my dream since I was really small. Mama told me that dreams were just food for heartache, but I didn't believe her. I didn't say so, though. She didn't take very well to anybody disagreeing with her, but I let her think that she was right. And I never stopped dreaming."

I nodded, knowing what it must have taken to tell me that one disloyalty. "I think it's all right to have dreams. As long as you're willing to put the hard work into making those dreams happen."

"I'm ready to jump, Miss Earlene. I really am. I can taste it so bad, it hurts."

I hid my smile and patted her helmeted head. "You're not ready, Lucy. But we'll get you there. Promise."

We'd taken a few more steps toward the ring before Lucy stopped suddenly. "Miss Earlene? Sara left her favorite doll on her raft in the pond. She remembered when we were eating lunch. I told her she could get it after our riding lesson. Do you think she went back to the pond instead? I hope not because she can't swim. She always has to wear her floaties and she doesn't know how to put them on herself."

The summer air seemed to go suddenly still; even the cicadas stopped their eternal whirring. *The pond.* I'd only walked by it, not interested in going swimming if only because a bathing suit gave no camouflage for my scars. But when I thought of Sara, and her beloved doll, I knew she'd gone to retrieve it.

I started to run, adrenaline making me oblivious to the pain in my knee. "Lucy — go find your father and tell him to go to the pond. Now."

I didn't stop to see if she followed my instructions, I simply ran harder in the direction of the pond, cold sweat beading on my forehead. I reached the far side of the water, opposite the decking that had been installed on the edge, connected to a jumping platform, where brightly colored floating toys bobbed in the dark green water. "Sara!" I shouted, my panic making me jerk my gaze from one end of the pond to the other without focus.

"Sara!" I shouted again, forcing myself to calm down so I could pay attention to what I was seeing. A flash of hot pink caught my eye on the jumping platform. I might have seen it at first and dismissed it as another water toy, but this time the tiny white hearts on her bathing suit caught my gaze and I began running again, skirting the side of the pond.

Sara was stretched out as far as she could go, reaching for her doll floating on her raft just beyond her reach. "Sara, don't — I'll get it."

Sara looked back at me and smiled, then returned to her mission of saving her doll. I saw her toes flex, absently thinking how her toenails matched the color of her bathing suit right as her supporting arm gave way.

I shouted her name one more time before she tumbled forward into the pond, the small splash seeming much louder in my ears than it should have. I sprinted to the end of the platform but held myself back. Maybe I'd finally learned my lesson about looking before I leapt, or maybe I knew the stakes were so much higher this time. Either way, I stopped to stare at where I'd seen Sara go into the water, peering into the murkiness, where I saw only a hint of disappearing pink. Keeping my eye on that point, I held my breath and stepped into the water next to where I thought she would be.

I opened my eyes beneath the water, the sun illuminating the three feet above my head as my feet touched the bottom. I swirled around looking for Sara, stirring the lazy sediment and stilling my panic. I knew she was near me; I could hear frantic kicking. All I needed to do was hold my breath and still my panic and the voice inside of me that was telling me I couldn't do it.

I thought of Helen and how she could hear things even before Mardi and I closed my eyes, focusing on what I could hear. At first, I thought it was my own heartbeat, the soft fluttering swish of blood. I closed my eyes tighter and listened for it again, the sound coming from behind me. My chest began to burn, reminding me that I hadn't taken a big enough gulp of air before I'd jumped in. But I was so close; I could feel her now, her thrashing slowing. I blew air out of my mouth, lessening the burn for a second, then twisted toward Sara. I reached out into the darkness, feeling the cool wash of water on my face, teasing me with a memory.

My fingers closed on a soft Lycra ruffle and I tightened my grasp, pulling Sara toward me. With her cradled in my arms, I opened my eyes and watched the sun push the darkness away from us as I lifted off the silted floor, moving us toward the murky light. We burst through to the surface with a loud gasp of air.

Tucker and Lucy were just reaching the platform, Odella close behind them, running so fast that I thought for a moment they couldn't stop before they reached the water. Tucker knelt on the edge and reached for Sara as my fingers grabbed hold of the platform to keep me from slipping back into the water. She was coughing and spluttering and clinging to her father as he held her tight and kissed her temple before handing her to Odella, who wrapped her in a large pink towel.

Then Tucker leaned forward and lifted me up, too, as if I weighed no more than Sara, and I felt myself enveloped in his arms, too, exhausted yet exhilarated, remembering the teasing memory I'd had in the sanctuary of the still water: the blind reaching for Sara and the confidence of knowing I had just the one chance gave me the same feeling I got from landing the perfect jump.

I rested my head on Tucker's shoulder as we both looked at Sara, clutching tightly to the doll that been the instrument of near disaster, and I knew with a sudden clarity that I'd just done something extraordinary.

CHAPTER 16

Lillian walked down the hallway to the girls' bedroom as fast as her arthritic joints would take her, her cane tapping impatiently on the carpet runner. She threw open the door and went in, blinking at the bright sunlight streaming in from the windows and illuminating the colorful palette on the walls and furnishings.

Sara sat propped up in her bed on large, fluffy pillows with her father in a chair on one side and Earlene on the other. At Tucker's insistence they'd taken Sara to the emergency room to make sure she hadn't inhaled any water. Satisfied with her clean bill of health, he'd brought her home and put her to bed to rest.

Now, judging from the rosy circles on Sara's cheeks and the piles of her favorite dolls and stuffed animals crowded around her in the bed, she seemed no worse for the wear. In fact, if Lillian had to guess, she was enjoying the attention. Even the sodden doll clutched in the crook of Sara's arm seemed to have a smug look about her, as if finally they were getting their turn in the spotlight.

Tucker stood and offered her his chair, which she thankfully accepted. After leaning her cane against the bed, she took Sara's small hand in hers and had to fight back tears. She knew what burying a child was like, knew already what needed to be done to survive it. But Tucker was still slipping on the ice of his first great loss, and she closed her eyes in a prayer of thanks that not only had Sara been saved, but so had her father.

"Don't cry, Malily. Me and Samantha are fine."

Lillian looked up and smiled, noticing that Sara and her doll Samantha wore matching nightgowns. She squeezed the small hand. "Yes, I know. But you have to promise me that you'll never go near the pond again without an adult, and never without your floaties. And maybe Samantha should stay inside the next time you decide it's time for a swim."

Sara's blue eyes widened, working out something in her head. "Do you think that's what happened to Mama? That maybe she fell into the river by accident and nobody was there to pull her out?"

Lillian's gaze rose to meet Tucker's, and she was surprised to see calmness where she'd expected the ghost of old grief. Maybe with Sara's accident he had finally begun to see that life continued after a fall, and that the hands that reached to pull you out didn't have to be your own.

Tucker pushed Sara's blond hair from her forehead. "Maybe. But what matters is that Earlene was there and that you're safe now. Just promise me that you'll never, ever go near the water again without an adult with you."

Sara rolled her eyes in such a perfect imitation of Lucy that Lillian almost laughed. "Like I would, Daddy. It's not like I had any fun or anything. And now Samantha's hair is all stiff."

Earlene leaned forward to take the doll to examine the hair closer. "We could try to shampoo it. Or we could call the manufacturer and see what they suggest."

Sara smiled brightly and reached out her arms for her doll. Earlene stood to tuck the doll back into the crook of Sara's arm and pull the sheets up. As she leaned over Sara to kiss her forehead, the chain around her neck slid out of the collar of her blouse, and

Lillian stopped breathing. The wings of the gold angel charm twirled, teasing Lillian with each twinkle of light it reflected from the window. Her hand reached for her own angel charm, and as her gnarled fingers grasped it, she caught Earlene's gaze and held it.

Slowly, Earlene sat down, her own hand tucking the charm back out of sight, but it was too late. Lillian had seen it, and along with it saw her own past and the sudden realization that seven decades could be reduced to the blink of an eye, or the reflection of sunlight on the wings of a gold angel.

"Where did you get that?" Lillian asked, her voice sounding horrifyingly normal.

Earlene lifted her chin in a way that was so reminiscent of Annabelle in a stubborn mood that Lillian wanted to laugh at her own stupidity. It had been there the whole time — the familiarity, the unexplained connection she'd felt. The moonflowers. Maybe Lillian had known all along, but like a child opening the door to a darkened closet, she'd been afraid to look inside, not really wanting to know. Because once she saw what was on the other side of the door, she knew what would have to happen next, and she wasn't at all sure that she was ready.

"My grandmother left it for me when she

died." Earlene's jaw didn't waver, but remained set in the endearingly familiar way.

"Perfer et obdura; dolor hic tibi proderit olim," Lillian said slowly, her mouth rusty on the old words. "Do you know what it means?" She still held on to a thread of doubt that maybe she was wrong, that maybe this girl wasn't who Lillian thought she was.

Earlene's gaze never shifted as she answered. " 'Be patient and strong; someday this pain will be useful to you.' It's Ovid."

Tucker looked from Lillian to Earlene and then back again. "Earlene said that it was a fad when you were younger — that lots of girls had them. Right?"

Lillian found herself staring out the window toward the alley of old trees, the stiff limbs reluctantly shifting in the wind, going where they didn't want to go. She closed her eyes, felt the ache in her fingers, and knew what it was like. After a deep breath, she said, "There are only three that I know of. And they all say the same thing because they were all engraved at the same time." She looked back at Earlene, who was studiously avoiding Tucker's eyes. "Which one is yours?"

Lillian saw the old familiar jut of the chin again. "Annabelle's. Annabelle O'Hare Mercer was my maternal grandmother."

Lillian nodded, feeling surprisingly calm as if none of this was news to her. "And your real name is . . ." She found herself unable to say it, the unknown darkness behind the door seeping towards her.

"Piper Mercer Mills." Her chin wobbled just a little as she said her name, the little movement revealing how hard it had been for her.

This time, Lillian did laugh — great gasping laughs of relief, and of the inevitability of everything. Since receiving Piper's first letter, she'd known this would happen, regardless of her efforts to the contrary. If she believed in such a thing as karma, she would have agreed that this was it, that all past sins would come back to you regardless of how many hours spanned the commission of the sin and the reckoning. And she laughed with joy, as if having this girl in front of her was like having Annabelle back, and knowing that to find the truth, Annabelle would have done exactly what her granddaughter had done.

Tucker gently disengaged himself from the head of the bed, where the now sleeping Sara had been resting against his chest, and stood. Color flooded his face, and even under the circumstances, Lillian found any emotion besides sorrow there a welcome sight.

"Piper Mills? You're Piper Mills?" His voice was hard, and Lillian wasn't sure if he was angrier at Piper for her deception, or at himself for his gullibility.

Piper stood, too, and faced Tucker. She reached a hand up to touch his arm, then dropped it when he flinched. "I'm sorry. I never meant to deceive anyone."

Tucker's expression was mocking. "Really? Then what exactly were you trying to accomplish?"

For a moment, Piper looked as if she were unsure of the right answer. "I needed to know about my grandmother. I wrote to Lillian three times — the first two letters were ignored and the third was replied to by you stating that your grandmother was too sickly to meet with me and that she didn't know who my grandmother was." She lifted her chin a notch. "And I knew both statements were untrue."

"So you figured you'd just come here, lie about who you are, and try to get what you wanted."

Piper clasped her hands together in front of her. "At the time, I couldn't think of another way to gain access to your grandmother." She shot an apologetic glance at Lillian.

"You couldn't or you didn't bother to find another way?" He shook his head and started to say something else, but his gaze fell on Sara, who had fallen asleep. Quietly he said, "I can't. . . . I have to go." Without looking at anyone else, he touched Sara gently on the forehead, then left the room, passing Helen in the doorway.

"Piper?" she asked as she stepped into the room.

"I'm here with your grandmother and Sara." Piper moved toward Helen, took hold of her arm, and brought her back to her vacated seat.

Before sitting, Helen grabbed Piper by the shoulders. "You told them?"

"Not exactly. Lillian saw my necklace."

Helen fell inelegantly into her chair. "Oh, wonderful. I told you that you needed to tell them before they found out."

"You knew about this?" Lillian tried to show her indignation but she wasn't all that surprised to find out that Helen already knew Piper's secret. She'd always seen things more clearly than anybody else.

"It doesn't really matter, Malily. You both weren't completely truthful, were you? She just wants to ask you about her grand-

mother, all right? And I know that you know who Annabelle O'Hare was because she's all over your scrapbook — at least the parts you've shared with me." She leaned toward Lillian. "This whole situation could have been avoided if you'd simply told her yes when she first asked. Annabelle is gone — what harm could it do?"

Lillian thought back to the time when she was eight years old and she'd fallen off her horse and landed on her back, knocking all the air from her lungs. As she'd gasped for air she'd wondered if it were possible to drown on dry land, and found herself wondering the same thing now. A calmness descended on her, making her think of drowning again, and of Susan, and she wondered if this was how Susan had felt after she'd stepped into the cool waters of the Savannah River.

Lillian had the absurd notion to laugh again, as if it were the only normal response to the vagaries of life — as if Sara's brush with death had been a necessary reminder of how fleeting this life was, and how it could disappear in the same amount of time a moonflower bloom took to close in the bright light of day.

Schooling her face to hide any emotion, as she'd been taught, Lillian said, "If it's any consolation, I recently told Tucker that I'd changed my mind, that I wanted him to contact Piper. He said that his phone calls to the home number she'd given us went unanswered. He was going to write a letter. I suppose it's unnecessary now." She paused to let her words sink in. "I'm not really sure why I changed my mind, only that Annabelle and I used to be friends. I suppose I was curious." She focused her attention back on Sara. "Not that I think it matters now. I doubt Tucker will want her to stay."

She fought to control her expression, feeling elated and disappointed at the same time. Her thoughts warred between wanting to free herself from the weight of her memories, and clinging to the Lillian Harrington-Ross she had created, the woman who claimed no regrets.

Feeling much older than her ninety years, Lillian leaned over and kissed Sara's soft cheek. Then she stood and straightened her skirt. "This has been an overtaxing afternoon and I need to go lie down for a bit before supper. I don't know if we'll speak again, Piper, so I'll tell you good-bye now."

Piper just stared at her. "But you didn't ask . . . why."

Lillian raised an eyebrow, an expression that had once made people back down. It

381

had never worked on Annabelle and it didn't seem to have any effect on her granddaughter, either. "I assumed because Annabelle had passed, and because you were feeling guilty that you hadn't had the time when she was living to discover her story."

A pink flush flooded Piper's cheeks. "I didn't even know she had a story until I was given the letters that she'd written to you here at Asphodel, asking for forgiveness for something she'd done. But you wouldn't have known that, would you? Because all were marked 'return to sender.' "

Lillian fought the urge to sink back down into her chair but managed to remain standing. "Is that all?"

Piper's eyes narrowed. "No. I also found torn pages from a scrapbook the two of you shared with a girl named Josie, and a necklace you called Lola. You were best friends, the three of you. Then Tucker wrote back telling me that you didn't recall knowing my grandmother, and I knew you were lying. I wanted to know why. And I also . . ." She stopped abruptly, her gaze darting away.

"And also what?" Lillian asked, focusing on standing and breathing evenly.

"Nothing," Piper answered, and their eyes met again in an understanding of secrets kept, the shiny thing seen at the bottom of a well, too dangerous to obtain. "But don't you want to see Annabelle's scrapbook pages again? Was she really so unimportant in your life that none of it matters now?"

She was so tired of thinking, of being the keeper of secrets. Of being the last one left. She took a deep breath and met Piper's gaze. "Annabelle was like a sister to me once. So be careful what you say. And what answers you want to find. You just might discover that you were better off not knowing."

Lillian touched her granddaughter on the shoulder. "Helen, please help me to my room. I'm so exhausted all of a sudden. Then you can call Emily to come sit with Sara so she doesn't wake up alone."

Piper's voice was even, leaving out the desperateness Lillian knew she felt. "But can I stay?"

Her exhaustion allowed Lillian only a small shrug of her shoulders. Feeling like a coward she said, "It's not up to me. Speak with Tucker."

With a final glance at the sleeping Sara, she let Helen take her arm, and the two of them, each helping the other, left Piper standing in the middle of the room looking so much like Annabelle that it made Lillian want to laugh again.

■ ■ ■ ■

I watched them leave, feeling as if I'd been winding a jack-in-the-box, my emotions fluctuating between excitement and trepidation while I waited for the box to spring open. Yet unlike a child's toy, I had no idea what was inside the box, and was still unsure of whether I really wanted to find out.

I still remembered my conversation with Lillian the first time I'd come to supper at Asphodel. She'd said that there was nobody left who knew the truth. And I thought again about the blue baby's sweater and blanket from my grandparents' house, and how Lillian had lied about remembering my grandmother. *The truth.* Maybe it was my fear of the truth that had kept me from blurting out my discovery of the newspaper article about the baby found in the river. Or maybe it was because now that I'd found a surrogate family, I wasn't ready to lose them so soon.

I left the house, aware of the black clouds gathering overhead, and went to the one place I knew Tucker would have gone — the one place I had always been drawn to when I needed a place to think. The stable doors were open on both ends, creating a clear view from one side to the other and I easily spotted Tucker at Captain Wentworth's stall. I knew he could hear me approach, but he didn't turn to acknowledge me.

Captain Wentworth nickered softly in greeting, as if to make up for Tucker's rudeness, and Tucker stepped back as I reached for the horse. "Hey, boy. You being good?" I rubbed his nose and watched his ears twitch like antennae.

Tucker surprised me by speaking first. "It must have been a big joke to you every time I asked you about your riding experience. God, how stupid I must have looked to you."

I faced him. "No, Tucker. That wasn't it at all. I felt ashamed, and I wanted to tell you so many times. I did. But I kept on imagining . . . this. How angry everyone would be with me. And I didn't want to . . . to lose what I've found here. A sense of belonging, and of being needed and respected again. I haven't had that in a very long time."

He ran his hands through his hair. "But Piper Mills, of all people. Grand Slam champion and Olympic hopeful, for crying out loud."

Captain Wentworth nudged Tucker's arm.

"Sorry, boy. I don't have anything for you right now. Maybe later." He stroked the long neck, but his eyes focused on me. "So why did you do it? Why did you lie?"

I turned away, still unsure of my answer. I looked down at my shoes, now covered in shavings and dust from the stable floor, and breathed in deeply the smells of my childhood and the part of my life before the accident. A life that seemed so distant now that it was hard to imagine it had once been mine. I took a deep breath and faced him again, trying to put into words something I was just beginning to realize myself.

"Because I wanted to wake up. Because I heard the world snapping outside my tiny life and I wanted to be a part of it again. Because I missed jumping insurmountable obstacles and cheating disaster every time I landed. And because there's more to life than regret but I'd much rather live the rest of my life regretting that I got caught trying to do something stupid rather than regretting that I never even tried."

Tucker stayed where he was, leaning against Captain Wentworth's stall. Captain Wentworth had lost interest in our conversation and had returned to his feed bucket, as if deliberately giving us privacy. "The stupid thing is that some small part of me does understand," he said quietly.

And I knew that he did; it had been almost two years since Susan's death, yet his former life must have seemed as alien to him as my own was to me. Maybe he'd also heard that snapping, but had been unsure or unable to figure out what to do about it.

"But why now? Your accident was nearly six years ago."

I took a deep breath, trying to decide what parts I should tell him, and what I should leave out. In the end, I told him everything: about my grandparents' deaths; about the hidden room and the knitted blanket and sweater; about the letters my grandmother had written to his, asking for forgiveness, that had been returned unopened; and about the torn scrapbook pages and the necklace. And then he moved forward and touched my arm, showing me that he might still be angry and wasn't sure he'd be able to forgive me, but that he understood with the empathy of someone who'd been stumbling in the dark and would reach for the first glimmer of light regardless of its source.

He drew his head back, his eyes never leaving my face. "There's something else though, isn't there? Something you're not telling me."

I looked at him in surprise. "Why would

you say that?"

He raised an eyebrow that reminded me so much of Lillian that I almost smiled. "Because it would take more than just an interest in your grandmother's story to entice the Piper Mills I've read about. Impossibly high jumps, sure, but not a cross rail. I'm right, aren't I?"

I thought of denying it, and not just because I'd withheld the same knowledge from Lillian. It was more the threat of the unknown — of the certain understanding that my grandmother knew something about that baby, and had maybe had a part in its fate. I met Tucker's gaze, seeing the boy who'd been afraid of thunderstorms as a child, and how he still wore that vulnerability close to the surface of his skin. It connected him to me, as if reaching out to him could heal the parts of both of us that had once seemed damaged beyond repair.

I took a deep breath. "In my grandmother's scrapbook, I found a news clipping from nineteen thirty-nine about the body of a black baby boy found in the Savannah River. The scrapbook stops before the date of the article, so there's nothing in it that might give me a clue about who the baby was or why my grandmother would have kept the newspaper clipping. But there had to be a reason."

A slow rumble of thunder rolled overhead and I watched as Captain Wentworth stilled, his ears alert.

Tucker's gaze didn't move from my face. "Before Susan . . . died, Malily suspected she might have found a letter Malily wrote to Annabelle, apologizing for a lie. I don't know what it was about — Malily wouldn't tell me. But it might explain why Susan just . . . changed. Almost overnight. She stopped sleeping, and spent most of her time in the office in the cottage where you're living now. She started using again; I was sure of it but I couldn't find any evidence. And she kept poring over papers and Malily's scrapbook and letters. She was obsessed. In the beginning, when she seemed to be identifying herself with Malily as a younger woman, both her doctor and I initially thought it was a good thing because she seemed to have found something that filled the void that she'd been used to filling with pills. And then . . . something. Something that made her just snap."

I looked at him in horror. "And you think it could somehow be related."

He shrugged. "I don't really know what to think. All I know is what you've told me, and what my grandmother told me. What if

Susan found whatever it was that linked their stories together; and what if it was bad enough that it sent her over the edge?"

"Like the deliberate death of a child?"

He stared at me for a moment, his eyes cold. A flash of lightning ripped through the sky outside, and the horses shuffled in unison, sensing change like blades of grass in a strong wind. Tucker shot a glance through Captain Wentworth's stall to the small window, watching the gathering storm.

"So what now?" I asked carefully, unsure of my own footing. "Lillian didn't ask me to leave. She assumed you would do it for her."

Reluctantly, he dragged his eyes from the window opening, and I saw the struggle there — the same struggle I imagined a horse made when presented with a higher jump. Sometimes, all it took was the right lead and the conviction that flying was sometimes allowed. "I'm not sure," he said slowly. "And I don't think Malily is, either. She asked me to find you, you know. She'd changed her mind. But now . . ." He shook his head. "Now I think she'd probably choose to die with a clear conscience, but I don't think she wants the world to see what she's been keeping hidden under her bed all these years, either."

I steeled my voice so it wouldn't break. "I need to do this, Tucker." I took a step forward. "Lillian said that she's the only one left who remembers the truth. I want to know what that truth is. I *need* to know. I owe it to my grandmother."

His jaw clenched. "You lied to me. With Susan . . ." He shook his head. "I can't abide lying. I don't know if I can trust you."

I shifted my feet, reminding me of the horses and the oncoming storm. I waited, afraid of what he'd say next.

"But I can't forget that you saved Sara's life, either."

The wind blew harder outside, pushing against the wood of the barn and lifting my hair, reminding me of riding into the wind on the back of a horse. And for a brief moment I allowed myself to imagine riding again. I waited for the fear to come, the indecision. But instead I felt only emptiness, with neither passion nor glory, and for the first time since my accident, I saw possibility. "Can I stay? Please? At least until I find the answers I need." The desperation had crept into my voice but I no longer cared.

Without answering, he shot a glance outside to the darkening sky. "It's getting ready to storm." He stood close to me and I closed my eyes for a moment, smelling the rain and the horse and Tucker, and my world snapped for a brief moment. He touched my arm and I opened my eyes, but he didn't say anything else as lightning flashed in the distance.

"Helen told me that you were afraid of thunderstorms."

He shifted away, and he was lost for a moment, revisiting places I couldn't see. "I'd forgotten that," he said, just as the first fat drops of rain began to hit the dirt path leading from the barn. He reached out his hand. "Come on. We'll make a run for it before it starts pouring."

I hesitated for a moment, reading more into his words than I should have. Then I grabbed his hand and followed his lead, and couldn't help but wonder as we ran toward the old house with its odd alley of trees if it was already too late.

CHAPTER 17

A whippoorwill called out in the night, re-assuring me that I wasn't alone. The storm had continued long after Tucker brought me back to the cottage, cleansing the earth and the air and matching my mood of renewal. I hadn't been to confession for years, and for the first time in a long while I felt the lightness of spirit caused by unburdening myself and saying penance.

But the storm continued to ravage the night, robbing me of a much-needed but elusive sleep. When it subsided I was wide-awake, my thoughts focused on my grandmother's scrapbook pages. I needed to finish reading them in the hope that I would be given another chance to speak with Lillian. Tucker had yet to answer my question, and it was still uncertain if I would be welcome at Asphodel after tomorrow.

I listened to the rain drop from the eaves of the house and the whippoorwill calling again into the clearing sky and began to read.

February 4, 1937

Lillian is missing. Again. It's not the first time and I'm sure it won't be the last time, but it is the first time her father's ever caught her. Her father arrived this morning, sweating and flustered and demanding that I go fetch her so that he could bring her home. I haven't seen Lillian in almost a month, but I had a good idea where she was, and it wasn't in a place or with anybody her father would have approved of. So I lied. I've gotten quite adept at lying lately, and I place all the blame at Lillian's feet and on my own inability to admit to myself what I really want out of life.

Things have changed for all of us. I think it began the night of Lily's comeout ball, but maybe the winds of change had begun to blow long before that. I suppose it's all part of growing up in an uncertain world. I yearn for social equality for all men and women, just as I yearn to be a doctor to minister to the most needy. But I can't seem to keep my dreams on a steady course. I feel as if I spend most of my time helping Josie and Lily determine their own courses; I'm proud that they turn to me, that they respect my resourcefulness and intelligence. But I can't help but sense that if I don't begin to focus on my own needs, they will be forever lost to me.

I told Mr. Harrington that Lily was making her rounds to all the society ladies in town, and that I hadn't gone with her because I was needed to tend to my father. This all began when he'd told Lily that he expected her to be married within the year, after which she quietly went to her room without argument. He didn't find her missing until that evening when she didn't appear for supper, and he assumed she'd come here for me. He had half of it right, at least.

I calmed him down and told him that my father had developed a bad cough that had sent him to his sickbed for the first time I could remember (which is true). I explained to Mr. Harrington that I needed Lily with me to help care for my father, who doesn't seem to be getting any better. I assured him that my father would undoubtedly be up and about by the weekend after an extended and much-needed rest and then we would send her home. I can only hope that gives me enough time to find her before it's too late and her reputation is beyond repair.

I admit, too, of being a bit jealous of Lily. She is not afraid of following her passion, regardless of the consequences. I fear consequences a little too much, I think, which makes me hesitate. Lily claims that kind of behavior will get me stuck in the middle of the road in the face of oncoming traffic. Yet I fear that her relentless pursuit of passion will find her in a place in which she will have no way out. I suppose when we're old women we will look back together and she will laugh at me and claim that her life was fun with no regrets. And I will look back and wonder if I ever did anything passionate enough to warrant any regret at all.

The only other event of these past four months that bears recording is that Freddie has made me an official member of the Savannah chapter of the National Association for the Advancement of Colored People. It is his goal to register every black man to vote in accordance to the fifteenth amendment granting this right, despite the social and legal pressures that keep citizens from the polls each election. Since Freddie has already captured the notice of those who would prefer that he cease and desist in his efforts, we decided that I could do it instead. I have access to all of the colored homes in the poorest neighborhoods because of my father, and it would be an easy thing for me to do.

One of Freddie's associates who'd been registering voters disappeared last month and two weeks later they found his body washed up under the Houlihan Bridge. I understand how dangerous the job is. I also understand how dangerous it would be for my own soul if I did not seek equal access to representation, education, and employment for all citizens. Lily calls me two-faced because I don't embrace the entire Negro cause since I still live in my nice house with my colored servant. I tried to explain that I don't embrace any cause; I just understand the desire to be something more than what we are by birth, and support the means necessary to elevate us all.

I selected a bell charm for Lola to exemplify my life these last four months, mostly to annoy Lily by suggesting she has a wedding to begin planning for. She needs to settle down soon, before it's too late. And when I know she's safe, and Josie is in New York pursuing her singing career, I can begin applying to medical school and see where that takes me.

I awoke with my face pressed against the pages of my grandmother's scrapbook, Lola held tightly in my hands. I'd been dreaming of Mr. Harrington knocking on the door, but it wasn't the front door to the house on Monterey Square that he banged fat fists onto but instead the door to the secret room. I waited and watched in the darkened attic, seeing the door open, but awakened before I could see who'd opened it. Blinking my eyes, I spread my palm and found the bell charm nestled between a miniature sixteenth note and a plump golden heart, representing the three women whose lives were recorded on the linked chains.

"Piper? Are you in there?"

I sat up, my head groggy and my eyesight blurred as I strained to see the clock on the kitchen wall, and then shot up out of my chair when I realized it was after ten o'clock in the morning.

"Piper?" I heard again.

I pivoted toward the front door of the cottage and saw Helen in the doorway, a bundle of papers held with both hands.

"Did you drive yourself?" I immediately felt foolish, knowing it was ridiculous but also realizing that I wouldn't put it past Helen to be so industrious.

She laughed, then took a step forward over the threshold. "No, Emily did. Odella gave us some supplies and Emily's getting them out of the cart. I'm sorry for walking in like this, but Emily peeked through the kitchen window and saw you there, sleeping. We thought it would be better to awaken you now before you developed a permanent crick in your neck."

I rubbed my neck, feeling the stiffness from having slept in an awkward position. "Thanks," I said. "Is anything wrong?"

"No. I just wanted to make sure you were still here. I figured you went to go see Tucker last night and I wanted to make sure that he wasn't pigheaded enough to tell you to leave."

"Not yet. He's still thinking about it. He's pretty angry, and I don't blame him. But I think he understands why."

She tilted her head to the side, reminding me of a flower as it bloomed, unable to hide its secret beauty any longer. "Yes, he would.

But he doesn't forgive easily. You'll have to earn his trust back."

"I know. I just hope he gives me a second chance. He said he couldn't abide lying."

Her sightless eyes drifted behind me, almost making me turn to see what she could. "Because of Susan. I don't think he ever really figured out who she was. I always thought that Susan was trying to outrun her past by inventing new ones. And when she couldn't run anymore, she used drugs to help her forget."

I leaned against the table, unable to completely shake my grogginess. "Why would she want to reinvent her past?"

Helen shifted her eyes back to me and shrugged. "I don't know. She never spoke about where she was from, or her family, other than they were from New Orleans." She smiled. "That's where Mardi gets his name — his full name is Mardi Gras Cotton Picker. But that's about all we knew of her. She never visited any family; she always said they were all gone. We sent word when she died, but no one came to the funeral."

"How sad," I said, taking her elbow and leading her to a chair at the kitchen table.

She sat and looked at me expectantly. "I have a favor to ask, but first I have a little peace offering."

For the first time I noticed what she held in her hands and I bit my lip when I saw what she was handing out to me.

I took the scrapbook pages, my hands not quite steady. "Are these Lillian's?"

She nodded. "But not all of them — just the ones we've already read. Malily doesn't know I took them — yet. Odella helped me sort through them. I promise to tell Malily later. But I wanted us to be on the same page, so to speak."

I looked down at the old, weathered pages, recognizing the torn edges where they'd been ripped from the book. But the handwriting was different — softer, with more loops and slants whereas my grandmother's writing had been compact, with small, bold strokes.

"I don't want you to get in any trouble with Lillian."

She turned her green eyes up to me. "Malily's always been the one to tell me not to hesitate when it comes to something I want. Besides, I know that her silence isn't about protecting her. It's about protecting me. And I don't need protecting; I haven't for a long time now but nobody seems to realize it."

I touched her hand. "Thank you," I said, placing the pages on the table next to my grandmother's, feeling an odd sense of satisfaction at seeing them together.

Emily appeared at the door. "Is it all right if I bring these things in and unload them in the kitchen?"

"Go right ahead. Do you need some help?"

"Nope. Got it. Don't want you to strain yourself before we start today's therapy session."

I jerked my gaze to Helen. "Excuse me? I didn't schedule anything."

Emily looked genuinely surprised. "Helen said you were ready to start. I'm sorry — I hope I didn't misunderstand. . . ."

Helen interrupted. "You didn't. The girls and I decided that it was time for Piper to begin walking straight again. And Tucker agreed."

I stared at her for a moment while the blood flooded my cheeks. "You decided? It's none of his business — or yours, for that matter."

Helen simply smiled. "Ah, she roars. I thought you could. I knew Piper Mills could but I'd never seen Earlene Smith show any emotion. Glad to know it's there. But, yes, Tucker and I dared to butt our noses into your business. Sorry."

I looked at Emily, but she just shrugged

and moved to the kitchen counter, where she dumped the bags and began emptying them. They were right of course, but I'd never taken well to people telling me what to do. Which is why I'd been a great competitor: when people said something was too hard, I'd wanted even more to prove them wrong.

"What makes you think that I haven't already tried therapy and it didn't work?"

"Because you're still limping. Badly. It doesn't have to be that way, you know. If I thought there was something I could do that would improve my sight just a little, I'd do it, no matter how uncomfortable or painful."

Shame replaced my anger, but I didn't say anything.

"You need to get riding again, Piper. It's who you are, regardless of who you used to be. And you need to strengthen your legs so you can do it."

"I'm not riding again," I said, sounding less convincing than I'd hoped, but still feeling shame and a desire to make it up to Helen. "But if it makes you feel any better, I'll work with Emily today. And hopefully it will only take one day because Tucker might decide that it's time for me to leave Asphodel."

"Oh, it will take more than a day," Emily piped in as she opened the refrigerator to store a gallon of milk.

"Fine, fine," I said. "If it will get you off my back. But it won't make me change my mind." Then I heard Helen's words again — *It's who you are, regardless of who you used to be* — and I realized that being blind must be an advantage when it came to seeing into people's hearts.

Helen leaned forward. "He won't make you leave, you know. He cares too much about you. He's just deeply hurt right now. He'll get over it."

I felt my cheeks flooding with color and I was glad she couldn't see them.

"Are you blushing?" Helen asked.

"How on earth did you know that?"

She laughed out loud. "I didn't — but you just told me."

I couldn't help but smile. "I don't think you're right, Helen. But I'd like to stay. I've become . . . attached. I somehow can't remember my life before I came here."

Helen reached for my hand and squeezed. "And we can hardly recall what it was like before you came, too."

As if she could sense another blush, Helen changed the subject. "Do you have any of your grandmother's scrapbook pages you

404

could share with me? Odella could read them to me so I'll know the other side of this story."

"There're more than two sides of their story; we don't have Josie's pages. She was the third friend, the one who went to New York in nineteen thirty-nine — the year my grandmother's pages end. Anyway, Josie became pretty famous in her time. There's quite a lot of information on the Internet about her and her recording career. But I assume she took her pages with her."

Helen blinked slowly. "So will you let me see your grandmother's pages?"

I felt a small frisson of panic, as if I were being asked to bury my grandmother again. But I glanced at Lillian's pages and knew it was a fair trade-off. "Is that the favor you were going to ask?" I blew out a puff of air, oddly relieved that I wasn't alone in this anymore. "I'm not finished yet, but you can read what I've already read and I'll give you the rest of the pages when I'm done. If I'm not still here, I can drive them over to you and we can make the switch."

"All right. Or when I'm done with the first batch, you can read the rest of them to me." She frowned. "Although I have to say that I'm surprised that you haven't already read everything."

I stood and took a large bottle of detergent from Emily and stuck it in the cabinet under the sink. "I am, too," I said, pausing to look outside, where the sun had almost finished erasing the previous night's storm. Emily went outside again to get another load from the golf cart.

"Pandora's box," Helen said softly.

I turned to face her. "I don't really . . . ," I began.

"Yes, you do. It's not your nature to hesitate, I would think. Hesitating before a jump could be disastrous, couldn't it? But you've had these pages for a long time now, and you still haven't read them."

I opened my mouth to deny it again, but her next words stopped me. "Every day, I face the unknown. But I refuse to be afraid of it because then I'd be too paralyzed to get out of bed. And that's a horrible way to live, whether you're blind or not." She placed her fingers on the table, the tips touching the scrapbook pages. "But you need to know your grandmother's story. We both need to know the truth."

Her hands found the stack of read pages and she began to absently thumb through them, pausing when she reached the blank pages in between which I'd placed the newspaper clipping. I watched as her hands touched it, the long, manicured fingers lighting briefly on the clipping before moving to the edge of the page, and then hesitating. She returned to it, then looked up at me expectantly. "What's this?"

I paused only briefly before answering. "Pandora's box," I said. "It's the newspaper clipping about the baby found in the river."

She was silent for a moment, and we both turned as Emily reentered the cottage, her arms filled with more bags. "Does Tucker know?" Helen asked.

"Yes, I told him yesterday when I came clean about everything."

"And you're still thinking your grandmother might have had something to do with this story."

"Yes. There had to be a reason why it was in her scrapbook."

Helen frowned. "Or maybe Josie was involved; she and the infant are of the same race, after all. Have you had any luck researching this?"

I shook my head. "I haven't had a chance to. I was planning on going to the historical archives this week. You can come along, if you like. I can read to you whatever I find, and maybe you can help me put something together. Or we could just ask your grandmother. I think that's the real reason why I haven't gotten further with my research. She knows the answer to every question raised in these pages."

She picked up the newspaper clipping, holding it as gingerly as a newborn. "I'm going to show her this, and ask if she knows why it was with your grandmother's pages. I'll let you know what she says — if she agrees to tell me anything." Helen stood. "I can't help but wonder if Susan found out about this, and maybe the truth behind it affected her deeply — deeply enough to start using again." She shook her head. "I'm not going to tell Tucker that. Not yet. He feels guilty about enough things that I don't want to burden him with anything more."

"But what could he feel guilty about? Susan's unhappy childhood and drug-abuse started long before he even met her."

She looked startled. "I wasn't referring to Susan. I was actually referring to myself."

She started to move away, but I touched her gently on the arm, holding her back. "What do you mean?"

Her eyes darkened. "I caught measles from Tucker, and that's what made me blind."

"Measles?"

Helen shrugged. "My parents didn't believe in vaccinating us. They brought measles back with them from Africa and Tucker got it first. He was in isolation — our dad's a doctor, too, which is why Tucker was cared for at home — and everything was fine until we had a bad thunderstorm. He came to my room, scared, and I let him crawl into bed with me as we always did. And when I got sick, I tried to hide my symptoms because I didn't want to get Tucker in trouble. That's why I got so much sicker, because it was so far along before I got treated."

"But it wasn't his fault." I shook my head, remembering the look on Tucker's face when I told him that I knew he'd been afraid of thunderstorms as a child.

"Yes, well, you know that and I know that, but guilt is a funny thing. So let's just wait a bit, see what else we can find out. But first, I'm going to go lie down on the sofa and watch my soaps while you and Emily work. And then I'm going to go find Malily and see if she can save us some research time."

I helped her to the couch and placed the TV remote in her hands, admiring her silk knit dress and also the way this blind woman seemed to be the least handicapped person I knew.

■ ■ ■ ■

Lillian fingered a rose bloom as she sat on her favorite bench in Helen's garden. She'd retrieved the full-bloomed head from the ground, as if it had been so full of its own passion and beauty that it had burst from the stem. The edges had started to brown and furl, and as she stared at it, she wondered if she should give it another day or two of life by bringing it in and sticking it in a glass of water. In the old days, she would have scattered the petals on the ground to enrich the earth; but life seemed so much more fragile to her now. She contemplated the rose in its final, glorious bloom before dying, and wondered what form her own death would take, and if she'd have a chance for one final burst of understanding.

"Malily?"

Lillian turned to see Helen hovering at the gate.

"I'm in here. On the bench."

Using her cane, Helen tapped her way on the slate path, knowing to turn right when the path turned to brick. Lillian had designed the walkway for just that reason for the granddaughter she loved as a daughter.

Without offering assistance, knowing it would offend Helen, Lillian waited for the cane to strike the line of rocks in the path to indicate she'd reached the bench. She slowly lowered herself onto the bench next to Lillian, then rested her cane on her knees.

"I smell dirt," Helen said, tilting her nose into the air, her creamy skin glowing in the late afternoon sun.

Lillian eyed the bags of topsoil propped against the garden wall and the pile of it spilled onto the path. "Piper's been busy. The pansies were getting too leggy, so we decided they needed to go. She's coming up with a redesign of that section with new flowers."

She felt Helen looking at her. "I can't believe you're trusting somebody else to redesign part of your garden."

"She was taught by a master — the same woman who taught me everything I know about gardening. Her grandmother, Annabelle O'Hare."

Helen nodded, not saying anything because she didn't have to. It had always seemed to Lillian that to make up for Helen's lack of sight, she was given an extra sound track inside her head, to hear everything that wasn't said out loud.

Eventually, Helen said, "Piper spoke with

411

Tucker last night. He hasn't decided yet if she should leave or not."

Lillian let out an inelegant snort. "He knows what he wants. He's just afraid to say it. Susan taught him to doubt his own feelings and to hesitate when it comes to getting what he wants. But he's learning. And I have no doubt that Piper will stay, regardless of whether or not I think she should."

"And you don't think she should?"

Lillian looked down at the crimson bloom in her hand, the redness of it making everything else around it pale. "It's not up to me, is it?" She twisted the bloom, feeling a sense of inevitability, of Annabelle's part in sending Piper into Lillian's life to tidy up an unfinished past.

After a few moments, Helen spoke. "Piper gave me pages of her grandmother's scrapbook to read, and I gave her your pages — the ones we've already read. Once we're caught up, we're coming to you so we can read the rest of yours. Please don't be angry. But I think you'll agree that it has to be this way. You've been silent for so long, Malily. And it's my story, too."

Lillian raised an eyebrow, remembering too late that the movement would be lost on Helen. With a long sigh, she said softly,

"I suppose you're right. I won't like it, but I'll do it for you."

Helen reached for her hand and held it, and they were silent for a long time. Eventually, Helen turned to her. "Out of curiosity, Malily, when do your pages end?"

Lillian stilled, trying to think of why Helen would be asking, and trying not to imagine the worst. She didn't pretend to think about it; she remembered the date as if it were yesterday. "September third, nineteen thirty-nine."

Helen was silent for a moment, and Lillian tensed. "Something else I've been thinking about, Malily. You were married the following year, which makes me think that you'd have a lot to write about. But instead you stopped — and so did Lillian — within months of each other. Surely there was a lot more to be said about your lives."

Lillian lowered her head, shading her face in the shadow of her hat brim. "It was a busy time. I felt that I'd become a woman, and the scrapbook and Lola were childish things to me. I didn't need them anymore."

Helen nodded, then reached into the pocket of her knit dress. "Piper found this with her grandmother's pages. It's dated September eighth, nineteen thirty-nine."

The sun dipped lower in the sky, and the

evening breeze from the river rushed over them, tossing the rose bloom from her hands and making the ancient oaks in the alley begin a faint, whistling cry. Lillian knew what it was before she touched it, although she'd seen it only once before. She grasped it with shaking fingers, glad Helen couldn't see. "This was with Annabelle's things?"

"Yes. Piper told me it was stuck between two scrapbook pages, as if it were hidden on purpose."

"How odd," Lillian managed, her fingers shaking so hard that the words were now a blur. She'd always imagined this moment differently; despite the hours and the years of silence that separated them, she'd always thought that it would be Annabelle she'd unburden her sins to. Annabelle in her self-imposed role of martyr would have understood, and chased the demons away. But Annabelle was gone, leaving only Lillian with the truth.

She took her time finding her voice. "Was there anything written on the pages? Any words of explanation?" Her hands ached, nearly masking the ache that pressed against her heart.

"Nothing. And Annabelle's scrapbook ends in July of the same year." Helen faced her, the breeze lifting her hair, reminding Lillian of when Helen was a little girl and had become Lillian's hope that she'd been given another chance.

Helen continued. "I think Piper believes that her grandmother might have known something, or might even have been involved. That's the reason why she's been dragging her feet in reading the scrapbook and researching further. She's afraid of what she'll discover."

Lillian fought to control her voice. "What about you, Helen? Are you afraid of the story you don't know?"

The whistling in the trees became louder, saturating the air with discordant notes and an unease that seeped into Lillian's skin, shrinking it tightly against her bones.

"No, Malily." Helen's green eyes widened, reminding Lillian again of an innocent child. "Because I know you. More than my own mother, I know you in my heart. You saved me, remember? When I was so sick and burning up with fever, you picked me up and put me in your car and drove me to the hospital. And then you slept in my room until the fever was gone, and you held my hand when I woke up and it was dark. You saved me then, too. Do you remember that? Do you remember what you told me?"

Slowly, Lillian nodded. " 'Where there is life, there is hope.' "

"It gave me hope; it helped me not be scared of a darkened world. So no, Malily. I'm not afraid of the story I don't know. Nothing you could ever tell me would make me not love you or think less of you. You're who you are today because of what you did in the past. I can only feel proud to be your granddaughter."

A cicada whirred in the magnolia tree, its last song to the fading sun. Lillian had been waiting for this moment for so long, felt as if each hour leading to it had been counted. But now that it was here, the words were as lost to her as Helen would be if she spoke the truth. She'd not anticipated this — only a letting go and a freedom from the burden she'd carried for seventy years.

A small line appeared between Helen's brows. "So who was the baby, and what connection did he have to Annabelle O'Hare?"

Lillian felt the charm, cold and heavy against her skin. *Be patient and strong; someday this pain will be useful to you.* The words she'd lived by for so long felt meaningless now as the lie fit itself to her tongue, flattened by the threat of facing death alone. A story untold seemed suddenly like a small price to pay.

"A girl in trouble is a temporary thing, they used to say. Perhaps a young girl saw no other alternative than to end her shame."

"Was it Josie's baby?"

Lillian stared at Helen for a long time, trying to find the right answer. Instead, all she said was, "I don't know. She could have kept it hidden from me; I didn't see much of her that last year before she went to live up north."

Helen nodded, thinking. "Did you know about the secret attic room in Annabelle's house?"

Lillian weighed her words, each heavier than the last. "Yes. She showed it to me once. She wasn't sure why it was there or what it was used for. Why?"

Without answering her directly, Helen said, "Piper and I are driving into Savannah tomorrow. We're going to see the house and the attic room and then do research at the library. I'll let you know what we find."

"Yes. Please do."

"And when we get back, we'll come see you and we can read more of your scrapbook. Because that's the real story, isn't it?"

Lillian nodded, feeling weak. *Because I know you. More than my own mother, I know you in my heart.* "Does Piper have Lola —

the necklace — with her? I'd like to see it again."

"I'll tell her to bring it."

They sat for a moment, immersed in the night sounds and the sighing oaks, breathing in the heady scent of the blooms that surrounded them.

Helen sighed. "I love the way it smells in here. I think it will always be my favorite place in the world."

"Mine, too," said Lillian as she stood, her bones screaming in protest. She picked up the small garden shears that had been next to her on the bench and approached the rosebush, its crimson blooms glowing softly in the last light of day. She searched for stems holding buds without color, wanting ones that weren't expending energy required to sustain a vibrant bloom, then neatly clipped them off at the bottom.

After removing the thorns, she returned to Helen and opened her hand, placing the clippings gently inside. "Keep these wet with damp paper towels and give these to Piper, if you would. They're for her grandmother's garden. I'd always meant to give these to Annabelle and never had the chance."

Helen closed her fist around them, then tilted her face up to her grandmother. "Why not? Why didn't you have the chance?"

Because I didn't have the courage to tell the truth, she wanted to say. She shifted her gaze to the moonflowers, which had begun to unfurl their petals, opening up to the growing darkness. "Because I saw too much of myself in Annabelle. I needed to separate myself from her. So we parted ways."

Helen was silent for a while. "But what was she asking forgiveness for in her letters — the ones you returned unopened?"

Night edged its way into the garden, falling softly over the roses and sweet autumn clematis, bleaching the colors from the flowers and replacing them with shadows. "I don't know," Lillian said, her answer fortified by the first lie, making it easier. "I suppose I never will. She must have thought that she'd done something to sever our friendship, but there's no way of knowing. Poor Annabelle."

Helen stood, too. "Is it dark yet?"

"Yes. The moonflowers have bloomed."

Helen stepped forward and Lillian guided her hand to the milky white petals, the same way she'd guided her through her first months of blindness and every pivotal moment in her life since then. *The daughter of my heart.*

Helen smiled. "I can still see them, you

know. I haven't forgotten."

Lillian looked at her but didn't smile back. "There are some things that should never be forgotten." *Like the worth of an old friendship, and a secret to take to the grave.*

Lillian took Helen's hand and tucked it into the crook of her arm, then led them both out of the garden guided by the glow of the distant moon and the sound of the old oaks crying for old friends and to a river that flowed over a bed of silt and secrets.

CHAPTER 18

I awoke early, eager to head downtown. I hadn't heard from Tucker, and I was using the reprieve to do as much research as possible. Because I had another hour before I had to pick up Helen, I reached for my grandmother's scrapbook pages, impatient now to get through them. I had a sense of urgency that had eluded me before, and I wasn't sure why. Maybe it was Lillian's increasing frailness, or maybe it was the sense I'd had ever since pulling Sara from the pond that I still had the potential to be more than ordinary.

I'd left the scrapbook pages and my grandmother's box out on the table, since I didn't need to hide them anymore, and turned to the page where I'd last stopped. I looked at the photo that had been stuck at the bottom that I'd barely glanced at before if only because I assumed I wouldn't know anybody pictured in it. But as I sat down to resume reading, something about it caught my eye again and I lifted the page closer to see it better.

The photo was of a small group of men. I recognized Freddie immediately as the tall, handsome man in the back row. The rest of the men were black except for one white man, and all were dressed in three-piece suits and hats, a few of them sporting pocket watches. I scanned the anonymous faces, and my gaze paused on the white man, wondering why he looked familiar to me.

He was very young, the shade of his hair in the black-and-white photo hidden by his dark fedora. But then my gaze fanned down to his clothing and my eyes caught on his watch chain and the golden key fob that dangled from it. I squinted my eyes to see it closer, trying to recall where I'd seen it before. And then I remembered. On his last visit, I'd seen Mr. Morton pulling out his old watch, and had seen the key fob. I smiled to myself, recalling what I'd read in my grandmother's scrapbook, about how he'd been sweet on her. I tapped my finger against the photograph, thinking. He knew a lot more about my grandmother than he'd let on, and he fully expected me to figure it all out on my own.

Shaking my head, I leaned forward and began to read.

December 30, 1938

It's been nearly two years since I last wrote in this book. I haven't had the heart to. So much has happened, and most of it nothing I wanted to record, so I left the book under my bed, hoping to forget about it. Even Josie and Lily seem to have forgotten about it. But I feel as if this last vestige of our youth must not disappear, and so I pulled it out this morning, and dusted it off so that I can continue with our story.

Father has never fully recovered from his bout with pneumonia. His doctor thinks it might have settled in his heart and he is in a weakened state. Any exertion exhausts him, although I help him practice walking around his room three times a day. But it is obvious to all of us that he will not be able to work again. We are all devastated. We'd never thought that he could be reduced to such circumstances. He was always so strong, and such a presence that when he became ill, it never occurred to us that he might not fully recover.

I was at his side through much of his

illness, when he passed through delirium and mumbled things that didn't quite make sense. But there was one feverish utterance that shook me, and for a moment I knew it had to be the high fever. But he said it again, and squeezed my hand, as if to make sure I understood, and I was made to understand that he thought he was about to die and had to unburden himself to me. I sat next to him for a long time after he collapsed into an exhausted sleep, pondering his words, knowing them to be true. So much made sense suddenly — things I should have seen but hadn't. I'd been blissfully unaware of all of it, ignoring the clues that had been right under my nose for as long as I could remember.

I was angry at first, angry at his cowardice. He'd only told me because he expected to die and wouldn't have to live with the repercussions his confession would cause. How unfair to me, and to everyone else, that we were not given a chance to come to terms with the new order of things, or to prepare ourselves for what must follow. Whatever that was to be.

The only thing that is certain is that Lillian will be pleased. She has made assumptions that weren't true — thank-fully — and now she will know that she was wrong and I can be exonerated. When Lillian takes possession of this scrapbook and reads it, she will ask me what I'm referring to. I might even tell her. And hopefully we can both laugh at our misunderstanding and resume being as close as we once were, before matters of our hearts took precedence in our lives. Or maybe I'll make her wonder.

My father's lawyer, Mr. Morton, has told me that the house is paid for and that my father had investments besides stocks, so I will have a little income to live on comfortably if I'm frugal. I've never been a spendthrift, never desiring to dress in the latest fashion, so this shouldn't be a problem. My only thoughts now are for my father's patients, and who will treat them now.

Mr. Morton's son, Paul, is a courier in his father's law office and has become a good friend to me despite the fact that he is five years younger than I am. He thinks that I should go to medical school. He, too, is a friend of Freddie's and has become quite committed to our cause. I'm not completely sure, however, if his commitment is more for the cause or for what Freddie refers to as Paul's "unrequited" love for me. I tell Freddie he's being foolish. I think I will be a confirmed spinster and bluestocking if I cannot marry for love.

There's been no more talk of Freddie returning to England to complete his education and I now know why. And without my father's income from his medical practice, I cannot pay Justine as much, but she insists that she does not want to leave my employ despite the fact that this means she can no longer afford Josie's voice lessons. I feel strongly that Josie needs to continue. Unfortunately, this means I will have to sell my beloved horse, Lola Grace, whom I have been stabling at Asphodel. I won't be able to get a high price for her, but I cannot afford to feed and stable her, and I have little time to ride anymore. I will miss that the most I think.

I told Paul — to whom I've confessed everything — that I will apply to medical school as soon as Josie is settled in her new career and Lily is married. They are like frayed ends of a rope, and I'm the knot that will tie us all together.

That's why I chose the sailor's knot as my charm for Lola. Ties stronger than friendship bind us together now, and I doubt they can ever be broken.

The sound of tires crunching on gravel brought my head up, and I spotted Tucker's Jeep outside. Peering out the window, I saw Tucker in the driver's seat with Helen riding shotgun. I jumped out of my chair and opened the door just as Tucker was reaching up to knock. We stood still, facing each other, neither one of us stepping back.

His hair was wet, as if he'd just stepped out of the shower, but his eyes were bloodshot and there was the faint scent of alcohol on him. "Rough night, Tucker?"

He rubbed his hand over a clean-shaven jaw. "I've had rougher." He dropped his hand and we remained staring at each other.

"Have you come to ask me to leave?" I asked, crossing my arms over my chest so he couldn't see them shake as I waited for his answer.

He looked as if he wasn't really sure of the answer. "No, I'm not."

"Why?" I wanted to take back the words. I'd never known how to stop when I was ahead. It had always created a nice point spread between me and the number-two spot, but it just didn't seem to translate as well in social interactions.

"Because you saved Sara's life."

I hadn't expected that answer and I struggled not to drop my gaze.

He closed his eyes for a moment and I saw his exhaustion and the lines of grief around his mouth, which seemed to have lessened since I'd first come to Asphodel. "Because I feel as if we're all stuck in the same place — me, Sara, and Lucy — but that — how did you put it? — the world seems to be snapping outside our walls." His smile was sad. "Malily doesn't believe in regret. Maybe if I find out what happened to Susan, I'll discover that maybe I don't really have anything to regret."

I wanted to touch his face, but I kept my hands tightly wrapped around my arms. "So you're not still angry with me?"

"No, I'm still pretty furious. But I have to get over that because Lucy and Sara would never forgive me if I was the reason you went away." Shoving his hands in the back pockets of his jeans, he indicated the Jeep. "I'd like to see the hidden room. And the rest of it. I might be able to help."

"I'm assuming Helen's on board with this?"

"Yeah. She suggested it, actually. Helped me see that this could be what I need right now. What we all need." His eyes met mine.

"If that's all right with you."

I nodded, and managed a small smile. "That's fine. I could use the help."

"Great." He motioned toward the Jeep again. "Come on, Helen hates to be kept waiting."

"So, does this mean we have a truce?"

He held the door open for me, his brow furrowed. "For now. Just don't lie to me again, okay?"

I nodded. "Hang on a second — I have to get something for Helen." I ran back to the table and picked up the pages I'd just read.

As we began walking toward the car, he said softly, "I was home by midnight, by the way. You can ask Emily, who let Lucy wait up for me. I was there to tuck Lucy into bed."

I just nodded, but felt an inexplicable warmth flood my face. I ducked my head as I climbed into the backseat of the Jeep and greeted Helen. After waiting for Tucker to climb in behind the wheel, I handed Helen the pages. "Are you and Lillian all caught up?"

"Yes. She was tired last night, but she insisted that we read all of your grandmother's pages. I shared them with Tucker, too. She did ask if there were any more; she doesn't remember reading past what we already have, so this will be a nice surprise for her."

"There's some interesting stuff in the pages I just gave you, and I think I have a good place to start my research."

"Like what?" Tucker shifted the Jeep into first gear and we sped down the gravel road toward Asphodel's front gates.

"Well, I've been wondering how Freddy paid for his education in England and how Josie paid for her singing lessons. They're the children of a housekeeper, and no matter how important the housekeeper was to the O'Hares, I can't imagine they could afford to pay her that much money."

"So who did?" Helen tilted her face up toward the open roof of the Jeep.

"I don't know — yet. I was hoping that we might be able to find their birth certificates in the archives. Finding out who their father was might answer a lot of those questions."

I sat back against the seat, my thoughts dancing with the rush of air coming through the open windows. I wasn't sure what I'd find, but I wasn't afraid so much of the unknown now. Maybe I was just beginning to realize that discovering the past couldn't change it, nor could the knowledge erase the hours between as if they'd never happened at all.

Helen kept her face tilted upward, feeling the warmth of the sun as they headed down the old Augusta Highway toward Savannah. She loved the feel of her silk skirt brushing against the bare skin of her legs, and the way her hair whipped around her face. She remembered how when she was a little girl her mother had always braided her long, wavy hair so it would be easier to manage, but as soon as her mother would leave, the braids would come undone. Helen was still convinced that there was nothing as lovely on earth as the feel of your hair blowing about your face.

She listened as the sounds of the highway softened to those of the intimate city of Savannah, with its manicured squares of flowering hedges and native trees filled with mockingbirds, and Forsyth Park's gardens bursting with fragrant blooms that Malily refused to admit she'd borrowed the idea of her scent garden from, insisting it had been the other way around.

Piper sat forward in the backseat so that her head was close to the front so she could talk. Helen half listened to Tucker and Piper's conversation, noticing how it was less strained, and wondering if they'd finally noticed that by staring into a mirror, they saw the other.

"Take a left here on Bull Street, and the first square is Monterey," Piper said. "Go around to the other side of the square to East Taylor. My house is the first one on the right."

"I just need the address. I used to live here, remember?" Tucker's voice lacked the sharpness Helen had grown used to, and she wondered if it was because of Piper or because his guilt had finally reached its expiration date.

The car stopped and Tucker shut off the engine. After a moment, he began to describe it for her. "It's a three-story Savannah gray brick, with iron stair railings and a white columned portico with an iron balcony above it under one of the second-story windows." He paused. "And there's a large side yard that looks like it might have once been a garden."

"What's in it now?" Helen asked.

"Nothing but weeds and dirt," Piper answered slowly from the backseat. "It used to be as beautiful as Lillian's."

Helen turned her face toward Piper. "Malily gave me a few rose clippings from her garden to give to you and I have them with me. She said she'd always meant to give them to your grandmother but never had the chance. Maybe you'll have time today to plant them."

Piper's voice sounded unsure. "If I even remember how. I can have George water them while I'm gone."

"George?" Tucker asked as he exited the Jeep and then helped Piper out of the backseat. Helen listened as he came around to her side and opened her door. "Who's he?"

Piper didn't answer right away. "George Baker. He's . . . an old friend. He's related to Mr. Morton, my grandfather's lawyer, and he's been sort of taking care of things while I've been gone. He's even been helping with some of the research."

Helen held on to Tucker's arm as he led her to the sidewalk, feeling him tense. "Just a friend?" he asked, his voice sounding forced and making Helen smile.

"Earlene!"

Helen turned in the direction of the male voice as Tucker stopped walking.

"George," said Piper, "I didn't expect to see you here today."

Footsteps approached on the sidewalk. "You asked me to hire a cleaning crew to deep clean the house while you were gone. I'm sure you didn't want me to give them a house key, so I'm just here to unlock the house for them."

There was a short pause, during which Helen felt Piper's uncertainty although Helen wasn't sure why. She liked the man's voice. The accent was old Savannah and as deep and warm as the pond water in the middle of summer. "Are you going to introduce me to your friends?"

Again Piper paused. "I'm sorry. I guess you just surprised me. This is Dr. Tucker Gibbons and his sister, Helen."

She felt Tucker shake George's hand and then she held out her own. George's skin felt smooth, the fingers long, his grip firm. She smiled brightly at him. "It's a pleasure," she said. His grip lingered a little longer than it should have before he dropped it. She was used to that when people realized that she was blind.

"They know who I am, George. I told them."

"Well, that's a relief." He turned to Tucker and Helen. "I tried to tell her it wasn't a good idea, but trying to tell Earlene Mills not to do something is a lot like trying to tell grass not to grow."

"You call her Earlene?" Helen asked.

"Yes, he does. And I find it annoying but I can't get him to stop," Piper interjected.

"It's her name, and I think it suits her better than Piper. Piper's not even her middle name."

"I wondered about that," said Helen. "How did you get Piper from Earlene?"

They began moving forward and Tucker indicated that they were in front of the steps and needed to climb. She was surprised to feel George on her other side taking her elbow.

"I didn't," said Piper from ahead of them, jangling keys. "My grandfather started calling me that when he realized I had potential in equestrian eventing. He thought it was a champion-worthy name."

Tucker's arm tensed under Helen's hand. "To go with the empty living room wall, I suppose."

George stopped and Helen realized they'd reached the top of the steps. She listened as Piper stuck the key in the lock, opened the door, and stepped inside. Her footsteps clicked across wood floors.

George sounded surprised. "She told you about that?"

There was a short pause before Tucker answered. "Yeah. She did. Her grandfather was a real piece of work."

"He loved her, though. In the only way he knew how. My grandfather was a good friend to both of her grandparents. He said

435

Jackson Mercer was a tough guy to get to know, but his one soft spot was for his granddaughter."

"Are y'all going to stand outside all day or do you think you want to come in?" Piper's voice carried from inside the house.

The three of them wouldn't fit through the door at the same time and Helen was amused that George resisted relinquishing his grip, making Tucker step back. George escorted her across the threshold, careful to watch her footing, then led her into the house.

"Miss Gibbons, your green dress matches the shade of your eyes exactly, and I have a feeling that's no accident. I had an aunt who lost her sight when she was only in her forties. She'd been a very attractive woman, too, who liked to dress, and she saw no reason to quit just because she could no longer see. And she taught me a very important lesson."

"And what was that, Mr. Baker?" Helen asked, enjoying the sound of his voice.

"That a blind woman sees a lot more than you think. And that my aunt knew just where to swing her purse when I accidentally swore in her presence. The woman never missed."

Helen laughed, remembering something

Malily had read from her scrapbook, something about dancing with Charlie and how it made her feel breathless, as if she'd found a little bit of extraordinary. She wondered if she was feeling a little of that now.

"Please call me Helen."

"Only if you call me George."

Tucker touched her arm. "Sorry to interrupt, but Piper's showing us up to the attic. The stairs are steep, so hang on to my arm."

She allowed Tucker to lead her up the stairs, wishing George would say something again so she could listen to his voice. The house smelled old and musty, the scents of oil soap and dust saturating the air. The stairs creaked like an old woman, and Helen wanted to ask Piper to open up all the windows to let out the sad, stale air. Tucker described everything to her as they passed rooms down a narrow hallway, but he didn't need to. She could picture the antique furniture, the polished hardwood floors, the outdated upholstery and flowery curtains. It made sense to her that Piper had only ever considered this house to be a place to sleep; her life had occurred far beyond these walls.

Tucker made her climb in front of him when they reached the attic stairs because they were steeper and narrower, and she wondered if he was thinking of her safety or merely forcing a distance between her and George.

She knew they'd reached the attic from the wall of heat that seemed to slam into them as they stepped through the threshold.

"Hang on. I'll open the windows," Piper said, her footsteps moving to the opposite side of the room.

"You might want to consider putting air-conditioning up here, Earlene, especially if you plan to continue using it as storage. All your ribbons and trophies are up here and I'm sure you don't want those to be ruined by the heat and humidity," George said as he managed to move between Helen and Tucker.

Tucker walked away. "Pretty impressive collection, Piper." Helen heard a cabinet door being tugged open. "Nice cover photo of you on *Eventing* magazine." He cleared his throat. " 'Piper Mills wins Eventing's greatest prize, the Rolex Grand Slam,' " he read out loud.

George turned to Helen. "That's consecutive wins at Kentucky, Badminton, and Burghley. She was the first person to ever do that."

"They expected Fitz and me to do it again in two thousand four and make the Olympic team," Piper said.

"But you had your accident," Tucker said softly.

"Yeah. At the Kentucky Rolex Three-Day, during the cross-country portion. I made a stupid mistake." Piper's voice was lighter somehow, as if the burden of loss and regret had at least packed its bags although not completely left. She walked across the attic and Helen heard the cabinet door shut with a final thud.

"It's hard to believe that I've managed to have such an accomplished athlete give beginner lessons to my daughters." Tucker's tone was light, but couldn't disguise the fact that he hadn't completely forgiven Piper yet.

"You didn't mention that, Earlene. It's hard to imagine that you'd voluntarily go anywhere near a horse," said George.

Helen listened as Piper walked around the perimeter of the room, opening windows to create a cross-breeze. Warm air blew over Helen's face, and she turned to catch the breeze head-on.

"It's . . . complicated. And I don't want to talk about it right now." She banged on a window and it opened, creating a strong movement of air. "George, let's show Helen and Tucker what we found."

George led her forward. "We pushed aside

this armoire and found a door behind it. Mr. Morton, her attorney, gave Piper a key after her grandfather died. He'd instructed Mr. Morton to deliver it to Piper following his death. I guess her grandfather didn't want to have to answer any of her questions."

"Or maybe he didn't know the answers," Tucker said as he followed them through the doorway and into the airless attic room. "He might have been doing just what his wife had asked him to do."

It was even more stifling in the hidden room, but Piper made no move to open the windows, as if she wanted to spend as little time in there as possible. "What's in here?" Helen asked, pressing her hand to her nose to smell anything but the heavy dust and sadness that seemed to linger still.

Piper's voice was matter-of-fact. "There's a small single bed, stripped of all of its linens. There's a small table beside it with a washbowl and basin, and an empty chest of drawers." She paused and Helen heard her swallow. "Behind the door is a baby's bassinet, where I found the hand-knit blanket inside. The yarn seems to be identical to the yarn used to make a baby's sweater that I found in my grandmother's trunk. There's also a basket in front of the windows with a stack of old magazines." Helen listened to the rustle of paper. "There's a *Good House-keeping* on top from nineteen thirty-four and a *Life* magazine beneath it from nineteen thirty-seven."

Tucker stopped in front of Helen and she heard him pivoting, studying the room around him. "I've never seen one of these; I've only read about them."

"One of what?" asked George, patting Helen's fingers that rested in the crook of his elbow.

"A disappointment room. My partner in the medical practice — the psychiatrist — he's the one who first told me about them. They were created to hide imperfect children — basically any child with a mental or physical defect. They would be fed and clothed, but they remained in their little rooms, hidden from the world and never acknowledged."

"Like Margaret Louise," interjected George. "I was doing some research for Piper and came across her name. She's listed in the family Bible as having been born in eighteen ninety-eight, but there's no official record of her having lived at all. This room could have been created for her, and family members would have known about it. And maybe that would explain the

441

bassinet and the blanket. I haven't had a chance to check the burial records at local cemeteries, but I think I'll start with Bonaventure Cemetery."

"Their burial records are easy to access," said Piper, sounding thoughtful. "But what I'd really like to do is sit down with Mr. Morton. I think he knows a lot more about all of this than he'd like me to believe. I found his picture this morning in my grandmother's scrapbook. He was apparently working with her and Freddie Montet in the NAACP chapter here in Savannah."

Helen turned around to where she knew the door she'd entered was and slid her hand down the wood. "There's no door handle on this side."

"No, there wouldn't be," said Tucker. "A disappointment room was just another name for a prison, really."

Helen took a few steps to the right and her hand brushed against wicker. "What color was the blanket?"

"Light blue, like the little sweater I found," Piper said.

Tucker moved to Helen's side. His voice was agitated. "But what does any of this have to do with Malily?"

The hot air in the room settled heavily on Helen, like a winter coat worn on an August

442

day. But it wasn't just the heat; there was something else in the room that wearied her. Maybe it was the stark picture she had of it in her head, of the bare mattress and the empty bassinet; or maybe it was a lingering despair that had never been allowed to leave.

"I'm not sure," Piper answered. "All I have are the letters my grandmother wrote to her, asking for Lillian's forgiveness for something. I haven't spoken to Lillian yet about any of this, but Helen has and we're both convinced that Lillian isn't going to tell us anything she doesn't want us to know. She wants to tell her story — the one that's recorded in her scrapbook. But both her scrapbook and my grandmother's end before the baby was found in the river. Which means the end of the story will be whatever Lillian chooses to tell us."

"Did you ask your grandmother about any of this?" Tucker asked, his voice strained.

"Not until it was too late. I'd been knocking around this house with my grandfather for nearly six years and I didn't think to look in my grandmother's trunk or ask her about her life until after my grandfather died. I took the sweater to my grandmother in the nursing home and she seemed to recognize it. It . . . it made her cry."

"Did she say anything?" Tucker asked.

"Yes. She did. She said, 'He's gone.' "

Tucker walked across the room toward Piper. "That was all? She didn't say anything else?"

With a voice thickened by tears, Piper said, "She did, actually. She said something about . . . about how every woman needs a daughter to tell her stories to. I left then. And two days later she died."

Helen's skin felt as if it might sag from the weight of the room. She remembered those words, of course. They were the same ones she'd heard from her own grandmother. There were so many missing pieces to the puzzle that it was hard to focus on just one. She touched the wicker bassinet again, as if it might hold an answer for her, or at least a clue. Her fingers plucked at a loose strand, pulling it free from the weave until it stood alone. *What's missing?* she asked herself, wondering why the unwoven strand held such significance to her. The answer sidled up to her and shook her.

Helen turned toward Piper. "What about Josie? We haven't talked about her at all — probably because we don't have her scrapbook pages. But she's as much a part of all of this as Malily and Annabelle. She was mixed-race but her skin was dark; couldn't the baby have been hers? Maybe the three of them made a pact that they would never tell anybody about what happened. That's why they tore up the scrapbook, and went their separate ways."

"It's possible, I suppose," said Piper. "She did leave for New York around the time the news story appeared. But Josie's dead. And there's still the fact that my grandmother wrote to Lillian, asking for forgiveness for some unknown sin. There wasn't any mention of Josie."

Helen turned to Piper again. "Maybe Josie had children — a daughter. And maybe she told her daughter the story."

"And maybe none of this is connected at all," Tucker said, and he sounded hopeful. Almost as if he couldn't believe that his grandmother could have been involved in anything as horrible as a room that hid things not fit for the outside world, or the mystery behind a baby found in the Savannah River. Or that Susan had known, and the knowledge had killed her.

"I'll have a lot of research to do today, then," said Piper. "The library on Bull Street has a local-history room as well as quite a few genealogical resources, where I might be able to find more information on Josie. Then I'd like to go to the Georgia Historical Society at Hodgson Hall on

Whitaker Street to see what else I can turn up about my grandmother and Josie and see if I can find any more news articles about the baby."

George stepped forward. "Earlene, come on. What are we — chopped liver? You have here six willing hands to help you, so please let us. Why don't we split up? Helen and I can make a visit to the library, and you and Tucker can go to Hodgson Hall. We'll get twice as much research accomplished in half the time. As long as you tell us what we need to be looking for."

Helen looked away, not wanting anyone to see her face. He'd said *six willing hands,* not four. She pressed her hands together, if only to keep her from doing something stupid like cry.

"All right," Piper said. "If everyone's in agreement, we can do that."

Tucker and Helen murmured their assent.

"Let's go then," said George as he touched Helen's arm and led her through the door of the small room and back into the attic.

They waited until Tucker and Piper followed; then Helen paused, turning slightly back toward the secret room. She thought she'd heard something — something that sounded like a baby's crying but could have been a bird in the chimney or the moaning eaves of an old house.

With a shudder, she turned her back and allowed George to lead her from the attic, aware all the time of the little room with more secrets than could be contained in a mere span of years.

Chapter 19

I'd made the walk so many times from the house on Monterey Square to Forsyth Park that I probably could have made it with my eyes closed. In my early days in Savannah, when I was just starting to learn the secrets of her garden, my grandmother would take me to the park to study the flowers. We didn't study them as a botanist would, captivated by their propagation and their ability to survive in the heat of summer. We studied them instead as a photographer would, focusing on the individual elements of each bloom: the shell-like interiors, the tiny veins inside delicate petals, and web-thin stamens that most people never bothered to see. But the beauty of the flowers was dependent on these elements, and my grandmother and I would smile at each other, sharing our private knowledge of the wonderful, secret world of the garden that seemed to exist only for us.

Tucker and I walked without speaking, being careful to make sure our arms didn't touch. As we passed the edge of the park along Gaston walking toward Whitaker, Tucker finally spoke. "You and George, are you . . . ?"

I almost choked. "No. Definitely not. I think he would probably like to, but, well, no. If I had a brother, that's probably how I would feel about him: nice enough, but not somebody I'd want to kiss."

Eager to change the subject, I turned to Tucker. "I appreciate you doing this. I know you have other places you could be."

His pace slowed. "Please don't make me out to be some kind of a hero. I have my own reasons."

"I know. Because of Susan. But I still think you're a bit of a hero."

He stopped and I stopped, too, and we faced each other on the sidewalk. "Why?"

I didn't even have to think about my answer. "Because you get out of bed each day. Because you try. Because you love Lucy and Sara even though you're still not sure how to show it. But you try."

He stared at me, his eyes darkening, and I wondered if I'd made him angry again. Finally, he said, "I could say the same thing about you, Piper Mills."

I blinked in confusion and looked away, then continued walking toward Hodgson Hall, feeling his presence next to me as he caught up.

I'd become a regular fixture at the Georgia Historical Society during my years of burying my past life by hiding in someone else's as a genealogist. Tucker and I climbed the familiar broad brownstone stairway with heavy curving balustrades to the solid mahogany doors tucked under a two-columned portico.

When we entered the great hall with its soaring three-story-high ceilings, Tucker stopped and looked up. "I guess they're pretty serious about their history here." I followed his gaze to the wall above the entrance, where engraved in gold leaf on red mottled marble were the words *No Feasting, drinking, and smok-ing or amusements of any kind will be permitted within its walls.*

I put my finger to my lips. "Quiet. They'll ask us to leave."

He raised an eyebrow, then rolled his eyes in an exaggerated version of Lucy's favorite move, and I had to cough to hide my laughter. Shaking my head, I led him over to the reference desk to show my ID and sign in.

I was already a registered user, and after doing an online search of their catalog, I'd called in ahead of time so that the boxes and folders of information I'd requested had already been pulled from the repository. I clasped my laptop — one of the few articles for note-taking actually allowed in the library — and we headed through the main hall with its large, vaulted windows, which had been designed in a time when there was little artificial light or ventilation, and into the reading room. We sat down at one of the four large tables made of slabs of solid walnut supported by cast iron, and stared at each other over the boxes and folders that had been pulled for us.

"What do we do now?" asked Tucker.

I slid a large box across the table toward him. "These are all from various personal collections housed here. I asked for them to be pulled because they contained newspaper clippings and obituaries from the years nineteen twenty-five through nineteen sixty. I want you to look for anybody with the last names of Montet, O'Hare, Harrington, or Ross — either birth or death information. My preliminary online searches have only shown Josephine's death information, but only because she was relatively well-known at the time of her death. But I can't find any of her birth information, and there's nothing on Freddie, which makes me think that he used another last name for legal documents. Anyway, after we verify that we're looking at the right person, we'll look through the newspaper obituaries on microfiche. That's where you find all of the interesting data — as in remaining family, where they were living, and where they're buried."

He frowned. "What will you be doing?"

"I'll be upstairs going through microfiche. They've got death registers from nineteen nineteen to nineteen ninety-four, so I'm bound to find something — assuming I can find the right name."

He continued to regard me. "You've done this a lot, then."

I nodded. "Kept me busy."

Tucker eyed the boxes in front of him. "What time does the library close?"

"Five o'clock. And at four forty-five they'll come and start making you pack up. They're very strict about it."

Sliding the box toward him, Tucker said, "Then I'd better get started."

I made my way to the microfiche machines and, after retrieving the films for the dates I'd requested, worked in relative silence for several hours and through lunch, my stomach rumbling its protest but I was unwilling to stop. I was no longer afraid of discovering my grandmother's story; I was simply eager to know it. Somewhere in the last months I'd begun to see my malaise of the last years as less of an inevitability, or a genetic response to failure. Instead, in discovering my grandmother, I realized that I'd inherited a lot more from her, and my curiosity and need to push further and get there faster might even be related to the drive she'd once had as a young woman.

My stomach rumbled again and I thought of the granola bar I'd tucked in the pocket of the sweater I'd brought to keep me warm in the cool air-conditioning. But the staff's eagerness to keep the researchers alert by the near-arctic temperatures was matched only in their desire to keep crumbs off of rare manuscripts and documents, and the first sound of a crinkling wrapper would bring staff from all corners of the building, resulting in us being tossed out on the sidewalk.

I went back to work, blinking my tired eyes and sighing in frustration when I realized we only had two more hours until closing. My first perusal of the death register had yielded nothing unusual, only the death information for the fathers of both Lillian and Annabelle. I could find nothing for either Josie or Freddie, although I did find the death register for their mother, Justine.

The only alternative that I could think of was to guess Freddie's birth dates and start flipping through the birth registers in the hope that my guess had been accurate.

It was nearly four thirty when I stopped, my finger held in midair over a page of scrawled names of the dead. I'd been focused on the death register of a woman with five different names, either given to her at birth or she'd been married multiple times, when it had occurred to me that we might know exactly where to look for Josie and Freddie, after all. Quickly, I shoved the book out of the way and pulled out the register containing deaths for the year nineteen eighty-one.

I flipped open the nineteen eighty-one book, the year of Justine's death — and found her name again, tucked in with the other Ms. In my experience in researching people's genealogies, unwed mothers tended to use creative license on their children's birth certificates to either hide the identity of the biological father, or protect their family name from scandal by using their middle or even their mother's maiden name as a last name for their illegitimate children. Still keeping the name in the family, but not close enough to warrant scrutiny.

I scanned the entry again. Justine's middle name had been Marie, but her mother's maiden name was Latrobe. Looking around to make sure no one was watching, I pulled out my forbidden cell phone and sent a text to Tucker. "Check Latrobe for last name." Glancing at my watch again, I quickly skipped to the book containing the year of Josie's birth, nineteen eighteen, and flipped to the Ls.

A member of the staff approached the table. "The library will be closing in fifteen minutes. You may leave the books on the table, but you'll need to start finishing up now." Her smile indicated that we would be locked inside the frigid library with the documents if we dared to linger any longer than the five o'clock closing.

I nodded, then quickly went back to the book again, looking for the last name of Latrobe. I knew the information would still be here after we'd left, but I'd have to wait two more days before the library reopened the following Tuesday. Despite all of my foot dragging up to this point, I didn't think my patience could take having to wait even one more hour.

I felt nearly weak with relief when I found

what I'd been searching for. The same staff member appeared again in the reading room doorway. "We're closing. It's time to leave."

I stood as I scanned the entry quickly, not having time to take notes on my laptop, and instead committed the information to memory. I stopped, forgetting to breathe for a moment as I recognized a familiar name.

"My friend is downstairs," I explained. "I'll just go get him and we'll leave together." Without waiting for an answer, I headed down the stairs.

Tucker stood as we entered and smiled. "All done? If not, we can come back on Tuesday if we need to."

I stared at him dumbly, irrationally thinking that the overhead lights that were now being shut off should be shining with brighter intensity or at least flashing on and off to illustrate my discovery.

With Tucker taking hold of my elbow, we were escorted out by two staff members and a security guard, who made a great show of jangling keys and locking the door behind us. I stopped on the front step, unable to go any farther without sharing my newfound knowledge.

I faced Tucker, my hands grasping his upper arms. "Leonard O'Hare was Josie and Freddie's father. Being a doctor, he must have filled out and filed the birth certificates himself so nobody would know. Josie and Freddie were Annabelle's half brother and half sister."

He raised both eyebrows, then tugged on my arm. "Let's keep walking. I think I found something, too, and I don't want anybody else knowing."

I walked with him down the steps, impatiently following him as he led us into Forsyth Park, finally stopping at a bench near the fountain. Looking around us, he said, "Sit down."

I did and waited for him to join me. We must have been walking relatively fast because I was a little out of breath, but was surprised to find that my knee wasn't hurting me as much as it should have been. I wondered if the exercises Emily was forcing me to do might actually have been doing some good.

"Do you think Lillian knew about Josie and Freddie's father?" he asked.

"No, I'm pretty sure she didn't. I guess we're going to have to tell her." I squinted at him in the bright sunlight. "You said you found something, too."

He waited for a moment before reaching into his back pocket and pulling out a yellowed newspaper clipping.

"You stole something from the archives!" My outrage raised my voice enough to have several passersby glance in our direction.

"*Shh,*" he said. "I only borrowed it. I promise to be there at ten o'clock sharp Tuesday morning to put it back where I found it. But there was too much information for me to memorize and not enough time to jot it down, so I borrowed it."

"If they find out, they'll never let me back in." I tried not to let my curiosity overtake my indignation, but I failed. "So what is it?"

"Well, when I got your text, I knew immediately where to go. A good friend of mine in med school was a Latrobe, so I guess when I first saw the name on a folder, I went through the whole thing to see if it might be the same family. It wasn't, but the name and the folder I'd pulled it from sort of stuck with me." He handed the clipping to me, a look of smug satisfaction on his face. "This was one of the items in the folder. It must have been filed there by accident because of the last name."

I smiled, my guilt lessened somewhat by the promise of discovering something new. Taking the clipping, I held my breath and began to read. It was an obituary for Justine Marie Montet, who'd died on May twenty-fifth, nineteen eighty-one, interred at Laurel Grove Cemetery in Savannah. Predeceased by her son, Frederick Latrobe, and daughter, Josephine Montet of New York City and survived by granddaughter Alicia Montet Jones, of Tattnall Street, Savannah.

I looked up at Tucker. "Josie had a daughter, who lived in Savannah and might still be here." I looked back again for the street, ready to start walking there now.

"Am I forgiven then? Because if I am, I have something else, too."

My indignation all but forgotten, I held out my hand. "Show me."

From under his shirt he produced what looked to be a photocopy of an official document. At least he hadn't folded it up to fit in his back pocket. He handed it to me. "This was clipped to Justine's obituary."

It was a copy of Freddie's death certificate. I glanced at the birth and death dates to see if they corresponded with what we knew about Freddie, then let my gaze roam over the document to see if I could find whatever it was that had made Tucker borrow it.

"Look at the cause of death," he said.

My gaze went back to the correct box. "Suicide. By hanging." I closed my eyes for a moment, and shook my head. "He was only twenty-six years old. What would have made him want to kill himself?"

"Piper, it was Georgia in nineteen thirty-nine and Freddie was a black man. It's entirely possible that it wasn't a suicide. Your grandmother mentioned in her scrapbook that he was involved in registering black voters. Back then, men would have killed for less."

I sat back, my mind spinning. "Josie's daughter — what was her name?"

"Alicia Jones."

"We need to see if she still lives here — and it should be easier because we have the street name, too. I know I'm pushing my luck, but let's look in the phone book and see if we can find her. If not, I'll go online. I hate to pay for that kind of information, but if I need to, I know a great search engine."

He stood and reached for my hand. I took his and let him pull me up. "You're pretty good at this stuff, Piper."

"Thanks," I said, feeling oddly pleased. "A lot of it is dull and routine, but every once in a while you're given a little bit of a mystery to solve, and it makes everything else worthwhile."

Tucker didn't move away. "I have a feeling that you'd be good at anything you set your mind to."

I looked away, embarrassed. "Come on.

Let's get back to the house to find what Helen and George turned up and to see if I can locate Alicia Jones."

We walked the short blocks back to Taylor Street, and I didn't think once about how hot it was or even if my knee hurt. I was too busy thinking about what Tucker had said. *I have a feeling that you'd be good at anything you set your mind to.*

I practically bounded up the steps when we reached the house and then fumbled impatiently with the keys to get inside the front door. Helen was laughing, although it sounded a lot closer to giggling, in the front parlor, and when I walked in I found her and George sitting on the love seat and her hands were clasped in his. He didn't even have the decency to drop her hands when he spotted us.

"Hello, Earlene, Tucker. We were wondering what was taking you so long. I was just telling Helen about a few of my court cases, some of which have been rather humorous." He patted Helen's hand and then stood. "So, did you find out anything new?"

I plopped down in my grandmother's armchair. "Quite a bit, actually. I discovered that Josie and Freddie were my grandmother's half siblings. Apparently my great-grandfather had a longtime relationship with their mother and employed her as his housekeeper to keep it simple."

"I wonder if Malily knew," said Helen, a line between her eyebrows.

"From what I've read in the scrapbook pages, I don't think she knew," I said. "But we need to ask her. Might make her tell me more than what's been written."

Tucker sat down next to me in my grandfather's chair, the one positioned to directly face the empty medal wall. "Helen should go with you. Malily's never been able to tell her no."

I nodded, then turned to George. "Were you and Helen able to find anything new?"

George gave me a smug smile. "As a matter of fact, yes. We make quite the team, I'll have you know. She takes excellent shorthand and has a very precise memory. I told her she should be working in a law office somewhere to utilize her skills."

I forced myself not to grit my teeth. "What did you find out?"

"After going through miles of microfilm — it's very hard on the neck, you know. . . ."

Helen interrupted George with a hand on his arm. "We found the burial record and plot for Margaret Louise in Bonaventure. She was buried in nineteen twelve, which predates the magazines that are up there, meaning the room served another purpose after Margaret Louise died."

"Any luck with more news articles about the baby found in the river?" Tucker asked.

George shook his head. "No. Archives for the *Savannah Morning News* for the time period we're looking for are sketchy at best. A bad flood destroyed about a year's worth of stored newspapers prior to them being stored on microfilm. Some of the major news stories, obits, and the like could be found in other sources, but not so much the little news tidbits."

I swallowed my disappointment, focusing instead on the one last piece of information we'd learned. "We found Justine's obituary, and it said she was survived by Josie's daughter, Alicia Jones on Tattnall Street. There's a chance she could still live there, so I'm going to go see what I can find, starting with the phone book." I stood, heading for the kitchen.

Helen stopped me. "Did you find out anything else about Freddie?"

I paused on the threshold. "That he died when he was twenty-six. The death certificate says suicide by hanging."

Her cheeks paled. "How sad. After reading about him, I was starting to feel as if I knew him. I didn't expect . . . that."

"Neither did I. Although Tucker pointed out that a black man, especially one with his background, found hanged wasn't all that unusual back then. Paying somebody to fudge the cause of death wouldn't have necessarily been a big deal."

"No," she said softly, "it wouldn't have been." George took her hand again, and I left the room to make a phone call.

The phone book was where it had always been, on the top step of the kitchen stool tucked beneath the ancient princess phone with the long, tightly curled cord in mustard yellow. My grandparents had been frugal; despite their being comfortably off, spending money to replace something that worked perfectly fine had never been on their agenda.

I flipped the thick book open and found the Js, rapidly moving my index finger down to the top of the *Jones* list, saying the names quietly to myself, and simultaneously searching for Tattnall Street. The listing, when I found it, seemed innocuous enough, a single *Jones, A.* but my heart began to pound a little louder in my chest.

Lifting the receiver from the cradle, I held it away from my ear for a moment, listening to the dial tone as if it were a voice from the past. Then I slowly dialed the number.

The ringing sounded unusually loud, and I let it ring five times before an answering machine picked up. It was an electronic voice, so I was unable to determine the gender or anything else about the person I was trying to reach. At the sound of the tone, I left a message explaining that I was the granddaughter of Annabelle O'Hare and that she and Josie Montet had been close friends growing up. I asked that if I had reached the home of Josie's daughter, Alicia, to please call me back. I left my cell phone number, then hung up, my hand lingering on the receiver for a long time, listening to the quiet of my grandmother's kitchen, and feeling her presence.

When I rejoined the others, they looked at me expectantly. "I got an answering machine, so I left a message. I guess I'll just wait and see if she calls back before I decide what to do."

"And if she doesn't call back, you'll hire on as her housekeeper to find out what she knows that way?"

Tucker's face was deadpan, but when Helen began to laugh he smiled. "Sorry. I couldn't resist." He stood. "I guess we should head back. Malily hates eating alone."

Helen pulled out a card from her purse

and handed it to George. "Call me."

I moved toward the doorway again. "Give me about fifteen minutes, okay? I have something I need to do."

I went out to the Jeep and pulled out the rose clippings Malily had given to Helen, wrapped in damp paper towels. I brought them back to the desolate garden, where the empty soil waited, trying to decide where to plant the roses. I chose the back wall, where they could grow wild, just as my grandmother would have done, untamed and unruly; her garden was the only place in her life where she allowed herself to revisit her past.

The door to her garden shed stuck tight, but I managed to dislodge it by tugging. I found my grandmother's tools, her trowel and her gloves. Even her large-brimmed hat. I left the hat behind, but put on the gloves, feeling my grandmother's hands on mine as I pulled them over my fingers that were shaped like hers. I attacked the soil with the trowel, scraping off the hardened topsoil and digging deeper to moist earth, exposing its secrets. I placed the clippings far enough apart so that when they grew they wouldn't crowd one another, then tightly packed the earth around them to keep them upright.

I knew I wasn't done. They'd need more

nurturing, more direction. I might even have to move them once I determined where the sun would hit them. As I sat back on my heels and studied the tightly closed buds that reminded me of a newborn's eyes, I knew I'd done something good. Like learning to trot before cantering, it was a place to start. My grandmother had been a horsewoman and a civil rights–crusader, and she had once wanted to be a doctor, but her garden was her story, and I made a silent promise to her that it wouldn't be forgotten.

I replaced the trowel and the gloves, gently touching the hat before I tugged the door shut. I exited through the garden gate, pausing long enough to take in the lonely rose clippings against the back wall, the late-summer sun casting giant shadows like a bridge from one life to another.

Chapter 20

Lillian sat in her chair by the window as night fell, listening to the whippoorwill calling out to the darkening sky. She pushed aside the tray of uneaten food that Odella had brought up, tossing a bite of chicken to the waiting Mardi, who'd been sitting patiently as they'd both waited for Tucker's Jeep to return.

Tucker had called earlier to let her know that there'd been an accident on the highway, so they'd turned around and had dinner in Savannah. It hadn't mattered. It had been a long time since Lillian had had an appetite, and now she just used food as a buffer against the medications and alcohol that seemed to be the only things getting her through her days.

Leaning forward, she rubbed her swollen knuckles, feeling the shifting of the seasons in her bones. Like the weathered oak trees in the alley that never alternated colors or dropped their leaves, they showed the approaching autumn in more subtle ways — a change in pitch to their nightly cry, and an almost imperceptible change in the angle of their arch. It was almost as if the oncoming cold of winter alerted them to hover closer to the earth and to one another to help face whatever came next.

Lillian sighed, missing Charlie again. He'd been the one who'd protected her, who'd sheltered her from the storm even when she thought she didn't need it. She'd been thinking a lot about him lately, and she didn't know why. He'd been gone for almost fifteen years, and in the time since he died, she had only thought of him with the same nostalgia one might feel for a favorite dress that no longer fit. It was the scrapbook, of course, and all of the memories it brought forth — the good and the bad. And all the things that weren't written on the pages, but were inscribed instead on the years themselves, as permanent and irrevocable as surviving beyond everyone you'd ever loved.

She turned her head, hearing the sound of a car approaching the house, followed eventually by the front door closing and footsteps climbing the stairs. Despite her sense of foreboding and inevitability, she smiled. Piper with her bad leg wouldn't take the elevator any more than Annabelle would have.

Mardi ran to the door before anyone knocked, then launched himself through the opening crack as soon as Lillian called out her permission for them to enter. Tucker, Helen, and Piper stood clustered in the doorway like children sent to the principal's office, and it made Lillian want to laugh, realizing how very reversed their situations really were. She was the one who should be afraid, after all.

Lillian indicated the sofa and wing chair near her and they found seats, Tucker and Piper together on the sofa and Helen in the chair with Mardi's head propped on her lap. Piper handed her more scrapbook pages. "Here're more of my grandmother's pages. I've got one more left. I haven't read it, but I'll give it to you as soon as I'm done."

Lillian regarded Piper with surprise. "You're prolonging it, are you? Afraid of what you might find?"

Piper's eyes met hers with a question, but she didn't look away. "No. Not anymore. I think I'm hesitating now because I don't want to say good-bye. It's the last thing I have of hers." She reached behind her neck. "Well, almost."

Gently, she unclasped the chain, then held the necklace in front of her, the gold charms seeming overly bright as they reflected the lamplight. "I think Lola belongs to you."

Piper stood, then waited in front of Lillian until the older woman realized what Piper was trying to do. Lillian bent her head forward and waited for Piper to clasp the chain behind her neck before stepping back and sitting down again.

"I've made a list of the charms along with when they were added and by whom. There's still quite a few I'm unsure about — although I assume most of them are Josie's since we haven't read any of her pages — yet."

"Yet?" A butterfly settled in Lillian's stomach, beating its wings against her past.

"I think we've found Josie's daughter. She lives in Savannah. If it's her, she might have Josie's pages."

Lillian sat back in her chair. "Alicia," she said.

"You know her?" Helen asked.

"No. I just know of her. I followed Josie's life. Knew she had a daughter, and that Josie had named her Alicia." She smiled to herself, remembering when she'd read the birth announcement. "Alicia is my middle name. I always thought that was Josie's way of telling me that she hadn't forgotten me."

"But you had no other contact with her?"

Lillian's knuckles began to hurt and she rubbed them, trying to make the pain go away, and knowing that nothing would ever take it away completely. "No. We'd made a clean break. There was no more contact."

Piper leaned forward, her elbows on her knees. "Was it Josie who added the baby carriage charm to Lola?"

How easy it would be to say yes. Lillian shook her head, the effort exhausting her. "No. Alicia wasn't born until nineteen fifty and we stopped adding to Lola when we split up the scrapbook in nineteen thirty-nine."

"So who did?"

Lillian fisted her hands, wishing she had a drink. As if reading her mind, Tucker stood and moved to the wet bar, then poured her a generous glass of sherry. She took her time sipping from the glass, her eyes never leaving Piper. "That would be jumping ahead in our story, wouldn't it? We've still got a few more pages in Annabelle's scrapbook, and you've got most of mine still to read. That way you'll have all the information you need before you start jumping to conclusions. But maybe that's your nature. Is it, Piper? To jump ahead of yourself before you're prepared?"

She watched as Piper's cheeks darkened. Before Piper could defend herself, Tucker stood again. "That's enough, Malily." Tucker moved back to the wet bar and poured three more glasses of sherry.

Lillian looked down at her hands, knowing he was right. "All right. Why don't you tell me what you learned today? I'm eager to hear how events have been distorted by the historical record." The weight of Lola on her chest surprised her. It was the weight of years pressing against her chest, pushing the air out of her lungs.

Tucker brought over the drinks and Helen clasped hers with both hands as she spoke. "Why don't you read from your scrapbook first? You haven't gotten very far."

"My eyes hurt, and it's hard for me to read the handwriting. Why don't we have Piper read it?" She wasn't sure why she'd said that, only that she realized how much Piper sounded like Annabelle, and how when she'd been ill, she'd enjoyed listening to the sound of Annabelle's voice reading to her. It was a rare place in her memory, a place untouched by adulthood.

"I'd be happy to." Piper stood and moved to the desk where Lillian had motioned.

"The pages are stacked in order from the

top. Thumb through them to find where you stopped. I didn't write every time I had Lola, so I don't have as many pages as Josie and Annabelle." She took a sip from her glass. "They had a gift for turning the mundane into something exciting to write about. I preferred to live an existence that was a bit more exciting, and precluded the need to share lest all my secrets be exposed."

Piper glanced at her, then leaned over the desk, and Lillian noticed how her hair fell over her shoulders, the first time she'd seen it loose. It softened her, shadowing the blunt edges and angles of a woman who'd once jumped tall obstacles without blinking an eye.

Sitting back down next to Tucker, Piper cleared her throat and began to read.

June 14, 1937

It's been a year since my debut and Papa is getting impatient with me. I can't explain to him that my future isn't solely in my hands, that I wait for my love to offer for me, to take me away so that we can live together finally as man and wife.

I've told no one except this book, so Josie and Annabelle are left to wonder when they read this. It's remarkable that the sisters of my heart don't yet know the depth of my love, or the secrets in my heart. They only know that Charlie makes me laugh, and loves to dance and has already promised me that he will love me forever.

Sweet Annabelle, I think you suspect my secret, but your loyalty keeps you silent. Or is it jealousy? Your clandestine activities to help those less fortunate amongst us are admirable, but I'm afraid they won't keep you warm at night. Take care, my friend, that you choose wisely.

I'm afraid these affairs of the heart have cooled our friendship, and it grieves me. That's why I invited Annabelle and Josie to Asphodel last month. Our friendship is meant to last forever and I'd hoped we could recapture some of our childhood. I think we did, too. We went riding again, just like old times and even got Josie to sit in a saddle, although she never went faster than a slow walk. But Annabelle flew over hedges and gates — scaring the life out of me and Josie — but she was a queen on her horse. The very best. And I remember thinking at the time that I wished for her in life what she felt at that moment — sheer joy and passion at having found the thing that makes her heart beat wildly. People live their entire lives without discovering what that is, but she's found it by helping others. And by flying over hedges on the back of a horse.

And then we went to the county fair and all the men couldn't take their eyes off of us — it was so flattering! Annabelle did exchange words with a young man who said unkind things to Josie, but she put him in his place so he didn't bother us again. Annabelle's like that — when she speaks, she speaks with authority and people listen. I think that will help her when she becomes a doctor and has to tell people what they need to be doing.

They had a singing contest and Annabelle and I made Josie perform. She didn't win, and we suspect it was because she was the only woman of color who participated, but we all knew she was the best. The girl shines on stage and it's only a matter of time before somebody important hears her sing and decides to make her a star.

The fair had just finished the new dance pavilion and we didn't lack for partners, if I may say so myself. We tried cotton candy for the first time and Annabelle enjoyed it so much that she went back for seconds. When we went on the Ferris wheel, the spinning and all that sugar was too much for her and she barely made it out of our car before she threw up behind a bush. She was embarrassed but I laughed, and that made her laugh, too, and it was just like old times, with the three of us together.

We grew close again, didn't we? Until Freddie returned to Asphodel to break in a new mare my father managed to acquire from a bankrupt lawyer. And things grew awkward between us again. I wish he hadn't come. Because friendships are forever, regardless of any matters of the heart.

Piper was silent for a moment before she looked up. "There's another entry. Shall I go on?"

With their nods of assent, she continued to read.

April 9, 1939

She stopped, looked up at Tucker. "That's the year Freddie died, isn't it?"

Tucker nodded, and Piper's gaze fell back to the book but she paused for a moment, filing away the information, before she began to read again.

My father has stopped writing for me to come home. I've told him that Annabelle is still busy nursing her increasingly frail father and exhausted from all the extra work that has fallen on her shoulders.

At least that wasn't a complete lie. She has taken upon herself the burden of running the household and nursing her father, but she also seems to hold a great deal of anger toward him. When I ask her about it, she gets upset with me, so I've stopped asking. I think they might have had an argument that has yet to be resolved, and she can't bear to think about it. Several times she has taken me aside and tried to tell me something, but has so far been unable to. But sometimes she has a gleam in her eye, like she knows something that I should know, but she harbors her secret in an attempt to best me. I hope, with time, it will be easier for her and she can unburden herself to me. I owe her that, at least, considering everything I'm asking her to do now.

I've told my father that I would like to stay for at least another six months —

for reasons obvious to us here but not to him. I told him that I'd like to find employment, and it's easier here in the city. And Annabelle does need me after all, though I could never tell my father why.

Papa tells me that Charlie comes to Asphodel at least once a week on the pretense of visiting my father but everyone knows it's to find out about me. Papa said that Charlie's bank is doing well, considering the times, and it's quite plain to anybody with eyes that Charlie needs a wife and that he's already decided on who he wants.

Charlie would make a good husband, I know. When I think of him, I remember him at my come-out, and how he danced and made me smile. It wasn't that long ago, but it feels as if it happened in another lifetime, and a part of me wishes that I could go back, that we could all go back and be the people we were before. But that's impossible now.

Piper stopped and looked across the room to Lillian. "There's an envelope here that's come loose from the page." She glanced down, holding the paper as if it were a delicate flower petal. "Is this the letter Susan found?"

Lillian swallowed, the necklace heavy on her skin. "No. That's from Charlie. Go ahead and read it."

With clumsy fingers, Piper slid the letter out. "It says, 'Marry me, Lily. Come home and marry me. My heart is quite lost to you, and there is nothing you could ever say or do that would cause my opinion of you to sway. I love you, sweet Lily. Come home to me and be my wife.' "

"Did he ever come to Savannah to see you in person?" Helen placed her untouched sherry on a side table and sat on the edge of her chair.

"Every week, I think. But I would never see him. Annabelle would have Justine make excuses for us so that neither one of us would have to face him. Sometimes he'd sit on the porch for hours waiting for me to change my mind, but I never did."

Piper used both hands to swipe her hair from her forehead. "But I thought you loved him. And you did end up marrying him the next year. So why did you make him suffer?"

Lillian leveled her with a stern gaze. "You're jumping ahead again, dear. Be patient."

Piper didn't back down. "I'm not jumping

ahead. I'm just trying to fill in the empty places you seem to be skipping over. Like the letter that Susan read that you told Tucker was an unsent letter you'd written to a friend. Was it intended for my grandmother? And is it in here?"

Lillian continued to watch her, wondering who would back down first, and not at all sure of the answer.

Tucker placed a hand on Piper's arm and she looked at him for a long moment before sliding back in her seat. She cleared her throat and began to read again.

Annabelle shared a secret with me today. She led me up to the attic and made me help her shove an old armoire away from the wall. A locked door had been hidden behind the armoire, but Annabelle had a key. She said she'd found it with her father's things as she and Mr. Morton were getting his papers in order. Before she opened it, she told me that she thinks she's found the answer to all of our problems.

On the other side of the door lay a sad little room. A small bed with sparse furnishings was all it contained, but I understood immediately what she meant. A person could live here without the interference of prying eyes from the outside world. If a person wanted to disappear for a period of time, this would be the perfect place.

I feel better now that our predicament has a temporary solution. I might even be able to sleep at night, if only we knew where Freddie was. Josie tells us that neither she nor Justine has seen or heard from him since I've come here, and certainly Annabelle and I haven't either. Unless Annabelle isn't telling me everything. But I can't be angry with her. She is being more like a sister to me, and I can't be anything but grateful to her.

I only added one charm this time: a golden key. It's to symbolize the key to our sanctuary, and to the locked door of our future. For all three of us that future is a mystery, and I wonder which one of us will be the first to figure out how to unlock it.

Helen had moved to the floor by her grandmother's chair as if the story being told was theirs together, that anything revealed would be about them. She placed her hand over Lillian's. "We went into the secret room today, Malily. We believe it was probably built for a little girl born in the late eighteen hundreds, Margaret Louise O'Hare. Piper found a blue knitted blanket there. And she also found a blue baby sweater in Annabelle's trunk. Whose baby were they for?"

Lillian turned, listening to the sound of the clock, the necklace pressing down on her again as she struggled to find words.

"Would you like us to leave now?" Piper stood, as if she could feel, too, the need to end the story now — now that it still had the chance for a happy ending. Annabelle had been that way to the end, unable to believe that the worst thing that could happen to you could happen twice.

Lillian shook her head, feeling as if the ticking from her bedside clock was louder than it should have been, the passage of time echoing through the still room. "No. Not yet."

Piper's hand reached up to the angel charm around her neck. "My grandmother, Annabelle, she was a good friend to you?"

Lillian nodded without hesitation. "The very best. Even when I didn't deserve it. I was jealous of how close she and Freddie worked together with the movement. I was excluded from helping because of my father and his association with the Klan, not that I think I was so brave back then to be of

much use, anyway. So I tried to make Annabelle jealous by flirting like crazy with that
boy from the law office. He was a lot
younger than us, but I think she had a
tender spot for him."

"Paul Morton?"

"Yes. That was his name. Nice-looking
young fellow. I think he had it bad for Annabelle, too. But she never said anything to
me. Allowed me to make a fool out of myself
without any repercussions." She smiled to
herself, remembering. "Josie and I used to
say that we were the stones and Annabelle
the mortar. She kept us together."

Piper and Tucker exchanged a glance.
Piper stood and moved to sit on the footrest
of Lillian's chair. "We found the birth
records for Freddie and Josie today."

"Yes?" This wasn't a direction Lillian had
anticipated.

"Did you ever know who their father
was?"

Lillian shook her head. "It didn't really
ever concern me. Since I was very little and
began visiting the O'Hare household with
my father, Justine was there with Freddie
and Josie. There was never a father. He
simply didn't exist, and to my young mind
it never occurred to me to ask. Why?"

Piper cleared her throat. "Dr. Leonard

O'Hare was their father. Josie and Freddie were Annabelle's half brother and half sister."

Lillian stared at her for a long moment, not comprehending at first. The ticking of the clock was more insistent now, each tick louder than the last, the sound coming from very far away. She shifted her head. "But Justine . . . She was . . . she was his housekeeper."

"Apparently she was more than that, Malily," Tucker said gently.

"Did . . . did Annabelle know this?"

"According to her scrapbook, we think she didn't find out until her father was so sick with the flu."

Lillian's gaze darted around the room. *Couldn't they hear the clock ticking?* She jerked her hand out toward the sound of the clock, succeeding in knocking it to the floor. She held up her hand to stop Tucker, who'd already stood. "Leave it."

Piper spoke again. "Annabelle or Josie never told you?"

Lillian stared at Piper for a long moment, seeing her friend Annabelle — the friend whose loyalty she'd taken for granted, who'd taught her how to cultivate tea roses and who'd known how to keep a secret. "I don't think Josie knew. And Annabelle never told me." She closed her eyes and laughed, the sound brittle and hollow. "I was jealous of Annabelle. I thought she and Freddie . . ."

Helen leaned forward. "But wouldn't she have told you? You were like sisters. I would have thought she'd confide in you about her feelings."

Lillian gasped, the memories of her youth cold and unyielding against the reality of her frail body. "Yes. She would have. I know that now, but back then . . ." She shook her head, still unable to tell the rest of the story. The ticking from the clock, although now muffled, continue to reverberate through her head.

Tucker stood and moved to press the buzzer on the wall by her bed. "I'm calling Odella. You're not looking well, Malily. We can continue this tomorrow after you've rested." After murmuring something in her ear, he lifted her as easily as one of his daughters and brought her to the bed. Piper approached and adjusted the pillows under her head and placed a blanket over her legs, her touch soft and reassuring as Lillian had known it would be.

Lillian nodded, feeling the tiredness now in her bones. She welcomed it, this respite from the pain. But there was something new, too. She felt lighter, somehow. As if the secrets that had long anchored her to this world were slowly fraying, like a ship breaking its moorings as it slid out to sea.

She turned her head and blinked at the watery image at the foot of her bed. Annabelle sat there, her knitting needles flying, the ticking of the clock having eased its way into the clicking sound of needles. Blue yarn spilled on the white chenille bedspread, only Lillian knew that it wasn't the right bedspread. *Always knitting, Annabelle. Always that incessant knitting as we'd waited those last months for news of Freddie. How I'd hated it. And how I hated you for having something to keep you busy besides regret.*

She heard Helen whisper in her ear before kissing her cheek. "Good night, Malily. We'll see you in the morning." Lillian closed her eyes and the sound of the knitting needles ceased.

Piper took her hand and Lillian managed to hold on to it, pulling her closer. "Stay. Please."

Piper sat down on the edge of the bed, not releasing her hand. "Okay."

Lillian waited for Tucker and Helen to leave before speaking again. "I need you to do something for me."

Piper nodded.

"In the top drawer of my writing desk is

an old framed photo. I need you to bring it to me."

Piper stood and did as Lillian asked before resuming her seat on the side of the bed. "When was this taken?"

Lillian smiled, smelling again Charlie's cologne and hearing the magic of Josie's voice. She felt her in the room, too, knowing that if she turned her head she'd see Josie and Annabelle at the foot of the bed, just as she remembered them during those long months of waiting.

"Right before my come-out ball. It was the happiest night of my life."

"Then why do you keep it in your drawer instead of where you can see it?"

Lillian sighed, not remembering ever feeling so tired. "Because of Annabelle. I didn't want to see her anymore."

Piper lowered the frame, letting it rest in her lap. "Why? Please, Lillian. Please tell me why."

Lillian clutched at the necklace around her neck, her fingers sliding along the charms, finally settling on the key. She wrapped her hand around it, feeling the edges of the charm biting into her skin. "Maybe you don't want to know. Did it never occur to you that you might not really want to know what some of those shadows are you see in the dark?"

Piper dislodged her hand and stood, averting her head so Lillian couldn't see the tears pooling in her eyes. "No. Not anymore. I need to know. I need to know because . . ."

Lillian managed to sit up a little, giving strength to her voice. "Because why? Because you want to know what changed your grandmother from an intelligent, vibrant young woman into the timid shell she was when she died?" The sound of the knitting needles began again, frantically clicking against each other.

Piper's breath stuttered. When she turned around, Lillian expected to see a shattered expression; instead she saw the Annabelle she'd known, the friend who fought until the end. Piper came close to the bed, her eyes bright with tears and confusion. "Maybe that's part of it. But mostly . . ." She stopped, her chest rising and falling as she tried to catch her breath. "Because mostly I want to know that I'm different than her."

The click of needles stopped abruptly, and Lillian listened as the silence was filled with another sound she couldn't yet identify. Something low and murmuring, reminding her of a moving river, heard from a distance. "But you're not, are you? Because if you were different, you'd still be jumping fences."

Piper turned to her, her face rigid with anger. As if Lillian hadn't spoken at all, Piper asked, "Why did you come to stay with Annabelle for so long? Was it because of your father's association with the Klan? Or was there something else? And what about the baby in the news clipping? Whose baby was it, and how did he end up in the river? Is that what was in the letter Susan read?"

There was a soft knock on the door and Odella entered. Lillian closed her eyes again, relief and exhaustion washing over her. *So tired.* "You're jumping ahead again, Piper. Just like Annabelle . . ." She kept her eyes closed, waiting until Piper turned away.

"Wait." Lillian held up a finger. "The frame. I want it next to me. On the table."

After a short hesitation, Piper did as she'd been asked. "You're wrong, you know," Piper said quietly as she settled the frame on the bedstand.

Lillian smiled, letting the approaching sleep begin to numb her limbs and her mind. "Then prove it."

Piper stiffened and moved back, her presence by the bed replaced by a bustling Odella.

"Do you hear them, Piper?" Lillian tilted her head, listening to the voices who spoke with words she couldn't understand.

"The trees?" A line formed on Piper's forehead as she turned her head to listen. "I don't hear anything. Maybe it's just the wind. Or maybe your hearing is going."

Lillian smiled at Piper's back as the younger woman retreated, watching as she moved to the door and closed it behind her, unaware of all the ghosts now crowding the room or their silent nods of approval.

CHAPTER 21

I ran down the stairs, ignoring the protest in my knees. I'd been dutifully doing Emily's exercises and my joints did bend more easily and with less pain. I knew now that I would probably never walk normally again, but the realization came with some relief. Now that I knew the worst of it, I could focus on making it better. Like an alcoholic continuing to drink so he doesn't have to face the real problem, I'd relied on my limp to show the world physical proof of why I couldn't ride anymore. And I couldn't help but think how disappointed my grandmother would be that I had chosen to live that way.

I heard Tucker and Helen talking in the parlor, but I slipped past the doorway, unwilling to speak to anybody after my conversation with Lillian. I was unsettled, suddenly feeling the earth's gravitational pull, wary that it might stop at any moment.

Because if you were different, you'd still be jumping fences. Lillian's words taunted me, and I walked faster as if physical exertion might distract my thoughts. I left a note on the kitchen table telling Odella that I would return the golf cart first thing in the morning, then left out the back door.

It was full dark now, the house illuminated with spotlights, the alley of oaks towering in front of me. I paused by the sundial, feeling silly at my reluctance to continue forward. An owl hooted from a high branch of the nearest oak as I studied the sundial again, recalling the English translation. *Time flies, but not memories.* I wondered if my grandmother had ever paused at this exact spot and contemplated the words on the sundial as I did now, and understood how very true they were.

The cloudless night lay still over the oaks and old house and as I moved forward under the canopy of trees, I pushed on the pedal as far as it would go. I couldn't shake the feeling of expectation, as if the trees were watching me, and waiting to see what Lillian's words would make me do.

When I returned to the cottage I put on a pot of coffee and sat at the kitchen table, prepared to make a long night of it. I had one more page to read from my grandmother's scrapbook, and then I was going to reread everything, making more notes and checking dates. I was determined to discover Lillian's secrets before she had the chance to make me doubt my reasons why.

I set the coffeepot and my mug next to me and began to read.

July 7, 1939

So much has happened, and yet it feels as if no time has passed at all. I'm surrounded by people in my house, yet I'm all alone. If it weren't for Paul Morton's frequent visits, I'm certain that I would have lost all hope long ago.

Freddie comes sporadically, if at all, and always in the middle of the night. He's afraid for his life, but he tries to hide it from us. He wants us all to leave, to hide until after the next election, when new laws can be enforced, and not used against those they are meant to protect. But he forgets that memories run deep in these parts, and I'm afraid neither he nor his family will ever be safe, regardless of how far they run.

He did convince Justine to go to Virginia for an extended stay with her sister. I made it seem as if my father is getting better and will be able to protect us, but

I knew she wasn't convinced. But Freddie can bargain with the sun to make it shine, and she left. I feel relieved, knowing there's one less person I'm responsible for.

A farmhouse over in Effingham County burned two weeks ago, killing a black man, his wife, and three of their children. The official report was that a cow knocked over a lantern in the barn but Freddie knew the man, and knew he kept no cows. I rail against the injustice, and feel impotent with my situation. Freddie assures us that after we weather this storm, we'll find peace.

Paul Morton brings us food as I hesitate to leave the house now and don't want to draw attention to the amount of food I'm buying. He's been up to the attic room and bided his time there with conversation and magazines, and his company was greatly appreciated. He's written to several medical schools for their brochures and entrance applications and is having them sent to his house. For when I'm ready, he says. And I'm thankful not just for his kindness, but because he believes it's something I can accomplish.

It won't be long now. I've been knitting quite a bit because it keeps my mind off of things. Josie jokes that I've made enough sweaters and blankets to fill an orphanage and we decided that whatever color we don't need will be donated.

So we've been biding our time, keeping ourselves busy by worrying about Freddie, doing housework and recalling the happiest parts of our childhoods. It's sad because we're still young, but I feel as if we've been here forever, just waiting for our lives to finally begin.

I asked Paul to take a picture of the three of us in my garden — my favorite place in the world. My flowering azaleas and purple wisteria were photo-worthy, so I posed us in front of them, with Lillian standing behind us as Josie and I squatted in front. The flowers have done well despite the heat, and Lillian wore her new coat, ignoring the temperature. We all wore our angel charms and smiled for the camera, and I know it's a photo we'll look at when we're older, if only to remind ourselves how far we've come.

For Lola, I've borrowed an idea from Lillian and chosen two charms. The first is a rocking chair, because it reminds me of this waiting time. And a baby carriage, of course, for obvious reasons.

I jerked my head up, staring at my grand-mother's handwriting as if it weren't fin-ished and the script should continue down the page. My fingers traveled downward toward the black-and-white photo of the women in the backyard, Lillian wrapped in a bulky wool coat and scarf. Pulled over each collar was a chain with an angel charm, the dim sun glinting off of each one like a conspiratorial wink.

I stared at the photo for a long time, try-ing to see beyond the thick coat, and draw-ing more than one conclusion. Despite the lateness of the hour, I stood, intending to call Tucker and Helen and tell them what I'd read.

As I reached for my cell phone, it rang. I grabbed it and flipped it open before I re-alized that I didn't recognize the number.

"Hello?"

"Hello. May I speak with Piper Mills?"

I knew then, and I might have forgotten to breathe. "This is she. Is this Alicia?"

There was a brief pause. "It is. I'd like to sit down and talk with you, if you're still interested."

I leaned back in my chair, listening to the honeyed tones of Alicia Jones' voice as she gave me directions to her house, smiling to myself as I realized that I might have a chance to beat Lillian at her own game.

I'd been up for hours, having returned the golf cart and done my morning exercise by walking back to the cottage. I'd called Tucker and Helen both, reading my grandmother's last pages out loud, and telling them about Alicia's call, and made plans to drive into Savannah with Helen.

She was waiting for me by the sundial wearing a yellow silk knit dress with a wide tapestry belt, making me feel frumpy in my cotton skirt and cotton knit pullover despite the collapsible cane she carried. It even had a yellow tip to match her outfit. It had stopped striking me as odd that the first person I'd ever ask for fashion advice was a blind woman.

"You look beautiful, Helen," I called from the open window. "You'll have to take me shopping sometime."

Helen laughed as she waited for me to stop the car and help her in. "George has invited me to lunch, if that's all right with you. He invited you, too, but said he'd understand if you were too busy to join us. He'd be happy to drive me home."

Helen kept her face averted but I could see the blush blooming in her cheeks. "Yeah, I'll need to get back, so if he doesn't mind driving you, that would be fine."

"Please don't think that I'm rushing into anything. I'm not. I like George and it's been a long time since anybody who isn't related to me has paid me any attention. I like to enjoy myself, and to have a reason for wearing pretty clothes." Helen shrugged. "I like that he's related to Mr. Morton. He was a real friend to our grandmothers, it seems. And I think we should sit down with him and ask all of our questions. He's bound to know a lot more than he's told you."

I flipped off the radio. "He's on an extended vacation right now with his wife, but I've been sending e-mails on the odd chance he'll think to check it when they're in port. He communicated with me once through George, something mundane like where to find the circuit breakers. And then he sent me an e-mail last night answering one I'd sent to him, although it wasn't really a response."

"What do you mean? What did it say?"

"Perfer et obdura; dolor hic tibi proderit olim."

"Be patient and strong; someday this pain will be useful to you." Helen thought for a moment. "What do you think he's trying to tell you?"

"The same thing my grandmother was

trying to tell me when she left the charm for me. And I haven't quite figured that one out yet."

"Maybe Mr. Morton feels that you need to figure it out yourself without his help. Hearing it from someone else sort of loses its power. Kind of like Malily telling Tucker and me all these years that our parents loved us; it's just not as effective as it would have been if they'd told us themselves."

I reached for Helen's hand, and felt her squeeze back, accepting that I would understand more than most the missing part of the human heart rendered by the absence of a mother and father.

"Does Lillian know where you're going this morning?"

Helen shook her head. "Mardi and I went down to breakfast really early to get there before Malily did so I wouldn't have to lie. But I needn't have bothered; Odella told me that Malily wasn't feeling well and was having a breakfast tray sent up." Helen rested her head against the side window and for a moment I was fooled into thinking she was watching the traffic.

Helen continued. "I was relieved at first, and then I began to worry. Malily isn't one to admit to weakness and is always at breakfast, dressed with full war paint —

Tucker's words not mine — and ready to go before any of us. I'll just make a point to stop by when I get back, and bring the last of Annabelle's pages for her to read if that's all right."

"Absolutely. And I'm going with you. We'll finish reading her pages tonight, too. This has got to end. I can't stand the not knowing any longer. Besides, I've got projects waiting for me at home for a few of my genealogy clients. I need to get back."

Helen faced me. "I guess it's inevitable, but I somehow can't imagine this place without you. And the girls — it will be hard saying good-bye."

"I'll be back. Promise. I'll need to check on how the girls' riding is going, and on Captain Wentworth's progress, of course."

"Of course." Helen elbowed me in the ribs but I didn't say anything else as we continued our drive downtown.

Alicia Jones' house was located in a part of Savannah known as the Pulaski Ward. The street itself was brick paved and tree lined with wide neutral areas between the sidewalks and the street. Centuries-old row houses, paired houses, and five-bay center-hall houses, all beautifully restored, lined each side of the street, where a number of brick walled gardens hinted at what might lie behind.

Alicia's house was a tidy row house with a brick walkway bursting with late-summer pink crepe myrtles and boasting an historic plaque by the front door. She opened the door before I had a chance to knock, greeting us with a cautious smile and the sound of jazz music playing on a stereo inside the house.

She noticed my angel charm first, then reached up to touch her own. The wariness in her eyes lifted as she ushered us in. I made introductions before being led into a cozy living room with bright floral chintzes and framed posters lining the walls featuring jazz greats Ella Fitzgerald, Miles Davis, Cab Calloway, and a host of others I didn't recognize. A baby grand piano dominated the corner, the closed lid covered with photo frames. Over the fireplace was a framed record album, the edges of the cover frayed from use. I read the title out loud. *"Hunting Angels."* Below the title, in a large bold font were the words "Including the hit single title track and the number-one singles 'Time Is a River' and 'Moving On.' "

Alicia came to stand next to me. "That was my mama's first album. Almost went gold. Not that it mattered to her. It was always about the music. But this album" —

she tapped the glass — "was her favorite. Always told me that she said good-bye to a lot of ghosts while she was writing the lyrics." She motioned to one of the sofas. "Please sit down. I'll be right back."

I showed Helen to one of the sofas and then sat down next to her. She frowned. "That's an odd name for an album. What year did it come out?"

"Nineteen forty-eight. I only know this because I spent some time on the Internet after Alicia called last night. The album came out nine years after Josie left Savannah."

"I bet Odella has a copy. I'd love to listen to it." Helen raised her eyebrow as we turned our attention back to Alicia, who'd reentered the room with a tea tray.

"Your house is lovely," I said as I poured milk and sugar into a cup of tea for Helen and handed it to her. "I was admiring your piano. Are you musical, too?"

Alicia smiled. "Not like my mama, no. I can't hardly sing a note. But I teach piano. I figured out early on that I was a better teacher than musician, so I made the best of both worlds." She took a sip of her tea and gave Helen and me a considering look. "I'll admit to being a bit surprised to hear from you after all these years. After my

503

mama died, I wrote letters to both of your grandmothers, to let them know that she'd passed. She talked about them a lot in those last days — it was the cancer that got her — and I was surprised because she'd never mentioned those names before. That's when she gave me my angel charm and told me all about Lola." She shook her head. "I would have sworn that she'd had no past before coming to New York and singing in the Harlem Opera House because she never talked about any of that before she was dying."

Gently, I placed my teacup in its saucer. "Did either one of them respond?"

Alicia shook her head. "No. Neither one. I didn't know if Annabelle was still alive or not, but I saw Lillian in the papers all the time, so I knew she was alive and well. I had half a mind to just show up on her doorstep and ask her what's what."

A half smile twitched at the corner of Helen's mouth. "I've heard of that happening before."

Alicia pursed her lips. "Yes, well, I thought it just rude. Especially since my mama left something for her. And I explained that in my letter to her, too, but I guess she wasn't interested."

Both Helen and I gave her our full attention. Helen choked down a cookie so she could speak. "Was it her scrapbook pages?"

"Oh, no. She had my grandmama Justine burn those before I was born. I know because my grandmama told me. Said she regretted it until the day she died, seeing as my mama's story will never be shared. See, I wasn't the only one who believed Mama's story started at the Harlem Opera House. She came from Savannah — I knew that much, but you never would have known it to hear her talk. It was like she just wiped the Georgia clay from her feet and never looked back. That's why I'm here. Wanted to return to where we came from. I raised my children here." She indicated the piano and its collection of frames. "Three boys and one girl. They all still live here except for my youngest son. He's in Germany right now in the Army."

I slid my teacup and saucer onto the coffee table, not sure I could hold it without it rattling. "The thing you were supposed to give to Lillian — do you still have it?"

"Sure do. Figured I'd hold on to it for a while longer. Maybe write her again. She must be getting old though, hmm?"

Helen nodded. "Yes. She's ninety. But still relatively healthy, except for her arthritis."

Alicia stood and walked to a dark-stained

footed bookshelf tucked between the two long front windows. With both hands, she pulled out a thick, leather-bound Bible, then withdrew a yellowed envelope from between the pages. "I figured if I kept it here, I wouldn't forget about it."

She handed it to Helen. "I figure you can give it to your grandmother. See what she wants to do with it."

Helen nodded and slipped the envelope into her purse after a brief hesitation. She turned back to Alicia. "Did Josie ever say anything about her brother, Freddie?"

Alicia sat down again across from us and poured more tea into all three cups. "She had pictures of him. He was a fine-looking man, that's for sure. My middle son, Jeremy, favors him a great deal. And my oldest son, Frederick, is named after him." She straightened her shoulders. "I do know that he was one of the founding members of the NAACP chapter here in Savannah. My mama always said that's what got him killed. That and him marrying a white woman."

Helen grabbed my hand. "He married a white woman? Here in Savannah?"

Alicia nodded. "Not that they advertised the fact, of course. My mama said that the reverend who married them got raided, and his church burned because they found out he was marrying couples of mixed races. It was illegal here until nineteen sixty-seven, but there were some ministers who felt God was on their side in joining a man and a woman in holy matrimony, regardless of the color of their skin or what the law books said." Her dark fingers played absently with the angel charm around her neck. "Anyway, when he got raided, they took the marriage records. Found my uncle's name and decided to teach him a lesson. It was too late, of course."

"Too late? How?" I felt Helen's hand in mine again, squeezing my fingers.

"They were expecting a baby."

Helen's fingers squeezed mine tighter. "Who was the woman — his wife? What was her name?"

Alicia shook her head. "Mama never said her name. Everything associated with her brother's death was too painful for her. She never did talk about it. She only mentioned about his being married because of that big Supreme Court case back in sixty-seven that said people of color could marry who they wanted to and that the states had nothing to say about it. Made my mama cry, remembering her brother, who died because he loved the wrong woman."

"But you don't know her name?" I asked, but not because I didn't think I knew the answer. I said it only to fill the empty places in my head that kept knocking against the parts of the truth I still didn't know.

"No, I'm sorry. Like I said, it wasn't something she ever talked about. My grandmama always called that part of my mama's life the 'great sadness.' She said it was what made her music so poignant, but I think that's a horrible price to pay."

"And her scrapbook pages," Helen said, "all of them were burned?"

"All of them. I wish she hadn't done it, but my mama was a force to be reckoned with. If she said she wanted something done, you didn't go against her."

Alicia smiled, and I smiled, too, thinking of the three friends who'd lived in different times but had tried to be stronger than they were allowed.

"There's another reason why I wanted to meet with you today. We — you and I — are related. We found the birth certificates at the historical center. My great-grandfather was your mother's father. Leonard O'Hare was Josie and Freddie's father."

Alicia closed her eyes and nodded. "Well, praise the Lord. It's always a good day when a family gets expanded."

508

We stood and hugged and Alicia smiled in my face. "Although I can't rightly say we look like we're kin."

We both laughed as I helped Helen stand beside me. Helen extended her hand. "Alicia, it's been a pleasure meeting you. We'll have to have you and your family to Asphodel soon."

"Let's plan on it. And one more thing." She held on to Helen's hand a moment longer. "When you open that envelope, I want you to let me know what's in there. It's . . . it's all I have left of my mother, and there're so many missing parts to her story that I'm a little hungry to learn what I can."

"I know what you mean, and I certainly will let you know," Helen said before hugging Alicia good-bye.

We gathered our purses and Helen's cane, then left among promises to visit again soon. We rode in silence during the short drive to George's office, where I'd be dropping Helen off, listening only to the whir of the car's air conditioner. Helen spoke first, her voice thick. "She was married and pregnant, and she's never mentioned this to anyone before. Dear God." She shook her head but couldn't seem to find any more words to convey her surprise and hurt. She turned to face me. "So what do we do now?"

"We go see Lillian and ask her about Freddie. And then we're going to ask her what happened to their baby."

Helen nodded, using a knuckle to impatiently wipe under her eyes. She didn't look at me when she finally spoke. "I think she's kept quiet all of these years because of me."

"Because of you?"

"Yes. She and Tucker have always believed that they needed to protect me. Like being blind made me somehow more vulnerable or worthy of sheltering." She smiled to herself and smoothed her hands over the soft fabric of her dress. "It's funny really, because I've always thought it was the other way around."

We drove the rest of the way without speaking, our minds focused on the envelope in Helen's purse, and the untold story of three best friends and the secret two of them had managed to take to their graves.

CHAPTER 22

George dropped Helen off at the tabby house, where he'd spotted Emily pushing the girls in the tire swing Tucker had recently placed in the towering oak tree in the front yard. Helen invited George to stay, but he'd sensed that he'd only delay the confrontation with Lillian and that he might complicate things. He'd kissed her chastely on the cheek when he'd said good-bye, promising to call her later, and she could still feel her skin tingling.

After determining from Emily that everyone else was up at the big house, she took her cane and began tapping her way down the path toward the gravel drive. She heard Tucker and Piper speaking in the front garden near the stone bench where she remembered Malily planting the azaleas. They'd be dormant now, but for Helen they were always in the height of bloom, with showy purple flowers dancing amid the

511

shiny green leaves.

Mardi bounded over to her as she approached and the conversation ended abruptly. Tucker greeted her, then led her to the bench.

"Did you have a nice lunch with George?" Piper asked.

"Yes, thank you. We went to Firefly Café, one of my favorites. And it would have been the perfect date if he hadn't kept reminding me how bad cigarettes are for my lungs." She rolled her eyes. "So I told him fine, that maybe I'll stop. The girls have been wanting me to quit for forever, so maybe it's time I did." She kept her hand on Mardi's head, scratching him behind his ears, and wondering why Tucker and Piper weren't saying anything. She pictured them gesturing with their hands and eyes and decided to put them out of their misery. "Go ahead and say it. I can handle it."

"It's not about George, if that's what you're thinking," said Piper.

"I wasn't thinking anything, actually." She smiled patiently.

Tucker cleared his throat. "Piper told me about your meeting today with Josie's daughter. And about the envelope she gave you. Do you still have it?"

"Yes, of course. It's in my purse. Why?"

Again, Helen pictured the gesturing between Tucker and Piper, amused that they seemed to know each other well enough now to create an unspoken language. It had never been that way with Susan. Susan's attempts at communication, verbal and otherwise, had never appeared to work. Even with her own children, it was as if she were speaking in a foreign language.

Piper spoke. "Because I'd like to see it first."

Helen surprised even herself with her quick response. She held up her purse. "Take it, and read it. Malily had first dibs and she declined, remember? Even she wouldn't argue with that."

Tucker sounded agitated. "You're not even going to think about it first?"

"You think that I haven't been thinking about it all afternoon?" She shook her head. "Haven't you ever wondered, Tucker, why Malily drinks? Or why the blinds at Asphodel are always closed? Why would Malily, who loves the bright flowers in her garden, choose to live in darkness? She's punishing herself, whether she realizes it or not. That would be a horrible way for her to die."

Helen reached for his hand and laced her fingers with his. "And I understand your reluctance, too. Because the closer we get to the answers we're looking for, the more we'll understand about Susan." She leaned against his arm, remembering the brother who'd hung three of her paintings in his office and deserved more in his life than grief and unanswered questions. "Ignoring things never made them go away, Tuck."

" 'Never hesitate when it comes to something you want,' " Tucker said slowly. "Malily taught us that, didn't she?"

"Yes, she did."

Piper took the purse from her and removed the letter. Helen listened as Piper gently ripped the envelope open.

"It's another news clipping — just like the first."

There was a brief silence, and then Helen heard Piper sigh.

Gently, Tucker said, "Here, let me have it. I'll read it out loud for Helen." He began: "It's dated September twenty-ninth, nineteen thirty-nine. It reads, 'The Negro child pulled from the Savannah River three weeks ago remains unidentified. The medical examiner has confirmed that the male infant was a newborn and apparently born healthy. Cause of death remains inconclusive, although the examiner's report indicates the child died prior to being placed in the river. As an act of charity, the body was given into the custody of a Dr. Leonard O'Hare for a proper burial.' "

Helen remained thoughtful for a long moment. "Why would Josie have sent this to Malily?"

"Hang on," said Piper. "There's something else here in the envelope. It's a handwritten letter." Helen listened to the sound of crinkling paper and then Piper began to read.

Dear Lily,

My mother has always said that a heartbreak only makes your heart bigger, that someday all those cracks and holes will be filled in with all the joy and love you haven't had yet. Her words have helped us both handle the sad news about Freddie and the baby. I hope they can help you, too.

Charlie came and took you to Asphodel the next morning and I didn't get a chance to say good-bye to you or Annabelle. Charlie gave me the rest of the money I needed for a train ticket to my mother in Virginia and I left that same day. It's a lot closer to New York from here, and I think that's where I'll be heading next.

I got a letter from Annabelle last week

saying you won't answer her letters, so she sent me this in the hopes that I might be able to get through to you. We know her father gave the baby to Charlie for burial, but that's all we know. She'd like you to let her know where he's buried so she can plant flowers.

Annabelle is grieving something fierce. We always thought she was the strongest of us three, but there's something we missed. I fear her heart bleeds for the world, and all of its disappointments become hers. My mama said that she's heard stories of flowers and trees absorbing the sadness around them and turning black, still alive but mostly dead inside. And Mama thinks that's what's happening to our beloved Annabelle.

She blames herself, and only you have the power to forgive her. She is like the walking dead now. And that wonderful light that used to shine for all of us is flickering like a candle in an open window. Forgive her, Lily. She did what she had to do and saved all of our lives. She doesn't see it that way, of course, but that's what makes Annabelle so different from the rest of us.

You left Lola behind, and I gave it to Annabelle, hoping it will help her remember happier times.

And may the good Lord forgive us all.

Love,
Josie

Quietly, Piper folded up the letter and Helen heard her slide it back into the envelope. Her voice shook. "So what did my grandmother do, do you think, that she needed forgiveness for?"

"There's only one way to find out," Helen said. "Let's go find Malily and get this over with." She stood abruptly, not able to reconcile the memories of the grandmother who'd planted a garden for her with the woman who'd never found it in her heart to forgive a friend.

Tucker took her arm. "Are you sure you want to do this? It might be hard to hear."

She yanked her arm away from him. "I'm not a child, Tucker. And just because I'm blind doesn't mean I'm not strong. I was the one you came to when Susan died, remember? I grieved for her, too, but somebody had to be strong for the children and I was happy to do it. But don't treat me now as if I can't handle this."

He stepped back. "Go then." He softened his voice. "You've never really needed me anyway."

Helen reached out in her darkness for her brother, and he grabbed her hand. She threw her arms around his neck and hugged him tightly, remembering the little boy who'd been afraid of thunderstorms. "Yes, I have. And I always will. But in case you haven't noticed, my life has managed to be far less complicated than yours. Why don't you focus on you for now? I wouldn't mind a complication or two in my own life now and again."

She pulled away from him and turned toward Piper. "Come on. You and I are going up to Malily's room." She held up a staying hand to Tucker. "I think it should be just Piper and me. You know how Malily has always said that history is best translated by women. I also don't think she could stand to see the disappointment in your eyes."

"Or yours," he said.

She allowed herself to smile. "But that's where you'd be wrong. She doesn't think I can see anything."

"Fine, then. If that's what you want. Just . . . call me when you're done."

Piper stood and placed the envelope in Helen's hands. "I'll let you give this to her." To Tucker, she said, "Go see the girls. If you don't mind helping them tack up, they'd love to show you a few of the things they've learned this week. I've already told them I'm Miss Piper now — because I wanted my nickname back."

After a brief hesitation, Tucker said, "Sure, I'll do that." He started to walk away but turned back. "Go easy on her. She's an old woman."

Helen shook her head. "She'd hate to hear you say that. But, yeah, we will."

Piper took her arm and led her inside. They walked more slowly than usual, as if each realized that Pandora's box was about to be blown wide-open.

Lillian sat up in her bed propped against plumped pillows covered in the best Egyptian linen. Still, she couldn't get comfortable, and had rung for Odella so many times that Odella had parked a chair outside of the bedroom door to save herself the trouble of climbing the stairs again and again. This was the first time in Lillian's life — not counting when she'd had her children — when she hadn't gotten out of bed. She was too tired, all the thoughts in her head and words on the scrapbook pages warring in her brain, sapping her strength.

Annabelle's last scrapbook pages lay on the bedside table next to her, but the photo of the three of them in the garden at Dr. O'Hare's house on Monterey Square was now propped against the photo of her debutante ball. She'd had Odella pry the photo off the page using a nail file, the photo popping off the old glue easily. The edges of the photo curled inward like her memories, as if neither one could move forward past that time.

"Were you pregnant in that photo, Lillian?"

Startled, she looked at the doorway where Odella stood behind Piper and Helen. She'd known better than to ask Odella to prevent entry. The Annabelle she'd once known wouldn't have been deterred, and neither would her granddaughter.

Lillian leveled Piper with a stern gaze. "Yes, I was. I was in my seventh month then."

Odella raised her eyebrows, but Lillian waved her hand and she left, closing the door behind her. Not that it mattered; Lillian knew Odella would have her ear pressed to the door the whole time. Lillian watched as Piper drew a chair close to the bed and seated Helen and then did the same for herself.

Helen spoke first. "We visited Alicia Jones today — Josie's daughter."

Lillian raised an eyebrow but didn't say anything.

Helen opened her purse and took out the envelope. "She gave me this. It's from Josie. Alicia contacted you after Josie died to let you know that she had it, but you never wrote her back."

Lillian looked down at the soft blankets covering the bed, wondering whose old hands were resting there.

"Do you want Piper to read it to you, or would you like to read it yourself?"

Lillian's lips wouldn't move even as she saw Piper take the envelope from Helen and begin to read. She kept her head down until Piper had finished, absently wondering where the wetness came from that spotted the blanket and the pale mottled skin stretched over arthritic knuckles.

"What did you name the baby, Malily?" Helen's voice sounded removed, as if she didn't want to be there anymore than Lillian wanted her to be.

"Samuel. I named him Samuel Frederick Montet. After his father."

Piper stood, ready to ask another question, but Lillian managed to raise a hand, searching for a way to stall the inevitable, yet knowing it was like trying to stop a baby from crying. "You're jumping ahead again.

I've got one last entry in my scrapbook. Don't you want to read that first?"

Piper hesitated before nodding, then reached over to plump one of the pillows behind Lillian's head and to smooth the blanket over her knees. *Just like Annabelle.* Lillian reached out and touched Piper's wrist. "Stop."

Piper pulled back and sat down, wearing a wounded expression, misreading her actions. Lillian wanted to laugh, because of what she'd wanted to say. *I don't deserve your care and concern any more than I deserved Annabelle's.*

"Go ahead, Piper, and read. Even with my glasses on, I can't seem to focus on the words anymore."

Piper picked up the pages Lillian indicated, then began to read.

August 24, 1939
I'm not even sure why I'm writing in this book or collecting photographs and charms for Lola, except that Annabelle expects me to. She is our surrogate mother in the absence of our own, her quiet strength and determination in salvaging what is left of our futures a beacon for us but a burden for her, I fear.

I hate to disappoint her, so I write and collect. But I'm a woman now, and this scrapbook and charm necklace are childish to me. Annabelle seems to think that recording our lives now will help us share our stories with our daughters when the time comes, as if that's the most important part of our lives. I don't know about that. I've never known my mother or her stories; but again, maybe that's why I've always felt so rootless. And I'm left with wondering if my mother had a story to tell after all. So I'll write in this scrapbook and I'll find a charm.

I've been living in the O'Hare household again and I'm sure my father doesn't suspect the reason why. Dr. O'Hare is ailing, and without Justine to help, a great deal of the burden of caring for her father and the household falls on Annabelle. At least that's what I've told my father. But if he knew Annabelle, he would know I was lying, because she seems to handle all of her responsibilities without batting an eye. This doesn't make me feel less guilty for adding to her burdens, however, especially since she's the one who has to keep my secret from my father. If he found out, I don't know what he'd do. I don't think he'd harm me, but I am too afraid to think what would happen to Freddie and his child.

So this is best, to live in a web of lies for now. It is the mattress I sleep on each night in the hidden room, but I think we all realize how easily it might break.

Justine sends letters to Josie every week asking her to come to Virginia, too. Justine can't write, so she has to pay somebody to do it for her and mail the letters, so it's no little hardship. That's how badly she wants Josie to leave here. Annabelle and I agree that it's probably for the best, so we've begun to save up money for a train ticket. All that knitting Annabelle has done will finally pay off. Since I'm convinced the baby will be a boy, Annabelle's been selling off all the pink booties, sweaters, caps, and blankets she's made in the past few months. She laughs and tells me that it will probably be a girl just to spite us!

Justine gave us interesting advice: to loosen everything in the room — from bows to window latches to shoelaces — as this will promise an easy delivery. I don't have the heart to write back and tell her that it's not the delivery we fear, but the part that comes after.

Annabelle watches me, waiting. I no longer question her relationship with Freddie if only because he's shown his love for me in ways that have more to say about our feelings for each other than the ring I'm not allowed to wear on my left hand. I don't doubt her loyalty, either, and know she will do whatever it takes to keep us safe. But her eyes are hungry, hungry for the life she's always told us she's wanted. This passion of hers is stronger than any of ours, and it makes me worry. If her dreams are unfulfilled, what will it do to her? Her soul is too tender for the harshness of reality, and she clings too tightly to regret, always worrying what she should have done.

We have that in common. But so much is at stake right now that I've promised myself that I will no longer believe in regret. That I will not look back at the past and wish I'd done things differently. What's written cannot be erased. From this day forward, I will live in the present. If only I could get Annabelle to see it that way, too. Because she and I are so much alike in so many ways. And it frightens me. Maybe it's because we were both raised without mothers that's given us a perspective of us against the world. But my self-reliance seems selfish compared to her self-sacrifice, and I am ashamed.

Because we've sold my camera, I can't take a picture of this room that has become like a prison to me these last few months. But I'm here, and I've got time, so I'm going to use my poor sketching skills to show what the room looks like now: the iron bed, the wicker bassinet that one of Dr. O'Hare's patients gave him as payment years ago. I've even managed a plausible rendition of the chair and the window that remains covered day and night. Maybe someday, looking back, we will smile in remembrance, and say how brave we once were.

For the charm, I sent Annabelle out to Broughton Street to see what she could find. I told her what I was looking for and she brought back a charm of an unlaced boot. It's only gold-plated since we can't afford much, but it's perfect. It's my charm for an easy labor, but it also symbolizes our friendship — how we've loosened our hearts to make room for one another. It's what joins us together to weather any storm.

September 3, 1939

My pains started this morning, right after breakfast. At first I thought it was the poached eggs. Annabelle is a much better gardener than a cook, so when I started feeling queasy right after I ate, it was easy to blame it on the eggs. Even the beautiful arrangement of spring blooms she'd placed on the breakfast tray did nothing to ease my discomfort.

Annabelle, who's served as midwife for her father on more than one occasion, recognized what was happening and immediately set about boiling water and ripping sheets. She said she'd call her father when active labor started, but since that could be hours from now, we both decided not to bother him until necessary. He is still weak, but has promised to help with the birth.

We sent Josie to find her brother to let him know. He has been in hiding, so even she doesn't know where to find him, but knows who to speak to in order to get word out.

Annabelle said this could take some time and to try and keep myself occupied. I'm writing now but I can see that as the pains grow stronger and more frequent I will no longer be able.

527

I spent time reading over this scrapbook, and I'm glad that Annabelle has made us do this. It will be something we'll cherish when we're old. I read over my last entry, how I wrote about our friendship helping us weather any storm. How appropriate! Just as my pains started, the sky brought in thick gray clouds. A storm is coming, the thunder already on the horizon, the approaching sound sending waves of panic through me. I close my eyes, and lie back, and pray for the storm to be over soon.

Slowly, Piper lowered the page. "That's the last page. But that's not the end of the story, is it?"

The murmur of voices began again, the river of words that seemed to travel around Lillian and through her, too fast for her to understand them. But she thought she could hear Annabelle, telling her to breathe, that it would help take the pain away, and that one day the pain might be useful to her.

Lillian turned her head, the fine linen scratching her cheek, the bed now seeming to be a small, iron single bed instead of the mahogany rice poster. "No, it's not," she said, closing her eyes so she couldn't see the ghosts anymore.

Helen's voice came close to her ear. "What happened to the baby, Malily? Was it still-born?"

"You need to leave," Lillian whispered, hoping Helen would understand it was for her own good.

"Was he?" she repeated.

Lillian's eyes fluttered open and rested on her granddaughter. "If I tell you, will you promise to leave?"

There was a brief pause while Helen considered this. She nodded. "And Piper?"

"She wouldn't leave, even if I asked her."

Helen nodded. "Tell us, then. Was the baby stillborn?"

She closed her eyes again, remembering. "No. He was born healthy and strong, with all ten fingers and toes. He was perfect."

"Then tell us what happened, Malily. How did Samuel die?"

Lillian heard Josie's voice now, from behind her, mixing with Annabelle's like a chant. *Tell her.* She shook her head, trying to erase the voices. "Somebody turn on the radio. Please."

Piper stood and moved to the nightstand and flipped on the radio, the volume loud and pulsing. Josie's voice came through the radio, clear and sweet and full of all the hours lost between truth and regret. *Time is a river, and it ain't got no banks; I can't go nowhere but down, down to the place the heart breaks.*

Lillian jerked her arm from the blanket and slammed her hand down on the radio, shutting it off, the silence a solid presence in the room. "I need you to leave, Helen."

Piper and Lillian watched as Helen made her way to the door. She paused with her hand on the knob. "Did you ever love Grandpa Charlie?"

"I did. He was good to me, and I grew to love him."

"But Freddie was your true love. The one you really never got over."

She didn't want to answer, but she had no more time for secrets and lies. "Yes, he was."

Helen nodded. "I love you, Malily. Nothing I've heard so far and nothing you can say will change that." She rested her forehead against the door. "And I'm going to find out anyway. You were the one who used to tell me never to hesitate when it comes to what I want, remember?"

Lillian closed her eyes again. "You don't want this."

Helen opened the door and Lillian briefly glimpsed Odella standing and taking Helen's arm before the door closed.

Piper stood at the window, peering out at the alley of oaks, her body rigid with tension.

"You'll want to sit down."

Piper shook her head. "No, I want to stand."

The corner of Lillian's mouth turned up. "Annabelle didn't like being told what to do, either. Her only weakness was when she thought those she loved needed her. Always to her detriment, I'm afraid."

Piper returned her gaze to the window. "So what happened? After Samuel was born."

Lillian stared at the radio, still hearing Josie singing. *Time is a river. . . .* She didn't turn away this time, knowing there was no escape from the voices anymore.

"I need a drink."

Without pausing, Piper moved to the armoire and poured Lillian a sherry and brought it to her before returning to her position by the window. "Tell me."

Lillian drank the sherry in one gulp, and she felt the heat seeping into her veins, calming her. But the numbness evaded her, as if she were intended to feel every last word. She placed the empty glass on the nightstand and it fell over, but neither of them moved to right it.

"Samuel was born healthy. I'd known it was a boy. And not just because Josie told me she could tell because of the way I carried him in my belly. I felt him in my bones, the way a mother does." She smiled at the memory of her roundness, the swell of her belly and tenderness in her breasts. She'd been proud of the changes to her body. They'd made her feel older, more like a woman. Beloved.

"It was his body they found in the river, wasn't it?"

The warmth of the sherry made her limbs feel weightless, like she was floating in water, carried downstream. Her eyelids drifted closed and she was once again in the attic room in the house on Monterey Square, the window closed, locked in the stale, sweltering heat of the Savannah night. Her sweat had drenched the clean sheets Annabelle had put on the bed, the warmth of the baby tucked up next to her burning her skin. She spoke as if in the middle of a dream, feeling the heat and the damp sheets, the terror that gripped them when they'd heard the footsteps on the stairs.

"The baby was fussy. My milk hadn't come in yet, and I couldn't feed him. He kept crying because he was hungry, but he wouldn't suckle. Annabelle thought to let him suck water from a soaked rag, and that worked for a spell, but he'd get tired of that and start crying again."

"Did Freddie make it back that night?"

Her voice seemed to come from far away. "No. And not the next night, either. Things were bad right then. Two of Freddie's friends and a white man had been found shot to death in a car in a field over in Summerville. They'd been called agitators, going around to small towns and speaking out about their liberal views on the voting system and segregation. Views that back then could get a man killed."

The late-afternoon sun had begun to drift down the horizon, its orange light peering through the blinds that Piper had opened. It outlined her profile against the window, making her appear as if she'd been etched in glass, so fragile to look at, but how deceiving.

"Annabelle was beautiful, too. But her beauty was different than yours. She seemed so strong on the outside, that people never guessed how vulnerable she really was. How easily broken." She watched the younger woman for a moment, the delicate nose and cheekbones, the stubborn jut of her chin and the fisted hands that hid fingers permanently callused by holding a horse's reins.

"They never said that about you, did they? I'm sure it was a surprise to everyone that you stopped competing."

Piper's eyes were cold and unyielding. "Please don't change the subject. When did Freddie finally arrive?"

Lillian threw the blankets off of her, the heat overwhelming. "Why do you need to know this now? Can't you just leave it alone? Your grandmother is dead, and knowing the rest of her story isn't going to change that." Her words were slurred, her body trying to give up a fight her mind wasn't yet ready to.

"When did Freddie finally arrive?"

So persistent. Annabelle had been that way, too. Up until the very last letter Lillian had returned. Lillian lay back on the pillow, and went back to the small attic room, remembering the first flash of lightning that permeated the room with light before dipping them all into darkness again.

"I stayed in the attic room for two days, while Josie and Annabelle took turns watching over me, and making sure I ate. Sometimes they'd take the baby to stop his crying or to give him fresh water in a rag. Dr. O'Hare came up once to let us know that someone had come to the house looking for Freddie or for me, and he told them he hadn't seen either one of us for over a month. But it scared him enough to come up to the attic to tell us none of us should come out. That we should close the window because of the baby's cries. We'd already heard about the church fire, and the marriage records that were taken, so we figured if they were looking for me in Savannah, they'd probably already been to my daddy's and told him what they knew. It was only a matter of time, and we knew we had to get word out to Freddie not to come, that they'd be waiting for him."

"And then what?" Piper didn't turn around.

Lillian tried to keep her eyes open, so she wouldn't have to see it all again, but her lids fluttered closed, obliterating her comfortable bedroom at Asphodel and revealing the nightmare of a storm-ravaged night seventy years before.

"He came. We didn't know it was him at first. Dr. O'Hare had gone to the store to get food. He somehow managed to put the armoire in front of the door in the attic just in case. We sat in the dark taking turns holding Samuel and trying to quiet him, daring to open the blinds only a little. A black shelf cloud lay over the city, and Josie said it was a bad omen, that we needed to prepare for the worst."

"And did you?"

"What could we do? We had nowhere to go. We had to sit there and wait, and pray that Dr. O'Hare came back soon, and that Freddie knew not to come near." She waved her hand over the upended sherry glass. "I need another drink."

For a moment it looked like Piper would say no. Instead she pushed herself away from the window and retrieved the glass and refilled it, handing it to Lillian without a word. Then she returned to her post, watching the alley of oaks and the way the sun lay cupped in their branches as it began its lonely descent on a world that Lillian felt slipping away from her.

She upended the sherry like a shot glass, as she'd seen her father doing countless times without the tempering influence of a mother who would have ensured her daughter never had access to the vulgarities of men.

"And that's when Freddie came?"

Lillian tasted the alcohol on her tongue, knowing that no amount of drinking could ever take away the bitterness that lingered in her mouth still. "Yes, he came. He must have had Justine's key. He knew where we were — Josie probably told him — and he'd made it up to the attic before they caught up with him."

Piper was facing her now, the light from the window behind her darkening her face so Lillian couldn't see her eyes. "You . . . heard them?"

Lillian nodded. "We heard all of it. They beat him first, asking where his white whore was, and how they were going to teach her a lesson for defiling her race. He . . ." Her voice cracked, the memories like broken glass. "He never told them anything."

"And Samuel stopped crying."

Lillian slowly raised her eyes to Piper's, glad the young woman's face was blurred. Because every time she looked at Piper, she saw Annabelle the night of the storm, the night when they all left their girlhoods behind them.

Without averting her gaze, Lillian said, "Do you really want the truth? Because I could tell you the rest of the story where the ending is the same, but the bad guys are the ones in the black hats. And not the woman who held you as a child."

Piper slowly sank down in the chair by the bed and Lillian saw that her hands were trembling in her lap, as if she too could hear the cracking thunder and the sound of fists colliding with broken bone.

"I want to know the truth. All of it. My grandmother would have told me herself."

"If you'd only asked."

Piper's eyes flew to Lillian's face. She jutted out her chin. "Tell me the truth."

Lillian smoothed the blanket under her fingers, her skin numb. Her eyes didn't leave Piper's. "Annabelle was holding Samuel when he started to cry. She'd given him a rag but he didn't want it. He was so hungry. The storm masked it at first, but his screams were growing more frantic. We had no doubt that we would not live to see the morning if those men heard us."

She swallowed, her throat dry. She needed another drink so badly, but she didn't have the energy to ask. "So Annabelle covered his mouth with her hand, to quiet him. He . . . he stopped and we all dared not move as we listened to them beat on Freddie and raid the house. And then they left, taking Freddie with them, but we stayed in the dark room, listening to the rain and the thunder. We stayed there so long that dawn was breaking before we thought to move."

"Where was Dr. O'Hare? Why didn't he come back?"

"Oh, he did. Paul Morton found him in the front parlor. They'd hit him over the head with a chair and broken a rib. Paul was the one who came and moved the armoire and unlocked the door for us. He told us there'd been another lynching, that Freddie was dead. They were calling it a suicide. But we all knew the truth." She closed her eyes for a moment, dreading the act of opening them again. "And Paul was the one . . ."

She looked up, surprised to see that Piper was handing her a tissue and that her face was wet with tears.

"He took Samuel out of Annabelle's arms and gave him to me." Lillian looked away, unable to meet Piper's eyes. "He wasn't breathing."

Piper was shaking her head, her shoulders shuddering. "No. No!"

Lillian gazed past the young woman, toward the window, where she could see the brittle ends of the uppermost tree limbs. "She hadn't meant to. It was an accident."

Piper stared at her for a long time, horror and recrimination battling in her eyes. "And you've blamed her all these years. You could never forgive her, and that's all she wanted. It destroyed her, that guilt." She shook her head and swiped at her eyes with the back of her hand. Leaning forward, she said, "She saved you, and Josie. And you couldn't forgive her?" She pressed the heels of her hands into her eyes.

Lillian stared at Piper's bowed head, remembering their conversation about the moonflowers and how she'd called them courageous because they dared show their ugliness in the bright light of day. She almost told her the complete truth then, but hesitated still. She'd never been courageous like Annabelle, and that was why Lillian hid from the truth even now, when forgiveness was so close at hand.

"It wasn't about forgiveness, Piper. It was about survival. I saw my baby son's face every time I thought of Josie and Annabelle. That's why there was never any contact between us. Why we divided the scrapbook and never looked back."

Piper's eyes were reddened, and tears for a child she never knew stained her cheeks. "The angel gravestone in the cemetery. That's where they buried him."

Lillian nodded, pressing her tissue to her mouth. "My father allowed it, but only if I'd marry Charlie. He still loved me, despite . . . everything. And my reputation was saved because my father turned in Freddie's friends to the same mob that lynched Freddie."

Piper stood, her movements stiff.

"Are you glad now that you know the

whole story?"

Piper shook her head, agitated now. "But it's not, is it? What was in the letter that Susan found?" She moved closer to the bed, looking down at Lillian. "And why have you been living in the dark all these years? What aren't you telling me?"

Lillian watched her chest rise and fall, and thought of Helen. "There's nothing. I've felt guilt because of what happened to Annabelle, which I've tried to deal with every day of my life. But I forgave her long ago. I'd hoped she would have forgiven herself, too."

Piper looked at her oddly. "But she never knew you'd forgiven her, did she? So how could she ever forgive herself?" She looked away, sniffing loudly. "I need to go now. Should I send Odella in?"

Lillian managed a brief shake of her head before sinking down into the pillows. "No. I'm going to rest now."

Piper nodded and headed for the door.

"Piper?"

She turned around. "Yes?"

"I loved your grandmother like a sister. I never stopped."

"You had a funny way of showing it." Lillian thought she saw pity in her eyes. Quietly, Piper opened the door and left.

As Lillian's eyes fluttered closed, the words she'd been longing to say escaped her lips, spilling out into the empty room the way lightning in a storm diffuses the darkness for one brief moment, and then is gone.

CHAPTER 23

I stood outside Lillian's room, hearing the last words Lillian had spoken, not intending me to hear. *Forgive me.* The words chilled me, leaving me wondering for what she needed to be forgiven.

Odella had left, but Helen sat in the chair outside the room. From the stricken look on her face and her reddened eyes, I knew she'd heard every word. She raised her hand toward me and I took it. We stayed like that for a few minutes without speaking, as if in mutual agreement that their sins weren't ours. And that the fall of years was like pierced lace over old secrets.

I released her hand, then walked blindly from the house, not even aware of where I was going until I'd reached the stables. It might have been force of habit that made me seek out horses when I needed a place to think, but a part of my decision to stand in front of Captain Wentworth's stall had to do with what Lillian had said to me about my grandmother. Not about the horrible thing that had happened in a dark attic room years ago, but about the brave woman who'd fought battles that didn't have to be hers, and who'd remained a loyal friend to the very end. She was a person I was proud to have known, and to say she was my grandmother. If only I'd figured that out when she was still here to tell her.

The words that Lillian had said before continued to taunt me. *Because if you were different, you'd still be jumping fences.* I wasn't all that sure she'd said them to hurt me. She told me that she'd loved my grandmother, and I believed her. And maybe she understood that Annabelle wouldn't have wanted me to be sitting on the sidelines of life like she had, as if she wanted me to figure what had eluded her for so long, that disappointments didn't have a limit, but the number of lives we had did.

I rested my hands on the stall door, my knuckles white. *Because if you were different, you'd still be jumping fences.* I couldn't help but think that Lillian's words were meant for Annabelle as a form of forgiveness, too late to help my grandmother, but maybe not too late for me.

I looked into the stall, surprised to find it

empty, at the same time noticing the name tag on the door. *Captain Wentworth.* Gingerly, I let my fingers touch the engraved letters, thinking of Tucker ordering it for me.

"Captain Wentworth?" I called out, not expecting an answer, but eager to dispel the eerie silence of the stables. I emerged from the other side of the barn, the side that faced the riding ring, and forced myself to stop.

Lucy had managed to tack up Captain Wentworth by herself and lead the huge gelding to the mounting block, oblivious to his size and temperament in relation to her size and experience. I didn't run, not wanting to scare either one of them, but I walked rapidly toward the ring, where Lucy had already stuck one booted foot in a stirrup and was getting ready to mount.

When I was close enough, Lucy glanced at me and quickly lifted her right leg over the horse before I could say anything.

Captain Wentworth shifted uncomfortably, but remained still, allowing Lucy to gather up the reins and move him away from the mounting block in a smooth walk.

Keeping my voice down, I said, "Lucy, what do you think you're doing?"

"I'm riding a horse instead of a pony."

"Lucy," I said, my voice firmer, "that's not a horse you've been given permission to ride."

"But look, Miss Piper. I got on him all by myself and I'm riding him now. See? I can do it."

"Yes, Lucy. We never said that you weren't capable. Only that this horse is special and you're inexperienced. He was neglected and probably abused by his previous owners. Which means that his behavior might prove to be unpredictable if he feels as if he's being threatened in any way."

She smiled broadly beneath her riding helmet. "But I'm riding him, and he's listening to me. See?" Lucy squeezed her legs against his flank and Captain Wentworth responded by moving into a trot while Lucy posted, the horse's gait measured and beautiful, and I felt the old longing again. *I want to jump. I want to jump high.*

I began to feel uncomfortable. "That's enough, Lucy. Move Captain Wentworth back to the mounting block now, please."

"But look how good I am. See? I'm going to show you that I can jump, too."

Horrified, I looked around the ring and saw that she'd set up two cross rails — not inherently dangerous except for an inexperienced rider on an unpredictable and very large horse.

"I can do it. Watch!"

I stared in horror as her pigtails, as if in slow motion, bounced on her riding jacket. "Lucy, stop. Right now. This isn't the way to learn."

At Lucy's urging, Captain Wentworth picked up to a fast canter.

"Lucy — pull the reins to the left, get him to turn away."

But the little girl stuck out her chin and continued to move forward, somehow managing to stay in the saddle. I began walking toward her, controlling my movements so as not to excite the horse further, as she circled the ring one last time and Captain Wentworth began heading toward the first cross rail with no intention of slowing down to step over it. He was a show horse, and he was going to jump over any obstacle.

I made it in time to see Captain Wentworth clear the rail, landing with a cloud of dust. Buoyed by his success, he shot forward in an effort to gain more speed. His forward motion caught Lucy by surprise, and as I moved toward her, I watched her begin to slide, her slight legs easily losing purchase on the saddle with each movement from the horse. I jumped back as Captain Wentworth cantered in front of me, close enough that I could see the look in Lucy's eyes — an astonishing look of exhilaration with the beginning gleam of fear.

Stubbornly, she managed to hold on and even regain her seat in the saddle, but the horse was going too fast now for her to control him.

"Sit back, Lucy. Sit back!"

He sailed past the second cross rail, but my relief was short-lived as I realized he was heading for a four-foot vertical some-body had left in the ring. My mind moved slowly as I watched, impotent in my terror as Captain Wentworth got nearer with every intention of sailing over it, and Lucy equally determined to go over it with him.

Sensing Lucy's hesitation, the horse's steps faltered and he ran out of the jump, close enough to clip Lucy with the side of the boards and send her sliding to the ground. She landed with a solid thud and a cloud of dust, and I heard the *whoosh* of air rush from her lungs.

I reached her side before the dust settled, then knelt beside her to make sure I could see her chest rise and hear her breathe. The relief gripped me like a gloved hand but I didn't relax into it. "Can you hear me?"

She nodded, indicating her neck wasn't broken, and then I let out my breath before peering into her eyes to make sure they were focused and making contact with me. Her cheeks were pale, but she'd started to gulp in air and wasn't indicating any pain in her chest to show broken ribs. Methodically, I began checking her bones, one by one, just the way medics had done to me more times than I could count.

Her breath was becoming more normal and her eyes were following me. I cupped her chin in my hands. "Does it hurt anywhere?"

She nodded and I bit my lip.

"Where does it hurt?"

Her brown eyes were somber. "Everywhere."

I stifled a nervous laugh. "Yeah, I know. But does it really hurt in any one place?"

She shook her head.

"I'm going to take off your riding boots and I'm going to ask you to wiggle your toes, okay?"

Lucy nodded and watched as I took off one boot and then the other, smiling to myself when I noticed her socks had blue ribbons printed all over them.

"Let me see you wiggle your toes."

She did, and then we worked our way around her body, making sure everything worked by wiggling it on command. Captain

Wentworth stayed where he was, oblivious to the near trauma but I thought his arrogant head toss told me everything I wanted to know. *See? I could have made it.*

I helped Lucy to a sitting position and we sat there for a while to make sure she still felt all right. I stood and went to Captain Wentworth and allowed him to nuzzle me. I couldn't scold him; he'd done exactly what Lucy had wanted him to.

I turned to Lucy to see if she was ready to stand, and was surprised to see her scooting backward, away from Captain Wentworth. "Lucy?"

"I don't want to ride him anymore."

"What do you mean? Are you hurt and not telling me?"

She shook her head, her eyes managing not to leave Captain Wentworth.

"Then you need to get back on." Something stilled inside of me, like the stillness of the pond in the first hours after dawn. The words came to me, diluted and muffled as if they were coming from under water, but I heard them, remembered them as if they'd been spoken to me only the day before. "Or else you forget the reason you used to get up on the horse in the first place."

She stared hard at me. "But you didn't

550

get back on."

I stared back, realizing the words were spoken without animosity and matter-of-factly as only children can.

"That was different," I began.

"How?"

I wanted to stop and ask her how someone so young could be so wise, and how she knew about the argument I'd been having with myself for more than six years.

"Because . . ." I fumbled for words, realizing how easy they were to find. "Because nobody was there to tell me to."

She leaned back on her arms in the dirt, her eyes innocent. "But I'm here now. Why don't you get back on and start riding again, Miss Piper?"

I turned to look at Captain Wentworth, as if he could add something to the conversation. And then I remembered my other reason, as compelling as any other. I'd never admitted it to anyone, and had only begun to acknowledge it myself but there it was, the pink elephant in the middle of the room that I'd been trying to ignore.

I swallowed, trying to think of words an eight-year-old would understand. "Because I used to be really, really good, and people would come to see me and they'd all cheer and clap for me because I was that good.

But now . . ." I shrugged, wondering if even I understood. "Now I'm not great anymore. I'm probably not even any good, for that matter. I don't . . . I don't want to get up on a horse again after all this time and find out that I'm just another rider."

Her delicate eyebrows were folded sharply over her eyes. "But, Miss Piper, I'm here now. And I promise to clap and cheer for you if you get in that saddle right now and ride. And then it'll be my turn."

I looked at her, trying to find a way to win this argument, and I realized that I couldn't. I turned back to Captain Wentworth. His ears twitched and his tail moved slowly from side to side, as if waiting for my answer. His scar seemed more vivid, as if he were trying to show me that I wasn't alone. *Or else you forget the reason you used to get up on the horse in the first place.* Had my grandmother said those words to teach us both about persevering no matter how many times you fell off? And had she ever harbored hope that I could in turn teach her how very true they were? In that respect I'd failed her, but maybe Lucy was offering me a second chance.

Without thinking, I checked the girth. The saddle would be small, but I'd manage. I picked up the reins from the ground and began to lead Captain Wentworth to the mounting block.

"Miss Piper — wait."

I turned around. Lucy was standing, her stockinged feet in the dust, and she was handing me her fluorescent purple crop. I'd always wanted a colorful one as a young girl, and my grandfather had always said no, that they weren't for serious riders. But there'd been one wrapped under the Christmas tree one year with a tag that read from both of my grandparents, but it hadn't occurred to me until now who'd really given it to me.

"And this, too." She ran to the fence surrounding the ring and took an adult riding hat sitting on the top rail. "This is Miss Andi's — she left it here yesterday. It should fit."

With a nod of thanks, I took the crop and the hat, then led Captain Wentworth to the mounting block. I lengthened the stirrup leathers before placing my left foot into the iron, and before I could talk myself out of it, I threw my right leg over his back. He stayed perfectly still as we both got used to each other and I fought the urge to dismount again.

I wasn't wearing riding boots, so I was at a disadvantage, but I nudged Captain Wentworth into a walk with a slight pressure from my calves. Lucy backed up and lifted herself onto the fence so she could watch me, just as she'd promised. Today the familiar rhythm of the horse's gait and the sound of hooves on packed earth held no fear for me; instead they were like a lullaby sung by my mother but forgotten long ago. I allowed myself to be lulled, then squeezed my calves into his side a little more and began to trot.

Maybe this will be enough, I thought as I moved swiftly around the perimeter of the ring. Captain Wentworth's long stride covered the ground quickly, the wind washing over my face and into my open mouth, making me realize that I was smiling.

"Nice transition, Miss Piper," Lucy called out.

Yes. Yes, it was. I smiled more broadly and continued in a posting trot, feeling Captain Wentworth's restraint underneath me and my own restraint in the tension in my hands on the reins. *I want to move. I want to soar.* It was as if the horse had spoken out loud and I had shouted assent because I tightened my reins and signaled for the canter, feeling the horse reaching farther. My body adjusted to the rhythm as if it had never forgotten how, my heart adjusting to the joy of it as if it had.

From the corner of my eye I watched as Lucy opened the gate. "I think he wants to gallop, Miss Piper."

Unsure, I led Captain Wentworth in a canter around the ring twice more, but felt his pull, which matched my own. We both wanted to run as fast as we could, as if the years of being tethered had only made us want it more. Feeling as if we'd been meant to do this all along, I led him through the gate and pushed him into a hand gallop as we reached the fields behind Asphodel, hearing Lucy clapping and cheering as we sped by.

We ran until we were both covered in sweat, running until we'd outrun all of our demons and shed the ghosts we'd carried on our backs like a child collects rocks, heavy but without value. We ran until the blood flowed in my veins with the same rhythm of the horse's galloping hooves, and I could no longer taste the bitterness in my mouth.

Our energy expired at the same time, and I slowed him down to a canter and then a trot, then finally to a slow walk so we could both find our breaths. My knee felt sore, but not with the pain I'd feared.

We heard the clapping and cheering when we were still a good distance away and

Captain Wentworth lifted his head in regal acknowledgment as he led us back into the ring. I looked up in surprise when I realized Lucy had been joined by Tucker and Sara, and their cheering was as wild and enthusiastic as Lucy's.

Tucker met us in the middle of the ring but didn't wait for me to dismount. Instead he reached up for me and I gratefully slid into his embrace, glad for his arms around me, which seemed to be holding me up. "I can't believe I just did that." I pressed my forehead into his chest and began to sob, the tears cleansing me of all the regret and anger I'd collected since the night my parents had died and left me to believe that I was invincible.

I cried harder, remembering the grandmother who'd used her garden to try to teach me that I was wrong, that each year her blooms had to fight different enemies but if she kept the soil rich and firmly packed, and with the right amount of water, her plants would grow stronger each year, better able to withstand the onslaughts of nature. And I remembered, too, that she'd never given up on me.

I cried, too, for a little boy whose only sin was to have been born at the wrong time, and for the women who would have cherished him had he lived.

Tucker held me until my sobs stopped and my shoulders weren't shaking anymore. I felt his lips in my hair. "You were amazing," Tucker said, his voice close to my ear.

I pulled back to look in his eyes, and saw that he was smiling. "Really?"

"Yeah, really."

And it seemed the most natural thing in the world for him to lean down and touch his lips to mine, and just as natural for me to put my arms around his neck and pull him closer. It felt as if we'd found something we hadn't known was lost, tucked beneath years of grief and regret.

"Get a room."

We were suddenly reminded that we weren't alone. We broke apart and saw Sara with her hands covering her eyes and Lucy looking away. Even Captain Wentworth faced the other direction.

"Where did you hear that, young lady?"

I could tell Tucker was trying hard not to laugh and schooled my own face to a serious expression, realizing he was being a parent.

"Cable television," Lucy said, still avoiding looking at us.

Tucker nodded silently. "I guess I'll have to talk with Emily about that."

Sara ran up to us and tugged on Tucker's shirt. "Can we go eat now? Odella made lemon bars today and she said we can't have them till after supper."

Lucy walked toward Sara as if getting ready to leave. I put my hand out and touched her shoulder. "Wait a minute. I thought we had a deal."

She slid a wary glance over to Captain Wentworth. "I'll do it tomorrow."

"No. You need to get back on now."

She swallowed. "I don't want to."

"Lucy . . . ," Tucker began, but I put a hand up and he stopped.

"Why not, Lucy? Why don't you want to get back on?"

She shrugged. "No reason. I'm tired, I guess."

I went over to Captain Wentworth and adjusted the stirrups one more time before returning to stand in front of Lucy. "Why not?" I asked as I squatted down to eye level.

She looked down at her feet.

"Why not, Lucy?" I asked again, leaning toward her. "Because you're afraid?"

Her eyes rose to meet mine. "I'm not scared."

"Then get back on the horse and ride him." I put my hands on her shoulders. "Or else you forget the reason you used to get up on the horse in the first place, remember? I hadn't ridden a horse in more than six years because I forgot. Do you want to wait that long to ride again?"

Her eyes skittered over to Captain Wentworth, then traveled back to me. "Were you scared?"

I thought of how I had felt perched up in the saddle, how the barely restrained power of the horse had made me feel powerful and in control again, and the frisson of fear I'd felt before I'd lifted myself onto the horse's back when I thought that maybe I might be wrong, that maybe getting in the saddle again wouldn't be enough to take the pain away.

"Yeah, I was," I said. I stood and held out my hand. "Come on. Captain Wentworth is tired and wants a good rubdown and a carrot. Let's not make him wait, okay?"

She looked at Tucker for intervention, but he gave a quick shake of his head. "Listen to Miss Piper, Lucy. She knows what she's talking about."

"But I fell off," she said, and her voice held such surprise, as if she'd managed the impossible. She turned to Tucker, looking for sympathy. "I was riding Captain Wentworth, and I fell off."

Tucker's eyes slid to mine and I gave a

little nod, and was relieved when he didn't say anything, acknowledging that this was between Lucy and me. Although I had no doubt that he'd grill me about it later, and it made me want to smile.

"Yes, you did," I said. "And it was a nasty fall. You're lucky — you could have really been hurt. But you need to understand that it was your actions that caused it and not the horse's. You were doing something you weren't ready for, which is why you fell off. And to convince yourself that you can get back on a horse, you need to do it right now or you might not ever. That would be the real tragedy, wouldn't it?"

Her brow furrowed again, and I realized I'd used a harsher tone than I wanted to.

"Come on," I said gently. "You only have to walk and I'll walk right beside you if you want."

With a deep breath, she slid her boots back on, then took my hand and allowed me to lead her over to the mounting block. "I'm not afraid," she said again as she jutted out her chin and stared at the large horse. Without assistance, she climbed into the saddle in one quick movement, as if she were afraid that if she moved slower she'd change her mind.

"Do you want me to walk with you?"

She shook her head, grabbed the reins, and dug her heels into the sides of the horse. They ambled around the ring three times, Lucy's face regaining color and the stiffness in her shoulders and legs relaxing into the comfortable rhythm I'd been used to seeing with her.

"You ready to stop?" I asked.

She shook her head again and did one more lap.

"Good job," I said, helping her out of the saddle.

She surprised me by hugging me. I hugged her back and held her for a moment. Then she cupped her hands around my ear and leaned forward to whisper. "It doesn't matter to me if you never ride a horse again, Miss Piper. Because to me, you'll always be the one who made me get back on my horse the first time I fell off. I think that makes you pretty special."

I gave a half sob, half laugh and hugged her tighter. Then we headed together toward the barn to untack Captain Wentworth and rub him down. I stopped outside the barn for a moment while everyone else moved ahead of me and took a deep breath of air that smelled of fresh-mown grass. I looked over to the alley of oaks, where only the towering tips were visible, imagining that they looked different to me. The limbs bent softly in the breeze instead of rigidly defying it, the knobs at the base of each limb looked rounder. I smiled into the growing night, understanding casting a gentle glow over the house and fields of Asphodel. It seemed as if in defining the end of my own grief, the old trees had also discovered the end of theirs. With a soft sigh, I headed into the bright lights inside the barn, leaving the darkness behind me.

CHAPTER 24

Lillian's head swam as she pulled herself out of the bed, not knowing whether to blame the dizziness on the sherry or just the number of years she'd spent on this earth. She felt the ghosts in the room, too. Though she could no longer see them, she felt their recriminating gazes, heard the house breathe with expectation as if it, too, was waiting for the truth.

She dragged herself to each window, throwing open all of the shutters to let in the dying light of day, afraid suddenly of the encroaching darkness. She stared out at the alley of oaks, watching as the uppermost branches caught in the early evening breeze. But their movements were stiff and unyielding, as if they also waited for Lillian to acknowledge her ghosts.

Lola still hung around her neck and she lifted it off. She knew each charm by touch, had memorized the feel of each one along with their meanings and which of the three women had added it. Her fingers danced clumsily along each charm: the musical note, the heart, the rope. The baby carriage. She pressed it against her heart, willing the tears to come, but still, after all these years, they stayed in the place around her heart where she dared not visit, the place where regret lived. The place that, if examined too closely, would destroy her, as it had Annabelle.

There was a soft tapping on the door and she turned to see Helen enter the room.

"Malily? Are you awake?"

"Yes. I'm by the chair between the windows." She watched as Helen moved gracefully toward her, her face beautiful even with her drawn expression and reddened eyes.

She stopped a foot away from Lillian, her hand brushing Lillian's nightgown sleeve, and turned her face to the window as if sensing the light. "Have the trees changed at all?"

Lillian smiled softly. It had been an old joke between them. When Helen had first lost her sight, Lillian had been her eyes, describing everything around her. But Helen, who'd always been fascinated by the legend of the oak trees, had continued to hope that they'd get over their grieving and return to normal. On a nearly weekly basis, she'd asked Lillian if they'd changed back yet. It had been a while since she'd last asked. Maybe Helen had given up on getting a new answer. Or maybe she'd just got tired of asking. "No, not yet."

Helen handed her something and when Lillian took it she saw that it was a light blue hand-knit baby's blanket. Lillian's hand tightened around it, feeling instead Samuel's soft baby skin, and the thick hair that had covered his tiny head. She closed her eyes, trying to see her son and instead saw Annabelle holding Samuel in the room where he'd been born and where he'd died. *Annabelle's nephew. Samuel had been related to Annabelle by blood.* But Annabelle had never told her. As if the knowledge would have added to Lillian's grief somehow, and her friend had chosen to spare her. Even if it meant Annabelle would have to grieve in solitude, believing she'd killed her own nephew.

Lillian brought the blanket up to her face, trying to smell any trace of the little boy she'd known and loved for such a short time, but smelled only dust and old wool. And something else that she refused to recognize.

Helen reached out her hand and touched the glass of the window, her face registering surprise that the shutters had been opened before dropping it to her side. "Why did you want me to leave the room when you spoke with Piper? Did you think I'd be ashamed of you because you married a black man and had his baby? Or that you couldn't forgive a close friend? Do you know me so little that you think that any of that would make me forget what you mean to me?"

Lillian looked at her, not comprehending at first. It didn't surprise her that Helen had eavesdropped. It only surprised her that Helen hadn't guessed the truth.

"No." Lillian returned her gaze to the window and the darkening sky, the fading light reminding her of sand through an hourglass.

Helen didn't say anything for a while. "You didn't want me here because there's more to the story and you were going to tell Piper."

Lillian remained silent.

With a soft sigh, Helen leaned over and kissed Lillian's cheek. " 'Be patient and strong. Someday this pain will be useful to you.' " She pulled away. "Whatever it is can only make us stronger, right? So trust me that I'm strong enough to handle it, and that I love you enough now for it not to matter."

Helen turned and walked carefully to the door.

"How did you learn to be so brave?"

Helen didn't even turn around or pause when she answered. "From you, of course."

Lillian stared at the closed door, listening to Helen's retreat down the long hallway accompanied by Mardi's paws clicking on the wood floors. Lillian turned from the window and blinked, her vision fading in and out. She moved slowly to her desk with leaden feet. She'd never been this tired before, not even after childbirth. Each breath rattled in her chest; each movement was stiff and deliberate. Even her heart had to be reminded to beat.

She leaned on the desk with both hands, ignoring the pain, trying to catch her breath. The desk had once belonged to her mother, and when her father had given it to Lillian on her sixteenth birthday, she'd hoped that the secret compartments and multiple drawers would contain something from her mother: a note, a letter, a story. But the desk had been completely empty, and Lillian had spent a lifetime trying to fill it.

Mustering all the energy she had left, Lillian pulled open the middle drawer and gingerly slid her hand inside until she felt the release button, and pressed, wincing at the jolt of pain in her hand. She was rewarded with a slight clicking sound and when she reached farther, she felt the false side of the drawer bowing out, leaving just enough room for a piece of paper. Or an envelope.

She pulled out the envelope with her neat and much younger handwriting sprawled across the front, recognizing the address on Monterey Square by heart, even after all these years. The stamp in the top right corner remained uncanceled, but the seal had been torn open, allowing access to the letter inside.

The letter and its envelope had been in the desk almost since the time it was written, until Susan began her research into the Harrington family, and found instead the letter and Lillian's past. Holding the letter close, Lillian pressed her hands against her chest, feeling each breath as she summoned the strength to make it back to her bed. With faltering steps, she moved toward it, feeling as if hands were helping her onto the high mattress, settling the bedclothes around her.

She'd made her decision. The story belonged to a younger generation now, caretakers of the words left behind by three friends whose lives would always be intertwined. Helen and Piper were strong, independent women; they would understand. They would know how to forgive, and how to move on in a world that didn't always offer second chances. Curling onto her side, she cradled the letter like a baby. She would read it to Helen tomorrow, knowing now that it was part of the story she was meant to share, and that she'd raised a courageous woman who loved unconditionally, and who could face a darkened world without hesitation.

With a jagged breath she lifted her hand to the radio and turned it on, preset to the jazz station. Her hand fell to the mattress, the skin pale and bloodless. The volume on the radio was set low, and she couldn't be sure, but she thought she heard Josie singing again. *Time is a river, and it ain't got no banks; I can't go nowhere but down, down to the place the heart breaks. But then I see your face, and the angels sing, and my soul finds rest again in your embrace.*

Lillian smiled, her tiredness overwhelming her, welcoming it as a traveler welcomes sleep after a long journey. She allowed her eyes to close just for a moment, then forced them open again, listening to Josie sing, imagining she could hear Annabelle, too. Although night had fallen outside, the window she'd stood at shone with bright light, and Annabelle's voice was calling to her. Lillian rose from the bed, her stiffness and tiredness gone, and went to the window to find her old friend. The scent of the moonflowers hovered near as they opened into the night, sharing their secrets with anyone who braved the darkness to see.

Annabelle stood there, reaching out her hand and looking like the young woman Lillian had known. She glanced down at her own hands and they were young and beautiful again, the fingers straight and strong. Annabelle smiled and Lillian moved forward, surprised now that they were walking through the alley of oaks and Josie was there, too, still singing and holding her other hand. And as they walked together, Lillian looked up at the ancient trees and saw that they had finally changed. Instead of the gaunt, blackened branches, the wood was strong and supple again, each limb bearing the bud of new life, each shawl of moss swaying with the promise of forgiveness.

I slept soundly for the first time since my arrival at Asphodel. It might have been because my body needed rest after the physical exertion of riding Captain Wentworth the previous day, but I thought it was simply that my mind, having finally found the answers it had been seeking, shut down to rest, too weary to examine that last evasive question. Tucker and I had talked on the front porch the night before until about midnight, and I told him about Freddie, and the baby, and the night of the storm. There were no recriminations, no excuses or platitudes. We were forever tied to the players in the drama, but their tragedy wasn't ours — only the lessons learned.

I awoke before dawn, feeling too alert to go back to sleep, and went to the kitchen to go over my notes again. It wasn't until I was drinking my morning coffee that I remembered that I had dreamed of my grandmother again, but we hadn't been at my final riding competition. Instead, we'd been in her Savannah garden and we were planting moonflower seeds beneath the kitchen window. I'd looked at her face and she'd smiled at me and there were no words left to be said.

It was still dark when I heard a car pull up and I spotted Tucker's Jeep outside. I thought of Lucy and her fall the previous day and my heart lurched in my chest. I opened the door in response to his knock, and saw the drawn look on his face, the hollows beneath his cheekbones. "Is Lucy all right?"

He nodded. "Yes, she's fine. It's . . . Malily." He regarded me silently in the shadowy light of dawn, and I knew. "She passed away in her sleep last night. We're not sure when — she'd told Odella that she didn't need her anymore after she took her dinner tray."

I pulled out a kitchen chair for him; then I sat in the one next to his and took his hands. "I'm sorry," I said, feeling the weight of loss as if it were a physical thing. I knelt in front of him. "I'm sorry," I said again, knowing that any of the trite things people are supposed to say wouldn't fit here, or start to fill the ache in a grieving heart. But being near helped. I had the experience to know, after all.

He dropped my hands and leaned back in his chair, looking at me intently. "What is it?" I asked, sitting back in my chair.

He didn't say anything right away and then, "I thought for a long time about whether to show this to you." A soft smile illuminated his lips. "But then I remembered that you're Piper Mills. You don't break that easily."

"What is it?" I asked again.

"Malily left a letter. It was in her hands when Odella found her this morning. I have to believe that she planned on reading it to Helen today. But she didn't have the chance." From his back pants pocket he pulled out a yellowed envelope and I immediately recognized the handwriting on the front as Lillian's.

"It's addressed to your grandmother, but it was never sent."

He placed it in my hands and I took it, surprised at how light and inconsequential it felt. Slowly, I slid it out of the envelope and opened it up. After a brief glance at Tucker for encouragement, I began to read.

February 2, 1949

My dearest Annabelle,

It has been nearly ten years since we've last seen each other, but most of the time it seems as if it were only yesterday that we were riding together here at Asphodel or stealing cookies from Justine's kitchen. We had an idyllic girlhood, didn't we? You and Josie were the sisters I never had, and I will always be grateful for the friendship we shared. Please know that whatever you might think, I

573

hold you close to my heart. You were and always will be the bravest and strongest person I've ever known. If only I could have shared those qualities.

I know you've written to me. I sent your letters back, but not for the reasons you'd expect. You think that I hold you responsible for Samuel's death and that I haven't forgiven you for the events of that terrible night. But that isn't true. You see, I should be the one asking for forgiveness. My silence for these years has nothing to do with you and every-thing to do with my own cowardice.

The night after the storm, after they'd taken Freddie away and Paul Morton came to let us out of the attic, he took Samuel from your arms and gave him to me. He lay so still in my arms and we all knew him to be gone from us. You and Josie began to cry and Paul comforted you. But while you were mourning, I noticed a small flutter in his chest, a soft struggle for air.

I was elated at first, but something held me back from telling your father, who may or may not have been able to help. Something dark and hopeless.

You were always the dreamer, Anna-belle, and I the practical one. I could see my life with a startling clarity. Freddie was dead, and I was unmarried in the eyes of the law with a mixed-race baby. His life was over before it began, but I still had a chance to make a life for myself. To try and find happiness again.

So when your father came to take the baby, I wrapped him in one of the blankets you'd made for him and placed him in your father's medical bag. I discovered later that your father placed him in the Savannah River, and I pray every day that Samuel was sleeping with the angels before the waters of the river came for him. But the angels brought him back to us, didn't they?

I let you believe that you had accidentally smothered him, because somewhere in my weakened mind I thought that was so much easier to bear for both of us than the fact that I killed my own child. I know what I did was wrong, and I don't expect your forgiveness. All I can do is ask, and pray to God to have mercy on my soul. I pray for you, too, that you might find all the joy and happiness you deserve, and that you will be blessed with a daughter to tell your stories to.

I'm expecting another child now, and

am hoping it's a girl. I want to name her Annabelle if she is, although Charlie is adamant that she be named after his mother. So Annabelle will be her middle name, and she and I will have conversations like you and I used to, and I will teach her the secrets of my garden.

Samuel is buried here at Asphodel. I visit him every day and have planted moonflower vines near his grave. But they will not grow there, regardless of my ministrations, and I need your magical hands to guide them.

I've started this letter a dozen times and this is the first time I've finished it. I hope I can find your courage to mail it. And that you will see past all of my failings to forgive me. I am not whole without you, and Josie and my precious Samuel. I wonder sometimes how people can meet me and speak to me as if they can't see that I'm missing part of myself.

I manage to muster on. No regrets, remember? But that doesn't mean I don't grieve, or miss you, or wish for second chances.

Forgive me,
Lily

My lungs constricted, sucking all the

oxygen out of the air. I stood quickly, bumping the table and knocking over my half-empty coffee mug, but neither one of us moved. *Oh, God.* I needed air; I needed to breathe in the smells of summer grass and flowers; I needed to pretend that I'd never read that letter.

I'd made it to the front porch before Tucker caught up with me. I began to crumple and he caught me, bringing us safely to the ground.

"I'm sorry," he said, cradling me in his arms. "I'm so sorry."

I tried to tell him that I wasn't crying for myself; I was crying for the wonderful woman who'd been my grandmother and who'd died believing she'd done a horrible thing. And because of my own self-absorption, I hadn't known. I hadn't even thought to ask.

I peered up at Tucker, wanting to blame him because of his association with Lillian. "Did you know? Did you? And how could she say that she didn't believe in regret?"

He shook me gently, and I realized that I was on the brink of hysteria, feeling as if all of my newly won battles were now poised to begin the slippery backward slide on the slope of self-doubt.

"But it doesn't mean she didn't grieve,

Piper. She only believed in the impossibility of changing the past and focused instead on moving forward. But she grieved. There were signs everywhere. I even think that her devotion to Helen was because she felt Helen's blindness was punishment for what she'd done."

Tucker moved into a sitting position and he pulled me into his lap. "And no, Piper, I didn't know. If I had, I would have made her tell Annabelle. She wanted to." He moved my face so I would look at him. "She just lacked your kind of courage."

He pushed damp hair out of my eyes as I blinked up at him, recognizing the truth in his words but not yet ready to hear them. "Lillian's last words to me, when I left her last night, were 'Forgive me.' "

He nodded and placed a kiss on my forehead. "And you might not realize this now, but Annabelle also tried to live in the present, to move forward. I think that's why she tried to contact Lillian, and why she married your grandfather to start a new life. She was just less sure of how to make her heart believe it, too."

I leaned my head against his chest and stared at the horizon, where the sun had begun to rise, the yellow glow of dawn like melting butter on an open-faced sky, and thought of all the hours I'd spent with my grandmother in her garden and the lessons I'd learned without realizing. "Yes, she was," I said, my voice stronger. "It just took me a while to figure it out."

Feeling calmer, I faced him again. "What about you? That letter must have been what Susan found. What skewed her reality in the end."

"It's devastating for us to hear, but for Susan . . . she took it to heart as only a person as damaged as she was could. I think that's why she chose the river. Because of Samuel."

I pressed my face against his chest, wanting sleep, but knowing I'd still have to wake up eventually. I remembered the hours I'd spent sleeping following my accident, hoping I wouldn't wake up. But I wasn't the same person anymore. I was Annabelle O'Hare Mercer's granddaughter. "I'm sorry," I said.

Tucker tucked my head against his chest. "When I saw Lucy yesterday up on that horse after you convinced her that she needed to, I think I finally realized that whether or not we discovered the letter, it didn't really matter anymore. Susan chose her own path a long time before I ever met her. She was always beyond my help, but I kept seeing her failure as my own. I think I'd begun to feel that my success in life depended on whether or not I could make her better. And when she died, I blamed myself, believing it had been my fault."

He rested his head against mine, our eyes focused on the bright glow on the horizon. "But then I saw Lucy, how brave and determined she was, and Sara, how silly, and warm and charming, and I realized that somewhere along the way of me believing I had failed at something big, I'd managed to help create and nurture these two amazing people."

He tilted my face toward his, the pads of his thumbs rubbing away the tears on my cheeks. "And regardless of how angry I am with Malily for keeping her secrets for so long, I finally understand what she meant by not believing in regret. I think that to her life was about finding the extraordinary in every day. It was how she could sit in her garden on a rainy day and see the beauty in it. It's what got her out of bed every morning. That was her courage."

He brought his face closer to mine and I placed my hands over his. His breath brushed my cheeks as he spoke. "I wish I could change things for you, make it so this all doesn't have to hurt so much. But that's the point, isn't it? That one day we'll find that the pain we suffered was worth it. Your grandmother had that written on the angel charms, so she must have believed it, too."

I pressed my lips against his. "Thank you," I murmured, remembering my grandmother's wild lantana, untamed and unpredictable, just as life was meant to be. "Thank you," I said again, knowing that what he said was true, and hoping time would help me to accept it.

His arms came around me as we turned to watch the sun rise over Asphodel Meadows, illuminating its secrets as the moonflowers in Lillian's garden closed themselves against the bright light of day.

EPILOGUE

The sun glinted off of Lola around Sara's neck, illuminating each charm like chapters in a book. There were two new charms added on the gold chain: yet another horse, as a nod to Lucy's new mare, Jane Austen, and a tiny trophy for Sara, who'd learned to swim across the pond without her floaties not once, but twice. It was Lucy's turn to wear Lola, but I'd told her any jewelry visible to the judges would mean an instant deduction. With great fanfare and seriousness, she'd placed Lola around Sara's neck, extracting a promise that Sara would return Lola as soon as Lucy finished her three equestrian events.

The crisp fall air exaggerated the steam from our coffee mugs as Tucker and I sat with Sara between us in the bleachers in front of the beginner's ring, trying to ignore the wistful looks Lucy kept giving to the nearby covered ring, where the advanced riders conquered impossibly high fences and barriers. I nudged Tucker with my elbow, drawing his attention to the six people approaching the bleachers from the snack stand. George was using the cold weather as an excuse to place an arm around Helen's shoulders, and Mr. Morton was helping his wife negotiate her path between mud and horse droppings in her plum-colored suede ankle boots. She kept brushing away Mardi, who loped beside her, churning up red clay dirt like a small child in a mud pit.

Alicia was there, too, chatting with Helen and holding the hand of one of her grand-daughters. The little girl pointed at horses and tried to pet each one as they walked by. I smiled to myself, knowing that was just the beginning, and wondered how long it would take before I'd hear from Alicia about riding lessons.

They sat down beside us and Mr. Morton gave me a kiss on the cheek. We'd shown him Lillian's letter and he'd nodded once as if to set things into their new order, then moved on to the next topic of conversation. But he'd made a great show out of coughing, bringing out a handkerchief, and wiping his eyes. I'd patted his hand but looked away.

I'd read the letter to Helen, and she'd been silent for a long time. I thought then that I'd made the wrong decision in sharing it with her. But then she'd smiled and asked if she could place the letter on the back page of the newly reconstructed scrapbook containing Lillian's and Annabelle's pages. Sara and Lucy will be able to read it when they're older, after they've had the chance to learn on their own that disappointments are never permanent. And the large bouquet of tulips on Lillian's grave had been from Helen — white for forgiveness.

Mr. Morton came to the Asphodel cemetery for Lillian's funeral and for services for Samuel and Susan. The dark earth beside Charlie's obelisk was moved aside for Lillian, and Samuel's remains were exhumed and placed in the coffin with his mother. We moved Susan inside the enclosure, welcoming her into the family's stone garden, where her daughters could visit and place the flowers that they'd nurtured since seedlings. The girls and I like to visit at dusk and wait for the moonflowers that have begun to bloom finally on the vines Lillian planted. She has the perfect vantage point to witness the blossoming of the delicate flowers, courageous enough to open only at night without a guarantee that anybody will see.

The judge over the loudspeaker announced the equitation class, and I turned to Tucker. "That's Lucy. Wish us luck."

He kissed me soundly on the mouth, then took my coffee as I stomped down the bleachers in my mud-spattered boots and jeans and found Lucy already mounted on Jane and talking with another rider.

"You ready?" I asked, feeling the lurch of excitement in the pit of my stomach. She was only competing in the flat classes, but I couldn't still the thrill of being here again among the horses and the riders, the smell of horse and leather heavy in the air. But I was here only as a spectator and a cheerleader for Lucy, and for me it was enough.

"Yep." She said good-bye to her friend and then I led Jane toward the ring.

I patted her on the leg. "You remember what you need to do?"

She nodded and rolled her eyes. "Smile. Keep my shoulders back and my heels down. But when do I get to jump?"

I reached up and straightened her competitor's number, which had been tied around her chest. "Soon, I promise. But we're going to take it slowly, remember? I want you to enjoy riding — not just winning. That's the deal if you want me to be your trainer."

She rolled her eyes again, but this time she smiled. "But I wouldn't mind taking home some blue ribbons today."

"That's my girl," I said, tightening the yellow bows at the bottom of her pigtails as she gathered her reins and approached the ring.

The woman announced the class again over the loudspeaker, and Lucy and Jane entered the ring at a measured walk with the rest of the riders in her class, then pulled to a stop as they waited for the judge's signal to begin.

A trace of perfume wafted past me as a woman walked by, turning my thoughts to my grandmother's garden. I wasn't sure what I was going to do with the house, but I'd begun to restore the garden. The first frost was still ahead of us, and I'd mulched and tilled and planted my spring bulbs, and made plans for the lantana, smilax, and tea olives that my grandmother had loved so much. I'd started taking classes in landscape architecture at night, filling my time between the gardens at Asphodel and Monterey Square. It gave me more time with Tucker, too, as he'd returned to his medical practice in town.

Fall had already bleached the colors from the summer blooms, and as I prepared the gardens for winter, I felt closest to my grandmother, understanding more than ever the cycle of the garden: the barren earth that sleeps during the cold months and then erupts with life in the spring. I understand it now. Finally, I understand.

I waited at the fence as Lucy moved through the paces, listening to the instructions from the judge as she transitioned from walk to trot, then changed directions at the judge's cues. When she was done, Lucy guided Jane to the middle of the ring with the other riders and turned so the judges could read the numbers on their backs. I watched as her eyes scanned the crowd, searching until they settled on me. She seemed to relax and her smile broadened as she realized I was watching. I stood without moving, cherishing the moment, and remembering the woman who'd come to my first shows and braided my hair with gentle hands.

When the judge announced the results, Lucy winked at me before turning her horse toward the gate to exit the ring and accept her ribbon, gracious in her nods to her fellow competitors as she moved forward. I hadn't taught her that, or how to hold her head with grace, and I smiled to myself, feeling Lillian near.

Full darkness had already fallen when we returned to Asphodel. Sara rode with Helen and George, but Lucy slept on my shoulder between Tucker and me in the truck pulling the horse trailer, her three blue ribbons pinned to the jacket she'd refused to remove. The moon rose high in the sky, full and round with possibilities, outlining the branches of the old oaks and their sleeves of Spanish moss, transforming them into welcoming arms.

I rolled down my window, the puffs of my breath visible in the moon's glow. The trees were heavy with new leaves, the limbs no longer hovering over the drive but now waving gracefully as they bent gently to the earth, their season of grieving over. Even the wind as it made its endless circle through the branches had changed its sound, the whistling now a hum of voices, a new lullaby to remember years from now.

Over Lucy's head I leaned onto Tucker's shoulder and smiled up at him, feeling the rush of blood to my heart and head. Like a dormant garden I had found my way back from the fallow ground, my life the fertile soil in which hope can now flourish and possibilities bloom. I lifted my hand toward the moon, cupping it in my palm like a secret, then opened my fingers one by one until it slipped out of sight.

■ ■ ■ ■

CONVERSATION GUIDE
The Lost Hours
KAREN WHITE

■ ■ ■ ■

This Conversation Guide is intended to enrich the individual reading experience, as well as encourage us to explore these topics together — because books, and life, are meant for sharing.

A CONVERSATION WITH
KAREN WHITE

Q. Family secrets and hidden legacies are always intriguing. Do you enjoy these kinds of mysteries?

A. Definitely! I'm also a huge history buff, so combining real historical events with a family's legacy makes it more relevant, I think. It's fascinating to find a connection with our collective past — even if it's something as simple as matters of the heart.

Q. This book touches on many serious issues, including civil rights and, in particular, miscegenation. Has this always been an area of interest for you?

A. I'm always amazed how much I learn when I begin researching a particular historical period. I studied racial issues in school, but it wasn't until researching *The Lost Hours* that I realized how pertinent the struggle for civil rights would have to be in the parts of the book that were set in a segregated South in the 1930s. The characters lived in that time period, and I decided it would be a lot more interesting to immerse them in the middle of all the social unrest and see what happened.

Q. Piper's character was once an accomplished equestrian and an Olympic hopeful. Do you ride?

A. I was a casual rider as a teenager. However, my daughter is an avid rider and has been riding for the last eight years and would like to continue when she goes to college in a couple of years. We are literally surrounded by horse farms where we live, so I didn't need to go very far to research the equestrian aspects of the book.

I was also lucky enough to have a friend, Andrea Winkle, who owns several horses and rides daily. She was so very generous with her time and knowledge to help me with writing the "horsey parts" that I named the stable manager in the book after her.

Q. In this book you change points of view frequently, alternating between first and third person. What was your reasoning for this? Did you find it difficult to do?

A. I originally started writing the book all told in first person from Piper's point of view. But by the time I reached somewhere around chapter five, I realized how I needed to be inside of not only Lillian's head but also Helen's to give the reader more insight to the inner conflicts of all three women. I kept Piper's story in first person to let the reader know that although all three women are major players in the story, Piper is the primary protagonist.

The most difficult part of this was telling Helen's point of view. Because she's blind, being in her head yet describing what she's "seeing" or hearing was a huge challenge, but ultimately, very gratifying. I think Helen's a very strong character and definitely one of my favorites.

Q. Female relationships are often a focal point of your novels, and this book not only deals with the complexities of friendships between women but the sometimes intricate and difficult relationships between grandmothers and granddaughters. What inspired you to write about this kind of relationship?

A. Real life. Nothing about the story is autobiographical, but I did borrow from my own relationships with my mother and grandmother. I was close to my maternal grandmother because I'm so much like her. I think this put me at odds with my own mother, because she and I are very different.

I also have a sixteen-year-old daughter, and when I'm not being vexed by her attitude, I'm enjoying studying the complex relationship that exists between mothers and daughters that seems impervious to whatever time period one is raised in.

Q. Asphodel Meadows seems like a lovely place. Is it based on a real place?

A. It is, actually. Finding the house to fashion the fictional Asphodel Meadows after was one of those serendipitous discoveries during research. I was looking for a Savannah River rice plantation and discovered Hermitage Plantation. The plantation was known for producing the famous "Savannah gray brick," which was used to build many of the homes in Savannah. Piper's house in Monterey Square is actually made with Savannah gray bricks.

The house wasn't built in the traditional Greek Revival form of architecture, popular in its day, but instead was built in the English Regency style. It was well known for its beauty and its exquisite gardens, as well as its hospitality. Unfortunately, the house no longer exists today except in history books and memories.

Q. You have explored Alzheimer's and the difficulties of aging in this book. What drew you to write about this? What kind of research did you have to do?

A. My beloved grandmother is in the advanced stages of Alzheimer's. She's physically very healthy, but she's been in nursing care for about ten years now. I saw her for the first time since she's been in the nursing home right before I started writing *The Lost Hours.* Seeing her was difficult because what I saw was the shell of the vibrant and colorful grandmother I loved. And I mourned all the stories from her past that she could no longer tell me.

My great-aunt also died from Alzheimer's, so the disease has been in the forefront of my family's history for years now. Unfortunately, I didn't have to go very far to research this disease that I refer to as "the great thief."

Q. If there was only one thing you would like your readers to take away from this book, what would it be?

A. To connect with the older generations.

They have such stories to share with us! They are a part of our history and a treasure trove of not only what life was like before we came along, but also of our own personal journeys.

QUESTIONS FOR DISCUSSION

1. What does Helen's blindness symbolize in the book? Would she play the same role if she weren't blind?

2. Why does Lillian keep all the blinds and draperies closed at Asphodel?

3. What does the garden mean to Lillian? To Annabelle? To Piper?

4. If Piper had told the truth about who she was when she first arrived at Asphodel, what would Lillian's reaction have been?

5. Why do Piper and Helen form such a quick bond?

6. Annabelle tells Piper that history books are filled with men's stories of battles won and lost, but that women tell the stories of people's hearts. Do you agree?

7. What do the "old gentlemen" (the alley of oak trees) symbolize?

8. Why did Annabelle never talk about her past to Piper? What was she trying to tell Piper when she left Piper the gold angel charm?

9. Lillian claims that she doesn't believe in regret. Why? Do you agree with her reasoning?

10. In the beginning of the book, Piper is despondent, unmotivated, and essentially lonely. How does she change by the end of the book? What elements of her character were there all along and only rediscovered?

11. Lillian's secret, when it's revealed, is devastating to Piper and Helen, but they

ultimately forgive her. Were Lillian's actions justified? Would Annabelle have forgiven her?

ABOUT THE AUTHOR

Karen White is the author of nine previous books. She lives with her family near Atlanta, Georgia. Visit her Web site at www
.karen-white.com.